BLANK

SABRINA RG RAVEN

Blank

Published by Ouroborus Book Services
www.ouroborusbooks.com

Cover Design by Sabrina RG Raven
www.sabrinargraven.com

BLANK

CHAPTER ONE
Almara

When I was born my parents wept. Not in joy like most parents do, but in sorrow.

Everyone in the world is born with a tattoo that matches their soul mate's. We couple for life. I have no idea, even now, how it all works, how that soul mate is always close enough to be found, but I am *blank*. That is why my parents wept.

The hospital put me in isolation, capsuled in a humidicrib, encased in plastic, hoping that a mark would appear in time, like the spots of a Dalmatian puppy. But I remained blank. They took blood samples, and skin scrapes. They bottled my tears and called in healers. They genetically tested me, looking for missing markers and the like. They found nothing out of the ordinary. I was a healthy baby who grew into a healthy toddler.

My parents searched my skin a thousand times, praying that a mark would appear. It had never happened in my town – a blank child – at least not in the past 100 years of records. There were rumours, rumours that left me isolated and my parents embarrassed.

My sister was born when I was three. She had her mark emblazoned on her calf, the same place as my mother. They named her Joy, as they were finally going to be able to get past my deformity. My name, Almara, meant one who is alone. I guess they were right.

There was nothing but stories of people like

Eventually though I was ignored enough to make my life liveable. I went to school, but was sat in the back, so as not to disrupt the other children. I was a curiosity, but I needed more in my life than being the blank child. I worked hard at school and did as I was told. I got good grades and my parents were proud, but I was never acknowledged for my efforts. I was ten when I started looking through the town archives.

The archives were housed in the basement of the town library. The librarian, Mr Elwood, was used to me being in the building; it was a good place to escape the stares and whispers of the locals. My parents were content with me being there as long as I was out of their way and not getting in trouble. It was safe there and I felt safe too, surrounded by books and data drives.

I had asked Mr Elwood about the archived town records, but he would just ruffle my hair and tell me I would be bored in there, steering me towards the children's library. One day I overheard an adult ask for access to the archives and Mr Elwood shuffled through the stacks of books, leading the man into the antiquity section of the library. I followed behind, darting from shelf to shelf to stay out of view. When you spend your life trying to avoid stares you get good at walking as softly as a cat and blending in to the background. I was good at being ignored now.

The vanilla-like scent rose from the old pages of the antique book section, cracked leather sent swirls of warm dust into the air. I loved that smell. I heard the hushed voices stop as they drew up to a door. It was dark wood, with a metal keypad on the side. I darted to the next shelf to get a better angle on the keypad.

4-6-8-2 Mr Elwood typed in. 4-6-8-2, 4-6-8-2, I repeated in my head, locking the number away for next time. The man slipped into the room and banks of fluoro lights lit the white room beyond as the door swung shut with a sigh of hinges.

I scuttled a few rows over, just in case. Mr Elwood knew I loved the smell in here so I slipped a tome from the shelf and began to look it over. *A History of the Oasis*. Herios was my city, built on old forests with a thriving paper industry. I flicked through the pages, gently leafing through the history of my family home. We were Herians going back five generations. This book concerned itself though with wars and industry, and not so much the people or where the population originally emigrated from. I knew that most Herians were from the mountains and beyond; my family from the beyond part. I closed the book with a sigh and a small puff of dust, and was sliding it into its spot on the shelf when Mr Elwood appeared beside me.

'Almara, what are you doing back here?' he said with a smile as the book returned to its place in the shelf.

'Just soaking up the smell, Mr Elwood,' I replied with a laugh.

'A young lady like you shouldn't be digging around in the dust of these old shelves. Why don't you head back to the children's section? We got some new books in this morning that I just finished putting on display.'

'But the old books are interesting,' I said, trying to think of a better excuse. 'It's for a school report anyway. Just looking at the old history books. Stuff from before the war. If I could get into the archives...' I grinned, knowing his answer.

'We've spoken about that before. You don't need to go into the archives. Anyway, if you need pre-war history, you're better off going into the Libriophile system. The pre-war books are in there and much easier to read than these old things.'

'It's just not the same. And there's nothing else for me to do, so I don't mind spending the time.'

'Well, don't stay down here too long. You'll end up all dusty. Your parents won't like that.'

'Yeah, I guess,' I mumbled, knowing full well my parents wouldn't give a damn if I came home soaked in paint, let alone dust.

Mr Elwood smiled and wandered off, whistling a quiet melody that echoed through the shelves. I heard the town clock chime half past five. I had half an hour until the library closed. The archives would have to wait until tomorrow. I went to the history section and grabbed a few books to take home. I had read so many books on history that I didn't need the books, but I hoped to find something I'd missed about being blank in one of them. Maybe one day I would find answers as to what I was, and what being blank meant. There had to be more to it than meaning I was meant to be alone.

The clock chimed 6pm as I walked through the heavy doors of the library and down to the bus stop. The man from the library was there. I glanced up at him, trying not to draw attention to myself. I was envious of him. If I were an adult, Mr Elwood would let me into the archives too. He held a wad of paper in his hand, printouts of plain text, still curled on the corners from the warmth of the copier. I sat on the bench seat and tried to read the documents in his hand but he soon shuffled them into the bag he had slung over his shoulder.

The bus pulled up and we both got on. Soon I was home and sitting silently at the dinner table as my family talked over me as usual. I was their broken child and Joy had news. She had found her soul mate.

CHAPTER TWO

Joy was eight when she found her soul mate. He was six and named Wellen. He lived in the far district but soon his family would move so that he and Joy could grow up together. He was an only child so that was protocol, although my parents moving would have been considered fine I guess, seeing as I wasn't really needing to be considered. It's not as though I had a match. To them I was barely a person.

This was how it was. There would be a betrothal party soon. Not that they would marry for many years, but a soul mate was a soul mate and that link was established as soon as markings were matched. Being so young, this was seen as a good sign. Their lives would be long and plentiful together. Later matches were much more common, usually not being found until late teens.

I smiled in congratulations but it was like someone had punched me in the chest. One more blow to my deformity. I pushed my half-eaten dinner away and excused myself. My mother sighed and nodded her approval as I walked away. I couldn't handle the excitement. I knew I should be happy for Joy, but the hollow feeling in my chest was just too much for me.

I pushed my way into my room and looked at the pile of books on my desk. I grabbed the one on top and flopped onto my bed. How many times could I read it trying to find answers? After a few pages, I began to doze when a knock at my door startled me awake.

'Almara? Can I come in?' It was my mother. Her voice was soft and cautious, unsure of how I felt about Joy's pairing.

'Sure,' I mumbled, half asleep. I was not in the mood for this but what choice did I have? I pulled myself into a sitting position against my pillows as my mother settled at the foot of my bed.

'Almara, I need to talk to you about your sister.'

'I know, she's pairing. Her betrothal party will be soon and I will need to give a speech as her older sibling. It's fine. I'll do it.'

'No, it's not that...You can't be at the betrothal.'

'What? Why?' I surprised at the fierceness in my voice. Sure, I wasn't feeling all that good about being left out of tradition but she was still my sister.

'You're prohibited from being there. It's just the way of it. We were hoping to have more time to tell you.'

'But she's my little sister! I'm only ten! Maybe my marking will appear later. Everyone has them. That's what the history books say,' I spat, throwing the book I'd been reading at her.

'Almara...'

'No! I will be there. What else am I not allowed to do that you haven't told me about?'

'Almara, I... I don't know. Your father is looking into it. See if we can get you dispensation so you can be there.'

'I shouldn't need it. I'm her sister! I'm your daughter! I belong there as much as any other person.'

'We will talk about this more in the morning. I'll give you time to cool down.'

'Cool down? I am not going to cool down and forget that I'm a non-person because of a birth defect. If I am, it's as much your fault as it is mine!'

My mother recoiled like I'd slapped her.

'I'm sorry,' she whispered. 'I'm sorry that I failed you. If I could fix you I would. You know that, Almara.'

'There is nothing WRONG with me,' I screamed.

Mother stood and walked out the door, taking one last glance back at me before pulling the door closed.

I was awake now, all drowsiness flooded away with rage. I

had a lot of anger for a ten-year-old. I had to find out what I was. I had to. Tomorrow there was no school. Tomorrow I would go into the archives.

As the sun rose I snuck out of the house. Well, I tried; my mother was up, sitting in the kitchen over a cup of coffee. She was waiting for me.

'Almara, where are you going?'

'Does it matter? I'm not a person in this world, am I?'

'Sit down. We need to talk.'

'No. I need to get out of this house before I explode,' I snapped at her.

'SIT DOWN,' she barked at me. I don't think my mother had ever raised her voice at me. I pulled out a chair and perched on the edge of it. I refused to get comfortable as I knew what was coming was not going to be either pleasant or acceptable to my sensibilities, but I remained quiet and she just looked at me for a while. She looked tired, weary, her eyes sunken, the bruises of no sleep colouring the skin below her eyes. She hadn't slept either.

I opened my mouth to say something, too agitated to sit in silence, the code for the archives rattling through my head: 4-6-8-2, 4-6-8-2. She got there first.

'We need to talk,' she said, her voice back to the gentle tone I was used to from her, but I could hear a tremor in it.

'So you said,' I mumbled, beginning to fidget under the table.

'I'm going to have a talk with the town council today. The lawmakers have granted me a meeting.'

'About me?'

'Yes. About your status in our society. Not just for the betrothal ceremony for Joy but in general. There must be a precedent set and as much as it pains me to go against our laws, I don't agree that you are any different to your sister or the other children in this world. Blank or not.'

I didn't know what to say. My mother was a person who

never went against the grain, never spoke up, her quiet voice was always a sign of her docility not strength. My father was much the same. I was the thorn in their side and I always thought that if they had to make the choice they would choose the law over me. Maybe I was wrong.

'Uh...thank you?'

'You can't come with me though, and your father can't know. Not yet anyway. He believes we must follow what we are told, to the letter. I can't do that. You're my daughter and I can't let you miss out on things that are a part of all lives. There have to be other blank children out there. I can't believe you are the only one. I'm sorry though.'

'For what?'

'I'm sorry if something I did caused this...issue. I've tried to think about it, tried to work out what I did wrong. If I ate something that was wrong or I just did something...I don't know.'

'Mum, it's not you. I'm just different. You always told me I was just different, not disabled, not a freak, no matter what others said. I'm an anomaly.'

'And you are wiser than I am, it seems. Where are you off to this morning in such a rush?'

'The library. I want to get there as it opens so I can get the best books.'

'You and your books. Go, have fun. Don't forget to stop for lunch. I know how you can get lost in your thoughts. Can I give you a ride there or back?'

'I'll be okay. And Mum? Thanks.'

CHAPTER THREE

I got to the library as Mr Elwood was unlocking the door.

'You're here early Almara?'

'Early bird gets the best books... okay, that didn't work the way I expected. You know what I mean.'

He ushered me in as a group of university students began to file up the stairs. They always got here early so I knew I could disappear into the throng and sneak into the archives. I walked towards the children's section and into the reading alcoves. A few other kids ran in giggling, throwing themselves onto the beanbags on the floor, books folding under them. I winced at the damage they were doing. But I couldn't worry about that now. I pulled a novel off the shelf and tucked it under my arm and began to head over to the rows of antique books.

A few adults milled around in the aisles, but most of the students usually preferred the Libriophile system. Less effort was needed to search the database system for information and eBooks than was needed to trawl through the dusty books in here. But some knew that it held some hidden gems that could mean the difference in grades in their studies. I was in the row I had squirreled away in the day before and could see the door for the archives from here. I heard someone coming so pulled a book from the shelf, pretending to read. They walked past and I moved to the next row over.

It was empty, as were the next two rows, much to my delight. I wandered towards the archive door, my eyes darting from side to side, my ears pricked to hear the slightest noise of oncoming people. I heard someone clear their throat from a few rows over, coming towards me. I slid to the floor, resting my back against the wall under the keypad to get into the archives and pulled the book from under my arm and began to read.

I needn't have worried. The woman walked right past me, disappearing into an aisle five rows down without even a glance in my direction. I was invisible. I waited a few more minutes, and nothing but silence followed apart from the rustling of pages from rows away. I got to my feet, tucking the book back under my arm and turned to the keypad.

'4-6-8-2, 4-6-8-2,' I whispered on a loop under my breath. I hope I'd remembered it properly. Would an alarm sound if I got it wrong or would the door just not unlock? I took a deep breath, my heart throbbing in my ears, and punched the numbers in. I turned the handle on the door and at first it didn't seem to want to turn. A string of whispered expletives left my lips and then I heard a click, and the handle turned. I pulled the door open and slipped inside into the bright lights of the room beyond.

The door clicked shut behind me and I heard the lock reactivating. The room in front of me was bright. It was stark white in comparison to the old-world charm of the library building. Dark wood and rich carpeting gave way to white tiles and metal shelves. Five metres in was a set of stairs and beyond that, a room stretched as far as I could see.

Banks of computers were interrupted by more shelves and filing cabinets, all gleaming and striking in their order. I didn't know where to start. I realised I was still holding my breath. I exhaled and slowly made my way to the nearest shelf. My footsteps echoed across the cold tiles. The temperature in here was so much lower, goose bumps pricking at my skin. I pulled out the light jacket I had in my bag and pulled it on. It wasn't much but it would have to do.

The books here looked strange, and until I was up close to the shelf I didn't realise why. The covers of these books weren't made of paper or leather. These covers were metal; hinged folders made to resemble books, their spines blank save a number stamped into the metal. I shrugged and reached for the book nearest to me. 1251-235135-456. I recoiled at first as the cold of the metal bit into my fingertips. I pulled the book from the shelf and marvelled at the lightness of the volume. I had expected it to be heavy with its metal cover but although the cover was thicker than the leather covers of the antique books, the metal they were made of must have weighed barely anything.

I flipped open to the title page, not sure what I was expecting. *Laws and Protocols volume 456*. I looked at the other volumes on these shelves and saw that the last number of the books started at 001 and finished at 963. I went back to the book and checked for an index. Anything to help me locate a relevant book to look in but it seemed I was out of luck. Looking at the subject headings there didn't even seem to be any obvious grouping system for the subjects. This volume was about pet ownership and car licensing rules. How those two connected I had no idea.

I took a few steps to the left and pulled volume 568 from the row below. I opened it and again was confronted with random subjects: sewage and drainage regulations, and town parade ordinance. Who wrote these things?

I looked behind me and down the stairs to the banks of monitors. Maybe a search would help.

I put the metal cased volume back on the shelf, absent-mindedly wiping my fingerprints off the metallic cover. I wandered down the stairs and sat at one of the computer units. I could hear a hum of power but couldn't see a switch to turn it on. I tapped at the keyboard to no avail.

'Work, damn you,' I muttered.

Command not valid, said an electronic female sounding voice.

'Uhhh... Monitor on.'

The screen flickered into life. Okay, voice activated. This was new. I'd heard of these systems but then what was the point of the keyboard?

'Search blank children,'

4056 documents available.

That was certainly more than I was expecting.

'Search blank children, records of birth.'

20 documents available.

Better.

'Search blank children, records of birth, current.'

2 documents available.

'Show documents,' I said, not sure what the result would be of this command but what harm could it do.

Enter pass code.

Damn it. That was the point of the keyboard then. Could it be as easy as entering the door code? Would I be that lucky? I pulled the keyboard towards me, my fingers hovered above the number pad. Alarm bells rang in my head, imagining real alarms ringing if I entered the wrong code. Surely they would allow for human error and give a few chances before alarms would sound.

I tapped the numbers out carefully, making sure every keystroke was spot on. 4...6...8...2.

At first nothing happened, and then the screen went blank. I froze, awaiting the wailing of sirens and rushing of people. I knew I shouldn't be here, that much was clear. Then the smooth electronic voice came from the computer.

One document released. Document opening.

It worked! Well, it half worked, but this was the furthest I had ever gotten with my searches.

A large spreadsheet opened in front of me. The large monitor showed lists of names and lists of births and deaths. It seemed to be a full population record of the town. A new tab appeared for each year at the bottom of the page going back 20 years. This would take ages.

'Filter document, show blank children.'

Again the screen went blank for a moment. Maybe I had broken it. After a minute, I was thinking maybe I should give up when the document flickered back onto the screen. It was a single database. No tabs this time. There were a lot more names on it than I was expecting.

I hit the down arrow key on the keyboard and scrolled until I saw my name. There were still several names below mine too. These couldn't all be blank children. I'd never met another like me, and then I noticed the last two columns: status and deceased dates. Just the few names around mine made my head reel.

Name	DOB	Marking	Status	DOD
Brendon Polow	03.01.286PW	Blank	Secured	
Almara Henricks	06.06.286PW	Blank	Unsecured	
Sandrina Allan	12.06.286PW	Blank	Deceased	12.06.291PW
Belinda Fine	13.07.287PW	Blank	Deceased	24.09.290PW
Dianna Grid	06.06.287PW	Blank	Missing	
Paulo King	06.06.287PW	Blank	Deceased	04.05.288PW
Barry Lions	06.06.288PW	Blank	Secured	

Three deceased kids out of seven? Even I knew that was an awfully high mortality rate for kids under ten years old. But the status column certainly piqued my interest. Secured? Unsecured? What did that even mean? I scrolled back up the list skimming the column. At least a third of blank children born in the past ten years were deceased, several *missing* statuses peppered the report but most common was *secured*. Secured how? Secured where? And why was I one of the few *unsecured*?

I scrolled back up to the top of the page and pulled out a piece of paper and a pen from my bag. I began to write down the names and birth dates of the children marked as unsecured. It seemed the older the children got, the fewer they became. The oldest was 15. After that, deceased was the most common status.

Out of around 200 names there was a total of 24 names on my sheet of paper. 14 of them were under five. So where were the other 10 and why had I never seen them or met them? It was a big town but there were only three schools and gossip still flew hard and fast, especially among the mothers' circles.

Joy's betrothal announcement would already be in the ears of most school kids and their parents.

I needed to find out more about this secured thing.

'Search blank children secured.'

2 documents found.

'Search secured children facility.'

1 document found

'Open document'

Enter pass code

I typed in the same code as before and waited. The screen went black; I assumed it was loading and sat back waiting. Then the screen flashed red.

Security level incorrect. Please Enter pass code.

'Well, that's not helpful,' I mumbled under my breath. 'Override security code.'

Insert security override.

This was frustrating.

'Show sample document.'

Document description loading.

Blank Security Protocol

Facility location and listing security level 5.

Documentation contained is for use by Authority officials only.

Enter pass code.

Knowing I didn't have the security authority I sat there, not sure what to do next.

Enter pass code.

Why did it keep asking me that?

Enter pass code.

Uh oh. I started to panic, this didn't feel good.

Enter pass code. Code 645 protocol will activate in 10...

I smashed the keypad 4-6-8-2.

Code incorrect. Enter pass code.

The screen turned red. I jammed my paper into my pocket and stepped away from the screen.

'Shut down,' I yelled at the screen.

Command unavailable. Enter pass code.

'Exit database.'

Command unavailable. Code 645 protocol will activate in 5...

'Override code 645 protocol. Exit. Abort.'

The screen began to flash. This was not good. I looked back at the door into the library. A red flashing light began to glow above the door. That would make escape harder. I looked the other way into the rows of cabinets and shelves beyond the monitor bank. I was small. I could hide. I took off into the shelves as the alarm began to sound. My chair clattered to the cold floor as I heard doors begin to open from the walls of the archives and footsteps rush in.

I ran down the rows, my sneakers squeaking against the tiles, the sound drowned out by the alarms. As I slipped in between two large metal filing cabinets, I saw a glimpse of two people flash past the end of the aisle. It was so bright. There were no shadows to hide in. The sirens stopped but the red lights stayed flashing over the harsh white of the banks of bulbs inlaid in the ceiling.

I could hear yelling, voices echoing off the walls. I looked back up the aisle and realised that there was no way I would go unnoticed here between the cabinets. So far, my aisle was empty but I didn't know for how long. I looked across at the shelves running down the other side of my aisle. There was a gap but I wasn't sure if I could fit into it. I was small though and there was at least a semblance of shadow under there.

With one last glance, I rolled across the floor and squeezed in under the shelf, pulling my bag in with me. I tried to quiet my breathing but I'm sure that my heartbeat alone was vibrating its way across the floor and into the feet of whoever it was looking for me. No wonder Mr Elwood had never let me in here; he was just trying to protect me.

I closed my eyes and felt the tears welling, trying to escape in fear. My mother...what would they do to my mother?

The voices were coming closer to me.

'Down this aisle.'

I held my breath.

'Any word on an ID from head office yet?'

Spots began to dance across my vision from lack of oxygen.

'No ID but it was someone small, probably female.'

I tried to inhale as slowly and quietly as I could to refill my lungs. My hands were shaking.

'How did they get in here?'

'That fool Elwood probably. He's been out of the department way too long.'

I was managing to breathe a little easier now.

'It looks like whoever it was is gone.'

My hands still shook as I saw feet appear in my range of vision.

'Can't be. Internal lockdown means she's in here still.'

The footfalls stopped. A pair of black shoes stopped a few metres from where I lay under the shelf. I held my breath again. How silent could I be?

I heard a crackle of a headset but couldn't make out the words. All of a sudden, a hand clutched at my ankle. I screamed and grabbed onto the leg of the shelf.

'Almara Henricks, under the power invested in me by City Ordinance you are under arrest for trespass and treason against your City. You will remain silent unless asked to speak. As you are a blank child you will be remanded in a facility suitable to your condition until proceedings can be completed.'

I continued to cry out at my captor as I felt my body dragged into the light. I was small and nowhere near strong enough to resist, especially as a second set of hands grabbed at me, pulling me out from under the shelf. I thrashed against them, feeling my bag connect with the face of the woman holding my arm.

I felt something cold press against my neck, then a sharp, cold stabbing of a needle through the muscles and then everything went black.

Seven years later...

CHAPTER FOUR
Darnell

Darnell sat on the edge of the jetty at the lake. A makeshift fishing rod dangled from his fingers. The fish were not their usual active selves but he knew they were in there. He'd been fishing in this lake since he was six. His mother, Sharon, would be in the garden.

They'd lived up here in the mountains most of his life. His father had stayed behind in the City. Darnell hadn't seen him since he was a small child. His mother would occasionally go into the outskirts of the country town in the valley to get basic supplies they couldn't make themselves and his father would sometimes meet her there with money for when they couldn't swap goods for fresh vegetables or fish. Occasionally they would score a wild turkey but that was rare.

He felt a tug at the line and reeled in the fish. It was a decent size. Big enough for the two of them but he unhooked it into a bucket of water, re-baited the hook and threw the line back in. Any excess fish could be cured or dried. He didn't know what type of fish they were. His mother didn't know either but the white flesh was sweet, and when cooked over the open fire with some herbs and tomatoes made a delicious meal for them both. He hoped there would be potatoes too. He'd have to check the storage cellar.

Another fish, this one a little smaller, tugged at the line and he reeled it in.

'Darnell, come inside,' his mother called. He packed up his

fishing gear and headed towards the cabin. It wasn't much, but it had a well-stocked cellar and was warm enough in winter. He wished he could live in town, with other children his own age, but he knew it wasn't possible. His mother had been a town official and when he was born blank, she panicked. After months of testing the hospital had released him and his mother had run away with him at that point.

She knew what happened to blank children... at least in theory. A single report had been laid on her desk when she came back to work. If anyone asked her she would have said it was nothing, just the latest notes from the council meetings, but those few sheets of paper had been burned that night. A sick relative from across the mountains was the excuse they gave when she bundled Darnell and some meagre belongings and disappeared. She missed her life, the comfort of the City, the warmth of her soul mate in bed. He remained behind, his marking a daily reminder emblazoned across his face that he was alone. Her mark was on her forearm. She tried to keep it covered in front of Darnell so as not to upset him. He knew enough that he was why they were out here.

Before the war, this land had been a holiday home for her ancestors. During the war it became a shelter for her family to escape the bombs that destroyed the green landscape, tearing families apart. It was this shelter that inspired her to come here. Would they come looking for her? Maybe. Would they come looking for him? Yes. She had technically committed no crime by taking him out of the City but it was not the done thing.

Sharon ushered the boy through the door, wincing at the bony shoulder. They ate well but a life lived on the land was harder than she would have liked him to have and with his latest growth spurt his bulk had still not caught up to his height. His father was the same at his age – a bony beanpole. She pulled the door closed then slid the inner metal door closed. It may have looked like a wood cabin on the outside, but the inside was reinforced and every opening could be locked tight behind thick steel.

Without asking he began to fillet the fish he caught. *Such a good boy*, she thought to herself.

'Potatoes?' he asked, startling her back out of her memories.

'What?'

'Potatoes? Do we have any?' he asked laying out the last of the fillets on the chopping board and throwing the scraps into the rubbish bucket.

'We should. Go check. I'll get started on the rest of dinner.'

Darnell pulled up the trapdoor in the floor and ducked down the stairs as the light flickered on. She could hear him rummaging in the root cellar bins when there came a stomping sound from the veranda. Maybe an animal, she thought. They got deer out here occasionally. She went over to the peephole in the window shutter, but couldn't see anything in the dimming light. The hair on the back of her neck began to prickle. Something was wrong. She backed over to the cellar trapdoor and closed it, pulling the rug over it. They had discussed contingency plans before and she hoped Darnell would remember them.

'Mum?' she heard him call. 'Is everything okay up there?' She kicked at the floor three times. Danger. She kept backing up until she got to the kitchen cabinet. She pulled a handgun from behind the ceramic jar of flour and tucked it into the waistband of her pants. A knife was already strapped to her calf, inside her boot. Then she heard something she wasn't expecting, a knock on the door.

'Hello? Is anyone in there? I'm lost.'

Sharon breathed a sigh of relief and went up to the peephole again. She peered through it and saw a young woman dressed in hiking gear, a backpack slung across her shoulders and a slightly bewildered look on her face. They didn't get many hikers come through but occasionally they spotted someone travelling from beyond the mountains. A black curled mark swirled over her cheek.

'Hello?' the girl called again, knocking. The sight of the mark curling over her cheek brought a rush of memories of her soul mate and she pulled the metal door aside and opened the door.

'You're lost, dear?' Sharon asked. Her hand still hovered near enough to the gun, just in case.

'Oh, I'm so glad I found you! I'm trying to find the road back to the City. Can you point me right?'

'Sure thing,' she replied, pointing down the path to the left. 'You're a fair way out so the easiest way is to follow the path until you hit the hiking trail at the springs. From there, there are signs back to the town.'

'Could I trouble you for a drink of water? My bottle is empty and I'm no good at this camping thing.'

'Pass me your bottle and I'll fill it up.'

'I can't come in for a moment?'

'No offence to you, dear, but I'd rather you didn't. Feel free to rest out here on the porch.' She held her hand out for the water bottle but in a flash the woman had grabbed her by the arm.

'No offence to you, dear, but I'm coming in.'

The woman dropped the bottle and pulled a gun from out of a holster hidden below her shirt.

'Go inside and do as I say and you will be okay.'

Sharon wondered if she could reach her gun before the woman could shoot her but she knew she was no quick shot. The barrel of the gun pressed on the back of her head, as the woman reefed her arm behind her and pushed her into the house.

'Where is he?' the woman snapped. 'Where is the boy?'

'I don't know what you're talking about,' she said, hearing her voice tremble.

The woman smacked the gun against the back of her head. 'I'm here for the boy. Not for you, not to rob whatever valued items you have in this shack, just the boy.'

'It's just me here. I've been alone here for years.'

'Lies. I have come for your son and you will give him to me or I will shoot you and tear this cabin to shreds until I find him. Then I will shoot him too. My boss won't be as impressed as if I bring him back whole, but one less anomaly is one less anomaly.'

'Does threatening to shoot people normally work?'

'Yeah, most times actually.'

'Well, I don't know what to tell you. I've been here alone for years. My son died. The anomaly must have killed him. He got sick, I couldn't fix him, he died and is buried out under the vegetable garden. I can take you there.'

'Bullshit.'

'What am I supposed to do? Magic him back to life? I miss my son every day. I would have him back in a heartbeat if I could.'

'If he's dead, why do you stay out here?'

'Because I can't bear the thought of my soul mate seeing my face, knowing that I couldn't save our child. If you work for who I think you do, you know his remains would not be allowed to be interred in the cemetery. I need to be close to him.'

'Sit down,' the woman said motioning with her gun towards one of the wooden chairs. 'Sit there and don't move.'

The woman kept her gun raised as she backed into the narrow hallway, pushing open doors and peering into bedrooms. They were simple and the beds were made – Sharon had always insisted on the bed being made first thing in the morning. They kept everything simple, there was no sign that the bed was recently slept in and no clothes were piled on the floor like a normal teen's room.

They wore similar sizes as well and their clothes were simple jeans and t-shirts. Even if the woman saw clothes, they could be written off as her own. Sharon slowly moved her hand to the gun but the woman returned before she could free it.

'You have to come with me.'

'No.'

'What do you mean no? You have no choice in the matter.'

'You have no authority to take me anywhere. I have broken no laws.'

'You removed a child from the schooling system without permission.'

'Really? He died when he was five. Well before schooling age. I have done nothing wrong.'

'You have abandoned your soul mate.'

'Which is not illegal. I have had to leave but intend to return once the pain is less severe.'

'To be honest, I'm taking you in. Things have changed. You are going against the ways of our people. You need to return and go back to your life. If you choose to stay I will take you by force. I have my orders.'

'You have no authority.'

'Then I will be dragging you kicking and screaming from this cabin.' She stepped forward to grab Sharon but she was ready this time. Before the woman's hand clamped down on her arm, she had pulled the gun free and fired towards her captor.

A bullet pierced through her upper arm. Blood splattered over the cabin. She tried to step back to take a better shot but the woman fired first and a bullet pierced through the shoulder of Sharon's shooting arm. White, hot pain burned through her arm as the gun clattered to the floor.

'We can both play these games. Your problem is that I have a backup plan.' Using her good arm, gun still clutched in hand she pulled a walkie talkie from her belt.

'Bring them in. And bring me a med kit. The bitch shot me.'

Darnell's mother had staggered back to the kitchen bench where the filleting knife sat, still slick with scales and traces of blood. Her right arm was useless and she felt the cold sweat of unconsciousness touching at her temples. Spots danced in front of her eyes, she'd never felt such pain.

Her left hand felt across the bench until she felt the plastic handle. She pulled it towards her with her fingertips until she had it in her hand. She wouldn't be all that a formidable foe using her left hand but anything to give Darnell a fighting chance. They had spoken about this day. He would stay in the secondary cellar. The one set up as a bomb shelter behind the root bins. There was food and water in there for a few weeks and unless you knew where to look you'd never see the door. He would be safe as long as he did what she had told him to do. As long as he had the chance.

She blinked slowly. Fighting to reopen her eyes from the misty cloud that was settling over her, she took a glance at her shoulder. It was a mess. Her shirt was black with blood and the bullet had done some damage on its way through. She saw movement out of the corner of her eye as a group of six people dressed in black combat gear jogged down towards the house from the trees. Had they been watching? Had they seen Darnell? She thought she was going to throw up.

Before the group entered she had to make a move. She pushed herself away from the bench and staggered towards the woman, who had invaded her home; who had invaded the peace that she had worked so hard at for her and her son. The filleting knife was gripped in her hand, her knuckles white with pressure.

Sharon dove towards the woman, slashing out with the knife. She felt it pierce through the woman's throat. At the same time guns began to fire peppering her body with bullets. Both women fell to the ground, gasping breaths through mouthfuls of blood. One full of bullet holes and one with a filleting knife jammed through her throat. Her mark now smeared like paint across her face.

From below, Darnell had noticed the kitchen light dimmed as his mother shut the trapdoor. When he heard the three footfalls he knew something was happening. He slid in past the root cellars and into the secondary shelter.

He killed the lights in both and sat on one of the cot beds

against the wall after securing the entrance. *It might not be anything*, he thought to himself but the fear bubbling in his stomach told him otherwise. *Maybe mum had just been spooked by a noise*, he told himself. He put the bowl of potatoes down on the floor and lay down, folding his hands behind his head, trying to hold the bile that rose in his throat from bubbling into his mouth. He had never been this scared before, for himself or his mother. His breathing came in short, sharp gasps of panic. He closed his eyes and counted to ten in his head. He had to remain calm.

He knew he wasn't to move unless his mum came down and gave the knock. Otherwise he was to stay there for a week before investigating. He wiggled into a more comfortable position and was just thinking of things to do while he waited when he heard the first gunshots. He sat bolt upright, all pretence of remaining calm out the window. He had to fight the vomit rising up his throat. He couldn't be quiet, throwing his guts up. And if his mum had been hurt, he would not let it be in vain. He choked the bile back down again and gripped at the edge of the mattress til his knuckles went white. He mustn't leave, he thought to himself, fighting the urge to unbolt the door and rush up to his mother.

He swung his legs over the side of the cot again and tapped his feet in a steady staccato rhythm. Anything to stop him from getting up. He couldn't hear anything else. He waited, knowing that very few sounds filtered down into the secondary cellar.

'Come on Mum, come on,' he mumbled to himself, a mantra of hope when things were looking grim. Then the second volley of gunshots happened. This time louder and faster, semi-automatics or multiple guns. He clapped a hand over his mouth to keep from crying out. His mother... she had to have been shot. He got to his feet. He had to get the gun. Not wanting to draw attention to the room by turning on the lights, (he had no idea if the door blocked out light) he pulled a small pocket torch from his pocket and shone it around the room.

Shelves of food, blankets, water, batteries and other supplies lined one whole wall. His mother always said there was enough in here for a week of living if needs be but looking at the rows of jars and cans, he thought he could live comfortably down here for at least three months, longer if the need arose. Although he would probably go stir crazy long before then, the darkness feeling heavy on his shoulders already.

He knew what he was looking for but in the half light, with thoughts rushing through his head, he fumbled his way through the shelves, dislodging a can of peaches and nearly sending a canister of sugar crashing to the floor. He was still unsure how he had managed to catch them both, but with a sigh of relief, he pushed them back into their homes. Then he saw the box. It was a cereal box, colour faded and edges rounded with age. He pulled it from behind the cans of beans. It was heavy, heavier than any box of cereal.

He pulled the pistol out and then the clips of ammo that had been with it. They went into his pockets. The gun felt wrong in his hand. It always had felt wrong, unnatural and alien. He didn't like to use guns but his mother had shown him how. Just in case, she'd said. Now he felt he was going to get to know what she was talking about.

He could hear stomping through the floor, although the sound was greatly muffled by the shelter roof. Too many feet to be just his mother or a few wayward deer. Someone was up there. Only his father knew their exact location and if it were just wandering campers, the gunshots would not have happened.

He heard a thud as something heavy hit the ground. A cupboard perhaps, he thought. They were trashing the place. He hoped his mother was still alive. He had no idea how to go on without her. He could look after himself but he had never been truly alone for more than a day when his mother would take a trip into the town to meet his father.

He didn't even remember his father all that well. He had a

photo, propped on the mantel piece upstairs of a tall, dark haired man who was a little too thin for his own good but in that lanky stretched way, not just underfed. Darnell knew he looked like his dad, all except the absence of a mark curled across his cheek, and the bronze sheen to Darnell's skin that had come from more time outside in the sun than inside an office.

He sat back down on the cot bed, switching off the torch and placing the gun beside him on the thin mattress, where it sunk into the foam. He just had to wait. His stomach rumbled but despite its hunger, the bile of panic that had risen into his throat had pushed all urge to eat away from his mouth. He just had to wait.

It had been a few hours since the noises from upstairs stopped. He even heard someone in the root bins outside the door to the second cellar area. It had to be going on 10pm. He had not moved from the cot, his stomach grumbling at him, willing him to eat something, anything, but knowing that the taste of anything would make him throw up. He didn't need the smell of vomit cloying at his nose while he was stuck in here.

He pulled himself up off the cot bed, leaving the handgun where it sank into the mattress. He needed a drink. Turning the torch on, he shone the beam over the walls again until he saw the pallet of water. Large jugs sat on the lower shelves but a few slabs of smaller bottles were at the top. He put the torch between his teeth and tore into the plastic wrapped slab, pulling two bottles free. They weren't super cold but the lowered temperatures in the cellar had them cool and drinkable. He guzzled the first one down. He hadn't realised how thirsty he was. The second he opened and began to sip. His gut cramped at the influx of fluid. He really did need to eat something.

He sighed and grabbed a can of peaches off the shelf. May as well eat something I like, he thought to himself. They had always been a treat because they didn't grow naturally where the cabin sat. So it was only when his mother was able to get them from town that he had them. He laughed at the fact she had saved a whole bunch of them for the shelter, just in case. The laugh turned into a quiet sob. He was so alone now.

He couldn't stand the darkness any longer. Hoping the door seal would block out any light, he flipped the switch and bathed the room in a gentle yellow glow. He blinked as his eyes grew accustomed to the light and looked around. It had been a long time since he had actually come into this room and actually taken note of it.

The cots, four in all, lined one wall, a solitary white pillow on each and folded green wool blankets, old army issue he assumed, sat folded at the foot of the beds. White sheets, now tinged cream with age, were crisp and tucked neatly on the cots under another green blanket. Military corners, as his mother once described the perfect sharp folds. He asked her once if she'd been in the military but he'd never gotten a straight answer from her. The only scrunched cot was the one he had laid on, the pillow askew, the blankets rumpled, the black gun sitting sunken amongst folds of fabric. He turned away from it.

The other wall was lined with shelves, floor to ceiling. Gleaming silver cans, glass jars, ceramic containers marked flour and sugar and the pallets of clear water bottles. At the very end was a shelf with plastic tubs marked on each side with their contents: medical, clothing, tools, etc.

At the back of the room was a table. It was big enough for four people to sit around. Beside it sat two massive packs of camping gear, a set of drawers and a small bookshelf. She had been so prepared. He took his can of peaches to the table and sat down, pulling the top off the can. Spoons… they would be around somewhere. He pulled open the top drawer of the cupboard and lo and behold, there was cutlery. He smiled as he pulled out a spoon. Everything had a place. Everything but him. He sat quietly and ate the fruit, drinking the juice left in the can. He felt a little better. His belly had stopped growling and the rising nausea had subsided a little.

He was exhausted. The urge to go out and look to see what had happened was so strong but he had promised his mother that unless she came for him he would stay down here for a week. That would give some time for him to be safe. To escape from whoever was following him.

He needed to sleep but doubted he would. He got a book from the shelf near the table. So many classics, all favourites of his and his mother. A lone tear escaped down his cheek. He grabbed the remainder of his water and lay down on what he now thought of as his cot to read, the gun resting next to him. He opened the book but fell asleep before he had got to the second page.

CHAPTER FIVE

It was the longest week of his life, even including the one where they had been snowed into the cabin with nothing but each other to entertain themselves.

But that was the problem wasn't it, Darnell thought to himself. The two of them could have made it through in a flash. By day three he'd grown sick of tinned peaches and beans and started to actually make proper food. It was never as good as the things his mother could whip up from a few paltry cans but it was filling and he guessed it was healthy enough, even though he was still a bit wary of the tinned meat that smelled too salty and tasted like it had been made by someone who had never eaten meat in their life. He looked at the ingredients and although slightly relieved at seeing pork in the ingredients list, still didn't quite believe that pink gelatinous glob was once a pig.

He squirted more mustard onto the jelly-meat stew he had made. It was only just palatable. He had experimented with some canned vegetables he hadn't eaten before called brussels sprouts and now he knew why his mother had never cooked them for him before. Who ate these things? Or cared enough to put them into tins?

He sighed as he got up, pushing the bowl away from him. Maybe if he read a book or something it would distract him enough from the taste to not waste the food. He had already picked out the bigger chunks of sprouts but the flavour had permeated even the salty meat. He pulled a book from the shelf. He had looked at all the titles on the second day and seen that most the books were ones he liked. He sat back down and opened it. He was just about to shovel another mouthful of the stew when a piece of paper fell out of the book. This time he pushed the bowl even further away, dropping the book and snatching for the paper.

It brushed across the tabletop and began its gentle decent to the floor before Darnell snatched it out of the air. It was delicate paper, thin and almost see-through like tracing paper. The pale blue lines sung out across the page, a throng of his mother's careful handwriting perfectly aligned. He felt a sharp stab of worry for his mother, knowing she would have come for him by now if she could.

> *Dear Darnell,*
>
> *If you are reading this then my worst fears have come true and we have been found. I have told you about why we were here in the cabin and why you must always follow the rules but I don't think I ever really got the chance to explain what would happen if they came for you.*
>
> *You were born blank. You know that much. I told you that the Authority didn't take blank children very well and that you would always be viewed as flawed. I didn't want that for you. What I didn't tell you was that I was given information when you were born that made me fear for your life. So we came out here to the woods to live to give you a chance to get to adulthood.*
>
> *You need to get somewhere safe. If you are following the rules I set for you in emergencies, you will be in the second cellar for at least a week. This should give time for them to leave, but in case they are still watching the cabin, there is a tunnel you can use to escape. Take one of the camping packs with you. There is enough food for two weeks and essential tools. You cannot come back to the cabin. Make your way north to Ellintown. There is a man there named Oscar Greatfoot who will take you in and help you to get by. He runs the local post office.*
>
> *If you move the bookshelf away from the wall you will find a crawl space. After a few metres, it will open up into a tunnel that will get you out far enough away from the cabin to be safe.*
>
> *Do not worry about me. Do not come back for me. If I am*

*able I will meet you at Oscar's otherwise I wish you well and
will try to find you again.*

*I have taught you as much as I can and I hope it serves you
well enough to keep you safe.*

Love

Mum

Darnell sat holding the letter in silence. He felt panic rising up
in his chest. The letter fell from his fingers as he pushed away
from the table, and went for the bookcase. With a few good
shoves he pushed it away from the wall. There in the cement
was a metal plate, screwed tight into the wall. He rummaged
through the toolbox until he found a screwdriver that would
fit and got down to unscrewing the panel. It was hard work;
the screws had begun to rust over. Who knew how long this
panel had been closed for? Finally, pulling the last one free he
pried the panel off the wall. The light from the room
penetrated a few metres in and he could see where it opened
up to a full-sized tunnel. The walls were brick and the smell
was damp like wet leaves, the air stale.

Darnell pushed the screwdriver into the pack he was going
to take. With air that stale, the tunnel had to be closed at the
other end somehow as well and he didn't want to be stuck
with no way to open it if there wasn't a screwdriver in the
pack.

He still had two days before the week was up so he placed
the metal panel back against the hole so as not to tempt him.
He knew his mother wouldn't have told him to wait a week if
he didn't need to. No matter how frustrating it would be. He
grabbed a bag of dried fruit off the shelf and headed back to
his cot to read, the letter resting on the table.

***

Darnell woke with a start. He could have sworn he heard his
mother calling for him. He rushed to the cellar door and put
his ear against it. He knew sound did penetrate the door but

had no idea how loud it would be. He strained his hearing, hoping. He heard a whimper of sound but not sure what it was. He wanted to call out but unless he was sure it was safe he wouldn't.

Then he heard it clearer this time.

'Darnell? Where are you?'

It was a woman. She was close but it was not his mother's voice. He slowly backed away from the door making as little noise as possible. He sat on the floor, too scared that the cot springs would creak or the sound of the chair against the floor would carry through and out of the second cellar.

'Darnell! Get out here you little freak. I am not leaving without you.'

He heard a jar smash on the ground and a scream of frustration was accompanied by more jars hitting the cement floor.

He heard stomping as she went back up the stairs and then the footfalls as she walked through the cabin punching walls. He lay down on the cold floor. He shivered but he knew he must stay still and quiet, soon he fell asleep.

Darnell awoke to silence. Looking at his watch he saw he'd been asleep for over an hour. He sat up, his bones complaining after that long on cold concrete. He stretched as he got to his feet, his neck cracking from its stiffness.

He was still tired. Bed was the best option. He'd be quiet enough and unless she was close by he would risk the squeal of the cot springs. He lowered himself as slowly as possible onto the cot and pulled up the blankets. He was asleep in minutes.

Darnell had heard no noises from outside the second cellar for the last two days. He wanted so much to go upstairs and look for his mother but he had promised her he would follow her instructions to the word. He tidied up and made the bed, as he had every morning in here even if he did spend most his time reclining on the blanket with a book in hand. He had looked through the packs that morning to see if there were any differences between the two but found nothing more than a few different coloured shirts. He chose the one with the darkest colours as he intended to leave in the evening. He knew sundown was at around 6pm so at 5 he double checked he had everything ready to go.

He choked down a quick meal and moved the bookshelf over to reveal the panel in the wall. The entry gaped open, like the open maw of a monster. He took a deep breath and tossed the bag in ahead of him. He had located a torch on a head strap which he clicked on. He took one look back at the room he had lived in for the past week – the last remnants of his life with his mother that he had to leave behind, and crawled into the tunnel.

CHAPTER SIX
Zale

A scream echoed through the night. It was a curdled scream, the kind that only came from pain. The smell of seared flesh wafted on the air. Zale wrinkled his nose at it. Even after many blanking rituals he was still not used to that smell. It resembled burnt beef with overtones of burning hair and the sickly sweet metallic tang of blood. He fought the urge to throw up.

It was part of joining the group. They were a small farming community of those who chose to become blank. Their markings were removed with a burning knife. It both cut the flesh and sealed the wound, hence the smell.

It was okay when it was the adults. Those who chose to be here, like him. He and his partner, Allen, had fled the City eight years ago, after they had both turned 18. Their pairing was not destined, their marks did not match, and their love was unsanctioned. The marks always created breeding pairs. There were never any same sex marks, at least according to any town records that he had been able to find. After the war the population needed to be enhanced. If a couple couldn't bear children naturally, they would be inseminated artificially. That was the way of the world.

When Zale's betrothed, Alice, had discovered their clandestine affair, she had cried but understood. She promised not to report them and helped them to leave the City. There was a town, she had said, where love, not marks, decided pairings. And that town was here. Not so much a town but a community, a commune, set in an old army base now deserted, from before the war – Condor Point was its name.

They had settled amongst couples who had fallen in love with differently marked people. Here in Condor Point, children were born purely from passion, not duty, and it was one of those children who was being unmarked tonight. On their sixth birthday a Condor child would be made blank.

The smell of burnt flesh began to dissipate and the scream had dropped to sobs. The child would be fine. They got over it and their wounds healed well. The facial ones were the worst, and he would know. His hand went to the shiny patch on his face. It was pink and still felt tight to this day. With salves and time it would soften. Luckily Mazra, the mark remover, used to be a surgeon. She did good work.

Although the base was attached to the town water and electricity, the leader of Condor Point, The Colonel as he was known to the residents, discovered through old army records that Condor Point was a separate jurisdiction to all surrounding towns. It encompassed enough land (mind you this included the rather desolate salt flats that backed onto the barracks) to be considered a town in its own right. So they were left to their own devices most of the time unless the Authority poked their noses in.

The Authority were the overseers of the post war state named Oasis. Oasis was named such because after the desolation of the war, the area around them became mainly an unfertile dustbowl of salt flats and sand dunes. Inside Oasis was still lush with fertile soil and temperate weather. And the ten cities, including Condor Point, thrived. No one really ventured into the salt flats and those that did rarely came back.

Zale walked back to his cabin, the soft light of the lamp in the sitting room made the window glow warmly. He smiled. The scar across his face was worth it. He dodged a group of kids heading to the after party for the newly blank child. He could go if he wanted. They all could, but he couldn't handle the smell hanging in the air of their meeting hall – what was once Hangar Four.

He had just opened the door when the bells began to ring. Warning bells. The peals filled the air, travelling through Condor Point. The flood lights came on, illuminating the town in a harsh white light. Allen came out, holding a hand gun out to him. He held a taser for himself and a rifle was slung across his back.

'Main gate?' he asked Zale.

'I think so. That's where the bells started from.'

'Might just be some kids mucking around.'

'We could be so lucky.'

They began to jog towards the main gate when they heard the first gunshots. That was not a good sign.

'Bunker, now!' Allen called, spinning on his heel and pulling Zale by the arm, back past their cabin. They saw a few more people rushing towards the bunkers under Hangar Two. A teen couple sat huddled against the hangar wall. They were frozen in fear except for jumping every time another gun shot rang out through the still night air.

'Hey, you can't stay there, it's not safe,' Zale called, slowing reluctantly as the noises got closer.

The girl finally moved, turning towards Zale and Allen.

'His ankle, I think it's broken. He fell in a hole. I can't lift him! He can't walk. Please, I can't just leave—'

'Get out of the way. We can carry him for you.'

Zale tucked his gun into the waistband of his jeans and pulled Allen over to the cowering teens.

The girl scrabbled to her feet. He recognised her – Trella. She and her partner had arrived last year, beaten and bleeding from their home town. No wonder they were not leaving one another. Their love was forged in blood. The boy's name was Jonah.

'Jonah, listen to me,' he said, looking into the boy's distant eyes. 'Jonah, you have to put your arm around my neck.'

The boy didn't move.

'Jonah!' he snapped, slapping the boy's pale face. A pink hand print lingered on the pale skin. Jonah blinked a few times before seeming to focus.

'Arms, around my neck, now!' An explosion rang out in the distance. 'Now Jonah!'

The boy threw his arms around Zale's neck as Zale hoisted the boy up into his arms. Jonah winced but remained quiet. Zale nodded to Allen who grabbed onto Trella's arm as they resumed their dash to the bunker. It was hidden behind a utility panel. The gunshots were getting closer. They ducked into the bunker and pulled the panel back into place. They dashed down the sloped tunnel until they got to the main room where people, mainly children and the elderly, huddled.

He placed Jonah down on the floor as gently as possible and rolled up his pants leg. The ankle was extremely swollen and bruised and the foot sat at a weird angle.

'Any medics in here?' Zale called. An older woman came over, her hair dishevelled and her shirt sleeve torn.

'I used to be a nurse. What's wrong?'

He motioned to Jonah's ankle. Her eyes went wide.

'Oh, that's not good. We need some supplies. First aid kit in under that bunk bed.'

Zale ran and got it, hearing a wail of pain from Jonah. The nurse had removed his shoe and sock. His foot was even more bruised than his ankle.

'You did a bloody good job on your ankle, young man,' she said, flipping open the first aid kit. She gave him an injection and after a few moments she moved the foot straight. 'We'll x-ray this once we get the all-clear. For now, I'll splint it.'

Seeing everything was being looked after, Zale went over to where his partner sat. The room was too quiet.

'Should we go back out and help?' he asked.

'Let's just stay here until the all-clear is given. Don't want to show whoever is out there our safe place.'

'Trust in the almighty Colonel?'

'Always,' he replied patting his partner's leg.

And then the lights went out.

CHAPTER SEVEN

It was dark and getting stuffy in the bunker until the generator kicked in. It restored the ventilation but not the lights. They found some hurricane lamps and the older residents tucked the children into the cot beds and bunks. They soon retired themselves, leaving a small group of people up and about.

Trella and Jonah had fallen asleep against the wall, her head on his shoulder. Someone had thrown a blanket over them but the cold concrete still made for shivers. Zale couldn't sleep. He watched the hours pass, the clock on the wall opposite him ticking slower and slower. If he didn't know better he'd swear it was dying. He sighed; Allen snuggled up behind him making mewling noises. It was like having a giant cat in the bed with him. It was moments like this, he thought to himself, that made it all worthwhile.

There weren't many same sex couples at Condor Point. Even though most saw nothing wrong with it, so many folks were still scared of betraying their marked pairing. The idea of spending his life in a lie, as nice as Alice was, made him feel sick to his stomach.

He was so restless. Zale unfolded himself from Allen's arms and got up. The hurricane lamp was a warm but weak glow. There was a mess area in the bunker – a few tables and chairs, a bunch of soggy-looking bean bags and a book shelf? A toy box sat open in the corner, a few random toys spilled across the play mat. He'd never really looked around here before. Most times the all-clear was called before he'd had the chance or he was part of the response team.

He dragged a beanbag over to the bookshelf and plonked

down into it. He held the lamp up to the spines, illuminating the mix of old leather and cloth bindings. The bottom shelves were kids' books. The next four shelves were a random collection of novels and classical post war stuff. The top shelf held a collection of hand-bound, crinkled paper and leather books, held together with string.

He pulled one of the tomes from its place. On the cover was a plain stick on label, simply inscribed with A *History of Condor Point PW-PW32*. This looked interesting. The spine crackled as Zale opened the book. The leather cracked and the paper inside whispered at his fingers. The writing inside was in neat and tiny script and the ink was fading. He wondered if there were any pre-war ones. They'd be faded to all hell but would be mighty interesting if he could decipher the text.

He flicked through a few pages. Diagrams of the barracks were sketched in ink now faded brown with age. He turned back to the first page and began to read.

Zale was just finishing the first of the journals when he felt someone walking up behind him. A tiny hand fell on his shoulder.

'Excuse me, mister, do you know where my mummy and daddy are?'

He turned to look into a pair of big brown eyes framed with long dark eyelashes. The girl was about four. He knew her parents but hadn't seen them in the bunker.

'Did your mummy bring you down here, darlin?'

'She told me to go down the tunnel and find my Auntie Sam, and she'd be here really soon.'

'Is your Auntie Sam here?' Sam was pregnant so she should be in here unless she hadn't been able to make the trip. He hadn't seen her and he couldn't make her out in the minimal glow of the hurricane lamp.

'Yeah, she's having a baby soon. She's asleep. I'm scared and Mummy and Daddy never came here even though they said they would.'

'What's your name, sweetheart?'

'My name is Meg. Do you know my mummy and daddy?'

'I'm Zale and yes, Meg, I know your mummy and daddy. They'll be outside still if they aren't in here. They're very smart people so I'm sure they're safe.'

'I want to go out and find them.'

'We can't go out until the all-clear alarm sounds. It's safer in here for kids. How about we go get something to eat?'

'Okay, Mr Zale,' she said. He tucked the book back in the shelf and grabbed the next one along, shoving it into his back pocket and picked up the lamp. He held out his free hand to Meg. Her skinny arm reached up to his hand and he saw her mark, curling across her forearm. It was beautiful. More delicate than he had ever seen a mark be. It was a shame what it stood for. She looked up at him. He tore his eyes from her mark and shot her a smile. She grinned back and they headed to one of the store rooms.

He found some chocolate biscuits and juice boxes and they sat opposite from each other at one of the cold metal tables. The lamp light reflected off its surface throwing a glow over Meg's face and dark curls. She had that bleary look kids get when they were too tired but were determined to stay awake. She rubbed at her eyes in between bites.

'You have pink shiny skin on your face,' she said between sips of juice. It wasn't a question, merely a passing comment. He wasn't sure how or even if he should answer her, but she spoke again.

'That's so you can be with your husband, because you love each other.'

He smiled. Out of the mouths of babes.

'Yes Meg, Allen and I are very much in love.'

'My mummy has pink on her arm and my daddy's is on his leg. Mummy said pink is the colour of love, and once I have pink on me I can love whoever I want.'

'Are you talking Zale's ears off, Meg?' came a soft voice from just outside the glow of the lamp.

'No, Auntie Sam,' Meg said, but she looked down as though she'd been busted doing something wrong.

Sam's belly appeared before the rest of her, the bump large and protruding. She had to be due soon.

'She's alright, Sam. How are you? Ready to pop?'

'Three weeks to go. I swear there are two in there and they're dancing a salsa on my bladder. Only reason I woke up. But I'm glad I did. Meg, what did I tell you? Don't leave my side.'

'I was looking for Mummy.'

'Did you wake Zale up?'

'No, he was reading.'

'Please tell me that's true?' Sam asked. She looked so tired.

'Really, it's fine, and yeah, I was reading. I can't sleep. Thought a snack might settle her. She's just worried about her folks.'

'Meg, Mummy and Daddy will be fine. They've been outside when things have happened before and your mummy was hide-and-seek champ at school. I'm going to go to the bathroom and then we're going back to bed, okay?'

'Okay, Auntie Sam,' Meg said popping the last bite of cookie into her mouth. Zale did the same, watching Meg chewing furiously. She certainly was enjoying it. She swallowed just before a yawn hit her.

'Feeling sleepy now, kiddo?' She nodded at him as he yawned. She giggled.

'You're sleepy too!'

'I guess I am.' Sam came out of the bathroom then and scooped Meg up, placing her onto the floor beside her.

'Come on Meg, let's go back to bed. We should be clear tomorrow to go find your mum and dad so you need to get lots of rest.'

Sam guided Meg with a gentle hand on her shoulder. She turned and mouthed a thank you to Zale who smiled back.

With a sigh he got to his feet, cleared the rubbish into the bin and walked back over to the bed where Allen lay and turned off the lamp. He slipped the book out of his back pocket, sliding it under the cot then lay down and let his exhaustion take him over.

The next day he woke up without Allen's warmth behind him. He blearily opened his eyes and looked around blinking. Everyone was awake; it must be later than he thought. He glanced at the clock – 11am. He must have been tired. Why was everyone still here? He thought to himself. Surely the all-clear should have sounded by now. He looked around and saw Allen sitting on one of the beanbags reading a book.

They'd never been big on the television that streamed in the big cities. Old movies from before the war were always a nice treat but more of them were getting banned every year. They had a small collection saved on a few chip drives but books were always where they found comfort. He went and flopped down next to Allen.

'The all-clear not sound yet?'

'No. And no one will talk about it,' Allen said at a whisper.

'What do you think it means?'

'Either the Colonel doesn't want to risk showing the bunker to whoever is out there or everyone...well, everyone is dead or captured.'

'Pray for the former,' Zale whispered as he saw movement out of the corner of his eye. It was Meg, running full-speed at him, Sam waddling behind her as fast as her giant belly would allow.

'Mr Zale! You're awake,' Meg called, throwing herself into his arms.

'Meg, leave Zale alone,' Sam chastised, finally arriving at the beanbags.

'She's okay. Gotta burn that energy somehow.' Sam looked even more exhausted than the night before.

'How about you leave her with us and go get some rest? It looks like you need it.'

'Really? Are you sure?' she asked. The relief in her face sealed it.

'Sure thing,' Allen said with a smile.

Sam thanked them and waddled back over to the cot. She was asleep as her head hit the pillow.

'So, Mr Zale, can we go look for Mummy and Daddy now? I didn't want to ask Auntie Sam because she's so tired from the baby in her tummy. Now you're awake we can go look, hey?'

Zale looked at Allen, who frowned in response. Zale didn't even need to say anything. They had been together long enough that he understood what that frown meant. He was about to respond when Allen spoke up.

'Hey Sweetie, I'm Allen and who are you?'

'Hi, Mr Allen, I'm Meg. Mr Zale said we could look for Mummy and Daddy today.'

'Oh, did he now?' Allen said, throwing a look like daggers at Zale. 'Well, I'm sure he meant as soon as it's safe. We have to wait for the special announcement from the Colonel, okay?'

'But...'

'No buts. I'm sure your mummy and daddy would want you to follow the rules and stay safe. As soon as the going is good we will go and find them. Now, how about a story and then some lunch?'

Meg looked upset but nodded and joined Zale and Allen on the beanbags.

Sam joined them at 5pm, looking much more rested than she had this morning. She was just in time to help prepare dinner. Despite the firm words of several of the older Condor Point residents, she insisted on helping so they parked her at the table in the mess to cut vegetables from the root cellars. Despite stores of non-perishable items, there were always rolling fresh stocks of perishables placed in the bunker. Zale was glad as the idea of tinned meals never really appealed to him.

The volunteer cooks served a hearty dinner and Zale was pleased to see Trella and Jonah join them. Jonah was still a little pale but the pain relief the nurse had given him seemed to have alleviated enough of it and some makeshift crutches had been fashioned from things in the store cupboards. Meg was quiet now, eating by Sam's side. In fact, the bustle and noise from people cooking had all but disappeared once the meal was set. And it wasn't because people were eating. A few hushed whispers could be heard under the clattering of cutlery on plates but there was no conversation. No laughing and loud noises that so often punctuated a Condor Point group dinner. This was no full moon pot luck.

Zale heard the word dead too many times and when one young woman got up and ran to the bathroom in tears, Zale felt the throb of a headache beginning at his temples. He rubbed at them, his dinner forgotten, a bad taste in his mouth. He pushed his plate away with a sigh. Allen patted at his arm.

'You need to eat. We need to be strong and rested... just in case.'

'In case what?' Zale hissed.

'In case the all-clear doesn't come... You know at least one person will end up suggesting a recon mission. Half the people here are old enough to have great-grandkids and I bet most don't have weapons. If someone goes and we can't stop them, then we need to be able to protect who's left.'

'You wouldn't go with them?'

'If there's no all-clear, it's for a reason. If it gets to ten days or so maybe then, but look, there are enough supplies in here for a year at full population. I reckon we're at about forty percent population in here. Why risk it until we have to?'

'Fair enough.'

'Now eat your damn dinner then bed. I feel tomorrow will see the first wave of idiots.'

Allen smiled at Zale but it was such a forced expression. Zale sighed and tried to force down as much food as he could before the two retired.

***

Zale was woken the next morning by shouts. He opened his eyes to see Allen standing in front of the bed yelling at a group of five people.

'No, you cannot have the rifle and no, I will not go with you!'

'Look you little queer –'

'You stop right there old man. I may have a male partner but that is the right we fight for here. Freedom to love. Your wife wasn't your betrothed, your children are abominations to the City, but they're out there fighting for us, for you! So sit down and chill out and keep your archaic insults to yourself. We wait until it's safe. That's the Colonel's rules. Him and the Colonels before him.'

'I should knock you out –' the old man started.

'I would whoop your ass, now sit down, all of you.'

'You should respect your elders, son,' the man mumbled, walking away.

'Then give me something to respect you for. I just want to keep us breathing, you old fool.'

The group went and sat at one of the mess tables. Allen perched on the edge of the cot bed, rubbing at his eyes in frustration.

'Hey,' Zale said, before placing a hand on his back. Allen still jumped at the touch. 'Started a little earlier than you thought?'

'It's three-frikken A.M. They couldn't have waited til later in morning?' Allen was shaken; he hated confrontation. There'd been enough in his life with his parents before he left. He'd been betrothed since he was five. That was an honoured position. His betrothed hated him on sight. As they got older they hated each other more and more. Allen, because he had known he was gay, and her, because she wanted freedom. The betrothal felt like a jail sentence to them both, their parents not understanding that the more they pushed the two together, the further apart they had gotten.

Two weeks shy of her fourteenth birthday she disappeared. Her body was found by a fisherman three weeks later on the bank of the river. She'd tried to remove her mark, which was curled around her throat, but had cut too deep. She had bled out into the river, the cold water preserving her body well.

It was Zale whose arms Allen had fallen into. And now it was his arms that Allen returned to once again.

'Where's the rifle?' Zale asked.

'Hidden in a cupboard. Too many big ears to say exactly where.'

'Agreed. Now sleep. It's only going to get worse in the morning.'

They slept until 7am and woke to see the table of the five had grown to 10. A crowd was gathering around them as well and what were once whispered ideas were becoming what Zale's mother had called 'combative inside voices'. It seemed that two camps of people were becoming evident. The third camp was still in the majority – those sleeping, looking after children or the unwell and those who were attempting to get on with as normal a life as they could possibly manage in the bunker.

'I need a shower. Otherwise I might just join in that argument,' Allen mumbled, heading to the bathrooms. Zale sighed as he looked between the factions. He was glad for the weight of the handgun in his pocket. The safety was on, but knowing it was there was reassuring. He looked over at the growing group of arguing people. It was like a brewing storm and in the eye of it was the old man from this morning.

He was a long-term Condor Point resident but was one who kept to himself. Tyler? Tyrone? Something like that. Timon, that was it. He ran one of the greenhouses on the outskirts of the Point.

'He's been spending too long with the pumpkins, I think,' came a voice from behind the cot. Zale turned to see Trella. 'His head is turning into a gourd, hollow and full of mush and seeds.'

Zale laughed. She motioned to the bed next to his. 'May I?'

'Be my guest. That one's empty anyway.'

Trella sat and turned away from the group. 'I... we, just wanted to say thanks for the other day. Who knows what would have happened to us if we were left out there.'

'No problem. We Condor Pointers need to stick together. Thick and thin. And I'm glad we ended up in here, to be honest. How's Jonah's ankle?'

'Not pretty. It's a lovely shade of purple but the swelling is going down and he's doped up to his eyeballs pretty well. Not sure how much is left of that stuff but it should be enough for a few more days and Hannah – the nurse – said the pain won't be as bad by then.'

'Here's hoping for the all-clear so we can get the hell out of here.'

She nodded. 'It's not good, is it?'

'The lack of all-clear? No, it's not. I can't think of a single good reason it should still be unsafe.'

'Unless no ones left.'

'I'm trying not to think about it. The next Colonel was out there too, so we'd be leaderless.'

'Except for pumpkin head over there.' She paused, shaking her head. 'Well, I better get back to Jonah. He wants me to read to him because he's bored but too off his face to read himself. He's lucky I love him. Be safe.'

'You too.'

'Oh, and pass my thanks on to Allen as well,' she said with a smile as she walked away.

'Will do,' he called after her.

Allen returned a few minutes later, his wet hair falling in his eyes. He wore some old army fatigues and a Condor Point army t-shirt.

'Howdy soldier,' Zale said with a chuckle.

'It's the only thing I could find to fit me in the store cupboard. I had to get out of my old clothes, they were gross.'

'Pretty sure we're all gross,' he said, taking the dirty clothes from Allen and folding them up, tucking them under the bed.

They were interrupted by raised voices from the tables. A scuffle broke out between Timon and another man. A punch was thrown by Timon and the other man hit the floor like a sack of potatoes. Pumpkin head was stronger than Zale thought. He was glad Allen hadn't tried to fight him this morning. Allen was fast but Timon would have flattened him had he made contact. The man he had hit was twice his size. Zale's hand slipped into his jacket. He pulled the hand gun clear of the fabric but left the safety on. He saw Allen grip something in his pocket – the taser.

Timon grabbed his jacket from the table and climbed on top.

'Here we go,' Allen muttered, rolling his eyes.

'Condor Point residents – heed my call,' yelled Timon. 'We can't just sit and rot in here wondering what our intruders are doing on the outside. I propose an exploration out. A small group at first. I need five people who have stealth training. Hands-on combat training would be helpful as those with weapons are not cooperating.' He glared at Allen. 'So, who's with me?'

A few cheers went up along with several cries of *fool, death wish* and *idiot*. Timon got down off the table and moved towards the door to the tunnel.

'We stay. As soon as he's out the door I'm getting the rifle,' Allen said to Zale quietly, not wanting to rouse too much attention. 'Get Sam to come closer to us and bring Meg. We'll be safer together if things go sideways'

Zale hopped up and got Sam and Meg to follow him over to his and Allen's bunk. He motioned to Trella and the still zoned-out Jonah. As pumpkin head's group filed out, those who argued with them went back to their cots. Or sat at the tables. Zale saw a few grab kitchen knives on the way. Allen came back after a few minutes with the rifle slung over his back.

'I hope they don't think they can come back in,' yelled a man from the tables. 'They can stay out there and rot for all I care. Everyone's dead.'

Meg started crying. 'Are my mummy and daddy dead?'

'Hey asshole, there are kids in here. Keep your mouth shut,

okay?' yelled Allen.

The man sat down, but even from across the room they could hear him mumbling.

Great, thought Zale, a psycho inside with them too. Sam was trying to comfort Meg. After about 15 minutes, people resumed their quiet conversations.

Meg had settled and was over with one of the other children, playing, while Sam napped.

All of a sudden there came the noise of running coming from the tunnel. Zale clicked the safety off his gun but left it resting under the pillow he held on his lap. The door was locked from the inside. Whoever was on the other side began to bash their fists against the door. It echoed through the room.

'Let me in! Please, let me in!' called a voice. 'My daughter is in there, please!'

Meg spun around. 'That's my mummy!' She dashed over to the door but the angry man from before stopped her, grabbing her by the arm hard enough to redden her skin.

'No! It's a trap!'

'My mummy is not a trap!' Meg yelled as only a small child could. Hannah was just behind her and when the second round of shouts began she pushed the man aside and grabbed the handle.

'What's your name?' Hannah called through the door.

'Michelle. My name is Michelle Fenderland. My daughter is Meg. She's in there with Sam. Please let me in.

Hannah looked over at Meg. 'That's your mummy?'

'Yes Ma'am,' she squeaked, her face bright with joy.

Hannah opened the door, Michelle dashing in screaming.

'Run, they're behind me!' A gun shot rang out echoing in the hall. The bullet piercing through Michelle's stomach from her spine. She sprayed the group nearest the door, including her daughter, in blood. People dropped to the floor, except for Meg who stood there, dark rivulets of blood dripping down her delicate face.

The room went silent and to Zale it felt as though time itself had stopped. I couldn't move. He simultaneously wanted to run towards Meg, and to grab Allen and run into the depths of the shelter to hide. It was like no one breathed for several minutes.

A woman and two men dressed in black fatigues walked into the room.

'Everyone on the ground. You will be coming with us. You will not be hurt if you cooperate...' the woman yelled, breaking the silence. Now that it was broken, sound exploded from every direction as people scrambled and screamed and cowered in fear.

Zale got to his knees, still blocking Sam from view.

'Meg, come here,' he called. All three guns swung around to him. 'She's just a kid, let her come to me.'

Meg was wailing over her mother's body, her knees black with blood.

'She can move. No one else,' the woman said.

'Meg, come to me. Come on honey, come here,' Zale called over the wails. From the corner of his eye he saw Hannah get up to move towards Meg.

A bullet pierced through Hannah's skull with a wet thunk. She remained upright for a few seconds, her death on delay, only her head snapped back, then she fell onto the floor, the pool of blood under her head like a glossy black pillow. Meg went silent and turned towards the woman in black, pink streaks down her face, blood mingled with tears. The woman still had her gun raised.

'You killed my mummy! You killed the nice lady!' she screamed. Meg ran towards the woman, her little fists wet with blood, punching into the woman's side. Without missing a beat, the woman lowered her gun and put a bullet into Meg's head, blood spraying onto her pale skin. The woman wiped her hand on her pants as three things happened. Meg's body crumpled to the floor, screams erupted from the crowds and Allen got to his feet.

'I told you not to move!' the woman yelled over the din.

Zale tugged at Allen's shirt. 'Sit down. Please sit down,' he begged.

'You murdering BITCH! She was four years old!' Allen screamed as he began to get back down on the floor, dragged by Zale's incessant grasp.

Zale looked around the room. Most people were lying on the cold concrete floor. Sobs wracked their bodies in a mixture of fear and anger. Trella and Jonah were still sitting up, backs against the wall. Trella caught Zale's eye, nodding towards the cot. From his kneeling position he saw a flash of metal.

She had a gun. Jonah looked over and when he made eye contact, looked down himself, lifting his hand enough to show he had one too. Using hand signals they motioned to the man on the left and the woman. They would take them out. If he could take the other guy on the right out, they'd be safe...for now. Over the cries no one heard the safeties release. He watched Abagail's hand count down from five.

Five...

They gripped the guns

Four...

They braced their bodies

Three...

Two...

One...

They raised the guns in unison and fired. The Colonel's training had been worth it. Zale got his target in the head, Trella got her guy and Jonah, in his painkiller-addled state, still managed a shot to the chest on the woman. Her gun clattered to the concrete floor. She ducked down in a mix of pain and self-preservation.

Zale fired at her, the bullet grazing her leg as she sprinted out into the tunnel. Zale took chase, Allen calling after him. He dashed up the tunnel trying to get a clear shot but the woman was zigzagging as she ran. She jumped through the doorway to outside, the bright light blinding Zale to her position. He fired at the entry hoping to chance a hit.

He heard a grunt of pain but she kept running. He got to the door; a blood trail led out. He peered through the opening and saw her duck behind a building. He had just crawled through the door when an explosion tore through the tunnel behind him, throwing him clear of the opening. He felt the burn on his back as he smashed into the ground, sliding through the dirt. Then everything went black.

CHAPTER EIGHT
Almara

My name used to be Almara. I am now known only as prisoner 482. I have been here for seven years. I don't really know where "here" is because I haven't seen the sky since I was captured.

The hallways were white, the rooms were white, our facility-sanctioned clothes were black. They were the colours that painted my world ninety percent of the time. I saw other prisoners if our schedules crossed, leaving and entering rooms, but they kept our faces covered on the journeys and we couldn't see out of our rooms except cursory glances when they pushed food through the hatch. They kept us apart. We never spoke to each other. No one made eye contact.

They called this a containment facility. We called it the Cube. Well, I say we, the guards said so. They called themselves facilitators, but they carried tasers and batons.

They told me I was dangerous... to myself and others. I was an abomination. I was genetically damaged. The tests they ran were to 'fix me' and help fix others like me. They took blood once a week, skin and hair samples once a month. We got CT scans, MRIs, x-rays and other scans I don't know the names of. They didn't give us much information on the science side, and after a while I stopped bothering to ask.

The psychologists made me look at ink blob pictures, fill in quizzes, and they hypnotised me. They drugged me and tested my reactions. I was certain they also drugged our food or drink so we stayed placid. My mind was always a little fuzzy, my mouth a little dry. My eyelids always felt heavier than they should and when they made me exercise, I felt weak and got tired so easily, but it felt so good to move outside of a hallway or my tiny room that I pushed through it.

The gym was the only room with colour in the Cube, at least as far as I had seen. The ceiling was painted blue, the carpet a bright green, in some poor attempt at mimicking the outside world. Oh, how I missed the sun, the fresh air and a breeze rippling through my hair. Even temperature changes were something I missed, sweating in the summer or shivering in the cold of winter. None of these existed in the Cube.

I was thankful they had given me access to pencils and paper. I had been asking for paper for years. The pencils were used up quite quickly from using the walls as a canvas. I tried to draw my mother's face but I barely remembered her... I missed her so much. The picture on the wall had been a work in progress for a month now. It felt more like her every day. My father and sister had been wiped from my memory but my mother I had held onto. She was what kept me alive. I wondered what they told her had happened to me, or did they say nothing, leaving her wondering where I was, and if I was alive or dead?

Every day they taught us about the war. It'd been years since it ended, but the scars it left across the country were still affecting us today. The wastelands, reduced to deserts and radiation no-go zones, meant we remained unable to travel outside Oasis. People tried, but never came back. They told us what the radiation would do to us, if the lack of water and food didn't kill us first.

The war was started by the blanks, they say. An uprising of unmarked, fighting against the marked. They told me that the blanks were dangerous, that I was a remnant of chaos. I should not breed. I should not try and steal a marked person for myself or try to pretend I am normal, and blanks should never breed with other blanks. Chaos children, as they call children from two blanks, were aborted or euthanised at birth as they would be the ultimate downfall of genetics. I was a dangerous anomaly. Marked pairs were chosen by genetics to be the perfect pair, to create perfect children; that is how it worked and how it was meant to be, they said. Genetic markers – that's what they are. So two matching marks means two harmonious genetic codes.

I would only create damaged children. I asked them how a perfect pairing like my parents made me. They told me again that I am an anomaly and that my parents had been tested. I was a birth defect. Maybe my mother had a fall when she was pregnant, or ate something bad. Maybe I was meant to be miscarried. Maybe I was why my mother had so many failed pregnancies before me. I had been poisoning her. That was why my sister was marked normally. It was my fault and once I, the toxin, left my mother's body she was fine.

I hoped they would stop the lessons eventually but they just repeated them over and over again, the teachers different but always in the same white room, with white chairs and a white desk between us. I had loved learning before the Cube, and had loved school, but not anymore. I was shown black and white photos of riots; of corpses and propaganda. The monochrome images seemed almost unreal, the dark black patches of blood looked like spilled paint. I'd become immune to the images now. Even the massacres of children elicited no reaction from me anymore. I had noticed the children in the photos bore no visible markings but I had learnt not to speak up or ask questions. These were no classrooms – they were lecture rooms and I was not to interrupt.

Talking was for the psychologists and facilitator Ahn. Ahn was my sanity break. He was a facilitator because he needed the money and his marked paring had been ended early due to his wife being killed in an accident. Only people without partners or children worked at the Cube, he told me. That explained the bitterness in some of them. They lived on-site but in the sunshine. I told him how jealous I was of him having fresh air. He smiled at me but knew he was already breaking rules by talking with me like a normal person instead of a prisoner. I knew the pencils and paper were Ahn's doing. He gave me a wink the first day I got them along with my week's clothes and supplies. I never asked but he was the only kindness I experienced here. He told me I looked like his wife.

The war lessons continued. After the uprising and the first of the bombs, we, the blanks, felt that we were losing the war. It was because we were... we *are*, inferior to the marked. So we harnessed the beasts of the wastelands, the mutations that had been created by nuclear fallout and chemical warfare. I had never seen a beast and they couldn't show me a photo of one. They had been purged, I was told; like the blanks were. The beasts had strength and anger and the blanks used this rage to fire them up to battle the marked – to even the number. Most the big cities fell. Bombs tore through high rises and crumbled the roads. Some of the cities could still be seen far on the horizon in the wastelands, they said. I have never seen them. I doubted I ever would.

I asked what the war was about and how it started.

'You,' was the answer I was given. They didn't like questions, but when I first asked I was still young and still bristled about being here. Don't get me wrong, I still hated it here, but the fire inside was a mere ember of its former self. I asked them to elaborate. They told me that the blanks wanted equal rights; that despite their being inferior, they wanted to be considered as mutagen free as the marked. They wanted to be loved and to be betrothed like their superior brethren. They wanted to be free. But inferior breeding was not allowed. Before the war the population had gotten too large. The infrastructure of the food production network could not handle the sheer numbers of people. The unmarked were like feral rabbits, I was told.

By the time the war was over, half the population had been eliminated – mainly the blanks, who had been all but annihilated. The war was won and the marked had succeeded, the blanks and beasts either eradicated, captured or had disappeared into the wilderness and the wastelands. New communities sprung up in the regions between the zones. Our area, Oasis, had thrived. Communication had never been re-established. The wastelands had too much radiation fallout and it meant the genetic pool would be mutagen free marked people. No visitors meant the blanks could be controlled.

Controlled. That was what I was. My status was recorded as secured. I had been allowed to be free as long as I had because my mother had petitioned for a normal childhood. Puberty was the latest they allowed us to be free. After that there was too large a chance of us breeding with a marked person, or worse, another blank. Most parents were happy to hand over blank children to the authorities. The shame was too much.

'Are they killed?' I asked. 'The babies, do you kill them or raise them here in this hole?'

They paused too long after I asked this question. I asked it to several facilitators but all of them gave similar answers. All of them paused just a little too long.

'They die quite early. Inferior genetics do that. That you have lived this long is rare.'

After I initially asked, no amount of follow-up questions were answered. I could never get more out of them. I always had questions, but the more I asked, the more tests they ran on me.

'You're smart for a blank. Too smart for your own good. Most blanks are mentally disabled,' one of the doctors said to me. I would ask for books, I missed the stories of my childhood, but they would only give me textbooks full of their version of the war and how inferior I was. I would still read them, cover to cover, word for word, for something to do. Once again Ahn managed to help me by slipping me some thin novels I kept tucked in my pillowcase and behind the sink. Some I had read so many times, I could recite them word perfect. They were the reprieve from the Cube I needed.

Today, along with a fresh box of pencils, was a note. It was scrawled in black ink on a thin piece of notebook paper.

Don't do anything rash tonight. Trust me, you'll see. It's a test. Remain calm. Destroy this note.

The look in Ahn's eyes told me it was from him. He looked spooked. His eyes were too wide for anything but fear and panic. I wanted to ask him about it but by the time I'd looked up he was gone and he didn't bring me my lunch like normal. A thin sharp-looking woman called Morag slid the food tray into my room.

'Where's Ahn?' I asked, but she said nothing, not even making eye contact. 'Hey, Facilitator. Facilitate me! Where the hell is Ahn?'

'He's sick, you piece of blank scum. Now shut up and eat before I get you a dose of electroshock.'

I silently picked up my food tray and took it to my bed. Electro was not something I wanted. It hurt. It was not used for anything but pain. They told me it was for medical reasons, but electro therapy wasn't supposed to hurt. This made your nerves scream and your teeth clench on the biter so hard I was sure I had cracked a tooth last time.

I ate slowly, looking for abnormalities in the food but it was soup and bread and a bottle of too-sweet-to-be-real juice. I missed real juice. I'd forgotten what it tasted like but I knew I had loved it. I'd always felt sleepy after eating but not today. If anything, I felt energetic for the first time in ages. My heart started to race and I couldn't sit still. I tapped my fingers on my now-empty food tray. My brain felt alive. Was this the test? Were they hoping for aggression?

I heard a yell from down the cold hallway. An angry cry of freedom. The noises grew. Trays were being thrown through door bars, cups tossed through the food chute and voices – so many voices. How many of us were there in the Cube? I couldn't tell as shouts echoed around, swelling into a billion voices from each room.

I heard the facilitators stomping down the hallways,

banging their batons across the bars of the doors, calling for quiet. As they went past me I heard the buzz of the taser prod they used to subdue people. Anyone touching the metal of the doors were in for an uncomfortable lesson.

'Settle down, you freaks, or I will personally remove meals from you for a few days. How does that sound?' came the voice of one of the facilitators.

Her voice barely made a dent in the current noise. Expletives burst from a room to my right. It sounded so close. I'd been THAT CLOSE to another blank all along. Now I understood the hoods they made us wear on the way to other areas.

A scream rang out as a zap flew from the taser prod. One less voice called out. I hoped he wasn't dead. I wanted to look but I stayed on my bed. Must be calm. Mustn't do anything, I repeated to myself. My feet tapped on the floor, their steady taps only taken over by my nails rapping on the bed head. I could feel my pulse rising. My face felt hot. It was horrible. I dashed to the sink and splashed my face with cold water. I was almost surprised when it didn't hiss into steam on contact. The small mirror glued to the blank white wall above the sink reflected the red of my flushed cheeks. I shook myself, trying to throw the heat from my body. The movement felt good. I started to jog on the spot and felt the heat and pressure in my face start to dissipate. Okay, this could do. I tried to block out the screams from the hallway.

My forced sessions of exercise at least gave me stamina. I ran til my legs hurt, my feet ached as they hit into the concrete floor. My lungs began to burn and even in the air conditioning of the room, sweat began to pour down my face. A sharp pain shot through my leg and up to my hip, a stitch tore through my side. I collapsed onto my bed. I felt the stitch begin to relax as I caught my breath. Despite my energy levels still pulsing though my brain, the rest of me was settled a little. My muscles twitched in my legs.

I reached for the last of my juice, but thought better of it.

Whatever was screwing with me could be in there. It could be in everything. I walked shakily to the sink and rinsed my cup, filling it with water that I gulped down. Three cups later and I finally began to feel less pained.

The screams outside continued. The zap of the taser prod could be heard every few minutes but still it carried on. I lay on my bed and covered my face with my pillow. *Shut up, shut up, shut up, shut up, shut up, shut up,* I muttered to myself. Even with my eyes closed against the rough cotton pillow case, I felt my eyes uncontrollably darting left and right behind my eyelids, a red haloed imprint on my vision.

I have no idea how long I lay there listening to my teeth grinding, watching the corona of red in my eyes, as the muffled cries from the halls pushed their way into my head. My breathing was still fast and shallow. Then I realised I didn't hear the cries anymore. Were they all dead? I pushed the pillow off my face and onto the floor. The noise it made as it hit the floor sounded wrong. Then I saw why. There was a shallow pool of water covering the floor. It wasn't deep but it pooled at the end of my room, looking like it was trying to crawl the walls, it was getting deeper. I could hear splashed footfalls from the hall. A timid cry came from the room next door. 'Help, it's flooding!'

'It's just a broken pipe. Don't fret, freaks!' called the facilitator from a few rooms away.

Had someone ripped a pipe from the wall in a fit of rage-induced strength? I glanced at the piping running along the edge of my wall. It looked very solid.

The water flow increased. My rising body temperature yearned to lie on the floor in the cool water but some instinct told me to stay out of it. I reached down and plucked my shoes from the water before it soaked through the cloth upper. I slipped them on. I just had to, according to the voice in my head that mumbled advice to me through my rising stress. Then I heard the clank of the door barrels unlocking. The last thunk as it opened was followed by a death-like silence. They had to have all unlocked. I felt the rumble as the doors began to slide to one side.

From my bed I tried to look into the hallway. The doors were open, slid back into the walls. I had never realised how well-concealed the doors in the hall had been. The food slot and barred window cover must be seamless once closed. I had never seen the outlines of doors like this before.

I saw movement in the water and noticed a small boy in the doorway across the hall to the right. He looked all of eight years old. He was dressed like me, in shapeless black clothes, his bare feet making ripples in the water. It was deep enough now to cover his feet. He saw me and waved, his eyes wide. I motioned for him to away from the door. I mouthed GET BACK but it was too late... a facilitator had seen him and sloshed his way across the floor to the boy and slapped him across the face. He fell backwards into the water with a splash and began to cry.

'Shut up, kid. Go sit down.' The boy crawled away from my line of sight but I could still hear his muffled sobs.

Another voice piped up. 'There has been a malfunction to the doors due to the water. Please remain in your rooms for your own safety. We will use force if necessary to keep you in them.'

I saw the owner of the voice, a thin spindly woman I always thought of as a spider. She was nasty and brutal. I quickly learnt to stay away from her and say as little as possible to her. She saw me looking at her.

'What you looking at, freak? Get your filthy eyes off me. I will incapacitate you if I have to.'

I lowered my head so she couldn't see my eyes through my hair. My hair was long and now curtained my face from view but I continued to watch.

A male facilitator walked past carrying a large tube attached to a huge battery slung over his shoulder. What the hell was it? I watched as he stopped just up from the boy's room. He pressed a panel and a hatch slid up. He pulled a plastic stool down and placed it on the floor. I noticed his belt held more than the standard issue taser and handcuffs. What looked like a handgun sat on his hip. I didn't recognise the man and that worried me more. What was happening?

I was getting agitated. I needed to move but I didn't want to get onto the floor. The water was easily ankle deep now. I heard splashing from all down the hallway but I just couldn't see well enough. I decided to stand on my bed. Resting one foot on the bed head, I pulled myself over to the doorway. I gripped the doorframe for balance and peered out, as quickly as I could. I didn't want to get caught. There were so many facilitators. It had to be at least three quarters of the staff.

I wished Ahn was here but his warning still echoed through my head. IT'S A TEST. A test for what? I chanced another peek. They were all armed. Plastic stools sat in between each doorway. Before I could pull my head back in I noticed two things – each panel in the wall had a cord hanging out, the thickness of my arm, and secondly a baton was swinging towards my head. I snapped my head back as the baton hit the door frame. The concrete wall showed through the white paint now. My finger didn't move quite as fast. The middle of the baton smacked into my right little finger. The crunch of breaking bone mingled with my scream. I fell back on my bed, pain shooting up my arm. It was bleeding and a splash of blood streaked down the white wall. I clenched my teeth through the rage that I could feel swelling up in my chest.

Must stay calm.

The spider woman stood grinning at the door. I bit my tongue and took a big deep breath through the pain. I pulled a sock from the end of my bed where I'd left today's pair and wrapped it around my bleeding hand, trying not to move it too much. The aggression I felt rising in me was helping to dull the pain. I was sitting up when the spider woman finally left my sight. I heard a thump and a scream in the distance, then another. More followed, splashes punctuating some of the screams as my fellow blanks hit the water. I looked down;

it was even deeper. Heavy splashes walked through the halls. I saw the stranger walk past again. He looked into my room at the blood-splattered sheet and at me flushed and shaking, holding my bleeding hand. He laughed. I moved to dive at him but took a deep breath and remained sitting. I grinned at him, my teeth grinding together to keep from screaming or spitting at him.

His smile dropped from his face. I laughed at him. I'm sure I sounded maniacally insane. I felt my brain beginning to fracture. I couldn't stop laughing. He furrowed his brow at me. I realised then that he looked like a dog my neighbour had when I was a kid. Bruno was his name. This only made me laugh harder. I felt tears streaming down my face. A part of me thought, this was it. They had finally broken me. My mind had snapped.

'Shut up!' the stranger spat at me.

'Bad dog, Bruno!' I screamed back. I laughed even harder. 'Sit, Bruno, sit.'

What was I doing? I saw him draw his baton. I just couldn't help myself. 'Want to play fetch, Bruno? Bring me the stick.' I held out my bloodied, sock-wrapped hand.

'I'll give you the stick, you little bitch,' he roared as he threw the baton at my head. What possessed him to do something so stupid I'll never know. In my normal pacified state it would have knocked me out cold, but whatever they had laced us with had not only given me the reflexes to dodge the baton but to catch it in my uninjured hand.

He stood staring at me, seeing what I'd do. I was still partially in a state of shock from catching it. I slowly placed it in my lap and looked back at him.

'No fetch for you, Bruno. I'm going to keep this right here for now.' I held eye contact until he walked away, splashing down the hall. That had been a little close for comfort. I picked the baton up again in my good hand, weighing it up. This could come in handy if I didn't lose the plot and end up face-down in the rising tide of water. But why would he let me keep it? Was it a last toy before I got put down? I kept a grip on it but rested it back on my crossed legs. Breathe. I needed to breathe.

I closed my eyes, trying to block out the yelling that continued to be punctuated by screams and more splashes but much further off now. How many people were there here in the Cube?

Then the alarm sounded. A low steady beeping began to echo its electronic wail off the hard, white walls.

'What's happening?' called a male voice.

'Shut that noise up!' came another voice.

'Is there a fire?'

'Do we need to evacuate?'

'Are we going to die?'

The questions bounced between the beeps. The sound was only making everyone more agitated. I stood up on the bed again.

'Get in your rooms!' bellowed facilitator Bruno.

I watched them walking back to the plastic steps they had placed against the walls. Bruno I could see from my bed but I needed a better vantage point. I hopped over to my chair. It too was plastic, and a little wobbly from my weight hopping onto it. But it would hold me fine. I wasn't that big but the years of mostly sedentary life had made me less than slim. From here I could peer to see another facilitator on her plastic step. She looked panicked; something bad was going to happen and it didn't look like she wanted any part of it. I whipped my head around to look for the escape route I knew wasn't there. I clutched the baton til my knuckles went white. Over the alarm and the calls of my fellow blanks I heard Bruno call out.

'Stage one!'

He shrugged off his backpack that looked like a battery and placed it into the alcove with the switches. The tube hanging from the battery slotted into a hole above the long black cord coming out of the wall. What the hell was that? I heard the tube click into place and then a flurry of clicks throughout the hallway.

'Stage two!' he called. I saw him push a button on the wall and a hum began to thrum through the air. He tossed the black cable to the floor; it floated in the water, wriggling like an angry black eel. I saw a blue spark as the end of it flicked out of the water. I realised then what was happening. They were going to electrocute us all.

I looked around me. The plastic chair I was on was the safest option. The desk and bed had metal frames and even if I could reach my little bathroom without ending up in the water, I had no idea if electrical current could travel through porcelain. I grabbed my pencil and papers, jamming the writings into my pockets and jabbing my pencil into my hair. If I had the chance to run, I'd take it, test or no test. They weren't getting my thoughts on paper to use against me.

I wanted to call out. I wanted to warn the others but I knew if I did that I would be punished. THIS WAS A TEST. I looked out the door and made eye contact with Bruno. He looked at me quizzically, and then smiled. I closed my eyes and crouched down on the chair, my hands over my ears. I heard a muffled call of 'Stage three' and then screams. I didn't hear the splashes but I knew that people would be falling into the water. They were exterminating us. I could feel the electric hum through the air, the hair on my arms standing on end.

I willed them to stop. I bit my lip to stop from crying out. I could taste blood in my mouth and the salt of the tears that now ran down my face.

The silence came all of a sudden. It was heavier than the screams on my ears; the enormity of it cloaked me. I saw the water level begin to drop, a drain opening up in the floor. The last of it gurgled down and away but still I could not move. I crouched on my chair and trembled. I knew if I tried to stand I would likely fall. I did not trust my legs to hold me.

I heard the facilitators stepping down off their steps. The spider woman stopped at my cell, tilting her head at me in my crouch. She smiled that nasty, toothy smile of hers where she looked as though eating you alive was a viable option. Hitting the button outside my room, the door slid shut, the food and observation holes closed and I assumed locked. The lights in my room dimmed like they did at bedtime, a pale-yellow glow filling the room, making everything look vaguely jaundiced. I took a deep but shaky breath and tried to stand up. Despite the lingering shake in my legs this time I managed to stay standing. I could hear muffled noises outside my room. Only the sharp retorts of gunfire could truly cut through the soundproofing. I didn't want to even think about it. There were only residual droplets now, rivulets running towards the drain. I gingerly stepped down onto the floor. My heart was pounding in my ears like cannon fire again and I couldn't catch my breath. I did a quick dash to my bed and sat down before my legs gave out. My thighs were throbbing. I tried to calm my breathing, white spots flickered in my eyes and despite the temperature-controlled environment, I was sweating like a pig.

Finally, my breath slowed and my head cleared a little. I still felt jittery, my eyes wide. I swallowed hard, my mouth dry. It was then I realised I still had the baton clutched in my hand. I'm not sure how long I lay there clutching the baton but I listened to my breathing until the lights went out.

CHAPTER NINE
Darnell

It was dark and cold, and the densely growing forest dragged branches across Darnell's face. He was sure at least one of the branches had ripped at his coat, scratching his skin and making it bleed. He'd never been in this part of the forest. His mother hadn't let him wander too far. He knew why, but hadn't believed it until the attack. He felt tears prickle at his eyes. His mother was surely dead and he had no home. He was on the run and felt trapped in the situation he was in. He hated it.

He took a deep breath and pushed the branches away from his face. He'd been doing battle through the foliage for at least a few hours. *What time was it?* he thought to himself. He was exhausted. He leant against one of the large trees, kicking at the branches near the ground; stomping down the sticks there. He slid his way down to sit in the dark. In the light of his head lamp, he pulled a bottle of water and guzzled it down. It was cold out but the effort of his journey had left him parched. His eyelids felt so heavy. He felt sleep threatening to overwhelm him. His eyes slid shut and he drifted.

A rustle came from his left. His eyes flew open and he flicked the headlamp off. He heard the noise again, this time closer, noticing light coming through the thick canopy.

'Dammit,' he mumbled. He'd slept for way too long. He tried to breathe as quietly as possible but his heartbeat pounded in his head and chest so loudly he had no idea how it couldn't be heard echoing through the trees. A branch broke to his right this time – he was surrounded. He fought back a wail as a set of glowing eyes appeared on each side of him. He whipped his head from side to side; he was too scared to breathe.

Then from his right appeared a deer. He looked to his left as another deer, obviously not fazed by him in the slightest, pushed its head through the leaves. They nuzzled in front of him. He let out the breath he had been holding, as slowly and quietly as he possibly could so as not to scare his visitors, although he was the real visitor here, he supposed.

They began to graze on the crushed grass at his feet. He felt a laugh rising in his throat and his hands flew to his mouth to stifle the giggle. The deer's heads swung to look at him, their mouths still chewing. They looked at each other, then wandered away into the shadows.

He reached back up and flicked his headlamp back on. Despite the early morning sun glinting through the breaks in foliage, the light was so filtered by the time it got through to the forest floor that his lamp was still necessary. He had to get moving again; find somewhere safe. He got to his feet, brushing the dirt and leaves from his backside.

His mother had taught him survival skills and they had been using them daily for as long as he could remember, but he knew he'd been spoiled with their gardens and well-stocked pantry. The roof over his head and soft bed would be sorely missed, but for one more day with his mother he'd have given it up forever. He pushed on, breaking through the foliage snagging at his clothes. It was back-breaking work. He was fit, he'd spent his days swimming, chopping wood and hunting, but this was dense forest, not the copse of trees around their cabin. He tripped again, his foot catching on the undergrowth for the umpteenth time.

He was getting frustrated. This forest felt endless. From maps in the cabin he knew he was heading between the mountains and into the rural areas, smaller townships, farms and processing plants. Most the region's food came from here as well as fabric, furniture and building materials. This forest was constantly being replanted on the rural side so he knew he was still a while off this zone as the trees here grew in a random and natural formation. This was natural forest. Men grew trees in rows, nature did not.

He tripped again, this time on a rock. He looked down at it and saw that to his right were many more rocks. He must be nearer to the mountain than he thought. Carefully he picked his way over the stones, feet slipping and rolling on the pebbles that littered the ground. At last he came across the very thing he was hoping to find – a small cave in the stone wall rising to his side. It wasn't that deep – he could see the back wall in the feeble light off his headlamp, but it would give him cover and he'd feel much safer. He checked for signs of animals but it held nothing more than loose leaves and a few errant vines creeping their way in. He looked at his watch. It was nearly midday. He had put himself at risk walking during the day. He unrolled his sleeping bag and snuggled in, turning off his headlamp. He was asleep in minutes.

***

Darnell woke shivering, a noise just outside the cave drawing his attention. Voices – he heard voices. He could see a slight glow from between the trees – it was still daytime. The cold stone below him pumped its icy flow into him, his fingertips flushed a purplish blue from the cold. They might get snow this year in the valley. Normally it was just on the mountaintops but it was just so unnaturally cold for this time of year.

He needed to move but the voices outside worried him. He didn't think he was close enough to the rural settlements to be near a village, but could people live out in the forest? People like him? Or was it the people who shot his mother...?

He pulled his hands into the sleeping bag to try and warm them and stretched his back to limber it up from the cold. He tried to slow his breathing, see if he could hear what the voices were saying to work out if they were friendlies. His heart pounded so loudly in his head. He shook his head, trying to concentrate.

A giggle echoed through the cave from outside. *Was that a child?* he thought to himself. *Or was it a trap?*

'I found blackberries, Nisha! Come here!' came another child-like voice, a boy, he thought.

'But Mum wants us to go to the pumpkin patch,' the girl replied.

'But blackberries are awesome! We can get a pumpkin afterwards!'

He saw a flash of yellow as the girl ran past the cave entrance. They were kids! He breathed a sigh of relief. They must live around here. And he did like blackberries. He wiggled out of the sleeping bag and rolled it away, his bones cracking from being cold and stiff for so long. He stood and stretched, then slung his pack onto his back and looked out of the cave entrance. He could see a patch of yellow through the trees to his right. Nisha was the girl's name, he remembered. He could see her brother kneeling in front of a massive patch of blackberry bushes.

'Glad I stopped here, otherwise I would have gone right past them,' he mumbled to himself.

He couldn't see anyone else around. He got to about two yards away but the kids hadn't heard him.

'Hey, guys? Can I join you?' he said quietly, hoping not to startle them. The children both spun around, their eyes looking huge and bright against their dark skin. The girl had pulled a knife from the pocket of her dress and the boy held a small axe.

'Woah, it's okay, kids. Not going to hurt you. I'm unarmed. Just want to get some blackberries if you're cool with sharing your patch. My name is Darnell.'

'What are you doing in the woods? I've never seen you before,' Nisha said, still gripping the knife without a single tremor in her grasp. She was small but fierce. He wasn't sure of her age but she held that blade with no fear of using it. Her brother had now got to his feet and despite his small stature and that he had to be at least seven years younger than Darnell, he held that axe like he was determined enough to fell a tree in one swing.

'I lived on the other side of the forest, closer to the City,' Darnell explained hurriedly, before they could act on that determination. 'My mother died and now I'm travelling through to get a new start.'

Lowering the knife, but still gripping it firmly in her hand, the girl stepped towards him.

'If you try to hurt me or Neil, I will skin you alive. I'm small but fast and I could take on a City boy twice your size. If you are as you say, though, you have nothing to worry about, do you, Darnell?'

Darnell stepped closer, taking a big breath. *This would either work very well or he'd end up with a knife in him*, he thought. He held out his hand to her, a slight tremble visible, at least to him. 'Let's start over. Hi, I'm Darnell. Can I pick some blackberries with you?'

She slowly slipped the knife into the front pocket of her dress and took his hand. He noticed her other hand slip into the pocket, ready to defend herself again.

'I'm Nisha and this is my brother Neil. And yes, you may join us.' She smiled but it looked forced. She watched him pull his backpack off and set it against a tree to open it. She remained stiff and on-edge, watching as he pulled a pot free and zipped up the bag again. The berries weren't in full season but there were plenty for picking. He moved a few bushes down and began to rummage through for the fruit. He saw Nisha nod to the boy, who still stood, axe ready to swing. He smiled and dropped the axe and began picking again. Nisha relaxed, and soon they all were deep into the picking.

Darnell glanced over to them. The children were dressed simply but were clean and well-fed. They must be looked after.

'So do you live in the woods?'

'We have a small farm on the outskirts. Our mother plants crops further into the woods for us though as the soil is better,' Nisha said.

'How far is the next town from here?'

'I've never been but our mother can ride there and back in a day. Walking I guess about a day each way if you kept a good pace. There's a road of sorts that will take you there and a few smaller farms along the way might be able to take you in if you need a rest. We are wary along these parts but happy to pay a favour if we can and it is warranted.'

'You know a lot for having not left the area.' Darnell said with a smile.

'I'm fifteen, just look a lot younger. I also read a lot. We have maps of the farming territory my father made.'

'Hey, we're nearly the same age! I'm 17.'

'Wait, you're only a teenager too? And you're all alone on the road?'

'Yup, no choice. Can't go back to the City and Mum told me to go to the township of Ellintown. There's someone there that can help me get back on my feet.'

'Come back to the farm with us and I can show you the maps. I think Mum is taking some of the lambs to town tomorrow. It's not Ellintown but it's close. Ashwater is where she's headed but from there it's paved roads. I'm sure she'd be able to give you a ride if you don't mind the smell of sheep,' she said with a smile.

'You don't go with her?'

'Neil's only six, so she doesn't like him left alone. It's not safe.'

'Hey Neesh, is this enough for Amma to make us a pie?' Neil said, looking up at the pair. His dark skin was smeared with the darker berry juice. Nisha and Darnell laughed. Even his hands were stained.

'Despite how many you've eaten, yes Neil, it should be enough. How you will have room for dinner, let alone pie, after what you've gobbled down already, I have no idea.'

'I didn't eat that many...'

'Just smooshed them all over your face then, did you buddy?' Darnell said, ruffling his hair the way his mother used to do to him, hoping it would be taken as a friendly gesture. Neil wiped at his mouth and chin with one of his hands trying in vain to wipe it away, merely smearing more juice across his skin. Nisha shook her head with a giggle.

'Let's go get a pumpkin and head home before it gets dark.'

They dumped their blackberries into Darnell's pot and Neil carried it in his arms, a wide smile across his face. They marched single file through the trees to a large clearing filled with crops. Big orange pumpkins were filling a square of vines in the back. Neil put the pot down and ran off, picking tomatoes, herbs and whatever else took his eye on the way. Darnell followed Nisha to the pumpkin patch and came away with two giant orange globes in his arms. Neil met them back at the edge and dumped the armfuls of produce he had picked on the ground.

'Herbs in the pot Neil,' she said, pulling a cloth from her pocket. 'Heavy stuff on the bottom and the rest at the top of the bundle.'

He did as she said and Nisha gathered the corners of the cloth up like the hobo bundles from his storybooks, then swung it over her shoulder.

'Let's go,' she said, and they began to walk back to the farm.

'So is it just the three of you?' Darnell asked.

'Yeah, if you don't count the animals. Dad was working in Eventone Mill when there was an explosion. Not sure how much you lot in the City hear about our side of Oasis, but a lot of folks died. Dad went back in to try and help people out but the roof caved in.' He could hear a sob rising in her throat, he eyes glazed with tears that she wouldn't let fall. She swallowed hard and let out a long breath, composing herself best she could, and continued. 'Luckily, we were pretty self-sufficient, otherwise I don't know how we'd have survived. We don't get much money from the sheep but we get by.'

'Your mum sounds pretty tough. Just like my mum was,' he said, feeling tears pricking at his eyes. It still hadn't fully sunk in that she was gone. It only made him want to go on and follow his mother's every word. He had to be strong. He sniffled away the tears, unable to wipe them away with his arms full of pumpkin.

'You said your mum died?' Nisha asked, gently. 'Only recently I'll wager.' He nodded. 'It's okay to cry, you know. Your face looks like the one I wore for weeks after we lost dad. You aren't weak for being upset. Blocking it in does nothing but make you feel worse.'

He felt more tears threatening to spill forth but he shook his head and cleared his throat, trying to hide the tremble in his voice.

'Thanks. I... uh... it hasn't hit home just yet. I'll be okay.'

'It gets better,' piped Neil. 'It never goes away but you get better.'

With those words of wisdom he broke into a run. Darnell could see a corner of a fence from between the trees. Next minute a large, fluffy collie came dashing out from between the trees with a string of barks. Darnell recoiled in fear, stumbling back and landing on the dirt as the dog climbed on top of him. Nisha laughed and told the dog to get off and sit. He obeyed, but continued a wiggling vibration of excitement. Darnell had never seen a dog in real life before. They had no pets at the cabin apart from the chickens and even then, dogs were uncommon in the City, so people walking in the forest never had them. He wanted to touch it because it looked so soft, but didn't want to get bitten. He just sat frozen, staring at the creature.

'Darnell, this is Kutta, Kutta this is Darnell. He's a friend.' The dog barked in recognition, his tail wagging at a furious pace. Darnell jumped at the noise. Nisha laughed.

'You look like you've seen a ghost. Kutta will lick you to death before he hurts you. You can pat him, he won't bite.' Kutta barked again, Darnell jumped again.

"Kutta stay and be gentle,' Nisha said. 'Darnell is okay. You've never seen a dog before, have you?' Darnell shook his head. 'Put the pumpkins down,' she said before grabbing his hand and pulling him gently towards the dog, placing his hand on Kutta's head. 'He loves pats,' she said stepping back. Darnell stroked the collie's head. It was like satin, so silky and soft. He dropped onto one knee to get a good look at the dog, continuing to pat his head. Kutta bounced up and put his paws on Darnell's shoulders. He froze but couldn't take his eyes off Kutta's. They were big and brown. They felt endless. He laughed as the dog licked his face.

'He likes you,' Nisha observed. 'Come on Kutta, let's go get dinner.' Kutta barked and ran in a circle before loping towards the house.

Darnell felt more relaxed than he had in a long time. And a home-cooked meal would do him the world of good. Neil was in the front yard picking beans. 'Amma said to bring everything inside then come out and get some carrots.'

Nisha nodded and motioned to Darnell to follow her. The house was small but warm and it smelled amazing. A small woman stood at the stove, her long dark hair trailing down her back in a tight braid. 'Amma, this is Darnell. He lives out in the forest, he's trying to get to town. Plus he helped carry the pumpkins. Can he stay for dinner?'

She laughed and nodded, stirring the pot on the stove. 'I'll make up a bed for him too. Welcome to the family, Darnell. Feel free to call me Amma. Everyone does.'

He nodded dumbly. He knew good manners but wasn't all that socialised. He managed to smile and mutter a quiet thank you.

'You are a shy one, aren't you?' Amma said, taking the pumpkins from his arms. 'Nisha, go help Neil with the carrots and I'll keep cooking. Darnell, you're welcome to go wash up then have a seat. You look tired.'

'Uh, thank you Ma'am. I'm happy to help though. Uh, your hospitality is much appreciated.'

She smiled and nodded, turning back to the bench to start chopping up one of the pumpkins. Darnell followed Nisha into the garden and found Neil munching on a carrot.

'Neil, did you even wash the dirt off that carrot?'

'I wiped it off,' he said defiantly, taking the last bite. He pushed the end back into the dirt. 'I got plenty so we can go back in.'

Neil wandered back inside, arms full. Nisha and Darnell followed. Nisha sat on the top step.

'Sit with me a while. I don't often get to see people my own age.'

'I know the feeling. Mum and I were pretty isolated at our cabin. We saw the odd hiker but mainly it was just the two of us.'

'Is your dad...'

'Alive? Yeah, I think so. Haven't seen him in years. He used to organise supplies for Mum and me, but he never visited.'

'So he left his bonded mate? That's rare.'

'Mum had her reasons. She still loved him, but some things meant they had to live apart.'

'So you went with her?'

'I was one of those things. Dad couldn't come with us. Mum's family didn't even know where we were. They probably think we're dead.' Darnell felt tears prickling at his eyes. 'It was all my fault.' He shut his eyes, trying to fight back the tears, but once one escaped that was all it took to open the floodgates. He began to sob. Nisha started to rub his back to comfort him. His mother used to do the same.

'Shh, you can't blame yourself. Death is inevitable, especially when you aren't in the City.'

He shook his head. He wanted to tell her about himself. Tell her how it was his fault but when he opened his mouth, a mewling sob was all that came out, so he merely shook his head again. He tried to take a deep breath but it was a little choked. A few more attempts eventually slowed his crying to just rogue tears.

'We were in the cabin because of me. I can't tell you why, so please don't ask. If it wasn't for me she would have been safe in the City with my dad, but she wouldn't leave me. And now she's dead. And now I have no family I can run to and it's all my fault.'

'Darnell, what is past is past. It cannot be changed. I know that doesn't fix anything and I know it doesn't help how you're feeling but it's true. I don't want you to tell me anything you aren't comfortable talking about but I'm happy to stay up to listen if you need an ear. You're also exhausted and, I'll wager, hungry. Maybe with some food in your belly and a good night's sleep you will feel a little better.'

Darnell sighed and wiped the last lingering tears from his eyes. He nodded weakly.

'You know what? Stay here. Dinner is still a while off. I'll get some tea for us. My father always said a cup of tea helps melt the problems out of your mind.'

She disappeared inside. Darnell looked out across the garden and at the animals that grazed in the next paddock. The square of sky above him was getting darker. He leaned back, laying his head on the cool, dark wood of the veranda, closing his eyes against the breeze.

Nisha was right. He had to forget the past. He needed to be strong. He had to not waste the opportunity his mother had given him by sacrificing herself. The smell of turned earth reminded him of home. He started to nod off when he felt something wet across his face. He jerked up into a sitting position, eyes darting around. Next to him was the fluffy head of Kutta, his tail wagging back and forth sweeping the floor boards of the dropped leaves. He laughed and Kutta responded with a bark.

'Kutta, shush,' Nisha said as she exited the home, two steaming hot cups in her hands. Kutta dropped onto the floor, tail still whipping from side to side. He looked ready to pounce at any second. 'Go sit on your bed. Bed, now, Kutta.'

The dog bounded over to a large, stuffed pillow in the corner.

'I swear Kutta would try to play even if the war came again.' She passed him a warm mug. The steam rose lazily in the breeze and he smelled a rich scent, a mixture of flowers and herbs.

'I wasn't sure how you liked it so I made it sweet like Mum does.'

He took a sip and there was a burst of flavours across his tongue.

'It's great. What is it?'

'Mum makes it. She mixes black tea with herbs. It's got lavender, lemon verbena and chamomile in it. There's a few other things too. It'll help calm you. I've been drinking it most of my life. Here,' she said, handing him a jar. 'For your travels. It's already got sugar in it so you just add a teaspoon to hot water and let it steep for five minutes.'

'Thanks,' Darnell said setting the jar on the floor next to him.

'So did you live on a farm?'

'No, it was just a cabin with a garden. We were next to a lake, so we ate a lot of fish.'

'Ooh, we don't get much fish. It's too expensive at the market unless it's tinned. Nearest lake is a day's walk at least and I wouldn't have a clue how to fish if I tried.'

'It's pretty easy. I could teach you.'

'But you'll be gone tomorrow.'

'I'll come back. I want to go back to the cabin in the long run. It's home. You could come visit. I'll teach you to fish and how to fillet them. I can't promise what the garden will be like by the time I get back but the cabin has a well-stocked larder.'

'That would be nice. Like a holiday away.'

'Mum talked of holidays. I've never really had one I guess. Where do people go now that we're so isolated?'

'I've never been anywhere either. I found a book from before the war that spoke of people going across to other countries. Not just regions but whole other lands! Isn't that exciting? Have you ever heard of the ocean?'

Darnell shook his head. 'Not really. I remember seeing the word but most the books we had were just stories.'

'We have an Atlas. My father found it in the basement of the old mill he worked at when he was a young man. The pages are really brittle so I rarely touch it, but Mum lets me take it down occasionally. Oasis is in the middle of a huge part of the world surrounded by water called the ocean. The water is bigger than the land. And there are huge fish in it called whales!'

'Whales I have heard of. Moby Dick was a whale.'

'Who?'

'It's a book my mother read me when I was younger. A big white whale named Moby Dick that lived in the sea.'

'Sea is the same as ocean!'

They laughed together. 'I wonder if we will ever see the ocean?' Nisha said quietly.

'I doubt it. There's no way through the wastelands, Mum said. Radiation and the beasts, with no food or water, and it certainly wouldn't be safe. The war rendered it dead.

'I dream of travelling over it. Flying like a bird.'

'Flight isn't allowed. Not since the war. What if you crashed in the wasteland? What if we're the last region left and the wasteland stretches forever?' Darnell said.

'I can still dream. It's been years. We have created so many things since the war, why has no one looked at fixing the wastelands?'

'Because the fence is there to keep us safe.'

He felt the words coming out of his mouth. They were City-sanctioned lessons, yet he was so anti-sanctioned himself. His lack of marking made him an enemy to the Authority of Oasis, to their history. If she asked about his marking, he would have to run. He felt the weight of his knife against his ankle. He couldn't hurt them but he could scare them enough to escape.

'Darnell, are you okay? You've gone pale.'

He shook his head of the thoughts that clouded him. 'Sorry, zoned out a little.' He swallowed the last mouthful of tea, now nearly cold. Trying to concentrate on thinking clearly, he cleared his throat and looked into Nisha's eyes. They were dark, almost black. 'Sorry,' he mumbled. 'I guess I'm more tired than I thought.

'That's okay. Do you think the beasts still roam the wastelands? No one's seen one since the war.'

'They're surely still around. I read a report Mum had. There are heaps of them. They apparently patrol the wasteland, just out of eyesight. The defence department has been monitoring them.'

'How did you get that report? It sounds classified.'

'Mum used to work for the Authority. There was a plan put in place after the war, to monitor the wastelands. There's a whole section on the beasts.'

'Does it say what they are? How they came about?'

'Super-weaponised and irradiated humans. Not sure on how they made them but they're huge and strong and super ugly.'

'My dad used to say they were why blanks were so dangerous and why we separated from them. It's only because their genetics are so messed up that they can do stuff like that. That's why the regions were made in the first place. I guess the blanks live in their own versions of regions. Dad said after the war they were banished from the surviving regions but surely they don't live in the wastelands?'

'I don't know,' Darnell argued, remembering to tread carefully. 'They're people too, remember. I mean the beasts are monsters but the blanks are human. They must have some food and water source.'

'They were terrorists. I heard they cut out people's marks and hung them out like flags. They hated the order of the marked. They wanted anarchy. People having babies wherever they liked, no genetics taken into account. Our genetics are more stable and are made to create an optimal person. Why wouldn't someone want the best for their children?'

'Freedom? I mean, isn't that what we fought for? The freedom to remain marked and follow through with how we chose to be? So if we can fight for that, surely that means that we fought for freedom, so that should include freedom to love who we want.'

'That's not right, Darnell. The marks are there for a reason. Don't you want a genetically balanced child?'

'I want a happy child. A happy and healthy child. That's all. If they love their marked companion, fantastic, if not they should have that choice.'

'Your parents are not matched, are they? That's why you and your mum were living in the cabin. You were an unauthorised child?'

'Something like that,' Darnell mumbled.

'Well, don't make the same mistake. It's no life for a child and I know from experience.'

'Were your parents...'

'My dad's parents. We live out here because the City still deems us mutagen risks for two more generations.'

'That's why you live out here?'

'Yeah. The City doesn't mind Amma but us kids are deemed unclean.'

'What about meeting your matched partner? What happens to them?'

'I don't know. I guess when I'm older I'll have to talk to the Authority. Amma said we may not have matches anyway. Unclean DNA and all.'

'What if you fall in love?'

'What with? A pumpkin? A sheep? Not much choice out here. You're the first visitor in a year apart from Authority officials.'

'Wait, Authority officials come out here?'

'Sometimes.'

'Why? Why would they come out here?'

'I guess they're checking in on Mum. She gets an allocation of supplies every few months because it's just her looking after us. They talk to Amma occasionally, hushed voices and stuff. She said it's because they're asking about Dad. Don't want us hearing anything. Sometimes they take kids into the City if their parents can't look after them. They'd leave me but they could take Neil. We should be okay though. Amma does a good job looking after us with so little.'

Darnell went to say something but before he could, they heard footsteps behind them. He snapped his head around but it was just Neil.

'Dinner's ready,' he called before dashing back inside.

'You're so jumpy. Be calm. It's safe out here. You're safe here.'

Nisha pulled him to his feet and led him inside. It was warm and the whole place smelled warm and cosy. They ate as a family, something Darnell had never done before. Neil chattered away, full of energy. Darnell had to laugh. He didn't remember the last time he had that much energy. It was refreshing and welcome. Neil's constant chatter meant no one asking him questions. As the meal wound up he found himself nodding off at the table. He knew he should travel by night but a cart ride with Amma would cut days off his trip and put distance between him and those people quicker than any night walking.

'I think someone is ready for bed.'

He heard the words but it took a few seconds to realise they meant him. He struggled to open his eyes and managed to see Nisha hop up from the table. Amma took him by the arm and pulled him to his feet.

'Sleep times now, my boy. We've set you a bed up near the fire. I'll wake you for breakfast before we head off in the morning.'

Darnell plonked himself onto the sofa and Amma covered him with a blanket. He couldn't keep his eyes open any longer.

***

Darnell awoke with a start. He had forgotten where he was, but after a brief moment of panic he remembered. A noise had woken him. It was still dark in the house and he could see no light from the window. His instincts on high alert, he reached for his knife, slowly drawing it. There it was again; a steady thumping like quick footsteps. The fire had died down so he could only just make out the shapes around him. He reached for his headlamp, but too late remembered it was stowed in his bag. Silence fell and he could hear how loud his breathing was. He shifted his weight to prop himself up for a better vantage point when the noise started again from near his feet. He squinted in the dim light but could see no movement.

Slowly turning himself around on the couch to get a better vantage point, he wracked his brain as to what could be making the noise without any visible movement in the embers' glow. Had the people who had killed his mother been hiding, waiting for an excuse to move in on him?

He crept to the foot of the couch and peered over the edge, knife gripped in his white knuckled grip. There was something there. As his head became visible the noise started again and he nearly fell off the couch onto the floor from his shocked jump. Then he started laughing. It was Kutta. The dog's tail thumped on the floor again as it wagged in a blur. He could only see the white patches of fur on Kutta, but his tail was flying.

'Kutta, you nearly gave me a heart attack,' Darnell whispered.

Kutta bounded forward at the sound of his name and licked Darnell's face. He slipped his knife back in its sheath and sat up. The dog leapt onto the seat beside him, curled up in a ball and rested his head on Darnell's lap. Darnell sat stroking the dogs head; it was very calming. When he moved back to the cabin, when things had settled down, he would get a dog. He would need the company.

He dozed on and off with Kutta's warmth a comforting weight on his lap. He heard a noise from the kitchen and felt Kutta lift his head then jump off the couch. He fought the urge to lie back down and snuggle back into the blanket. He stretched and got up. Kutta came trotting back into the room and curled up in front of the fire on the thick but worn rug there. Behind him was Amma with two steaming hot cups of tea.

She passed one to him and took a seat. She was dressed ready for the cold outside. A thick woollen beanie and a scarf enveloped her, a pair of jeans and heavy boots finished the look.

'Morning Darnell. We'll head off in a few minutes. Get a strong start. We can eat on the way then stop for lunch.'

He nodded, still sleepy, the tea filling his chest with heat.

'Have you ever bridled a horse?'

'Never been all that close to one to be honest, apart from pictures in books and the odd rider going past on the trails.'

'Okay, well you can load the wagon while I get the horses ready. You can lift heavy things?'

'I'll manage,' he said with a smile. They finished their tea and he gathered his bag. He pulled his boots on as Amma picked up a heavy pack and ushered him out the door, shutting Kutta inside.

'He'd follow me all the way to town if I let him.'

They got the cart ready in silence, Darnell packing crates into the cart and tethering the sheep into the back, while Amma bridled the horses. When they were ready she climbed into the driver's seat and motioned Darnell to join her; and in the darkness of early morning the set off down the road.

CHAPTER TEN
Zale

Zale's head was pounding. He groaned trying to lift his head – it felt like it weighed a tonne. His mouth was dry and full of dirt. He spat into the ground, mud dribbling from his lips. He tried to remember what had happened but everything was still a blur and his ears rang like church bells in his skull.

The light was blinding when he finally managed to peel his eyes open. It was like a dagger into his head. He felt hungover but like he'd also been thrown off a roof for good measure. It still hurt too much to lift his head so he tried to move the rest of his body. His right arm seemed fine but his left hurt like a bitch. If it wasn't broken it was most certainly sprained. His legs ached but he could move them well enough. If he had fallen off a roof, he'd come away with minor injuries, some gravel rash and a mouth full of dirt.

He tried opening his eyes again, slowly. Blinking at the bright glare. He was outside. *Where is everyone?* he thought. Normally an accident brought the town running. He felt so stiff. He had to have been out for a while. Through the glare he lifted his head and propped himself up on his good arm, still too shaky to attempt getting up off the ground. He spat out more dirt, his mouth still gritty but finally not feeling like it was made of sandpaper.

'Allen?' he croaked. Not much sound came out. He coughed to clear his throat and tried again. 'Allen?' He closed his eyes for a few seconds and opened them again, trying to focus his vision. He was looking at the main warehouse, he thought. The high, white wall was splattered with dirt and tiny burn marks.

Holding his injured arm against his chest he slowly managed to fold his aching legs under him into a sitting position. He turned and looked behind him and what he saw brought everything flooding back.

What used to be a door leading to the shelter was gone, replaced by a black, smoking hole. Debris lay around him on the ground.

'Allen,' he whispered. He tried to get to his feet but the pain in his arm made it hard. He looked at his arm, blue bruising spreading across his wrist. He tried to wiggle his fingers but they didn't respond apart from a sharp twinge.

Zale finally manage to scramble his way up to standing. His head spun and his vision was still not one hundre percent. Unsteadily, he walked towards the remains of the tunnel entrance but the rubble was blocking the tunnel below. He needed to find someone to help him clear it. It would be impossible with only one arm.

He spotted the blood next. The woman. The woman who had done this and had shot Meg. He wanted to go after her. He could follow the blood trail from the gunshot to her leg. Zale realised that she was probably long gone. He had no idea how long he'd been out and he would need to find his gun. Why they had come in, caused havoc and left, including leaving him alive, baffled him. He should be dead.

He shook his head as a last attempt to clear it and started heading towards the med centre. He could get his arm strapped up, get some painkillers into his system and hopefully find enough people to help clear the tunnel. They would need medical staff any way.

The door to the med centre was open, the plastic curtain beyond was still. He could hear the beeping of machines from beyond but not much else.

'Hello?' he called into the quiet. He heard a rustling noise from inside. He looked down at himself – covered in dirt and blood. Not all that hygienic but he needed help. He stuck his head through the plastic and looked down the ward. Curtains were drawn around beds, but the lights were all on.

'Hello?' he called again.

'Zale?' came a quiet voice from halfway down the ward. He saw movement from behind a curtain and an older woman in scrubs poked her head out, a scalpel clutched in her gloved hand. It was Dr Schonell.

'Yeah, it's me. I'm alone. I think those people are gone. I need some help.'

He saw her visibly relax, her hand dropping to her side. She hurried towards him.

'Who were they? Did you see anything? They came in and shot Dr Farrel. Told us if we moved they'd blow us up.'

'No idea. Authority Army by the looks of it. They had grenades too. The shelter entrance has been destroyed. I was on my way out, following one of them when the grenade went off. Must have landed badly. My arm; I think it's broken.'

'Go out to room twelve. I'll come in and x-ray it soon. I just want to check the other room. They didn't go in there luckily. If they had, they might have killed more.'

'What? Why?'

'Blanks. If they were Authority, that's the only reason I can see them being here.'

'Didn't realise we had any blanks. Thought we were all just anti-matched.'

'Go to x-ray and I'll tell you more when I get there.'

Zale turned and left the room, heading to the hall beyond. The med centre was eerily quiet. There was no bustling in the halls and only occasionally a cough from a patient. Where were the nurses? The other doctors? He reached room 12 and pushed open the door. The light above flickered like a sputtering candle. He heard a gasp and saw a flash of white dash behind the imager.

'Hey, it's okay. I'm a Condor Point person. Broke my arm.

Dr Schonell sent me here. The people are gone.'

'I have a knife! The all-clear hasn't sounded. How can I trust you?' came a young man's voice.

'Peek out and look at my face. If you don't recognise me, you'll recognise the scar on my face from my mark being removed.'

A mop of dark hair came from around the machine. His face looked familiar but he was certainly new to town.

'See, just me and my broken arm. I'm Zale.'

The young nurse got to his feet and placed what looked like a large kitchen knife on the desk in the room to his right.

'I'm Greyson.'

'Newbie?' Zale said seeing the tip of the man's mark poking out of his sleeve.

'Yeah, I was a nurse at Westpoint. Came here with my sister Amy. Both of us have lost our pairings and we wanted the chance at a family.'

'This isn't the welcome you should have had. You okay?'

'Yeah, Amy is in a ward down the hall. So we're both okay. Well, she's not hurt, not from this. It's just a sprained ankle. Sorry, I'm babbling.'

Greyson ran his hand through his hair. Zale noticed his hand was trembling. He looked down at his own hands and saw that his weren't much better.

'Let's get that arm x-rayed,' Greyson said, motioning to the machine. It was big and clunky and most definitely old, but it was still a digital imager. Greyson painfully stretched out Zale's arm onto the plate and stepped into the room at the side. The light flashed and then he motioned for Zale to join him.

'No break but it's certainly not happy. The doc can give you something for the pain and I'll strap it up for you. It might just need a bit of support. Come on, there's some strapping tape in the splinting room.'

Zale followed him to the room down the hall where Greyson pulled tape around his wrist. Dr Schonell came in as

Greyson cut the tape.

'Not broken then?' she smiled, passing Zale a small bottle. 'Painkillers. Thought you'd need them either way. They shouldn't make you too drowsy.' Greyson passed him a cup of water, which Zale gripped in his sore hand. He placed it on the table and shook two pills into his mouth.

'Is everyone secure?' Greyson asked.

'All the blanks are in the isolation unit. If they come back, the biohazard signs should keep them away. Old Mr Amstead is not impressed with being locked in but the sedative I gave him should calm him down. Last thing we need is him causing a fuss. He already made two of the children cry.

'How many blanks do we have here?'

About thirty. There's twenty-six in isolation. So a few may have ended up in the bunker or are hopefully hiding somewhere.'

Zale felt his stomach twist at the reminder.

'The bunker. We need to get down there. There was an explosion. Are there any people in here strong enough to move rubble? The doorway to the tunnel collapsed.'

'Greyson, go through the wards and gather anyone who can help. Mrs Norris is not well enough despite what she will tell you. Then see who has weapons they can grab on the way. See if anything here can be used as a weapon. I'll get med kits and see what else I can find. I have three tranquiliser guns and I know there's a few hunting rifles in lockup from people carted in with hunting injuries.'

Dr Schonell and Greyson both ran off in different directions leaving Zale sitting in the splinting room. He tried to make a fist, but the clenching of his hand made a sharp pain shoot up his arm. Luckily, it wasn't his shooting arm.

He jammed the pain pills in his pocket and checked the handgun was still in his waistband. He wasn't even sure how many bullets he had left. A single spare clip was in his other pocket. Hopefully he wouldn't have to use it.

His and Allen's home had no other weapons save the knife

in the kitchen and a baseball bat he'd brought with him from his old life.

Walking out of the room he turned towards the end of the hallway to see Greyson walking towards him with a group of four people, one of whom looked like he had a cold at least, the rest seemed to be uninjured, so hopefully they would be enough to dig through the rubble. Dr Schonell jogged towards them, heavy-looking bags and med kits weighing her down. She passed a khaki duffle bag over to Greyson.

'All the guns I could find, a few knives and the tranq guns. I don't even know how to shoot so I'll stick to fixing people.'

Greyson nodded and looked expectantly at Zale, wanting him to lead the way.

'Oh, I'm going first, okay. Stick to the walls, be quiet and try to keep up. Don't shoot unless you have to. Gunfire will draw attention if any of them are still around. People are going to be scared. There may be some Condor Point people hiding and they may freak out seeing us stalking through with guns. Keep them low, but ready.'

Zale walked around the back of the hospital and kept to the wall, the others following in a procession. He looked around the corner, but saw nothing. If they kept to this side of the compound, they would be able to get to the bunker without going through the residential area. This meant less chance to spook the locals. The less casualties the better.

They were heading towards the school and library buildings. No one should be there unless they were hiding inside. The path behind the building was well-worn from kids running back and forth during school days but the storage shed was surrounded by long grass.

Zale saw movement behind the shed nearest to him. He stopped and ducked down. The others followed suit. A shadow fell amongst the grass and the top of a blonde head poked out for a second before disappearing behind the shed again.

'That was Lucy,' Dr Schonell gasped. She stood to move

forward. Greyson grabbed at her coat.

'Don't, it might be a trap.'

'He's right,' Zale said. 'They used that tactic to get into the shelter. They don't care who they hurt.'

'Lucy,' she whispered as loudly as she could. 'Lucy come out here if you can.' No one moved. They finally heard the rustle of grass. Zale stood and began to circle around the shed from the other side, in case there was one of the armed personnel behind there with Lucy.

As the little footsteps dashed through the grass, he took the last step around the back of the shed, gun drawn. But there was nothing there. He heaved a sigh of relief and walked around the other side of the shed back to the group. He felt a prickle on the back of his neck. Something was wrong. He felt the shadow on his face before he saw it, looking up in time to see one of the intruders throwing themselves off the shed roof towards him.

The intruder's body smashed him into the ground. He felt the air pushed out of him, and saw stars before his eyes as his head hit the ground. A cold blade pressed against his throat.

'Where is she?' the intruder spat into Zale's face.

'Who?' Zale choked out.

'I will slit your throat. Where is she?'

'I don't know who you're talking about, man. Who the fuck are you guys?'

'I KNOW you've seen her!'

Zale felt the pressure on his throat as the sting of the blade breaking the skin began. A shot fired and the intruder's body fell onto him, the knife skittering to the ground.

'Are you okay? Please say you're okay?' came Greyson's panicking voice. Zale tried to get a sentence out but all he managed was a whimpered 'help'. Warm blood was dripping on his cheek and was getting closer and closer to his mouth. Finally, the weight was pushed off him, a few lingering drops fell across his lips. He sputtered, spitting the blood as far as he could, then wiped the remaining onto his sleeve. He looked at the body. It was shot through the temple. Well aimed.

'Thank you, Greyson. I assume it was you? Do much hunting where you're from? That's a bloody good shot for a nurse.'

'Beginner's luck,' he mumbled, tucking the gun into his coat pocket.

'Is he dead?' one of the men asked, a rifle trembling in his hands.

'I hope so, seeing I have half his brains dripping down my face and he has an extra ventilation hole in his head,' Zale said, wiping his face with the bottom of his shirt. He felt it would never be properly clean even after washing it a million times over with bleach.

'I'm sorry,' came a tiny voice. It was Lucy, one of Condor Point's children. 'I'm so sorry. I didn't know he was there, honestly.'

'It's okay, Lucy,' Zale looked at the group. They really couldn't spare anyone. 'Do you think you could make it to the hospital all by yourself?'

'Can't I stay with you? I promise I didn't know the man was there.'

'You'll be safer at the hospital. I need you to go there and sit in the waiting room. Can you do that?'

She nodded her tear-streaked face.

'You run and don't stop until you get there, okay? It's not very far.'

With a look of determination, she took off down the path.

'Will she be okay?' Dr Schonell asked as soon as she was out of earshot.

'Who knows? I hope so. She's a good kid. Maybe she'll find a patient to look after her. Sneak her some jello.'

'What about him?' she asked, inclining her head towards the corpse of the intruder. 'We can't just leave him there.'

'Yeah we can. He can rot there for all I care. We have lives to save. We can dispose of him once I know our people are safe. Until then the birds can pick his bones clean if they wish. Let's go.'

Zale fought the urge to kick the body as he walked past, instead he spat next to it, the taste of blood still on his lips.

They met with no one else on the way to the bunker. A few people peeped around corners and over window sills, but no one came out to ask where they were going or what duty lay ahead of them.

The quiet was much worse than the sounds Zale had been expecting. His eyes couldn't stay focused; they flew wildly, rooftop to shadow, looking for more of the black-clad intruders. A hand gun lay in the grass near the bunker, its handle sticky with blood. This was the woman's gun. He put it in his other pocket. It still had some ammunition in it. Spots of blood touched the blades of grass heading towards the fence. He would follow her, but first the rescue.

She would be long gone by then, but he knew he had to try and find her... find something to make some sense of the insanity of the past two days, and she wouldn't get far on foot.

The blackened rubble marking the old entrance to the bunker seemed much worse now his vision had cleared. The soot markings showed a blast radius of at least two storeys. The bunker would be filled with debris. Anyone near the tunnel door would be injured at least. Even if they had managed to get the bunker's inner door closed there may have been people in the tunnel. Had Allen tried to follow him? If Allen had been in the tunnel... Zale didn't want to think about it.

'We need to start moving the rubble. Be careful. I have no idea how the tunnel was reinforced or what type of explosive was used.'

The group set to work, the pile of debris not seeming to get much smaller despite how much they moved. He helped as much as he could with one hand, but kept getting distracted by wandering thoughts of those trapped inside. The air filters should keep it breathable in there but flashes of injured people sped across his mind.

After what felt like hours they had cleared the doorway enough to glimpse into the blackened tunnel. Sweat dripped down Zale's face and stung as it hit the shallow cut on his throat. The lights were gone in the tunnel. The bulbs had shattered and filled up with soot. Zale could see a patch of light through the gloom. The blast door was open. His heart sank.

'Dr Schonell, I think we need to brace ourselves for a lot more injured than I thought or hoped. It looks like the blast door was open when the tunnel blew. Who knows how much flew inwards.'

She nodded at him and started to head towards the tunnel.

'Wait!' Greyson yelled. 'It's not safe yet. We need to check the roof and remove the rest of the rubble in the tunnel.'

Zale ignored this and began to climb over the broken cement and twisted metal. 'Hello? Can anyone hear me?' He rushed forwards. 'Allen? Please, Allen, answer me!'

'Get out of the tunnel Zale,' Greyson called. 'It's not safe.'

'I need to get in there,' he called back. He stumbled over a brick and his foot slipped out from under him. He heard the rubble begin to shift behind him. Clambering back on his feet, he pushed off the broken pile of concrete next to him. A chunk dislodged and an avalanche of concrete began to tumble down. He heard Greyson yell from behind him but the words were drowned out by falling rocks. He threw himself down the tunnel just before the roof collapsed behind him, blocking him off from the outside world.

CHAPTER ELEVEN
Almara

It stayed dark. Our meals came in what I assumed was a regular time frame. It was hard to tell. Even with the food hatch open, only a red glow of the safety lights filtered through. It threw a surreal, blood-soaked glow onto the door around the slot and I could just make out the outlines of the furniture around my room and enough to see the food on the plastic trays delivered three times a day. I was wary of the food after the drug-induced haze and subsequent withdrawal from before when the lights first went out, but I needed to eat. Being weak and feeble wouldn't help me if they pulled another stunt.

It'd been three days if the meals had been on a proper schedule. Dinner was at 6pm so it was early evening now. The plate of tough meat, from what could have been our fellow blanks as far as I could tell, was tasteless and overcooked. The mush with it was most likely supposed to be potato. Without colour, the food all tasted the same, bland and powdery. Maybe it was all made of recycled paper.

There were no study sessions or exercise room times. The facilitators didn't say a word. There was nothing more than the scrape of the panel as they shoved the food through and the slight squeak of the food trolley's wheels on the cold floor. Writing in this light was not easy but I kept at it, despite the scrawl being almost illegible some days. It was what kept me sane in the silence of red.

I pushed my food tray away. The tray and plastic plate and fork clattered to the floor. It echoed in the silence. I lay down on my bed to stare at the black of the ceiling, white dots floating across my vision in the gentle red glow. I don't know when I dozed off but I woke to the rattle of the manual key lock. It was an override measure. The power being out must have locked the doors but it wasn't as though there had been any attempt to free us or even inform us of what was happening. The world could be ending and we'd still be in here expecting our tasteless meals and fresh clothes every day, none the wiser. We were seen as less than animals.

'482 please stand away from the door.'

In my half-asleep state, I stood and did as instructed. The behaviour was something ingrained in me.

'482 are you clear of the door?'

'Yes, facilitator,' I mumbled. Then it dawned on me. I knew that voice. It was Ahn.

The door opened, the red glow in the hall intensifying, flooding into the room. I tried to hide the smile on my face. I was relieved to see someone who didn't completely think of me as scum.

'Almara,' he whispered. 'Grab anything you care about and put your shoes on. I'm about to lose my job.'

I bundled my papers up and jammed the baton I'd scored into the waistband of my pants. I felt my adrenaline surge, but this time it was the real thing, not the artificial drug they had laced us with before lights-out.

Ahn stood in the door for a moment. I could see he was scared but he was my ticket to freedom. I'd see the sky again. I may even get to see my mother again.

'Place your arms by your sides to be hooded.'

He continued the procedures. Were there other facilitators in the halls? Apart from food delivery, I'd seen and heard no sign of them since the lights went out. But I trusted Ahn. He slipped the hood over my head.

'Hold your hands like I've cuffed you,' he whispered. 'You

might need your hands free. I don't know if this will work but we should have a clear run.'

I nodded my hooded head, staying as silent as possible. If we looked like procedures were being followed to the letter, it would feel like procedure. That would keep us safe and mostly unnoticed for a while at least.

He held my hands behind my back and pushed me from the room, our footsteps squeaking on the now dry and cold floor. It took me so long to learn to walk in the darkness of the hood without stumbling when I first arrived at the Cube. But now it was second nature. I never thought it was a skill that would truly come in handy, but I realised now I was more surefooted than ever before. I never thought I'd need it but I also never thought I'd get the chance to be free either. I imagined a life of lessons and tests before they inevitably dissected me like a lab rat.

Ninety-seven steps to the elevator. I had counted them thousands of times but this time instead of stopping Ahn turned me and we continued down another hallway. After a few minutes walking, he stopped me and took the hood off. I was momentarily blinded by the lights in the hall way. But blinked away the glare enough to make out a door.

'I hope you like stairs,' he whispered.

He opened the door and pushed me through it. Just inside the door were two backpacks. He passed one over to me. It was heavy but manageable. I was not sure I'd feel the same about it after however-many flights of stairs we had to climb. I peered up the stairwell. It looked like it went forever into a blinding glare of fluorescents.

'How far down are we?'

'Ten floors to the surface.'

'Won't we be seen?' I whispered as we began up the stairs.

'No one uses the stairs here. Everyone is much too accustomed to the luxury of the lifts. Plus, no cameras in here.'

'But what about when we get to the surface?'

'This stairwell opens out separately to the main building. It edges the main compound. I have a change of clothes for you in the bag. You can change upstairs. We have a new staffer so I should be able to get you through the checkpoint into residential using her ID. Don't talk; let me do that. There's procedure but it's pretty lax to be honest. It's also dark enough to get us out of residential without too much fuss. They won't suspect anything but we need to be quiet and fast. We don't want to push our luck.'

'Won't they notice I'm gone?'

'Due to the lockdown there's less patrols. Next one isn't for four hours.'

So we ran. Despite exercise room days, I still began to feel the burn after three flights. My chest hurt as my lungs tried to suck in as much air as possible. My legs throbbed. I'd certainly feel the aftermath of this in the morning. The adrenaline kept me going but only just. The glaring white of the stairs and walls were blinding and felt endless. I swear we'd run fifty flights already but the stairs continued.

Finally the door to outside appeared. I was getting dizzy from lack of breathing. I slowed, pulling myself up using the handrail to pull myself along.

The backpack was making my shoulders ache. If I stopped though I felt like I'd never get moving again. I'd just melt into a puddle on the floor and run all the way back down the stairs. My legs felt like jelly. We got to the landing and I leant against the wall.

'We can rest for a few minutes then you can get changed. There's water in the bag too.'

I slid down the wall I had leant against. That was a bad idea but I had no choice. I pulled the bag off my back and riffled through it. There were a few bottles in there amongst packets and other items. I twisted the lid off, which took more energy than I thought possible, and downed half a bottle in one massive guzzle. My chest still burned but I could feel the air becoming part of my lungs again. I tried to stand but my jelly-like legs were having none of that. My thighs burned and my calves were throbbing with a heartbeat of their own – and one having a panic attack to boot. The idea of getting back up to get changed did not appeal.

I grabbed the uniform out of the bag and pulled myself up on the railing. I nearly fell as my legs protested the length of rest I had given them but I held on until I had my balance back. I pulled off my top. Ahn looked away politely. I didn't really care though. I had no qualms of stripping down to my underwear in front of him. The facilitators, him included, had seen us all naked at least once for medicals. I pulled on the facilitator uniform. It was a little big, but not enough to draw attention to the fact I was wearing what amounted to a costume rather than a work uniform. The pocket didn't have a name embroidered on it but the small white cube of the facility was stitched into it. No name, just a cube.

The fabric was soft. Not just new. It was a change from the rough, worn fabric of our facility-issued clothes. I went to shove them into the bag when Ahn held out his hands.

'Give them to me.'

I passed them over and watched as he popped the vent of the wall open and shoved the bundle of fabric in.

'Shoes next.'

I passed him the slippers they made us wear and pulled on the socks and rubber-soled shoes that matched his own. The bag was a little lighter now. Ahn threw the shoes in after my clothes and pushed the vent back into place. The shoes were the right size at least but they were hard from being so new. It would take some time to get used to their rigidity. By then I would have worn them in. They rubbed against my heels. I hoped that I wouldn't have to run too much more. I bent the toes of the shoes, trying to limber them up a little.

'Ahn, what happened to the others? Did they die after the test?'

'I can't tell you,' he mumbled.

'You can break me out of the Cube but you can't tell me about the CHILDREN that were electrocuted in front of my eyes. The ones I nearly became one of?' I knew I was getting too loud but the rage in me was rising. 'I have been here for years. For nearly half my life. They have been here for who knows how long. I could have died!'

'But you didn't. That's why I had to get you out.'

'That makes no sense!'

'I… This is the best I could do. Open your bag.'

'What? No. Answer my question! How many innocent blanks have they killed? HOW MANY!?'

'I can't tell you any more. We need to move. It's not safe here.'

'When we're safe you have to tell me. You have to give me something.'

'I'm giving you your freedom. Your life. Your free will. Do you want it or do I march you back down to your room and let the Cube decide what happens to you?' he snapped at me.

I didn't know how to respond to that. He was helping me and I was laying all the blame on him for what I had been through.

'I'm sorry, Ahn,' I whispered. 'I'm sorry. I… I'm just so scared.' I felt tears prickling at my eyes. Ahn put his hand on my shoulder and looked at my face. The tears broke and spilled down my cheeks as he made eye contact.

'I had to save someone. Even if it is only one life, I had to try… We have to go. Get your bag. We will be walking to security. Stay silent. Here is her ID card. Kelly is her name. If they ask, you've transferred in from Western after your mate died in a factory accident. That's all you should need to know but I'll try to work around it so you don't need to say anything.'

I nodded, wiping the tears from my face and smoothing down my hair. He opened the door and held it open for me.

'After you, Kelly.'

With a deep breath, I stepped out into the dark, cool night. I felt a breeze on my face for the first time in so long. I could smell the grass beneath my shoes and the sweet air as it blew the scent of flowers over to me.

I heard noises I had forgotten about; birds and the scratching of tree branches against the buildings. It was rather overwhelming. I wanted to lay down on the cool grass and let the chilled earth seep into my very bones. Instead, I breathed in deep, inhaling as much of the black sky as I could.

Stars. The tiny pinpoints of light glittered in my eyes. It was mesmerising. I felt lightheaded and began to sway off centre. Ahn grabbed me by the shoulders.

'You need to focus. Take a deep breath and try to look like you work here. A slightly vacant look usually does the trick.'

I closed my eyes; the red glow behind them subsided.

'Okay, let's go,' I said, striding forwards with my shoulders back, trying to look confident but keeping my face as neutral as possible. We walked around the corner of the building. The stark white of the Cube rose to my left. It was an imposing creation. I began to look up at its size and I felt I might never see the top of it, but far in the distance a corner stood out, stark against the night sky. A shiver ran through me. I never thought I'd see a building reach into the distance like that again. A thin path ran around the perimeter, framing the structure and cutting through the dark sea of grass.

On this side of the building, spotlight-illuminated doors punctuated the plain expanse of wall. There were no windows on the upper floors. It seemed that even those who worked in the Cube didn't get to see the sky when on duty either.

I could see the fence ahead of us, the path deviating from its frame shape and heading towards a large gate. Two facilitators stood on each side. They held guns, and I could see tasers hanging at their waists. A control booth sat behind them, the light dim, the shadow of a reclining figure silhouetted against a bank of monitors.

'The monitors. Would they have seen us?' I asked.

'They're for the fences only. Stop people coming in. There's no way to get out without help so they just look out.'

'Has anyone ever...'

'A brother of a resident tried to break in a few years ago. Got as far as scaling the fence before he was arrested.'

'Arrested? What happened to him?'

'Before my time. There is the Black Sphere Institute. Political prison on the edge of the Badlands. It's more of a dome. Only seen pictures mind you. Apparently, there is a second half to it. The bottom dome is anti-grav suspended animation. For high level prisoners. Top half is training for Spherers.'

'What are Spherers?'

'I shouldn't say. I only know because my mate was in the Authority.'

'Did they kill her?'

'I don't know.'

'You came here for answers.'

'I came here in hopes to save a life because I couldn't save hers.'

We walked on in silence. At the gate we had no issues. Ahn was greeted with a high five from a man named Arthur. He introduced me as a new staffer. They didn't even ask my name. Two of the facilitators were more interested in lighting their cigarettes. The spark of flame made me jump but no one else noticed. We passed through the gates. It seemed too easy.

We walked through a village of little white cubes; each numbered in grey on the side with numbers almost as tall as I was. We approached number 82 and Ahn stopped.

'Come inside,' Ahn whispered. 'Stay quiet though. We don't usually have guests.'

He scanned his card and the door slid open. Inside was sparse. A low single bed, white linen. Two chairs and a table stood in neat a kitchenette, and a two-seater couch was against a wall with a door to one side. A bathroom was illuminated behind it.

'Sit down and pass me your bag.'

I sat on the couch as I passed him the backpack. Ahn dumped the contents of a box into my bag.

'There's food for a week, two if you stretch it out. Water

filter-enabled bottle, two changes of clothes and a thermal blanket. There's also a taser. I don't have access to a gun. I wouldn't know how to fire it anyway.'

'Same here.'

'The taser is easy to use. Point and pull the trigger. Just don't zap yourself.'

I wanted to laugh but didn't have it in me. I saw Ahn trying to smile at me but his dark eyes betrayed any humour he was trying to get across. He zipped up the bag and passed it over to me. I slipped it to the floor near my feet. It was heavy again but I'd manage.

'What's the plan?'

'We head north. There's a community of people who welcome blanks and mark removers. They'll take us in.'

'We? You're coming with me?' I muttered, pulling the pack closer to me like a security blanket of sorts.

'Once they check the cameras, they'll see me leading you out of your room and not returning you. I don't want to be here anymore anyway.' He pulled a bag from under his bed. 'We need to go soon but this part should be relatively easy. It's getting to the camp that will be hardest. It's a week's walk at least. It's too dangerous to steal a vehicle. We can try to hitch a ride when we get a little closer to town but the rest will be run at night and hide during the day. If we are separated just keep going north. Do you know how to work out directions using the sun and moon?'

'In theory, but I haven't seen either the sun or the moon in several years. Not sure I remember what they even look like anymore.'

'Damn, I knew I should have got a compass for you. Let's go. Stay close and don't let them get near you. If you hear dogs or alarms we are in serious trouble.'

'Dogs? They still use them?' I asked, standing up and shouldering my pack.

'Security relies on them. They're bio-teched in the Sphere with night vision and have been altered to hunt to kill. We will have some hesitation from them to start with because of the uniforms, but once they DNA-lock on us, while we are in this compound, they will attack.'

I nodded, not knowing exactly what I was getting myself into, but the idea of finally being out of the Cube was enough motivation for me.

Ahn ducked out the door and I followed close behind. The damp grass between the buildings dampened the bottom of my trousers and I revelled in the sensation. The reality of everything was almost overwhelming but I had to concentrate. I could savour the outside world once I was safe and far away from here.

I saw the fence loom above us as we walked. Barbed wire topped the five-metre fence and the chain links were small – too small to easily climb. I couldn't see a gate. Ahn motioned me to a darkened corner behind a humming metal box. I felt the static in the air but Ahn seemed unfazed by the tingle. He opened the small panel on the side marked with the word FENCE stencilled on it in faded black paint. Ahn flipped the switches in here methodically until the static had reduced, but the box kept humming like it was full of bees.

Ahn tentatively touched the fence. It had no reaction on contact so he pushed at the edge of the wire near the support pole where it came away. It had been neatly cut along the metal.

'Quick, go through, just in case the backup kicks in.'

I pushed through, my bag snagging on the wire. I felt my heart jump into my throat. It was just the fence. I knew it was, but even so, I felt so on edge for a second I waited to hear the barks of a dog and feel a taser shoot through me. I thought I would throw up. I pulled myself free and stumbled onto the grass outside the fence. It was longer and my hands were wet and smeared with dirt, as was the uniform I wore.

Ahn came through next with a little more grace then helped me to my feet.

'Follow me,' he said, and we began to run.

CHAPTER TWELVE
Darnell

Darnell had heard the phrase 'the road is long' in books his mother had given him, but never really understood how long it could truly be until now. They had been on the cart for two hours of endless dirt road, flanked on both sides by trees... and more trees. The occasional road led off to small houses and farms but mainly it was just more trees. The only other signs of life they'd seen had been birds overhead and the startled faces of deer from the undergrowth.

'Not many people live out here, hey?' he asked Amma. The silence had been long but comfortable enough.

'Most live in the cities where living is easier with technology and paperwork. Even the farms are part of the cities now. The big ones anyway. CropServ looks after most the farms used by the factories and cities these days so they have modern housing even for those doing the old-fashioned work. Most of the farming is done by machine now too. Only a few folks live off-grid. Most of us not by choice.

'I don't even remember the City. I've never seen more than photos.'

'You were young when your mother and you moved, then?'

'Yeah. It's going to be a bit of a shock to the system I fear. All the machines and stuff.'

'The City is busy. Lots of people and not much room. We're going to more of a township so it won't be as bad but it still might be a little daunting for you at first. You can stick with me if that will help acclimatise you.'

'Thank you, Amma. Eventually I will need to get to Ellintown. Is it more of a township or a City?'

'It's on the edge of the City. More tech than a town but not quite as many people. Enough for you to get lost in though. I assume you need to go unnoticed as much as possible.'

Darnell's head whipped around, eyes wide.

'It's okay. I don't know what you're running from or why. Nor do I care to know. Your business is yours alone. I just know that look on your face. You were out in the woods for a reason. Most of us are. So if you need to hide, you can.'

'I...'

'Shush child. I don't need to know. Do you have any money? I can't imagine there is too many days' worth of supplies in that bag and the closer you get to the towns the less things there are to forage for. Stealing would draw too much risk and would therefore be unwise.'

'I have some credits. My mother kept a stash to get supplies. Not sure how far it will take me but it should be enough until I get where I'm going. From there I guess I'll have to get a job. Mum's friend will help me, I suppose... I hope.'

'Well, worst case, if you can, come back to our farm. We don't have much but with an extra set of hands, we will have enough to go around.'

'Thank you, Amma,' he mumbled. She was so kind. She didn't even know him and she didn't care. He had no idea how to respond to such kindness.

'It looks like we're about to have some company,' Amma said, nodding at the road ahead. Darnell looked up to see three Authority enforcers riding towards them. They stuck out, their uniforms too crisp, their horses too clean, the bridles too new for folks living out in the forest. Everything was factory-made.

'Stay quiet. Let me do the talking. They're probably just

doing cargo checks. Making sure there's no contraband in the cart.'

'But I'm contraband,' Darnell whispered.

'Today you are my farm hand, Edward. They shouldn't ask much more. Just stay calm.

The horses approached and the closest rider held up his hand for them to stop, Amma reined in the horses to a stop as they pulled up beside the riders.

'Morning, Ma'am. City Authority. Just need to do a cargo check.'

'Good morning, officers. Feel free. Only a sheep and some produce back there.'

One of the officers, a blonde man with ruddy skin, dismounted and walked over to the cart. The sheep bleated at him – unhappy with being interrupted. The officer threw back the cloth covering the crates of produce, picking up a turnip and turning it in his hand as though looking for a hidden button. He tossed it back in but it rolled off the top of the pile and down beneath the sheep's feet. It bleated loudly and tried to reach the turnip to eat it, pulling hard against its tether rope.

'No! Bad sheep!' Amma yelled. 'Sir, please don't feed the sheep. Turnips will give him gas and I still have quite the journey ahead of me. I do not need musical accompaniment.'

'Sorry, Ma'am. Can we get your names for the ledger?' the second enforcer said, riding up to Amma's side of the cart.

'They call me Amma. This here is Edward, my farm hand. Orphan boy from out in the woods. Raised a bit feral. Can't talk but understands enough to be helpful. He's strong too, thank goodness. My boy is too young for heavy lifting and frankly, I am too old.'

'Poor kid. Nice of you to take him on. Most would let him starve.'

'Like I said, he's strong. Much more than I could hope for so he's good for heavy lifting and he has a way with the animals. They seem to like him.'

'Well everything seems to be in order here. Sorry for the

disturbance Ma'am,' the other enforcer said before mounting his horse. 'Before we go, how goes the road ahead?'

'Empty and calm save the odd deer. We have heard some wild boars at night though so keep your eyes peeled. They spook the horses something nasty and your City horses would probably react even worse. We certainly wouldn't want that, would we?'

'Thank you, Ma'am.' Then they rode past. Amma urged the horses on. Darnell turned and saw them ride out of sight.

'Raised by wolves, hey?' he said with a smile.

'It worked, didn't it? No questions asked.'

They sat in relative silence, bird calls and the sounds of the horses on the dirt the only background noises.

'We'll stop soon to stretch our legs. There's a small rest stop coming up. A few little cottages and somewhere to eat. Nothing fancy but they're good people. We'll be safe there.'

Darnell nodded. The movement of the cart was making him sleepy.

'You can curl up and sleep if you need to. I can wake you when we get there.'

He let his eyes close and next he knew Amma was gently shaking him.

'Wakey, wakey Darnell. We're here.'

He opened his eyes into the full brightness of the sun. He blinked at the glare. The clearing in front of them was the size of the lake. It was ringed with wooden cabins and massive gardens.

Beds full of vegetables. One little cabin seemed to be the main meeting place; chairs scattered around tables. Card games were being played over glasses and mugs, the remnants of simple meals pushed to one side. They looked up. The sun was right above them. His stomach rumbled. Climbing down he then followed Amma as she tethered the horses to a hitching rail.

'Stay close. Folks are pretty friendly here but you're still a new face. If you're with me, you'll be fine.'

'Amma,' called a deep voice from a neighbouring cabin. 'Your face shines as bright as always.'

'Mayor Coo, your warmth is ever glowing,' Amma replied as the man approached. They embraced and Darnell saw the man glance over him with a suspicious eye.

'And who is your young friend? He can't be Neil, too pale a skin. He little Nisha's betrothed or did you finally bring on a farm hand?'

'Just a hand passing through. Always welcome a little help on the farm. You know how it can get and Neil is still way too little to help.'

'When you bringin' your babbies back through here? Last I saw them Neil was a toddler!'

'You know the road isn't always safe. I'm not risking it. Plus the Authority seems to be on high alert. Last three trips I've been searched, plus they come to the farm too often for my liking. We are not criminals and shouldn't be treated as such.'

'Come, move into town here. We can build you a nice cabin. There's plenty of food and Corey's distillery keeps the Authority soaked enough with whiskey to keep them happy.'

'I'd never leave the farm. It holds too many of my heart's memories. As this place does for you, Coo.'

'As you wish. Come now, I was about to make some lunch. You and your boy look like a good meal would work well for you. I even have some meat we can get into.'

'Oh, we couldn't. Meat is expensive, Coo.'

'And I'm Mayor and the best hunter in these parts. I killed it so I get to share it.'

Amma laughed. 'Lead the way then, Coo, oh mighty hunter. Sure the Authority love you hunting instead of buying meat rations from the City.'

'Come on boy. Follow on in.' He stopped and turned to Amma. 'You trust the boy, Amma?' Darnell looked to Amma for her response.

'Yes, he has been affected by them too. He holds no love

there for them. I have seen it in his eyes.'

'Very well. We have matters to discuss then. Chatter from the City and the like. Join me in my gathering room,' he directed them into his house. He turned to a young man pruning a lemon tree. 'Artie, guard this cart with your life. All stock is counted.'

'Yes, Sir, Mayor Coo. You can count on me,' the young man replied.

'Always, Artie,' he called as he closed the door behind him. 'Dull boy but loyal and honest to a fault. Makes great apple pie too... Anyway, follow me.'

He pushed past them and they followed him into the kitchen. The cabin was sparsely decorated, the kitchen even more so. The benches were clean and devoid of objects save a cup that held a wooden spoon and a handful of chopsticks. Two pots hung from hooks near the stove. The open-faced shelves held little more than a handful of cans and a canister marked FLOUR. Coo opened the pantry door and stood looking into its empty shelves. A solitary jar of pickled onions sat near the back corner. A thin layer of dust coated it and the shelves around it. The only clean part was the floor. It was freshly swept. Coo dropped to his haunches and pried a floorboard up. Under it was a small metal keypad. He pressed some buttons and replaced the wood.

'Wha...' Darnell began.

'Shh,' Amma said, resting her hand on his shoulder.

Coo stood up as a series of clicks vibrated through the floor. It dropped down and slid into the neighbouring flooring beside it. Lights flickered on, revealing a ladder.

'After you, Amma. Boy, you go after. I'll follow.'

Amma calmly began to climb down the ladder.

Darnell looked down at Amma and back up at Coo. Panic began to rise.

'Don't run, boy. Artie will shoot you on sight if he sees you a-running.'

'Darnell, it's okay,' Amma assured him, 'it's not a trap. I

know that look in your eyes. Coo is on our side.'

'Is that why he just threatened to shoot me? Let me go please. I'm just trying to get to the City. That's all. I won't tell anyone about your secret dungeon. I just want to go, please.'

'Boy, go down the ladder. We can discuss this like adults. We can explain everything there. I promise. I don't want to harm you.'

'But you're going to?' Darnell's voice cracked on the last word. He felt sick. His eyes darted side to side, looking for escape, but Coo was a big man and he blocked the pantry door with his width. He felt like a trapped rabbit.

'Darnell,' Amma said. 'Just follow me. I promise you on my children's lives…'

Amma climbed down. Darnell looked into the opening. The room below looked like a lounge room. He could see a rug and the corner of a couch. He tentatively followed her down into the room, Coo standing over the entrance. He had nowhere else to go.

Coo followed him down. The panel slid shut. The panic began to rise again into his throat. He felt so trapped. The room was well-lit, the walls lined with shelves stocked like his cabin's larder. In the back was a small cot bed, a small card table and two folding chairs. The couch Amma sat on was a double, and a single matching couch sat next to it. Amma patted the seat next to her as Coo made himself busy making food.

'Breathe, Darnell. It's okay. This is a safe place. It is away from the Authority of the City.'

Coo brought a tray of meat, cheese and bread over to the table, a jar of tomato jam open next to it with a knife plunged into its redness.

'Eat please. I'll get us some water,' Coo said. Amma helped herself but Darnell was unsure if it was safe. He waited until Amma began to eat before reaching for food himself. He felt horrible for not trusting Amma after the kindness she had given to him the past day. He was hungry. Coo brought a jug of water and a stack of cups. He poured out the water placing full cups down quietly on the table. He took a seat in the single couch and sipped his drink. They sat in silence while Amma and Darnell ate.

Amma took a drink and looked at Coo with a smile. 'Thank you Coo; you can make a meal from anything.' He chuckled. 'You are too kind my dear. Now,' he said, turning to Darnell, 'young man, what is your story? Unmatched parents? Blank sympathiser? You're too young to be an Authority deserter, unless they're recruiting pre-schoolers now.'

Darnell said nothing. Despite Amma's affirmation of trust for Coo, he was new to both of them. His mother had drilled into him that his blank status could get him killed.

'Come on boy. I don't bite.' Coo paused. 'I'm ex-Authority. Was trained up and going for a rank when my sister had a baby. It was a little girl called Ava. She was a blank. The Authority snatched her. Said they were running tests. We never saw Ava again. It nearly killed my sister and her husband. She left him. Came out here. Closer to nature and all that shit. I followed her out here. Heard her husband disappeared too. My sister was never the same. Drank herself to death under Corey's bar. Found her next to the still. She was only twenty-six. She looked twenty years older. Age had not been kind to her. By then I'd officially resigned from the Authority. I'd never go back. I was trained in combat. I keep this place safe. The older Authority guys know to leave me well enough alone but the younger ones who get sent out here on patrol need to be put in their place. That's why I'm the Mayor. Not an official title or anything but I keep things in line. If only I'd been able to keep my sister in line.'

Darnell saw a tear escape Coo's eye and roll down his weathered cheek. 'They, the Authority, are not welcome here. Only those who think like us can stay. Those that can think for themselves. I would give anything for more time with Ava. My sister's name was Cora. My little Cora. My last memory of her was down in that still, the smell of alcohol and vomit, her skin greying and limp. Corey blamed himself. He normally locked the door to the still. Didn't want kids getting into down there. I mean everyone knew Cora liked her drink, but she was never cruel when she drank. She was always kind. She'd garden and paint. She'd play with the kids after school time. Never had a temper or raised her voice. I knew I should have cut her drink off but she was so sad without it. When she was drunk it was the only time I saw her smile anymore. The only time I ever heard her laugh anymore, and her laugh, it was like music. Corey nearly left the community after that but I made him stay. It wasn't his fault. It was the Authority's for taking Ava away from Cora.' His voice faltered, cracking on her name. He sniffed back the tears and wiped his face on his shirt sleeve. His hand was shaking as he took a drink. He coughed and looked up at Darnell, his eyes rimmed with red. 'So what's your story son?'

Darnell honestly didn't know how to respond. If Coo was lying he was a damn good liar. Darnell believed him but still had never put what he needed to say into words before.

'I... I...' Darnell's mouth felt dry. He took a gulp of water. It was too big of a gulp and too cold all at once. He sputtered into a coughing fit.

'It's okay, Darnell,' Amma said, placing her hand on his back to reassure him. She leaned back to let Darnell know he should continue. He put the cup back on the table. Now he was the one with the shaking hands.

'When I was a baby my mother moved us out to the valley. The cabin there had belonged to my great-grandfather. He was ex-military; convinced the war was going to start all over again. He built a bomb shelter and a massive larder. Mum managed out there with Dad's help to get it restocked and she learnt to fish and built us a big garden.

'When I was old enough she'd make me hide while she went to meet Dad for supplies. I don't remember him. I have photos... *had* photos back at the cabin, but I don't remember him as a person, just as a picture on the wall and in albums. I liked the cabin. I guess I knew no different, did I? But home is home. One day someone came. Mum got shot. I did as I'd been taught to do by her and hid. Now I'm heading to meet with someone she told me to find if this ever happened. An old friend of my parents or something.'

'But why? Why did someone from the Authority come out to your cabin in the middle of nowhere and shoot your mum?' Coo asked.

'I never said it was the Authority.'

'Who else would it be? A random bushwalker just wandered through the forest hoping to find a person to shoot? Saw your cabin and thought *Oooh goodie, a person to kill?* Of course it was the Authority. So why? Did your mum do something? Was she a criminal?'

'My mother was not a criminal!' Darnell spat. 'How dare you…'

'Settle, I merely asked. Why were they after you?' Coo said.

'I'm blank, okay? I'm blank. I have no mark.'

Tears streamed down Darnell's face. He closed his eyes and put his face in his hands.

The room was silent but for the sound of 'Here, look.' Coo said handed Darnell some papers. They were copies of old photos. The creases in the paper had worn away leaving no ink, scarring the images. The first was of a young woman. She had a wide smile and bright blue eyes. Her hair was flying in the wind, wrapping around her throat like tendrilly fingers. Her skin was pale, her cheeks pink. The other piece of paper was a picture of a naked baby. The child was giggling at the camera. Her skin showed no marks that he could see.

'Cora and Ava,' Coo said, barely a whisper.

Darnell handed the pictures back. 'I'm sorry.'

'You have done nothing wrong. There is nothing wrong with you either. Just because you are a blank does not mean you are less of a person. You are safe here and welcome. I won't let them take another blank from under my nose.'

'Uh, thank you, Sir. I have a place to go but your hospitality is much appreciated.'

'Where is this place you're going?'

'My mother has a friend, Oscar, in Ellintown. I'm to meet him there and he will help me.'

'How do you know he's still there? Or alive for that matter? When was the last time your mother spoke to him?'

'I… I don't know.'

'I'll take you. If you insist on going, I'd rather you have a way back to safety if the man isn't there anymore. Plus I can keep you safe. But today, you stay here, and tonight. We can head off in the morning. Amma you can head to your market. Boy, if you are going to Ellintown it'll be easier to head along the river. It'll detour a few towns and cut the trip in half. And if we get a good current may be faster than that. You okay on the water?'

'I can row a boat. Used to use one for fishing. I'm good at fishing.'

Coo chuckled. 'Well, I expect a fish dinner tomorrow. I should have a fishing pole we can take. I want you to stay down here until morning. We don't need people asking questions. You don't have a good poker face, kid. Can read you from a mile away. I'll get your things from Amma's cart. Amma, please help yourself to food for your journey, then say your goodbyes.'

***

Amma had left an hour ago. Darnell sat on the couch with his pack resting against the table. Coo had left him to tend to some preparations for their trip but had pulled a map from a shelf and spread it on the now cleared coffee table. His finger traced the blue line of the river. Coo had helped him pinpoint the settlement and he could see why the trip would be better by water than by land. The road, for there only really was one, wound through the forest and through seven townships, each bigger than the next, as they got closer to Ellintown.

The river ran through the forest, branching out to the

towns, but the main waterway of the river ran right past the docks in Ellintown. From there Coo said he knew enough folk that they should be able to locate the man without drawing too much attention to themselves. If the man still existed, that was.

Darnell tapped at the tabletop. He knew he was safe here but his heart still pounded every time he heard a noise above his head. Coo said this might happen and offered him a small bottle of what he called crystal whiskey from the still.

Post-Traumatic Stress he called it. PTSD. Coo explained that soldiers got it sometimes after experiencing something nasty. He was no soldier but the nasty part rang true. It was tempting to sample the alcohol, something that was never meant for drinking in their old cabin, only to be used as a disinfectant his mother said, but just the smell of it turned his stomach. It smelled like antiseptic to him, not something to be imbibed.

He took a deep breath and stood up. He'd already wandered the basement bunker a dozen times but he needed to move. Coo, of course, had locked him in. There were shelves of jars: jams, pickles, dried herbs and fruits and salted meats. Another side was all cans. These were labelled with commercial labels. These had been purchased from the City. He and his mother had a wall like this too. The last wall held supplies. Medical kits sat next to slabs of bottled water, swags, weapons and ammo, canteens and clothes. A lot was tightly enclosed in vacuum-sealed plastic bags. Boxes stacked on top were stuffed with other necessities. But there was order to the madness.

He shook his head as he went into the bathroom to splash off his face. On his way, he noticed a book that had fallen behind a box of medical supplies. Darnell tugged it from where it had jammed between the shelf and the wall. It was a small hardcover notebook, a rubber band holding it closed. It had a layer of thick dust coating it; the rubber band was brittle and cracking. Even after wiping the dust away, he had no clue what it was. Nothing was written on the cover. He took it back to the couch.

He turned the book over in his hands once again; he knew that if he removed the rubber band, there was no way of going back. It had no stretch left in it and he was pretty sure it would crumble first. It did just that. The rubber all but disintegrated as he tried to open the book. A sticky, discoloured trail remained across the dark blue over. The smell of mould and damp paper rose from the brittle pages. It wasn't that old, just overly damaged from its resting place. He peeled the pages apart as gently as he could. It was handwritten, black ink fading on the pale, off-white pages. Flipping through the book he saw it was edge to edge handwriting, minus a few inked sketches. He turned to the very first page. It was surprisingly almost totally blank except for one scribbled title in smeared black ink. 'The Life of Ava'.

CHAPTER THIRTEEN
Zale

Zale coughed as the dust settled behind him. He could see light ahead of him from the bunker, dust particles swimming in the air. He turned his head from where he lay to see nothing but blackness. The roof had totally collapsed.

'Zale?' came a muffled voice from behind the rubble wall. 'Zale, are you okay?' It was Greyson.

He got to his feet as carefully as he could but it wasn't easy or graceful with only one arm. He brushed his hand off on his trousers. It stung like hell. He realised the skin was cut up. Even in the half-light he could see it wasn't anything serious but he could only hope for better luck going forwards. He clambered over the rubble to the wall blocking the way out.

'I'm okay!' he called. His voice was hoarse from the amount of dirt and dust he had managed to ingest that day.

'We'll keep digging,' Greyson replied.

Zale nodded in the darkness. 'I'm going to go in. Be careful of falling debris.'

He turned and headed in towards the light of the bunker. He could see blast marks on the floor for a fair distance but someone had cleared the rubble and the blood from the floor.

He stepped into the main room and saw the aftermath. There were cots filled with bleeding people. Bandages soaking through. People sat by the wounded, cleaning wounds and redressing them. He scanned the faces. Where was Allen? He didn't see him amongst the wounded or the carers.

He saw someone running towards him from the other side of the room. It was Trella.

'Zale? Oh my goodness, Zale! You're alive!' She ran up and threw her arms around him.

'Allen. Is Allen...'

'He's got a few minor injuries but nothing serious. He's taken charge of the makeshift morgue.'

Zale let out a breath he didn't even know he had been holding.

'And Jonah? Is he okay?'

'Few cuts and bruises from flying debris. I think he was glad his ankle was as bad as it was so he didn't feel obligated to run after you. He's not... like you.'

'I need to see Allen.'

'It's not pretty down there. Luckily, there was a munitions room way in the back of this place. It's a level down so it's cool. But it's really messy. We didn't want to use any of the cot sheets to cover them in case we need them for bandages. The med kits aren't bad here but we're smashing through our supply of bandages. We put a few tarps down that were over the munitions but yeah, not pretty.'

'He's smart like that. His mum is a nurse. He knows triage inside and out and can repurpose anything he can find for helping injured people.'

'Just a warning, it doesn't smell too pleasant down there either. No decomposition yet but the blood smell is overpowering.'

'I wasn't expecting it to smell like a rose garden. It's okay.'

'Your arm; is it broken?' she asked, nodding towards the sling. He pulled it free and wiggled his fingers. He winced.

'Not broken but not very happy. I have some good painkillers that are certainly taking the edge off so I'm managing it. Falling in the tunnel on the way back in didn't help though,' Zale said, showing her the cuts and scrapes on his other hand.

'I'll get that cleaned up for you after you see Allen.'

'Speaking of clean-up – whoever did the clean-up up there did a good job. Great idea, less of a reminder of the horror.'

'Yeah, between the blood and rubble, it was not easy but it kept some people busy when they needed the distraction. Even though personally it made my stomach turn. That poor little girl. I'm glad her mother didn't see it. Her aunt is a mess both mentally and physically. She ran to the body behind you. When the blast went off a brick got her in the head. Didn't even knock her out. I think she was in so much shock, she barely felt it. She's probably going to lose an eye though or at least her sight if we can't get her to the hospital soon. We've cleaned it up best we can but she needs orthoptimol. The hospital has one of those orthoptimol med bots but yeah, time is certainly an factor.'

'And the baby?'

'She started contractions an hour ago. Luckily we have a midwife in here and baby is full term so that shouldn't be an issue.'

'I have Dr Schonell outside. They're trying to work their way through the rubble from the cave in in the tunnel.'

'They?'

'We rounded up a posse to help out in here. Not much by way of medical staff but people enough to help with the stretchers.'

'Allen's triage system is in place up there for the patients so we'll be able to get the worst of them to the hospital first. Any idea who our visitors were?'

'No. The blast knocked me out. I went flying into dirt. When I woke up most of them were gone including our lady friend, although she was bleeding pretty well. Another one of them jumped me on the way here, but he got shot.'

'I just don't understand…'

'Zale!' came a call from down the hall. 'Oh my god, Zale, you're okay!' It was Allen running full-speed towards him, arms outstretched like some slow-motion scene from an old film. He all but tackled Zale, kissing his face over and over. It was only Zale's repeated cries of 'ow' that made him stop and let go.

'Oh babe, what have you done to yourself?' he said, holding Zale at arm's length by the shoulders.

'The explosion sent me flying. I landed pretty hard I guess. Nothing broken. Don't fret. Just be gentle.'

'Gentle I can do,' he said, this time carefully leaning in and drawing him in for a deep kiss.

'I love you so much. I'm glad you're okay.'

'Same to you, hon,' Zale replied.

'So we're able to get out then? We need to get people to the hospital as soon as we can. Especially Sam. Both for her eye and baby.'

'Can't. The tunnel caved in behind me. I have a group of people trying to get back in. Dr Schonell is with them. So until then how can I help that only requires one load-bearing arm?'

'Want to play guard for the morgue? Penny Peters keeps trying to sneak in to see her son. She really can't do that. He was pretty close to the blast. A piece of shrapnel took the top of his head off and half his face with it.'

'How many are dead?'

'Fourteen so far. I guess we should be grateful it's only that many. Thirty-five injured to a point of needing medical attention in hospital, stitches, et cetera. Another twenty with minor injuries we've fixed up ourselves. Five that may not make it in critical conditions. They're all losing blood way too fast. The few in here with medical training are doing their best. We have one general practitioner, two nurses, an ex-nurse and a midwife. There's three ex-military out there but two of them are too injured to do more than bark orders. The only surgeon is in the morgue. Dr Wade had a heart attack or a stroke or something.'

'He was seventy-three. Is his wife here?'

'Yeah, she's on tea duty with the nanna patrol. They're keeping everyone fed and watered and distracting the kids best they can under the circumstances. Most of the kids just aren't coping.'

'Hon, they're kids. I'm not coping with this and I'm a grown-ass man. And here comes another person who is most definitely not coping. Penny alert.'

'Oh damn,' Allen sighed. 'Mrs Peters,' he said, turning to see the woman coming down the hall towards them. 'Mrs Peters. Penny, you need to go back to the bunker.'

Her dress was spattered with dark patches that could only be blood. Zale stepped forward.

'Mrs Peters, how about we go get you a nice clean set of clothes and a nice cup of tea? I'm sure Mrs Wade can fix you one.'

Penny looked up at Zale, her face pale, a splash of blood smeared across her face. He eyes were glazed.

'I... I... just need to check on my son. Billy came down here. He's hurt himself, the silly duffer. He just needs his mum.'

'Mrs Peters, Billy isn't down here. Billy is... gone.'

'Gone? Gone where? He should have told me he was going to go somewhere. Naughty boy. He's probably snuck out with that girl again. I wish he'd just tell me. She's lovely; you'd probably like her. Sarah is her name. Oh, he is so grounded when I see him.'

'Mrs Peters, let's just go back upstairs, okay?' He moved to take her arm but she looked like she had zoned out, looking through him rather than at him. All of a sudden, her eyes shifted focus back to his face.

'Oh, hello dear. I'm just looking for my son Billy. I know he came down here before. He's not feeling a hundred percent and I just wanted to see how he's holding up.'

Zale this time did put his arm in hers and turned her around. He knew logic would have no place in this situation. He needed to try again.

'He went back upstairs to get some fresh clothes for you. Let's go see what he found. How about that, Mrs Peters? I'm sure he found something nice and comfy for you in the storage room.' She looked at him for a few seconds then a smile crept across her face.

'Oh, okay dear. I know you, don't I? You're one of Billy's school friends. He hurt himself before. Is he okay? He's such a good boy.'

'Yes, Mrs Peters,' he replied, not wanting to answer any question too specifically. 'My name is Zale.'

'Oh, okay dear.'

He saw her eyes start to glaze over again. They managed to get to the door back into the main bunker room before she stopped. Zale nearly tripped as she stood rooted to the spot.

'Mrs Peters?' He eyes were blank. No one was home. She almost looked drugged. 'Mrs Peters? Are you okay? Mrs Peters, can you hear me?'

She started to tremble. Zale grabbed her by the shoulders.

'Mrs Peters, can you hear me? Penny! Look at me,' he yelled. She slowly raised her head and looked at him. It was like she'd been asleep. Her eyes came back into focus.

'Oh, hello young man. What on earth is wrong? Why are you yelling at me? Have you seen my son Billy?'

'Mrs Peters, we need to go back out into the bunker room. It's safer there. We shouldn't go down into the munitions storage. Billy wouldn't go to the munitions storage room, would he?'

'Oh, okay,' she muttered, starting to move in the right direction again.

Zale breathed a sigh of relief and led her to the kitchen area where he saw Mrs Wade. She looked up and nearly dropped the cup she was holding.

'Hey, Mrs Wade. Mrs Peters really needs a cup of tea.'

She nodded as Zale got Penny seated at one of the trestle tables. He kept one hand on her shoulder to safeguard her from wandering off again. Mrs Wade placed a cup of tea on the table in front of Penny.

'Hey, Penny. Just the way you like it. Black with two sugars and a dash of cold water.

Mrs Peters had gone back into glazed-over land again. The

cup sat untouched. Mrs Wade looked up at Zale. Her skin was crêpey and although dark, an ashen hue had crept across her.

'Her son is…'

'Yeah. She keeps trying to visit him. Thinks he's sick. Can one of your lovely ladies babysit her? Maybe someone who knows her well enough to hold her attention when she has her lucid moments. Allen is trying his best down there but he can't keep her away. She's most certainly in shock. She also needs to be cleaned up. She's covered in blood.'

Mrs Wade nodded. Her dark eyes looked so worried and her white hair was coming loose from its bun creating a cloud-like halo around her frazzled expression. He felt bad leaving Mrs Peters there but she needed someone she was more comfortable with to help her.

'I'll get Ellie on it. She's dealt with worse. She used to work in aged care. I'll be right back. I'll see if she knows if we have anything stronger than tea as well.'

Zale nodded and pulled a seat up to the table. His wrist was throbbing now but he needed to save the pain medication for when he would most need it. Who knows how long he would be down here? He did consider slipping one into Mrs Peters' tea but she wasn't drinking it anyway.

'Here, Mrs Peters. Have some tea.' He nudged the mug into her hand. No response whatsoever came from her. He gripped her hand in his. It was trembling again. If he just sat here and held it long enough maybe she would settle.

Mrs Wade and Ellie Crambol came back over. Ellie had to be in her eighties. Her skin was as delicate-looking as old paper, a deep olive brown from years of sun. She was tiny compared to Mrs Wade but there was strength in her despite her stature and age.

Ellie sat on Penny's other side and began to stroke her arm.

'Penny, dear. We need to get you freshened up. Looks like there's a stain on your nice dress. We need to get that washed so it doesn't leave a mark, okay?'

Zale pulled his hand out of Penny Peters' and stood up

quietly. He looked over at Mrs Wade who nodded and smiled in acknowledgement that they would be okay with her. He turned and walked back towards the makeshift morgue.

He had gone about halfway down the tunnel when he heard a strange noise behind him. It could only be called a wail. It was quiet and somewhat guttural to start, like a frightened cat warning away a shadow, and then the noise began to grow into a cry. It was like a siren, echoing off the concrete walls, barely human, a monster issuing a roar of terror. He turned and ran back to the bunker room in time to see Ellie tumble to the ground. The noise was louder now. He had never heard such a bellow from anyone before and hoped never to again. It just kept going.

Penny Peters stood at the table, her chair knocked aside onto the floor; the cup of tea, well forgotten, splashed a sepia puddle across the white tabletop, dripping onto the floor like the diluted bloody stains that had already become part of the bunker's concrete floor.

She was staring up at the ceiling, her mouth an open maw. The wailing sound was all her. Mrs Wade attempted to approach her but Penny's arm swung in a wide arc and knocked Mrs Wade to the ground as well. Zale ran towards her. He saw a few others tentatively coming closer as well, from where the cot beds were. Some of the children had broken away from the room they had made a creche and were standing in fear looking at the screaming woman; they had begun to cry themselves.

As Zale got within arm's reach he slowed to a crawl. He needed to be quiet. His approach was as slow and silent as he could manage. He saw people helping Mrs Wade and Ellie to their feet and pulling them away from the kitchen area. How Penny was breathing through the scream, Zale had no idea. He swore she hadn't taken a single breath since she began. Her shoulders rose and fell as if she was gasping for breath, almost like she was circular breathing without even knowing how. He got close enough and grabbed her from behind, holding her arms by his side. Her arms began to flail but he held on. Still the wail continued, angrier now than before but still inhuman. It was starting to hurt, his ears being this close. His wrist was throbbing in complaint at the pressure being put on it. He was going to feel this afterwards. He tried to drag her back towards one of the storage rooms, just to get her away from everyone, especially the kids. A few people now stood around not sure how to help. She was like moving dead weight. Zale could easily pick up Allen but this woman half the size was like trying to uproot a tree.

'Someone grab her legs for fuck's sake!' he called at the people.

Two folks rushed over. Each tried to grab a leg. The man, a stocky fellow in his forties who ran the storehouse, scored a flailing foot to the groin. He cried out and dropped to the ground in pain. He was not going to be of any help for a while. The woman whose face looked familiar as one of the new arrivals managed to snag both of Penny's legs and lift them from the ground. She was being kicked in the chest but still managed a decent enough grip. This could work.

This must be what it was like to wrestle a giant worm, Zale thought as Mrs Peters continued to thrash. They walked towards the storage rooms, Zale shuffling backwards. His ears were ringing from the sheer volume her screams had reached. It was ridiculous. He was sure she would soon start to hyperventilate. Whether that would make her quiet or in some bizarre way worse, he didn't know.

'Mrs Peters!' he yelled over the wail. 'Mrs Peters will you please shut the hell up!'

Her head snapped backwards. Her eyes weren't glazed over anymore, that was certain. Her pupils had dilated, hiding almost all of the blue that had been there before. Her head cracked into Zale's bottom lip, compounding the pain already radiating from his sprained wrist. In shock, he let go. She swung a hand at his face as she fell, adding what would surely be another bruise to his already battered face.

Her head hit the concrete with a sickening crunch. The woman carrying her legs dropped them, as the weight shift was just too great for her to keep her grip. But at least finally she had stopped wailing.

'Fuck!' Zale cried. He could taste the blood on his lip but was now more worried he'd killed Mrs Peters. Crouching next to her, he got close to her face. She was breathing, still at that rapid pace of gasps. Her mouth was open now in a silent scream, as if the fall had knocked out just her vocal chords. Her pupils contracted now into tiny pinpoints of black. The woman was crouched down on the other side of her.

'She's still breathing. Should we try and lift her?'

'She might have a broken neck. She landed head first,' Zale replied with a sigh. 'At least she's quiet.'

'I thought the same thing. Does that make me a bad person?'

'No. It makes you a human. Do you know if there are any neck braces in the medical supplies?'

'There was only one and we had to use it on one of the injured. He can't feel his legs so we have him fully immobilised. Who knows how much damage was done? He hit the wall so hard. He's burnt up pretty bad too. I don't even know his name. I barely know anyone. I'm Dina.'

'Zale. Nice to meet you, wish it wasn't in these circumstances. Dina, we need to make a makeshift neck brace. Any ideas?'

'She seems pretty docile now so could we just stretcher her?'

'We have stretchers spare but there was only one neck brace?'

'Injured come in to bunkers. They don't usually get new injuries once in here. I'll be right back. I know where we put them. Just keep her down.'

Zale nodded and looked back down at Mrs Peters. Her face was still a pallid shade of pale and her eyes were almost a silvery blue now. Her breathing appeared to be getting faster though. He hoped she wasn't having a heart attack. He had no idea if they had a defibrillator in the bunker or how to use it if they did. But he felt he had to do everything he could. This community was his family.

'Shhhh, it's okay Mrs Peters,' he said quietly, gently stroking her hair away from her face. She was starting to sweat. It certainly wasn't hot in here. Then he noticed she was also shivering. This was not good. Her body had finally caught up with her mind on the way to full-blown shock. As far as he could see there was no blood pooling under her head, and for that he was grateful. He was sure it would be bleeding though.

He saw Dina coming back with the stretcher and two helpers.

'Zale, this is Tony, he used to be an Ambulance driver in the City. He knows how to get her on the stretcher safely. This is Frank.'

'I'm just a farmer but I can lift heavy stuff. Thought you might need a hand seeing your wrist is all banged up.'

'Thanks guys. Where do we start, Tony?'

After a few minutes of positioning her and using a lunch tray to support her head and neck, the group managed to get her onto the stretcher. A small smear of blood was on the floor.

'Uh, what's the chance she's going to start that noise again?' Zale asked. 'Or start swinging at us? People are starting to stare and we don't need more of an audience'

'Honestly. She's so far into shock I don't know. I've seen people die from the stress it puts on them. Her heart is racing like mad, her body is trying to get oxygen but that panting gasp she's got going on isn't going to help. I think we need to get her somewhere very quiet, and unfortunately restrain her somehow. Frank, do you think you could lift one of the cot beds?'

'Sure can. Where do you want it?'

'I'll help,' Dina said.

'If we can get it into one of the rooms out back that would

be good. I haven't been back there. What are our choices?'

'There's a small room about five metres down that tunnel to the left. Looks like an office of some type. Should be room enough for a cot,' Zale answered.

Frank nodded and he and Dina went to get the closest cot. They began to carry it down the hall. Zale looked up at Tony.

'What type of restraints will we need.?'

'To be honest, in the state she was in, I'm pretty sure she'd get out of most restraints. Do we have some old sheets and some duct tape?'

'Old sheets in the store room. They're already being torn up for bandages so we should be able to snag a few pieces. Duct tape I actually saw in one of the storage rooms. Give me a few minutes. Yell if she… wakes up or starts swinging.'

'Will do.'

Zale got up and saw that one of the younger women had started a group of people tearing up the sheets to use as bandages and dressings. He approached them. They looked terrified and he was pretty sure the motions they were going through to make the bandages were just muscle memory of their task. They looked spaced out.

'Hey guys,' he said. One of the women yelped and dropped the sheet she was holding onto the floor.

'Sorry,' she mumbled. 'I'm just a little on edge.'

'It's okay, I think we all are. Just wondering if I can swipe one of those sheets there, and a pair of scissors if you have a spare set.'

'Help yourself to the sheets but no more scissors. Half of us are using knives we found in the storage room. There's a few in the box on the chair at the end of the table. Feel free to take one. Just be careful, they're very sharp. They're cutting the fabric like butter. At least it's making the work a lot easier for us, I can tell you that much.'

'Thanks.'

'Is she dead?' a redheaded teen boy at the other end of the table asked.

'What?'

'The screaming lady. Is she dead? She's quiet.'

'I think she's knocked out and in a lot of shock,' Zale said as he plucked a hunting knife from the box.

'That's Billy's mum, hey? No wonder she's lost it. His face was chopped in two. She wasn't too close but she saw it. She held his body and kept telling him to wake up and when they finally pulled it away, she just sat there all calm like.'

'Hardy, stop it!,' the young woman snapped.

'What? I'm just telling the man what happened.' He turned back to Zale. 'After about five minutes she just stands up and goes and stands in the kitchen like she walked in to do something then forgot what it was. After that every few hours she tried to get down to where the tall guy is taking the bodies,' he said.

'Yeah, Allen is my boyfriend.'

'You've got a good man.' The young woman said. 'I wish mine had been half as good. Allen's done a good job keeping most folk calm. We just wanted to help. None of us are old enough to know more than basic first aid so we're no help over there and to be honest I wanted to get as far away from all the blood as I could. Couldn't do the clean-up duty. Thought I would throw up and add to the mess. So when I heard they needed bandages, Trella told me I could use the sheets. These guys joined me. And we've been at it for a while. Looks like we might need them too.'

'Yeah we will, I fear.'

'So how did you get back in? And why aren't we getting out of here? Are they still out there? The people who did this?"

'I think they're gone for now. I came back in but the tunnel collapsed behind me. A group is trying to dig us out.'

'Did you kill her?' the boy asked.

'Kill who? Mrs Peters? No, she's still alive.'

'No, the bitch that shot the little girl. Please tell me you killed her?'

'She got away but she has a few bullet holes in her.'

'Good. I hope they get infected or she bleeds out.'

'I'm going to find her, don't you worry. But first I need to help Tony with Mrs Peters. Keep up the good work kids.' He left them to their sheet-cutting and rolling and went to hunt down the duct tape. He had picked it up when he heard a cry of his name.

'Zale! I need you. NOW!' It was Tony.

Zale dashed over to see Mrs Peters having a seizure. He dumped the sheet, knife and tape to the floor. 'What do I do?'

Tony was trying to hold her still. 'Put the sheet under her head. I don't need her to make that head wound any worse.'

'But her neck?'

'Fuck the neck. Another blow to the head could kill her. I'd rather keep her alive.'

Zale slid the folded sheet in under her head as she thrashed around. At least it might cushion the blow. People had started to watch now. A small group was gathering. Those that had been hovering over the dying and injured with sick interest were now creating a curtain of onlookers around Mrs Peters.

'Get away you sickos. Don't you have better things to do? Either help or fuck off!' Zale spat. Some of the crowd dispersed but still the curtain remained. At least the kids couldn't see this. Seizures were rare but scary enough when they weren't accompanied by all the mess of the current situation.

The seizure started to decrease in severity as Frank and Dina managed to push their way through the crowd.

'I honestly thought she was dead with the vultures hanging around,' Dina said, glaring at the onlookers.

'At least the kids can't see her,' Zale said.

'Small mercies my friend,' said Frank as he dropped to his haunches beside Tony. The seizure finally left her body. She was limp but still breathing in that panicked gasping way. Her eyes were finally closed, but her mouth remained open in a silent scream.

'Okay, while we can, let's get her into that room, onto that bed and restrain her so we keep her safe.' Tony took the top two handles and Dina and Frank took the back two. Zale gathered the supplies and moved ahead of them to clear a path.

'Move it or lose it folks. I have a very large knife and I am already very unhappy with the vulture population in this bunker. I do not need to create more patients. Let the stretcher through and none of you follows us unless you are medically trained and coming to help us. Got it?'

A few people nodded dumbly, a few more moved away, back towards the cots and triage area. People moved out of the way for Zale and once they had entered the tunnel, they seemed to have a smooth run into the room. They slid Mrs Peters carefully onto the cot, her head now on a yellowed pillow. It would have to do.

Tony took the supplies from Zale and began to cut thick strips of sheet with the hunting knife. It was quick work but Zale still kept an eye on Mrs Peters in case she had another seizure or all of a sudden woke up demanding to see Billy again. That was all he needed, that wail echoing in the tiny room.

Tony handed him the roll of tape and the knife. 'Hold these while I wrap her wrists.'

Tony got the wide strips of cloth and wound them around Mrs Peters' wrists. Next, he got the duct tape and used it to secure the wrist to the bed frame. He repeated this for her other arm and then her legs. It wasn't as secure as Zale would have liked but they'd get some warning before she started punching people in her fits of flailing and she wouldn't fall from the cot if she had another seizure.

'I need to get a drip in her. Dina, can you go get a drip for fluids? Not that we have much else. Does anyone know if she was on any medication or was actually epileptic?'

Zale shook his head. 'I think she was friends with Mrs Wade, but since Penny's husband died she's kept mainly to herself and looking after Billy. Dr Wade was her practitioner

I believe too, so we can't ask him.

'I'll go see if we have a spare IV,' Dina said, heading out the door.

'What about his nurse?' Frank asked.

'Cheryl! She would know. Frank, do you want to see if you can find her?' Tony said.

'Can do. I think I saw her over with the pregnant lady. That baby may just get born in this here shelter. Let me see what I can find out.'

Frank jogged out of the room. Tony was sitting with his back against the wall at the head of the cot. Zale was still crouched down by Mrs Peters' side when Trella came in.

'Oh shit, it's true. I went up to look for you, Zale. Allen was worried. I must have walked right past this room. Frank sent me down here. She going to be okay?'

'Who knows?' Tony said, his head still back against the concrete, his eyes closed.

'Was that noise before, her? I wouldn't let Allen go up. I was too scared.'

'Yeah the shock kicked in a bit. Then she lost it. We tried to move her but we dropped her when she cracked her head into my lip,' Zale said, sitting in the chair behind the desk. 'We were trying to get her moved when she had a seizure. She seems to be resting now but her breathing is still so erratic and she won't close her mouth,' Tony said.

'She might have lockjaw. My brother got that once,' Trella mumbled.

'Either way, at least with her mouth open we can see and hear that she's breathing,' Tony said. 'If I can get an IV into her for fluids, we should be okay until we can get her out. I can't believe they have adrenaline shots but no sedatives in this bunker. I mean honestly.'

At that moment Mrs Peters' eyes flew open again and the beginning rumbles of a wail began again.

'Nope. I'm out. I can't handle that again,' Zale announced, turning away from Mrs Peters.

'Is that how she started last time?' Trella asked.

'Yeah and it got to insanely loud quite quickly. My ears are still ringing from it.'

'How did you stop it last time?'

'Blunt force trauma to the back of her head. I really don't want to do that again,' Zale said.

'Uh, guys,' interrupted Tony. 'Guys, what the hell is she doing?'

Zale turned to see Mrs Peters' head whipping back and forth. Her body was rigid and then she started to cry. The wail turned into a sob. She was bellowing with sadness.

'This isn't the same. She's crying,' Trella said, her eyes wide with wonder.

'I can hear that,' Tony said, getting to his feet.

'No, I mean she's cry crying, sobbing. Her eyes almost look clear.'

Tony dropped down next to her and held her face so she was looking at him. There was no resistance, no flailing.

'Mrs Peters, can you hear me?' She continued to sob, her eyes now squeezed shut, tears rolling down her face. 'Mrs Peters, you've had an episode. You had a seizure and went into shock. Do you understand?' Tony said as calmly as he could.

She was still trying to shake her head side to side. Her mouth now was opening and closing like a goldfish, her breathing, although still gasping, no longer sounded like a panting dog, more like that of a long-time smoker trying to breathe.

'Mrs Peters. I need you to listen to me. I need you to tell me if you take any medications. Have you had seizures before?'

She stopped moving now and slowly opened her eyes as her breath hitched in her throat. 'No, I don't,' she whispered. 'My son...'

'I'm sorry Mrs Peters...'

'No. Please, no.'

'I'm sorry Mrs Peters, Billy didn't make it.'

She pulled at her restraints. 'Please let me move. I need to sit up.'

'Are you sure. It was for your own safety,' Tony said.

'Yes, I'm sure. My son is dead. I need to sit up. I think I might throw up.'

Tony cut the tape from her wrists and ankles as Trella passed her the waste paper bin in case she needed it.

'I need to see his body.'

'Mrs Peters, I don't think that's wise…' Tony began.

'He's my son and I want to see his body!' she shrieked as Frank came around the doorway.

'Ma'am, as someone who lost their son in an accident that resulted in similar injuries on the farm, I highly recommend you don't. At least not til we know how you're going to hold up. You've been through an awful lot already today.'

'I think I would be the best judge of that. Can one of you get me some painkillers and water? My head is pounding.' She reached back to touch the tender spot and looked rather calm when she saw her fingers now covered in blood. 'Oh, well, that explains the headache.'

'Let me get that dressed for you. I need to know a few other things to assess you, Mrs Peters.' Tony began.

'Please, call me Penny. I feel old enough as it is.'

'Penny. I need you to see if you can wriggle your toes for me and if you have any numb spots in your limbs.'

'My goodness, was this from the seizure?'

'You sustained a mild head wound during your fall. That combined with the nausea may mean you have concussion.'

She nodded. He began to dress her wound.

'There are no numb spots and I can wiggle everything, young man. I am so embarrassed and oh my goodness, look at my dress. How embarrassing. Did everyone see me?'

'It doesn't matter. As long as you're okay now. We can get you a change of clothes as well.'

'What will people think of me, though? Some crazy lady

having a fit in the middle of the shelter in front of everyone!'

'Ma'am, people will see you as a woman who witnessed her son and others, including a little girl, get killed today. Trust me, no one will think any less of you. More folk up there are concerned with your wellbeing than on gossiping about the state of your dress. Now I will go get you some water and see what painkillers I can rustle up for you. We have to have something. You're probably dehydrated, too. I think Mrs Wade was trying to get some tea into you but you weren't in the right state of mind to drink it. So you probably need a nice big drink of water, and probably an IV of fluids. It'll make you feel right as rain. Probably need food too.'

'No food, please. My stomach is churning like a blender. But thank you, Frank, water would be much appreciated, and no IV, there will be others that will need it more.'

Moments after Frank left, Dina came running back. 'Frank said Mrs Peters didn't want us to put an IV in, but I brought it anyway,' she said, holding up the IV. 'Good to see you up and about, Mrs Peters. You sure gave us a fright and a half. Sorry it took so long. They needed a bit of a hand. The bunker has a new resident. Sam just had her baby.'

CHAPTER FOURTEEN
Almara

My lungs burned. My feet hurt from the shoes I was wearing and I wanted so much to take them off and scrunch my toes through the wet grass below me. Ahn was pretty fit. He had broken a sweat but his pace only wavered when he turned to look at how far behind I was falling. We heard the dogs start to bark about an hour after we had gotten out of the compound.

Although they would be DNA-locked, Ahn doubted they would be able to follow us over water. We'd run through two streams now and my trousers were wet to the knees. My shoes made squelchy noises as I ran and I felt my wet-socked feet sliding inside every step. They would give up on us soon but I had no idea how much longer I was going to last.

It was then that I fell. I could have tripped or it may have been the sheer slipperiness of my shoes but I felt myself lose balance and fall, hands outstretched, the weight of my backpack only aiding my descent. My hands hit the grass, sliding in its dampness and sending the heels of my palms into the muddy soil below. It had been raining, Ahn said. And it was likely to rain more before we got anywhere safe. I'd forgotten about rain.

I felt my breath knocked out of me as mud splattered up my nose and into my mouth and eyes. I finally slid to a stop, my hands coming to rest against a thick tree trunk. My legs had begun to throb the second my weight was lifted off them.

I was not overweight but I certainly had not maintained the athletic energy of my pre-Cube days. But I guess that's what happens when you're sedated twenty-four-seven as I discovered we had been, save that night of death.

I just lay there. The energy to even keep my face out of the mud was draining me. I turned my face so I could see Ahn. He had come to a stop a few metres away and was walking back.

'If I knew you wanted a rest that badly... you should have said something,' he said with a smile. I was in no mood for his attempt at humour.

'I don't think I can move,' I mumbled.

'I hate to say this but you really don't have much choice, but we can reduce the pace for a while, at least until we get somewhere a little more covered. We're still five hours from dawn. We need to go for as long as we can in the dark. Here, let me help you up.' He held out a hand and I half rolled, half got dragged into a sitting position. At least I was camouflaged well. I was black with mud, including a good half of my face. I leaned against the tree that had acted as my brakes.

'Water?' he asked, holding out the bottle. I took it and had a few sips, trying to catch my breath through the burning feeling.

'I hate to say it but our outside time did not keep me fit and healthy enough for this sort of running.'

'You realise that's the whole idea? They let you do enough so your muscles won't waste away but not enough to be strong. Not unless you get moved out of the Cube.'

'Wait, people get moved out of the Cube?' I asked. He'd never mentioned this before but then again, how could he? I'd never seen my fellow blanks until the horror night.

'Well, technically not out of the Cube, but out of white level. There are two levels below yours. Red and blue. Blue is medical testing. I've delivered a few people there but never gotten too much of a look inside. There's rumours of gene splicing and trying to recreate the mutants in the wasteland in case they ever attack.'

'Is that where they sterilise us too?'

'Yes, although that happens to all blanks in the Cube, regardless of status.'

'Status?'

'You're white status. That means just a regular detainee, for now. You're kept docile enough to deal with and if needs be, action can be taken to test for moving to other statuses. Blue status is when they see something in your samples that make you a candidate for other tests. They're trying to work out why your body doesn't create a genetic mark like everyone else. Whether it's something missing or something added or just a fault in the DNA sequence is up for debate. Popular belief is that it's a missing part of the genome which is why blanks are easier to do splicing on and genetic manipulation.'

'So we become lab rats then?'

'To an extent yes. Blue status is not pleasant. I am glad I was never assigned there.'

'You said there was a red floor?'

'Red is five storeys under blue. The separation is solid concrete as red level is the training area. They push the blanks there. They enhance using tested splicing to see how far they can push the reds. It gets pretty brutal. They make the reds fight each other and run them ragged, pumped full of adrenaline. That's what the test was for. To see who could survive the adrenaline burst without having a heart attack or their hearts being weakened enough to be killed by that electric pulse they ran through the water.'

'So even white status are lab rats? How did you work there for so long?'

'I just kept reminding myself that once I had enough knowledge I could save at least one blank. It wasn't just my wife they killed. My little brother was a blank. He was taken at age five. I found his records once. He was blue status by the age of seven. '

'Did he...'

'He was mutated to the point where his organs failed. The bodies from blue status are burnt once they get as much information out of them as they can during autopsy. For all I know his brain is in a jar somewhere. He is nothing but a number in a ledger, a numbered file in a hard drive. It took me months just to find his name. It is written once. Once for the six years they had him there. After that, he was a number. Nothing more than a number to them. 942. My brother Lin was nothing more than 942 to every blue status staff person, every white status employee but me. The things they did to him.'

'Ahn I'm sorry.'

'I can't even visit a grave site. My parents made no memorial for him. The ashes are disposed of by the City. A truck comes and removes them every month. Whatever amount there is. Sometimes it takes the whole truck. My mother felt so much shame in my brother being taken. Not because he was blank, I don't think, but because he was taken in public. Right outside the school. She ended up in a hospital, unable to care for herself. It broke my father. And then when I said I was coming here, Dad didn't understand why. Mum did. Even in her drug-induced stupor in the care facility, she understood. She knew about my partner. She remembered how they took my brother.'

'She looked at me on the night before I moved out here and held my hand, looked me right in the eyes and, as lucid as I ever saw her, said to me, "You get them. Bring the City burning down." My father says that's the last thing she said. Hasn't spoken a word since. I've tried to call her but all I get is breathing on the other end. She knows if I had worried about her I'd have come home. She knew I had things to do out here. I hope I get to tell her what I've done before I lose the chance. She would be so proud.'

'I can't believe how many blanks there are. When I was a kid I thought I was the only one. And now to have glimpsed a small amount of us, it's just mind-blowing.'

'One percent,' Ahn said. 'Well technically one point three percent.'

'One point three percent of what?'

'Blanks. One point three percent of babies born in the past ten years have been blank. Half are taken at birth from parents who don't want them. They're taken right to blue status. They don't usually last a week. Babies. Just babies. The rest are usually taken before the age of five. A small amount come after school age. They're rare. Like you. They usually go to red status after a few years. That was why I wanted to get you out now. I think you were going to be on the transfer list this time.'

'Do any live normal lives? I mean, could a blank not partner with another blank?'

'And create more mutagen risk children? The City would never risk that. But some on record show as unaccounted for. Some end up living in the communities like where we're going. The City usually leaves them alone because the numbers are small and they keep to themselves. A few more slip through the cracks. Not sure what happens to them.'

'Did you ever try to hide your brother?'

'We kept him out of sight but he lived at home around the clock until he got to school age. Mum wanted him to go to real school. That's how she referred to it. Like home-schooling him wasn't real school. We lived in City One so it was not seen as proper. Mum thinks one of the teachers complained and then a car pulled up to the school and two Cube employees picked him up and put him into the car. His backpack and uniform were sent back to us the next week. No explanation.'

'The same thing would have happened to my parents.'

'Most likely. I remember seeing your admission file. You were one of the oldest we'd had come in fresh in a long time. They had to sedate you for weeks.'

'Do you think my mother and father would still want to talk to me?'

'Of course, but that won't be possible. It would endanger

their futures. They would already be on a watch list because of you.'

'But my mother…'

'Your mother deserves a normal life. You had a sister I remember?'

'Yeah, Joy.'

'Well, if she has a betrothed, your coming back could take away her right to partner. If they connect your parents with your escape they will be sent to prison for aiding a fugitive. Don't think that you're anything more than that to the Authority right now. I'd get prison. You'd probably go straight to red status or they'd remove you on the spot.'

'Remove me?' I dared to ask.

'Yes. "Remove" you. Kill you. It's not considered killing if the victim is a blank. Its referred to as removal as the City doesn't deem a blank a person.'

I was gobsmacked. So the City didn't even deem me human. I just couldn't process that. How many of the thirty million people in Oasis thought that way? A lot discriminated, that I remembered from my childhood, but I had thought they at least saw me as human, and not some beast with no mind of its own.

'We need to keep moving,' I mumbled, getting to my feet. My legs still burned but I was breathing normally again and to be honest, the idea of running until everything ached sounded like a great way to get my mind off being considered as less than vermin. I couldn't even be killed, just removed. I was a bit wobbly still and the dried mud cracked and flaked as I moved. I rubbed at the mud on my face, getting the larger chunks off but knowing that my once pale skin was now a lovely camouflaged greyish brown. I really hoped the first place we stopped had a shower although right now I'd settle for a river I could freshen up in.

We continued at more of a speed-walk than a run. My blistered feet complained regardless but my lungs were certainly happy for it. We occasionally heard barks way off in the distance but most of the noises we heard were purely animal.

'Do you know where we're going, Ahn? I mean not in the long run, but where we're going to stop to sleep?'

'If we keep a good pace tonight we should get to the outskirts of the CropServ 45 Plant. There's a small residential area there.'

'You're taking me, a fugitive, to a City-owned-and-run food plant?'

'CropServ 45 was closed last year after an accident damaged the soil. The plant is useless until they finish clean-up. The workers housing is right on the edge of the plant. We should be able to get at least running water and somewhere to sleep. Clean-up crews wouldn't be staying onsite but the power and water would be running. Our consumption won't make a blip on their usage reports compared to the soil flushing that's being done. It was evacuated so we might even find some supplies.'

'Wait, if it was evacuated, is it safe?'

'Technically no. But one day shouldn't hurt us as long as we don't eat any fresh food from there. Tinned and vac packed only. External things.'

'Comfortable shoes would be nice?' I said with a smile.

'We can scavenge before we leave tomorrow.'

'How are we going to get in to the buildings? Won't they be locked?'

'I have a plan for that too but don't stress. Now let's just concentrate on getting there.'

We walked for what felt like days but what I knew was only a few hours. The blush of the pink beginnings of sunrise was slowly spreading across what had been the dark and inky sky. The backlit fence, a silhouette of safety fencing with an inner barrier fence that was only waist high. Large signs hung from the high fence warning that the area was toxic and to wear safety equipment at all times. Smaller signs were below it but it wasn't until I was right in front of them that I could read it in the half-light:

Trespassers will be prosecuted by the Authority
to the furthest extent of the law.
This area is a City owned zone.
Authorised personnel only.

'We are going to get shot or turned into mutants, aren't we?' I said as Ahn started lifting the temporary fence panel.

'Not if I can't lift this fence panel out of the base. Want to give me a hand?'

'Why didn't you say so? Although I'm not sure how much help I'm going to be.'

I grabbed the other side of the fence panel. It was sturdy but with the two of us lifting, we managed to pull it out of the heavy base it was slotted into. It fell against the shorter barrier fence with a crash. I flinched at the noise.

'Should we not be just a tiny bit more careful?' I asked, climbing over the corner of the fence panel and into the area between the short fence and the taller fence panels. The grass had certainly taken hold here in this mini no-man's-land. It was knee-height at least.

'We need to put the panel back up,' Ahn said, pulling it up to vertical. 'Then they won't know where we got in if they manage to follow us this far. Although I haven't heard the dogs for a while.'

'What about people though?' I asked as he hefted the fence panel back into its base.

'That's my main concern. Technically, you are City Authority property. They might send Authority out after us. Now follow me,' Ahn said as he climbed over the shorter of the fences. It'd been a long time since I'd jumped a fence but I was now also considerably taller than I was last time so I made it over without too much effort, although I snagged my pants on a loose wire and nearly went tumbling, once again, to the ground. Ahn caught me and started walking towards the brick rows of buildings in front of us.

It reminded me of the Cube. Long white structures, which from the back had no distinguishing marks to show they were habitable; they looked almost like they were a storage facility or perhaps even a very long row of shower blocks. We walked between two rows and saw the front of the building was dotted with brightly coloured doors with assigned numbers painted on them. Dead pot plants sat outside some of the doors and one had a rocking chair, now weak from rain and too much sun, outside of it. It still rocked gently in the breeze but in the growing light of sunrise, I could see the rotted wood and peeling paint.

'Next row down,' Ahn said.

'They all look the same mostly. Why next row?'

'They would start from the back and work their way in. That will give us some warning.'

'Wait. What do we do if we hear them?'

'I would suggest run. If we are split remember just head north.'

I nodded and continued to follow him as we moved down the blocks of housing. The next row had less doors. They must have been bigger living suites. I saw a weathered teddy bear leaning against a door frame. It was leaning to one side, dropped in the rush of evacuation. I bent down and picked it up. The fur was crunchy from dried dirt. An eye was missing and a puff of stuffing was beginning to escape the hole.

'Poor thing,' I muttered, looking into its little face. It looked how I felt.

'Put that down, it's disgusting and dirty,' Ahn said as he approached the door to the residence.

'So am I, Ahn. Actually, I'm pretty sure this little guy here is cleaner than I am.'

He shook his head and began to jiggle the door handle. I realised none of the doors had keypads or fingerprint locks. They were all old-style door handles with key locks. I watched as Ahn dropped down to look into the lock. I couldn't see what he was doing but soon I heard a click and the door swung open.

I looked at him incredulously. 'How did you…'

'It gets pretty boring in the Cube compound. Took a Vidlink course on lock smithing. There's not many people who have key locks anymore but in case you want to transfer to different secure facilities, they run random courses to upskill us. That's how I found out they use key locks here.'

'Won't it look suspicious? That you did a course almost no one would use?'

'No, lots of people just work their way through the free courses before moving on to the paid ones. Helps if you want to transfer around.'

'Or if you want to become an expert at breaking and entering.'

'You know they genetic test for crime indicators before you can work in secure fields.'

'They also think that my genetics make me a monster so I'm not holding much sway to that testing anymore.'

He smiled at me and opened the door wide for me.

Still holding the teddy bear in one hand, its crunchy fur prickling my palm, I walked into the house. The sun was now high enough that the skylights let in a dim grey glow despite the leaves and dirt covering the clear openings in the ceiling. There was only one window, near the front door, and the shade on this was drawn tight. Ahn closed the door and pushed the bolt closed. He couldn't relock the door but the bolt was enough to be secure.

He flipped the light switch by the door and despite a few flickers, the lights in the ceiling came on. It wasn't as bright as I was used to in the Cube but after a night of running by dappled moonlight it was bright enough.

I dumped my pack on the couch. A puff of dust bellowed into the air, leaving specks in the light. There were three doors and an archway leading off from the lounge room. Through the arch was a kitchen. I smelled something unpleasant coming from in there. It wasn't too bad though and I could hear the gentle hum of the refrigerator. The solar panels on the roof were still obviously keeping the juice running, although why the City would leave it running mystified me. Despite the smell my stomach rumbled. I hoped there would be some supplies for us to dig into, keeping our rations for our journey ahead.

I headed towards the doors. The middle one opened to a bathroom. I flicked the switch and the light flickered on brighter this time than the one in the lounge room. I headed to the sink and looked at myself in the mirror. I was a mess. My hair was falling out of the tight bun I had put it in before we left, strands hard with a coating of mud stuck out around my face. I looked like I was wearing a mask, the mud was so dark. My eyes looked so bright against the greyish black of the dirt. I rested the teddy bear on the edge of the sink and turned the taps. There were a few clanks and gurgles before the water came but within seconds I had hot water. I was going to manage a shower that could scald the grime away. I checked under the sink and found towels and soap. The towels were a little dusty but were still softer than anything I'd felt in the Cube.

I left the teddy bear where he was and continued to explore. There was a washer and dryer in an alcove of the bathroom. I would even get fresh clothes. The dryer still had clothes in it. I opened the door and pulled out some t-shirts and pants. The shirts would fit me, the pants might. I would try them after I was showered.

I came out to see Ahn disappearing into one of the other doors so I chose the one not yet opened. Down a short hall was a bedroom. The light in here was bright like the bathroom. The bed was made, a green cover on the quilt and pillows. By the wall was a small desk, a few books scattered across it. A backpack sat next to it, unzipped, a notebook half out.

The walls were still the off-white that seemed to be the

only palette available to City employees' residences but the shelf next to the bed was painted yellow and held framed pictures and more books. I had missed reading so much. When I was a child I remembered many hours spent in the library. The library where they took my life from me.

There was a closet in the corner. The girl in the pictures looked about my age and I hoped her closet would hold something more comfortable than the horrible clothes I was in now. I opened the closet and looked in. It wasn't packed but I could see enough clothes that looked about the right size. I wouldn't touch anything though until I'd bathed.

Ahn came in at that moment, knocking on the door frame as he entered.

'I was hoping this was a second bedroom. You can have the master bedroom if you like. It's bigger in there.

'Too big might make for a hard night's sleep after what I'm used to. Anyway, I like it in here. Plus, I think I will be raiding this wardrobe.'

'Well the shower is all yours. I'm going to hunt through the kitchen and see what I can salvage. Might take a trip to the neighbouring residences as well. Before the sun is fully up and the work crew arrives.'

I nodded and followed Ahn out. I had a quick peek into the master bedroom. Ahn was right, it was bigger, but the colours were all City standard. I was much more drawn to the girl's room with its splashes of colour.

I headed into the bathroom and pulled out some soap and a towel. I gave it a shake until it looked as dust-free as possible and turned on the water. The room filled with steam as I hunted down some shampoo for my hair as well. The water was probably way too hot but I didn't care. I stepped into the stream of warmth, feeling the mud come away from my skin. The scent of soap was divine. It was floral and it lathered into handfuls of white bubbles. By the time I was finished my skin was red but I hadn't felt this clean in a long time. As I went to hop out and turn off the water, I spotted the teddy bear on the sink. Teddy could have a bath too. I hopped back in, lathered the bear up and washed away the dirt and crunchy feel of his fur. I wrung him out, apologising without even realising it and finally turned off the water. I dried myself and wrapped the towel around me.

Clothes was my next mission. I hoped the ones in the dryer would fit me. I pulled out a t-shirt and pulled it over my head. It was a little loose but it was comfortable and soft. I emptied the load onto the top of the washer and began to sort through it. I looked at the underwear but couldn't bring myself to wear someone else's. I hoped Ahn had packed some in my bag.

I found a pair of jeans and wriggled into them. Again, they were slightly loose but they stayed on. I would still rummage in the wardrobe for an alternative. I looked over at the soggy teddy bear and picked him up, tossing him into the dryer. At least he would be in a better state by the time he was done.

I tossed my dirty clothes into the washer and hoped I was pressing the right buttons. I heard the machine begin to fill with water and with that, was satisfied enough to move back to the girl's room.

I grabbed my bag on the way, noticing that Ahn was no longer in the residence. He must have gone for a scavenge. I dumped the contents of the bag on the bed and was happy to see Ahn had packed spare underwear for me. I put them on the desk and went to the cupboard. I was happy with the t-shirt but found a hooded jacket that fit well. It had pockets and felt warm but was still pretty light. I tossed that over onto the bed.

I finally found some cargo pants. They were black and had Youth Core embroidered across the back pocket. It seemed our girl was an Authority grunt in training. I pulled off the jeans and slipped into underwear and the cargo pants. They fit well and the pockets would be handy. I was hoping that when they evacuated she hadn't had her Youth Core issue boots on. If I could find them and they fit, I'd be in luck. I found some thick socks in the drawer inside the wardrobe then hit pay dirt.

There were two pairs of sneakers and one pair of slightly worn grunt boots. I checked the size and nearly let out a whoop of joy when I saw they were my size. I put three more pairs of socks in my bag and set the boots at the end of the bed. They were mine now.

I repacked my bag and was dusting off the bed covers when I heard Ahn come back in. He had a bag full of packets.

'Anything good?'

'Nothing fancy but heaps of freeze-dried stuff. It'll keep us fed. Found some tinned stuff before I went out too.'

Ahn got to bustling around the kitchen, whipping up a good but basic meal. Apart from the off smell coming from the fridge and its incessant hum, it wasn't a bad meal. Well, they always said freedom tasted good. I guess this was my first real meal of freedom.

We washed up and I went and got my laundry into the dryer. I pulled the teddy bear out. A little more stuffing was coming out of his eye but he was soft again and I could see he was a pale grey colour and would have been beautiful originally. I gave him a hug and went into the bedroom. I hopped into the bed and it was heavenly compared to the cardboard feel of the mattresses in the Cube. It reminded me of my childhood. The vague memories of a warm and cosy house where I was safe. I snuggled into the blankets with the teddy bear clutched to my chest and fell asleep.

CHAPTER FIFTEEN
Darnell

The book fell from Darnell's hands in shock. Ava. If she had been taken at such a young age how could there be drawings of her older? Was this the twisted fantasy of a bereaved mother? Was it shoved down behind the shelves so Coo would forget he ever saw it?

He picked it up and flipped through it again. The pages were headed with dates. Three quarters of the way through, he found a picture of a girl. Her face was slim and sharp, her hair tied back away from her face. The next page was headed "May 6, Ava age 18".

He heard the panel in the roof slide open. Coo was coming. He jammed the book into his backpack and zipped it up as though he'd just been sorting through his things. He was sitting on the couch by the time Coo had climbed down the ladder and turned to face him. He was dressed in black from head to toe.

'So, you ready to go soon boy?' he asked as he came and gathered the map. 'Do you have enough supplies, you think?'

'So far I have barely touched them thanks to Amma and yourself. And if all goes well I'll be on my way with Oscar.'

'Well, like I said, kid, if it doesn't work out, you've got a home here and I'm pretty sure Amma would welcome you back on the farm.'

'I do want to go home eventually. Back to the cabin. Once it's safe.'

'If they're hunting you as a blank, they don't give up until they see a corpse. No matter what your mama said to them. It may never be safe.'

'But it's my home.'

'Home is where the heart is, my pa used to say. You make a home of where you settle.'

'My mother was my heart, Coo. I will go back. One day.'

'Well, until that happens we need to head off. The current is strong but I feel there's rain coming in and I'd rather not be on the water, calm as it usually is, with a boat full of water. If we head off now we should make it to Fisher Caves. We can camp there for the night. It's dry and there's usually a fire pit set up. We may need to forgo that fish dinner though if it gets too wild. I hope you have some spare socks in that bag, boy.'

'Yes indeed. Mum always packed extra socks, even if we were just going into the forest for firewood or to check the rabbit traps. Said they might come in handy one day.'

'Your mama was a smart woman. Now let's get that pack on your back and get you up this ladder.'

Coo dashed up the ladder. He was quite quick for such a big man. Darnell hoisted his bag on his shoulder and climbed up, just squeezing through the hatch opening with bag intact.

Coo closed the panel and made sure it was secure. A black pack sat next to the door, along with a fishing rod, a rifle, a bow and arrows. He passed the rod and rifle to Darnell.

'Ever used a gun?'

'Only to take pot shots at cans. I'm much better with a bow.'

'Really, now that's a skill you don't see in the young ones these days. All the City folk are either guns if they're a grunt or nothing if they're a civilian. No one learns these skills in the City.'

'Well, I'm no City kid. Bow was cheaper than ammo and I learnt to make my own arrows even though they weren't that good. I managed to shoot a few fish in my time and I once shot a deer.'

'Fine then, gimme back the gun and take the bow and arrows.'

'Will we need them?'

'For food kid. In case we get stranded in the storm or something else untoward.'

'Do you think they're following me?'

'I think so far we're safe. Only folks that know you're here and that I'm taking you anywhere are people I'd trust with my life. If we go through my back door, there's only a few cottages to pass and most people further back from the garden circle usually keep to themselves. Else, they'll be at Corey's getting drunk.'

They walked through the kitchen and past the pantry with its secret door. At the far end was a laundry, an old washer sat on the cold concrete, a pile of laundry sitting on top of it in a wicker basket.

'Excuse the mess. Laundry day is usually tomorrow,' Coo said with a chuckle as he pushed open the back door to his cottage. Down two rickety wooden steps they went, a well-worn dirt path spotted with pavers led around the side of the house to an old clothesline pitched off the wall, rust stains bleeding down the boards. The path forked and ran further away from the settlement's centre and down between a tunnel of trees.

Darnell saw the cottages dotted through the trees, the path splitting off to each door. Coo was right, no one came out to bother them, although Darnell was sure he felt eyes on him as they passed the last cottage before the river. The curtains had twitched and he felt his skin crawl. Hopefully it was just a cat.

The path led through the grass to the boathouse and jetty. Despite the well-worn path, the grass either side was wild and snagged on his trousers as they passed. The boat house had a collar of this grass and sprays of ivy climbed its walls. The boathouse once had been painted red like the old barns from his story books. But now it was the same colour as the rust down the side of Coo's house.

'I know she doesn't look like much but our boat house is solid. Just needs a lick of paint but the ivy is too much a pain to remove and no one wants to just paint over the ivy. Don't you worry, the boats are in good condition. I make sure they're looked after. We do a good trade up the river.'

Darnell just nodded. His boat had been small and was usually tied to the jetty in summer, and in winter he'd pull it in to near the house and cover it with a tarp until it was time to repaint it and repair it the following spring. Coo pushed open the doors and he saw there were two boats in a dry dock. Both had wheeled dollies to get them to the water. Coo motioned for him to get out of the way and began to push the bigger of the two towards the river. Once he was clear, he called back over his shoulder for Darnell to get the oars.

Coo set the boat on the edge of the river and pulled the dolly back into the boat house.

'Hop in boy. I'll push her out.'

Darnell hopped in and lay the oars on the floor of the boat. There were two sets of oarlocks but both were crudely carved out of the edge of the boat. Coo pushed the boat out into the water and climbed in, sitting before he could cause too much of a wobble.

They locked the oars in and began to row. The pace was decent, not too strenuous, although Darnell was sure Coo could out-row him any day. He may not be Authority anymore but he obviously still did enough labour to keep himself strong.

Darnell was facing backwards at the head of the boat. He watched Coo for a moment, making sure he was matching his rowing rhythm before looking around. The forest was dark on either side and rose up in black pillars to the sky. The sky was rolling with clouds and he could see the sharp bursts of lightning in the distance. He certainly didn't want to be on the water when that storm hit.

The low rumbles of thunder had also begun. It reminded him of nights sitting by the fire with his mother, drinking soup. He always felt safe in front of a fireplace even when the lightning lit up the sky and nothing could be heard over the booming growls of thunder that echoed through the valley. A dog would have been a nice addition to their house. He wondered why his mother had never gotten one for added security. He'd read all the stories of brave guard dogs, and Kutta had seemed like he'd be smart enough to ward off people he didn't like.

'Don't stress boy. We should beat the storm to the caves. We might get a tad damp on the way but we'll be undercover by the time the lightning comes.'

They'd been rowing for a few hours when the rain began. It was a steady drizzle that eventually got heavier. The sky was now being lit by sheets of white lightning, although they were still ahead of the worst of it.

'Pull your oars in, boy, and try and rope the jetty coming up on your left,' Coo called over the rain.

Now this was something Darnell was unsure he could do. He held the rope in his hand but it didn't matter, the speed of the current pushed them up against the pylon of the jetty so it wasn't too hard to tether the boat. Darnell tossed his pack onto the boards and scrambled out of the boat. Knowing that the water was shallow enough to be safe, Coo jumped out and into the river. It wasn't the smartest idea with the current as strong as it was. Darnell would have been halfway around the bend of the river if he'd tried it, but Coo was steady. He took the rope and pulled the boat onto the shore. He grabbed his pack and then flipped the boat over so it didn't fill with water. He tied it to the dock but he knew if the storm was going to take it, no amount of precautions would stop it.

'Follow me,' Coo bellowed through the rain. The drops had turned from spits to massive bullets of rain. It stung at Darnell's face as he tried to keep sight of Coo through the downpour. He saw a cliff rising up in the trees, a gaping maw of open blackness waiting to swallow them up.

Coo dashed in and Darnell followed. He wiped the water from out of his eyes and saw Coo pull a torch from his pocket.

'If we go in a bit there's a nice open area. It's where a lot of the fishermen stay if they want an early morning round in the water.'

'Will there be anyone there?'

'Nah, no sane man would go out fishing with that storm rolling in, and City Authority leaves the cave well alone. Too far out of the way for them to patrol.'

The noise of the rain subsided the deeper they went. The torch barely lit enough ground to light the way but soon they turned into a wide-open cavern. Coo dropped his bag and tossed the torch to Darnell.

'Get the lighter from the front pocket of my bag and let's get a fire going.' He pulled a second torch from his pocket and found the fire pit. It was dry and was already stacked with wood, charred on its underside but still good. Coo chuckled to himself.

'Nice folk have left us a fire all set up.'

Darnell handed him the lighter and Coo lit some of the kindling underneath. Soon a fire was blazing and the cave was lit with a flickering orange glow. There was a pile of blankets folded roughly and stacked against one wall of the cave and someone had even left a saucepan and fork next to it. Coo tossed a blanket to him.

'Sit on this. The cold floor is no good for your ass. And get those shoes and socks off before you get sick.'

Darnell did as instructed and let the warmth of the fire dry him off the rest of the way. Coo whipped up a quick meal and they ate, the thunder rumbling all around them now. Inside the cave, it was not deafening but it was still enough to put Darnell on edge.

He lay down, trying to get comfortable on the blanketed stone. Oh how he missed his bed. He had just found a good position when he heard a scrambling noise.

'Coo,' he whispered. 'Did you…'

'Shush boy. Slowly get your bow,' he said, raising the rifle towards the cave entrance.

A man stumbled into the cave. He looked a little drunk, swaying as he walked in but something didn't feel right.

'Who are you?' bellowed Coo at the dripping wet man. The man froze and looked around the cave.

'Hey, no harm no foul my friends,' he said. 'Just went for a walk and got stuck out in the rain. Just looking for somewhere to dry off. Mind if I sit by your fire and warm myself? I'm catching a chill.'

'You been drinking? No sober man would go out with the clouds the way they were.'

'Maybe a little,' the man said, approaching. Darnell scurried back behind Coo. The man was speaking too clearly to be drunk. Coo's grip on his rifle had not faltered. He was going to stick with Coo's instincts on the matter. He doubted he could actually shoot the man but it made him feel a little safer.

The stranger crouched down by the fire and held out his hands to warm them. Darnell almost felt sorry for him.

'Now son, I don't mean to sound paranoid here, but what is your name and what were you doing walking in the woods this far out from a town with that storm rolling in?'

'My name is Marcus. I'm from Cribbins Valley. We were having a few drinks when my dog bolted because of the thunder. She'd rip your face off if you tried anything but the first roll of thunder and she's under the bed normally. She took off and I took off after her. Wasn't thinking straight. She's probably back home under the bed now wondering where in sweet hell I've gone.'

'It's not safe out in the woods by yourself. You Cribbins boys should know that after the last raid the City made on your lot. Growing tobacco without a City licence, so stupid. They let you make your own booze yet you grow tobacco.'

'Us boys like to smoke and the taxes are just too much. Cribbaco as we called it not only tasted better, but cost us near nothing to grow and the return was great.'

'How many of you lot got sent to the hole for that one?'

'Three from memory. I was lucky I just smoked it and wasn't growing or selling it. I'll stick to good old sheep thank you very much. Less effort and as long as we're under twenty head, the City doesn't care. Now are you going to stop pointing that gun at me and tell me your names?'

Coo lowered the rifle but still held it ready to fire. Darnell did the same.

'They call me Coo, and this is my son, Samuel.'

'Mayor! I didn't know you had a son.'

'Adopted. His folks died out in the mill explosion last year. I needed an assistant and, well, I always wanted a son. Nothing City official but my son none the less.'

'Well, come sit with me. I don't bite. Although when I see my dog I may give her a whoopin. Stupid mutt. Can barely herd the sheep. Not sure why I keep her. Now do either of you gentlemen have a cigarette or even a cup of tea I could snag? I feel frozen to the bone.'

Coo busied himself making a cup of tea.

'You're a quiet one there, Samuel. Cat got your tongue?'

'Just tired Sir. I've had a long day and we still have a long journey ahead of us once the rain clears.'

'So where are you and Daddy Coo off to?'

Darnell wasn't sure if he should answer but he didn't have to, as Coo brought the tea over and answered for him.

'We're off to see if we can find his uncle. Used to live in Ellintown, had a bit of money you see. See if he wants to help contribute to the boy's education at a City school.'

'Up the river was a smart idea. Nice and quick and twice as pretty.'

'That's the plan,' Coo said. He sat down on his blanket and lay the rifle across his legs. He wouldn't get much sleep tonight. Darnell, on the other hand, although still holding the bow and quiver in his lap, was starting to nod off regardless of how hard he fought against it. He had to wake up. He got to his feet and began to walk towards the cave entrance.

'Where you off to boy? It's still bucketing out there,' Marcus said. A rumble of thunder echoed though the cave as if to make his point.

'Just going to have a look and make sure the boat is okay.'

'It was fine when I came in. The wind isn't too bad so unless it gets hit by lightning it should be safe and sound. Don't worry yourself about it.'

'I'm just going to look anyway. Need to move. The ground is hurting my back.'

'I really think you should just come back to the fire. You don't want to get sick.'

'Why don't you want me to go outside?'

'What? I didn't say that,' he laughed. 'I just don't want to see you get sick.'

'I won't go out in the rain. I just want to go up the tunnel to the entrance. Really, it's fine.'

Marcus sighed. 'I really didn't want to do this. Please come back down here now boy. It's not safe out there. I may have lied. City is after me. That's why I was running. I may have been running some friendly bets that involved a City official or seven who unfortunately lost quite a sum of money.'

'You'll get ten for that at least,' Coo said.

'I may have also threatened one of them... well three of them. But they owed me money.'

'So City Authority is just waiting outside for you then? I'll tell them you're not in here.'

'I said don't go out there.'

'What else aren't you telling us?' Coo asked. His grip tightened on the rifle.

'All I'm saying is you need to stay in here. Otherwise untoward things may happen.'

'Yeah, to you,' Darnell said.

'No son, to your friend here,' the newcomer said, pulling a gun from his pocket and pointing it at Coo. 'Let go of the rifle my friend. And boy, drop the bow. Either of you move and

I'll shoot you both. Something tells me that Coo, you're the one I have to watch more so than your... son. Ha ha ha! That's a joke. Darnell Anderson. Father works for the City, nothing important, but easy enough to keep tabs on. Mother is deceased. Had an accident out at that little shack you were living in. What a shame. Now I've been told not to kill either of you, however don't put it past me. My hands are a little damp; my trigger finger may just slip.

'My friends will be here soon and you, Darnell, will be transported to the Sphere for the crime of treason against the City Ordinance. You, Mayor Coo, well I don't really care where they're taking you. His head is my pay check. Not yours. But if you don't come back to your little town, I guess people will start talking.'

'Just let him go,' Darnell said quietly.

'What was that boy?'

'Just let him go. Coo's done nothing wrong. I'll go with you peacefully, just let Coo go.'

'You aren't even human. You're a blank, why should I listen to you?'

'Because it's the right thing to do. He won't cause trouble, will you, Coo?' Darnell said, a look of pleading on his face.

Marcus stood up. Although the gun was still pointed at Coo, his attention was now solely on Darnell.

'Look you little maggot. I don't give a shit what you think about this old man. But he's going nowhere. And you are going into the Sphere for the rest of your natural life, whatever that is for freaks like you. Personally, I think they should put all you blanks outside the fence into the Badlands and let the mutants and whatever else roams out there take care of you. You might be lucky; the radiation might kill you first.'

Darnell saw movement from behind Marcus and tried not to focus on it. He hoped Coo realised what he was trying to do. Marcus twitched when Darnell's eyes moved but didn't turn around, next thing a shotgun blast ripped through the air. Marcus' handgun went off but the shot went wide, only grazing Coo in the shoulder. Marcus fell to the ground. Coo had got him in the face. Half his jaw was missing. The body twitched on the ground, a pool of blood spreading from where his face used to be.

'Grab your things, we need to run,' Coo ordered. A wet bloom was appearing on his shoulder.

'Are you okay?'

'It doesn't matter, just get your things. Carry your boots; we need to get out of here now.'

Darnell grabbed his boots by the laces, threw his pack over his shoulder and grabbed the bow and quiver. He reached for Coo's bag.

'No, just get out there. Stay quiet. See if this fool left a boat moored.'

He ran. The entrance to the cave was white with a curtain of heavy rain. The thunder boomed and lighting tore across the sky, momentarily blinding him. He ran past their boat, which was still where they had left it, but Darnell could see it had been smashed in the bottom. It would be useless to them. He ran over to it and grabbed an oar. In this rain the bow would be too hard to use but he had some strength from chopping wood so he could always swing the oar as a weapon. He started running towards the river and slipped, falling down and sliding down the bank towards the jetty. The river's wild water lapped at the very lip of the wood. It would soon swallow the jetty whole. He saw a rope tied around one of the pylons though and saw a small jet boat thrashing in the waves.

'Coo!' he called into the rain. He could barely hear his own voice. There was no way Coo would hear him. He went to scramble up the muddy hillside, slipping and sliding but still making some headway. It was like a muddy waterfall. He saw a figure approaching. He called out again, but a flash of lightning illuminated the figure's face. It was not Coo.

Darnell let himself slide back down the hill, but the figure was sliding after him. He ran for the jet boat. He had to wait for Coo. He couldn't leave him after he'd done so much for him. He heard the shot gun blast before he saw what had happened. The figure toppled face first down the embankment and into the raging water. He was taken by the current and Darnell saw his head go under but not come back up.

'Get in the boat!' he heard Coo shout as he ran past to untie the boats moorings. Another figure rose from behind the further pylon.

'Coo! Behind you!' Darnell screamed, running towards the shadow. He swung and connected with the head of the figure clad in black. He didn't hear the crunch as oar met with skull, but he certainly felt it as the blow reverberated up his arm. He felt a hand grab his arm and nearly swung again before he realised it was Coo.

'Get in the boat!'

Darnell did as he was told and jumped in, taking his oar with him. Coo jumped in behind him then let go of the mooring rope. The current took them in the right direction but Coo still managed to get the motor started. Their speed doubled. Darnell had no idea how Coo could see anything in front of him but it seemed not to matter as they flew across the waves. The lightning was the only light source now in the blackness and even with its frequency, Darnell was waiting for them to hit something.

He watched behind them for lights. Surely if City Authority was coming after him they would have search lights. Then again with the amount of lies Marcus had told them, he had no idea how sneaky they would be. Would they have night vision goggles? Heat sensors?

The boat felt like it was barely touching the water. It skimmed across the current, bouncing at times. Darnell held on for dear life. He felt the boat list to one side. Once, then again. It wasn't the right movement compared to what they had felt previously. He wondered if they had sprung a leak and water was getting in. He tried to see if there was any damage when he noticed a hand on the edge of the boat, then a second. Someone was trying to crawl in. Darnell didn't hesitate to grab the oar and bash it against the fingers gripping the side. The boat tipped badly as the person finally let go. Then it righted itself. It must have been the man Coo shot.

'Coo! That man!'

'That man was going to kill you. Let the fish have him.'

They bounced down the water for goodness knows how long but the lightning was less frequent now, as was the thunder. The rain still pelted down, stinging their skin. The water though had become a little rockier.

'Hold on!' Coo yelled as they went over yet another massive bump in the water. This time though it sounded more solid than usual. The boat began to tip and this time there was no stopping it. They had hit a curve in the river and without light to guide them Coo had turned too soon. Darnell felt himself go under the water as the boat capsized. It was just as cold in as it was being soaked by the rain. He couldn't see what was happening and felt the oar slip from his grip. He began to push himself up as fast as he could, he couldn't hold his breath much longer.

His head broke above the water and he choked in a few gulps of air, which were also partially mouthfuls of water. He tried to swim with the current and finally his foot felt land beneath it. Using the last of his strength, he pulled himself onto the bank and collapsed in a heap. He looked to see if Coo was nearby but in the dark, he couldn't see anything.

'Coo!' he called, but no one answered.

CHAPTER SIXTEEN
Zale

As Frank arrived back in the room with water and some painkillers, Zale made to leave. At the doorway he stopped and turned back to look at Penny.

'Will everyone be okay? I need to get back to the tunnel and see how they're going about getting us out.'

'I know you just want to see the baby,' Mrs Peters said, trying to smile. 'A new life when so many have been lost may be the best thing for this shelter. And Condor Point for that matter. Off you go. And… thank you. Thank you for taking care of me.'

'Any time, Mrs Peters. Now please get some rest,' Zale said before dashing out the door.

He really did want to see if there had been any headway in the tunnel. The announcement of a baby only exacerbated it. Not just to get the baby out but to try to keep the mother alive. If she'd lost blood, it could be that one thing that could send her into shock or kill her. He raced into the room to hear the cry of a baby. At least it sounded healthy, he thought, rushing into the crowd. Sam was barely conscious but he saw movement and there didn't seem to be any medical issues from the birth. Mrs Wade was shooing people away.

'Give the woman some space, for goodness sake. She just had a baby. She doesn't need you all gawking at her. Go do something useful.'

People began to spread out and wander back to the tasks

at hand. A few people sat by her bed still. Zale considered going up to say hello, but Mrs Wade gave him a stern glare so he turned back on course for the tunnel. There was a crowd around the door that, when they realised who was coming, turned and mobbed him.

'We hear a noise. Are they coming? Is someone coming for us?'

'Should we be digging from our side?'

'What happened out there?'

'Is that someone we know or those people again?'

The questions all came at once. Zale didn't know where to look. All this because they heard a noise. He felt fear go around the room. They thought they were under attack again.

'Shh. Everyone. One at a time. Today has been a little bit on the stressful side for me. Yes, someone is coming. They are trying to get through. The tunnel collapsed so I think we should stay out of it. Let them work safely from their side. If it collapses, it would collapse onto us. It's some people from the med centre. As far as we know, the others have left. And before one of you asks, no I don't know who they were.'

The group just stared at him for a moment, when one of the smallest of the group stepped forward.

'Is Mrs Peters okay? I mean, the screaming, and the fit?'

'She's recovering from that. I don't know about fine though, but she's lucid and being looked after.'

'That's good. Billy was my friend. The only friend I had here and because I had no family, Mrs Peters always looked after me. And now that Billy is gone...' She started to cry. Zale pulled her in for a hug.

'I know. It's going to be hard for a lot of people. But we will get through this.'

A lady in the group came and took the girl's hand.

'Come on, let's go sit down. Doesn't look like there's anything for us to do here apart from get in the way.' They walked off towards the kitchen area.

'Poor kid,' Zale mumbled. She wasn't all that much younger than he was but the look on her face was so innocent and scared. It had been that of a child, not a young woman. He looked at the others. 'Just stay here. I'm going to see how they're going.'

'Wait, why can't we come with you?'

'Because it's better if only one of us is disturbing the rubble in case there's a further cave-in. I don't want anyone else getting hurt.'

Zale walked up the tunnel towards the wall of rocks. It wasn't as dark as it had been but he still took every step gingerly and as gently as possible. There was a tiny beam of light shining through.

'Hey Greyson? You still there?'

'Zale? Yeah how is everything. We heard some screaming.'

'It's not pretty down here. We've got a fair few wounded and a newborn.'

'Was it Sam?' said Dr Schonell, through the hole.

'Yeah. She's not in good shape from the explosion but bub is pretty good by the looks of it. Who else is pregnant?'

'It doesn't matter. Sam was the only one close to full term. That's what I'd hoped.'

'Many casualties?' Greyson asked.

'Too many. My partner Allen is running a makeshift morgue but I'd much rather get those bodies somewhere refrigerated instead of laying uncovered in a munitions storeroom. And I fear with what I've seen of the injured we may lose at least one or two more before you guys break through.'

'Just get out of the tunnel and let us dig. Last we need is you getting knocked out by falling rubble.'

'Okay, find me when you get through. Think you'll do it by sundown?'

'Maybe. So far so good but now we're on the part that could be load-bearing. Get out of the way and let us work.'

Zale chuckled. 'Sure thing boss,' he called as he turned and left the tunnel. Two of the men were left at the entrance to the tunnel leaning on the blast door.

'Well?' one asked.

'Well, they're getting there. Few more hours. Can you guys make sure no one goes in there though? It's getting pretty touch-and-go with the roof right now. When they come through, I'll be down in the… morgue. Just head down the back tunnel and then down the stairs. You'll find us.'

'Will do. We'll keep the kids clear.'

'It's not the kids I'm worried about,' Zale said as he walked off. He went past the kitchen and grabbed some sandwiches that the nanna patrol had been working on and a bottle of water. He headed back down the tunnel looking in on Mrs Peters and Tony. Tony was leaning against the wall in a half doze and Mrs Peters had curled up on the cot bed and gone to sleep. Frank and Dina had disappeared. He hoped it was up back with whatever family and friends they had there. No one should be alone.

He rounded the last corner before the morgue door and found Trella sitting on the floor, halfway to the door of the morgue.

'Heya, what you still doing down here? Nanna patrol is making food and I'm sure your other half wouldn't say no to a sandwich.'

'I didn't want to leave Allen alone. I think it's getting to him, Zale. He's crying in there. I just can't go in. The smell is getting to me.'

'Go. Go be with your partner. I'll look after mine.'

'Thanks Zale. I think it's getting to me, too.' She pushed herself up of the floor and with a half-smile walked away. Zale approached the door to the morgue. He felt a chill that was more than just the air temperature.

'Allen? Honey? Come out and have a bite to eat.' There was no response. He put the plate and the water down, not daring to bring it inside with the bodies. It was bad enough anyone had to be near them.

'Allen, come on. You need to get out of there.' This time he heard a muffled reply and Allen came out. He'd been crying, his eyes rimmed with red. His hands were flecked with dried blood and so were his clothes. Zale didn't know which was worse. But he need to hold him. Zale pulled Allen into his arms and kissed him on the forehead. 'Honey, it's okay. We need to get you washed up though and you need a rest.'

'It's not okay. There are three kids in there Zale. Three kids under ten. That's not okay. There are people our age in there. That's not old enough to die. How could those people do this?' he sobbed into Zale's chest.

'I don't know, but when we get out of here I'm going after them.'

Allen lifted his head and looked into Zale's eyes. 'I'm coming with you.'

Zale knew this wasn't a request. When Allen set his mind to something, he was not an easy man to persuade otherwise.

'First, we need to get you cleaned up and away from this place, even if it's just to one of the offices down the hall. Is there a sink around here? Just to wash your hands.'

Allen nodded and pulled away from Zale's embrace. 'I'll be right back.' Allen went back as though to go into the morgue again but went further down the hall and into the next door. He came back a few moments later, with clean hands and a damp face. The cool water to his face had done nothing for the redness in his eyes but he looked a little less like he was going to crack at any minute.

They moved to an office down the hall with the food and water and ate in silence on the couch.

**

They were pulled from their absent minds by the sound of Zale's name being bellowed down the hallway.

'Zale! They got through! Zale, come on!'

Zale shook Allen awake – he could sleep through an earthquake.

'Come on, Allen. We can get out.'

'We can go get her.'

'Let's help get the wounded to the hospital first.'

They ran up the hall and met with the man yelling for them. They all ran together back to the bunker. There was a swarm of people milling around the injured and another trying to fight their way out. Greyson was trying to control them with no luck. Zale was about to step up when he heard a thundering voice above the crowd.

'Oi! If you folks are gonna act like disobedient sheep then we will have to treat you like disobedient sheep and I know a thing or two about sheep.' It was Frank. 'Now if you are not injured I want you to go towards the kitchen and make a nice tidy line.' Some people began to shuffle backwards. This was not fast enough for Frank. 'Come on sheeple. My nanny could walk twice as fast with her stick when she was ninety-five years of age and she'd wet her pants. Get moving!'

This got the people going and soon an orderly line was being formed. Zale and Allen kept to that side but milled by the line instead. They wanted to help.

'Okay. Now injured folk who can still walk themselves please form ANOTHER line down the centre of the room. If it hurts to stand stay where you are.' This time people moved. Frank seemed pleased.

'See, ya lazy folks. That's how it's done and half a them are a-bleeding everywhere. Now first up we need to get the bad ones out. We need strong people on stretcher duty from the kitchen side line. And no dawdling or dilly-dallying. Remember you are people not sheep. Act like it.'

Zale supressed a laugh at this. Frank must have been one hell of a farmer back on the CropServ sheep farms.

Within minutes, using the triage system Allen had put in place, the worst of the patients were on their way. Then those needing minor medical assistance went. Greyson was in charge of these and rustled up every person he could find that was first aid trained to help. Frank had turned Zale and Allen away. It seemed he had a plan for them.

'Next, nanna squad, I want you to take all the kidlets out

of here. I say take them to the school hall for now until we can locate parents and other folk. Now the rest of you can go. Please go to the town hall. Anyone you see on the way that belongs at Condor Point, send them there too. Hopefully the Colonel will show up soon or our leaders who all seem to have taken a little holiday.'

'Frank. What are you saving us for?' Zale called as he walked towards the burly man. His shirt was untucked now and Zale saw blood on his shirt sleeves. Frank had done quite a lot that day that not many people would probably ever remember past his sheeple-herding skills.

'Nothing pretty unfortunately. I need a list of the dead to pass on. I've got Greyson, Mrs Wade and Dr Schonell all taking roll call and where people are so we can try and make sure everyone's accounted for.'

'I have a list,' Allen said pulling a crumpled and overfolded piece of paper from his pocket. 'This is all of them that are in the morgue. I thought it would be needed. They'll need to be moved soon but they can last another day. It's cool enough but it won't smell any better then.'

'We will find folks to do that, don't you worry. I don't want you going back down there if I can help it. You seen too much death today, sonny-Jim. I'm going to do a sweep and make sure all folk are out then head to the town hall. You go on. I'll catch you up.'

'We'll help. It'll go faster that way.' Zale said, casting a knowing glance at Allen. 'We'll do storage if you can go down and do the offices and the morgue.'

'Sounds like a plan. Don't take too long in case that tunnel collapses again.'

Frank went towards the offices hall and the boys went to the first storeroom.

'Supplies?' Allen asked. Zale nodded.

'There are full soldier kits in the back here. Packs and all. I was rummaging in one before. They're behind a pallet of canned fruit so I don't think anyone even saw them.'

'Why were you behind the canned fruit?'

'I was on top of the pallet looking for chocolate. For the children.'

'For the children hey?'

'And maybe for me and Trella. Although she was looking for whiskey.'

'When did this happen?'

'Before you came back. I needed a break and was trying to be helpful.'

They clambered up onto the pallet of tinned fruit and jumped down behind them. Allen was right. The kits were fully stocked with rations, ammo, two hand guns, flashlight and a multitude of tools. In a crate nearby they found holsters for hand guns and pouches for ammo clips. They jammed as much as they could into two of the packs and hauled them onto their backs. They were heavy and Zale's wrist still throbbed when he moved it but they would be set for what they had to do.

'We need to hide these and go to town hall. We have to be there for the official roll call.' They came back out of the store and Allen pulled at Zale's back pack.

'Give them to me, I'll hide them outside while you check the rest of the storerooms. We don't want anyone getting stuck in here and we did promise Frank.'

'True,' Zale replied giving up his pack. 'Go. Be careful.' Allen took off at a run and Zale quickly checked the remaining storerooms, not finding anyone. He returned to see Frank walking in with Tony and Mrs Peters.

'Lucky we checked. These two were out like a light in that office we left them in. Where's Allen?'

'I sent him outside to make sure there are no stragglers around the shelter. In case someone was coming to look for friends or family.' At this Allen came bounding back down the tunnel.

'Come on. Let's get to town hall. We'll see where the Colonel is or at least the Condor Point Council is.'

It was dark out, the sun having set as the people evacuated from the shelter. Porch lights had begun to be turned on as people started to come out of their hiding spots. Frank spread the message as they walked through the middle of the town.

'Town Hall, folks. Everyone to town hall. Come on folks, safety in numbers. Let's get moving!' The chant continued the whole way. By the time they got to the town hall it was mostly filled with people milling around. A few people had pulled down seats for those needing to sit, and Zale saw some of the injured from the shelter along with other injured folks.

They looked up at the stage but so far none of the town council was there. People were getting restless. There were a few kids holding desperately to the hands of adults and clutching legs for dear life. People were wide-eyed and were either shocked into silence, sobbing or beginning to talk. Rumours were already flying about as to what had happened. Frank once again took charge, clambering onto the stage, his voice filling the room and making people pay attention.

'People! Listen up!' he began. People turned and looked, especially those he had called sheeple in the bunker.

'Quick rundown: We still have no idea who those people were or why they came here. There was an accident at the bunker. We have moved a group of folks to the hospital and those needing minor medical treatment elsewhere. I believe both lots have sent a roll call of names over. The children that were in the shelter have been moved to the school along with some of our older folk who have offered to look after them. If you wish for your children to join them, please feel free to take them to the school hall now. We may need to discuss some unpleasant things tonight.'

With this, a group of parents shuffled out of the building leaving only two children who were babies being cradled in their carers' arms.

'Now has anyone seen any of the council members? I'm looking for Adeline, Conrad, Geoff and Gracie. Anyone?'

'They weren't in the bunker,' a voice in the crowd called.

'Has anyone checked their houses?' a woman near the back called.

'Good question. Has anyone been near their houses?'

No response.

'Well, I'm going to need four folk who can run really fast. Do I have any volunteers?'

A few hands shot up and Frank sent them on their way to check on the councillors' houses. Frank sat down on the edge of the stage and people went back to talking. Zale was about to head over to Frank when one of the runners came back. His skin was white as a sheet. He was breathing hard and his eyes were wide.

'You... you gotta come. Come quick. I found them. Oh god I found them,' the boy stammered, gasping for breath. He took off again this time with a crowd following behind him.

Gracie's house was down near the entrance gates to Condor Point. She always liked to see the comings and goings of the community and was always the first out to welcome new people to the area.

Zale and Allen, who had been at the back of the room, saw it first. A spotlight was shining right on the gate, which stood open. Its crossbeam had new additions. Four bodies hung by the neck from the bar below the sign that welcomed people in. Someone screamed behind them. It was horrific. They had not died strung up. Their bodies were covered in knife slashes, their clothes hanging off their now half-naked and blood-stained bodies. Each had a bullet hole in their heads. They had been strung up after they were dead. This was a warning. As they stood there a piece of paper fluttered to the ground from Gracie's blood-soaked hand. Zale stepped forward to retrieve it.

'No!' Frank called as he got to the front of the crowd. 'It might be a trap.'

'Frank, it's a bit of paper,' Zale said, stepping forward again. Frank grabbed him by the shoulder.

'I said no. I know this style. It's a trap. There will be land mines. I'll show you.' He grabbed a bucket from beside Gracie's house and tipped the water from it. 'Everyone move back!' he called. There was a unanimous shuffle despite the crying coming from the crowd. He tossed the bucket in a wide arc. It hit Geoff's leg and fell to the ground below him. It was a few seconds later they heard the beep before the ground exploded in front of them, sending dirt and bits of flesh flying. A hand landed at Zale's feet. He jumped back. He would swear it moved. Once the dust had settled only the torsos of Geoff and Gracie remained. Conrad's body swung gently from the blast. Adeline's was mostly still. It was horrific. Zale kicked the hand away before he thought he'd throw up.

'How the hell did you know that, Frank?'

'We're a close community. First thing we're gonna do if we see someone hanging is cut them down. I'm right and you know it. And they knew it too.'

Frank took a step back and turned to the crowd

'We are a tight community who goes against City Ordinance of being marked. We are going against the one rule that our ancestors fought to retain for us. For those of genetic purity to create new life with their genetically marked partner. Some here have removed their marks as their rite of passage. As you can see I am one of them,' he said pulling his shirt down to show the knot of twisted scar tissue on his shoulder.

'Now I know they sound like mighty big words from a humble old farmer, but it's true. The Colonel is one of the few reasons they leave us alone despite flaunting our disregard for the law of the marked. We flaunt it by the scars we wear. Most of us anyway. And then we harbour those who are not marked. Some are our children. Some have come to hide out in a community where we value love and freedom despite the City Ordinance. We are near the Badlands so we are as far from the City as can be possible. That is why we are tolerated. But tonight that toleration seems to have come to an end.'

'Frank,' Zale yelled. 'How do you know all this? Who are they?'

'They're Sphere and I know because I used to be one of them.'

CHAPTER SEVENTEEN
Almara

I awoke to Ahn shaking me. At first, I had no idea where I was. It was dark, and the location was unfamiliar. I could see Ahn's face only because it was so close to mine. I jolted up to a sitting position, nearly headbutting Ahn as I did.

'Almara, we need to get going soon. It's nearly night time and I heard a noise.'

That certainly woke me up all the way. I pushed off the blankets I had cocooned myself in. I would certainly miss them. If I ever were truly free, I would make my first purchase a bed and blankets. I could dream anyway. I pulled on a fresh set of socks and the boots from the girl's cupboard. I wiggled my toes. They were a little loose but not enough to notice with the thick socks.

I scooped up my bag and jacket then stopped. I turned to see the little grey teddy bear sitting on the bed near the pillow. I must have kept a good grip on him all night. I saw that Ahn had already headed out to the kitchen so I grabbed the bear and pushed him into my backpack, down below the clothes. He was a waste of bag space. My brain told me this but I didn't care. He was a reminder now, a symbol of comfort and what I now had a chance of getting.

'I'll even get you a new eye one day, teddy,' I whispered as I zipped up the pack. I went to the bathroom to get my clothes that I'd dried but found them folded on the machine, the ID badge resting on top, melted on one corner from the heat of the dryer. I scooped them up and went into the lounge. I put my pack on the floor next to Ahn's overflowing one.

Despite the dust, I could happily live here, I thought to myself, looking around. I flopped onto the couch. Ahn passed me a bowl of something gloopy-looking but it smelled good and sweet and I was certainly hungry.

'It's porridge. I found some vacuum packs of it and a bottle of honey. Honey never goes bad, did you know that?' he said, sitting next to me on the arm of the couch. 'It's a bit hot but it'll fill you up.'

We ate as quickly as we could. The porridge was exactly as I remembered from when I was a child. When we finished, Ahn washed the bowls and put them away. He saw me watching him. I must have had a ghost of a smile on my face.

'What? They might come back someday, and we've already raided their pantry and stolen clothes. The least I can do is wash up.'

'I see you found something more comfortable to wear,' I said, looking at his faded black t-shirt and pants. I noticed he had on black boots much like my own.

'Was the dad ex-military?'

'Security for the crops I think. Found an ID but no gun or holster so nothing official. More likely just a supervisor role with boots to make him feel like big man on campus. They're a bit big but I have three pairs of socks on so I'm good. They're still more comfortable than the Cube-issued shoes.'

'I still have no idea how you could even walk in them. My feet are chewed up.'

'You going to be able to walk on them tonight? I think if we can make it to the shuttles we should be able to get as far as two days travel down in three hours,' Ahn said as he got up. He went to the window and flicked the curtain aside.

'Won't they be looking for us? Would a shuttle be safe?'

'The 1 AM from West forty-seventh is full of workers. We can blend in to the crowd. Once we get on the shuttle we just hunker down til we hit Northern Groves. It's not end of the line but it's a big enough station that we can mill with the crowds and get out. From there I think we might be able to hitch a ride if we can get out to the farmers roads behind the orchards.

'From there if we stick to the back roads, we should be okay, apart from patrols. We'll have to rough it in the forest for a few nights but that will be safest.'

I nodded and gathered my things. I pulled on the jacket and shouldered my bag. It wasn't much heavier but it would still kill my shoulders. Then I heard a noise. Ahn jumped and let the curtain fall, holding a finger to his lips. We heard footsteps. I dropped to the floor and Ahn followed. I hoped they hadn't seen the movement of the curtain. They walked past the door and continued up the pathway between the housing blocks. I breathed a sigh of relief.

'That felt way too close, Ahn,' I whispered.

'Let's stay still for a few more minutes. If the coast is clear again I say we dash.'

My heart was thundering in my chest. The sheer volume of adrenaline in my veins made me feel like I could run like the wind right now but I doubted my blistered feet and heavy pack would let that be even close to true.

The time ticked by. Ahn checked out the window again and this time slowly opened the door to stick his head out. I waited. He motioned for me to stand and next thing I knew we were running. The ground was damp. It must have rained that afternoon. I saw the storm clouds on the horizon, it had already passed us but certainly didn't look all that welcoming as the blackness rolled and churned in the sky past the mountains.

We dashed through the rows of housing until we got to a green warehouse building. Ahn dropped down between two industrial bins. I dashed in after him.

'Now comes the tricky part,' he said. 'We need to get to the fence but it's open and although its dark I don't know how many security grunts will be patrolling the area. We could run together or split, but I think one dash is safer than two. I need you to stand up in a minute and see if you can see the part of the fence near the flag poles.'

I popped my head up over the bin and saw three white poles standing near the fence. I quickly got back down and nodded.

'That's where we will jump over. There's nothing of value up there so there shouldn't be any guards.'

'What if the Cube has Authority onto us and they're patrolling the fence?'

'That's a risk we have to take. We need to get to West forty-seventh station. We should make it but we need to start now to give us allowance for any mishaps.'

'Mishaps. What do you mean mishaps?'

'If they've sent Sphere after us, we may get separated. If we do, follow the plan and remember, keep going north. You're aiming for Condor Point. Once you get out of the City proper and the CropServ farms, the little farms are full of decent folk who will help you out.'

'But we won't get separated. We'll stick together.'

'If we can. If it's safer for you to go on alone that's what we will do. I didn't break you out for you to be taken by Sphere.'

Ahn peered out from our hiding spot and got ready to dash.

'Stop at the end of the building,' he whispered.

I nodded. From there we could see where the flood lights over the fields reached. I feared it would be too far and once we got a look, my worst fears were correct. The flagpoles were outside of the majority of the light but our run would take us right through the edge of a flood. There were at least thirty workers on the side of the field that we could see. I didn't even know how far it stretched. How much security would be patrolling the edges and making sure no one was trying to get in?

'They won't be looking for people getting out, only people

getting in. If we sprint, they shouldn't notice. Throw yourself over that fence best you can and get to the ground. They won't see you past the grass and from there we can find a darker spot along the fence line to disassemble the outer perimeter fence. Okay?'

I didn't like it, but what choice did I have? Ahn had only been looking out for my interests since we got out of the Cube so I had to trust his instincts on this one.

'On the count of three… one… two… three.'

With that we were off. I almost wanted to close my eyes as we belted our way across the dirt and on to the damp grass but thought that ruining my speed by hitting a flagpole face-first was not ideal in our situation. It seemed the fresh air and un-drugged food was helping my mind stay alert so when I reached the flag poles, I ran effortlessly between them, dived over the fence and landed with a bellyflop on to the ground. I heard Ahn land a little more gracefully behind me. I'd winded myself. When Ahn crawled up beside me, I was still trying to get my breath back.

'You okay?' he asked, noticing my head still facedown in the wet grass. I groaned in answer. 'I meant for you to jump the fence, not dive over it sideways. Anything broken?'

'Just what little pride I'd gathered back since escaping,' I mumbled. I groaned again and lifted myself up into a crawling position. We began to crawl along the fence until we came to a spot that the light didn't reach all that well. We jumped up, and quickly lifted the fence panel out, jumped outside it and replaced it. Ahn started to run and so did I. It was then we heard someone yell. We weren't going to stay to see if it was over us.

There was a road ahead and Ahn ran towards it but stayed on the verge so if anything was coming we could dive behind the trees. He slowed to a walking pace and of that, I was glad. My feet, despite the thick socks, were sore from the blisters that had now burst on my ankles. They weren't going to feel much better over the next few hours either, but if Ahn's plan worked they would cut the travel time through the mountain passes to nothing.

I had heard that there were checkpoints on the road where they would ask for a City ID. My mother used to tell me about them as you travelled in and out of the main City areas. The capital was definitely somewhere I was wanting to avoid. It was close to my childhood home and as much as I wanted to see my family, I knew it would not be safe for any of them. I didn't even know if they were all alive. My head filled with thoughts of my mother in prison for going around the laws and keeping me at home and in school as a blank. How the absence of a tiny mark had made such a huge scar across my life... our lives. Would my sister be allowed to be betrothed now that I was running? Would they even be told I had escaped? Did they even know I was alive?

I stumbled over something as that thought crossed my mind and fell, again. The fact that I hadn't broken anything yet surprised me. I scrambled back on my feet and jogged to where Ahn had stopped.

'You okay? You seem to have two left feet.'

'Ahn, does my family know I'm alive?'

'What do you mean?' he said, starting to walk again.

'Ahn look at me. Does my family know that I am alive or would they have been told I was dead?'

'They wouldn't have been told anything.'

'What the hell does that mean? They think I just disappeared? That I was taken? That I ran away?'

'Officially, when it's an older child removed to the Cube, the parents are made to believe the child ran away. You were old enough then that that's probably the way it went down.'

'My mother wouldn't have believed it. She worked for the City. She would have found out. I found out about the other blanks. Surely...'

'She wouldn't have had clearance. She was probably demoted anyway to save face. Was she an official?'

'Yes. She worked for the undersecretary. She was one of his advisors.'

'She's probably a secretary or document filer now.'

'They wouldn't have hurt my family?'

'No, not if they're marked. Your mother may have had some unpleasant times but…'

'But what? What Ahn? You have to tell me. Would they have hurt my mother?'

'If she dug too deep I wouldn't put it past them to silence her in some way. They have the means and the money in the City. They aren't your family anymore. You need to let them go. If you mix them up in this, they will not have a future in the City. Or in the region at all.'

'In the region? What does that even mean? There's nothing left but the region. Would they have taken her to Black Sphere or are we talking some form of archaic banishment rubbish? Surely that's not a thing?'

'There are rumours of people being put out in the Badlands for indiscretions. I've never been told of a specific case but certainly, the rumours do fly. I mean that's what they used to do to blank children before the Cube was created.'

'They put babies into the Badlands because they were blank?'

'You must not have got to that part at school before they took you. I know it's not mentioned in the Cube. No point in making blanks want out even more. But they used to allow a blank to reach age fifteen. At that age, they were given a week's worth of supplies, a knife and a tent, and pushed out into the Badlands. Most died still clinging to the fence trying to get back in. We were told in school that the bones were there for about twenty years after the practice stopped and then they were just gone one day.'

'The beasts never get that close though, do they? I mean, wouldn't we have heard about sightings?'

'There are urban legends about them trying to scale the fences but my mother told me they were just stories to keep kids from trying to get to the fence, or worse, try and scale it for a dare. Look, some kids set off and who knows what happened to them. Most likely they died of radiation poisoning or dehydration, but hey, for all I know, there's a blanks region out there somewhere that picked up the strays or maybe the beasts really are human under the mutations and took them in as their own kin.'

'I don't know what's more barbaric – that, or blue and red status for blanks? The radiation, what does it do? Hasn't it been years?'

'The radiation used in the bombs of the Badlands was not normal nuke radiation. It also contained the mutagen that created by the blanks in the war. It not only made the mutation beasts but it made people get sick with incurable cancers, or sometimes their organs would just shut down. Even now, there's an exclusion zone inside the fence just in case. People who used to live off the edge of Oasis, just inside the fence, were still getting sick fifty years ago. There's a low brick wall that goes around inside the fence now and if you cross it they won't ever let you back in.'

'But the City technology? Can it not fix the Badlands?'

'It won't be safe for another thousand years they say, give or take. I know I wouldn't risk it.'

'Yet they'd send my mother out there for caring about me?'

'Your mother is a smart woman, yes?'

'Yes. Her IQ was 160, so extremely so. I remember being so proud to tell people that. But I imagine that, and the last few years would have made her quite stubborn. That's where my concern is.'

'Look, if she's smart, she'll lie and pretend she's accepted your departure. She'd look pleased that you will no longer be a burden or a smear on your family's genetics and lifestyle. Even if she is looking everywhere for you. If she puts on the right face in public and is careful with who she asks questions of, she will be fine. If she has half your tenacity she'll be safe.'

'Are you trying to convince me or yourself, Ahn?'

'Come on. We need to move. Less talking means faster walking.'

'That is the lamest excuse yet. But fine.'

I moved past him and kept walking in silence. I was pushing myself physically but it would be worth it if we got to the shuttle in time. So I walked.

***

After an hour or so I started to flag. I was tired... exhausted, actually. I had come even with Ahn but was going to soon fall behind.

'Stupid, stupid, stupid, stupid,' I muttered to myself. My feet hurt, the blisters on my heels long past burst and now rubbing raw flesh against my socks. They certainly did not feel soft and thick anymore. I stumbled again over some rock or branch on the verge. This time Ahn caught me. My breathing was beyond ragged. So much for fresh air giving me energy.

'You need to rest,' Ahn said, holding me upright.

'If I sit I won't get back up. My legs will melt into the ground.'

'You said that last time. Come on, a few metres in. Let's find you a nice soft... tree for you lean on.' He pulled me from the verge into the bushes and past a few metres of trees, leaning me against a tree where I slid down, the bark making rough scraping noises against my pack.

'How are you not tired?' I asked as Ahn pulled out some water for me and sat on a fallen tree trunk.

'I run a lot. Around the compound. It keeps me sane.'

'You just spend your spare time running and learning to pick locks?'

'Among other things. We don't leave the compound without prior arrangements sanctioned by the Cube. Family engagements and things like that. Unless it's something big though you stay onsite for security. Your only way out of the Cube is another facility-based job for the City. People can't know the true purpose of the Cube.'

'How have people not noticed a giant white Authority building? I mean, you told your mother.'

'I told my mother I was working for the Authority. I only knew what the Cube was because of my wife's clearance. She told me too much.'

'So the Cube technically doesn't exist.'

'Same for the Black Sphere. Both are listed on City maps as prisons. High security ones at that. It works well to keep it that way. No one goes to visit a prison unless they know an inmate. And Sphere is only for dangerous criminals.'

'You seem to know a lot. More than most.' I looked at him suspiciously. After all this time was he really trying to help me? Or was this just a game? Another test? Was I getting red statused and this was phase one of training?

'I told you. I read through my wife's work files before they came for her things. They didn't realise I had a key. She gave it to me in case anything happened.'

I didn't say anything. I was worried now. I got to my feet and picked up the long branch next to me. I would use it as a walking stick but now I also had a weapon I knew I could use. I tossed the water bottle back to Ahn.

'Let's move. I want to be on that shuttle.'

'Your recovery time is improving. The sedatives they gave you in the Cube must be wearing off.'

'Yeah must be,' I mumbled as I used the stick to get me to the verge. My breathing was better but my legs were still on fire. I wasn't going to let him know that. This time as we hit the verge I matched his pace. I didn't want him behind me now the seed of doubt was planted in my head. If he was going to cross me by returning me to the Cube after some bizarre real-world training I wanted to see it coming. I would not get trapped again. I never wanted to be helpless and scared again.

I had no idea how long we had been walking. My legs had become happily numb now and I could barely feel more than a throb from my numb feet. I saw lights ahead for the first time in our long trip. The shuttle station was packed. Ahn was right, this was a great time to mingle. We were dirty and exhausted-looking, but so were the throng of workers waiting to go north through the mountains to their homes.

'Lose the stick,' Ahn hissed as we began to move from the grass onto the paved road. A City bus was letting off a group of workers in black and navy uniforms. The colours would be dark enough that we could fall into line with them. BioServ was on the back of some of the jackets. This was the clean-up crew from the farm decontamination unit. I could smell the dirt on them and I was doubtful that two farms would be needing decontamination at once. It would hinder the food production too much, surely.

Ahn and I kept our heads down and fell into step with the group as it marched its way into West forty-seventh shuttle station. It was fairly packed. No one wanted to miss the last shuttle. That would mean a long sleep in the cold on the platform. I was jostled a little but nary was a sorry given. Men and women all in workers uniforms crushed to the front of the platform. I glimpsed a few security guards but they seemed more interested in smoking and chatting to each other than the people they were there to protect.

A bell began to ding above us and everyone on queue got into rough lines. This was second nature to them so I watched as Ahn was jostled into one line and me another. I looked frantically for him until I made eye contact. He nodded. I knew what I had to do if we were separated. And anyway, we would meet up on the other side of our trip. We were just lucky the City shuttles were free and had no identification registration required. Ahn's would be flagged, and I of course, had nothing. My prints, although recorded as a child, were probably long ago blacklisted into the oblivion of the records department.

We filed into the shuttle. I didn't want to go to the second level so I shuffled into a corner near the door and slid to the floor. Less likely to be seen but comfortable enough for the trip. I had no idea how long it would take or how many stops were ahead but I just intended to listen up for the station announcement so I knew when to get off.

The shuttle carriage was packed. But I saw I wasn't the only one sitting on the floor forgoing the hard, plastic seats the lined the sides of the carriage. People even began to sit on the stairs leading to the second storey. I hoped that from here it only got less crowded. I tucked my feet in under me and relaxed. I was used to confined spaces. This was going to be less stressful than I thought.

CHAPTER EIGHTEEN
Darnell

It was cold on the bank in the rain even though the drops were smaller and fewer than before. Darnell managed to crawl over to a tree to rest against. He needed to look for Coo. He pulled off his pack and fished out a torch. It probably wasn't smart to call attention to where he was but he was so scared that he needed light. He heard rustles in the bushes and strange animal sounds that he didn't recognise.

He swung the torch beam around and even though it tried its best, it barely cut through the rain. He needed to get up. Leaving his pack against the tree he started to scout the area. Down on the banks he saw nothing. The boat was long gone and if Coo had made it to land nearby, the rain had washed his footprints away.

'Coo!' he called. He began to shiver uncontrollably. The beam of the torch trembled through the air. 'Coo! Can you hear me?' But he heard no response. He walked up the river a little further when he saw something that might be helpful. A jetty.

He ran back for his pack and then took off through the rain to the jetty. This was at least a sign of habitation. He could go seek help. He had no idea how far they had come in the jet boat, but it had to have cut a chunk out of their journey. It certainly wasn't the port at Ellintown but who knew how close he had gotten? Darnell scouted around the jetty looking for any signs of Coo but found nothing in the torch light. There was a path leading away from the jetty. His best bet was to go to the township and ask for help. No one here would know him.

The path was gravel, and a lot wider than the one they had left from. He passed the boat house, this one a large metal shed with a guard's house in it. He glanced in but it was empty, the dim light inside showing a stack of newspapers and a pair of reading glasses. He considered going inside the boat house to get dry but if Coo was out there hurt, he wouldn't forgive himself.

He continued up the path and saw a farm house. Its lights were on in the downstairs rooms and as he got closer a shaggy dog stood up from his mat on the porch and wagged his tail. This would be as good a place to start as any.

He walked up the front stairs where he was greeted with a lick from the dog. It was old and dirty but he was happy that it was friendly at least. He ruffled the fur on the dog's head and said hello.

'Now dog, is your family as nice as you because I sure could use some help tonight?' Darnell said, looking into the dark brown eyes. The dog barked in return. He jumped still at the noise, and this dog was much bigger than Kutta so his bark was doubly loud. 'Shhhh boy, I don't want your family to think I'm going to break in. I just need some help.' The tail wagged again and Darnell heard footsteps behind the door.

'Now Roger, who do you have here?' asked a gruff female voice from the door. 'Looks like a giant drowned rat. So rat, what you doing on my porch at this late hour talking to my Roger?'

Darnell was a bit taken aback at the calmness of the lady. 'Uh... well Ma'am. Me and my friend Coo were in a boat and it capsized. I managed to get onto the bank and followed the road up here. I can't find my friend. Roger was just saying hello.'

'Useless guard dog. He's lucky I love him so much. Now did you say your friend Coo? That wouldn't be Mayor Coo from five townships down, would it?'

'Yes Ma'am. He was helping me get to my uncle's place in Ellintown. He's… really sick and dying and I'm the last family he had. We were trying to get there as soon as I could so I can see him one last time.' He felt the lie roll off his tongue effortlessly, but a pang of guilt still punched him in the gut.

'Silly old fool trying to row down the river in this weather. Trying to outrun it I'll wager. Come in boy and get into the laundry. We'll get those clothes off to dry. That pack of yours waterproof?' Darnell nodded. 'Good. Go get changed. Pop your wet things in the dryer then go sit yourself and those boots in front of the fire. I'll go rally some folk to go find old Coo. He's done some favours for those in this town so we will have enough folk for you to stay here. Now go through there.'

When Darnell emerged, still shivering, the lady ushered him to the rug in front of the fire and handed him a hot cocoa.

'I've reached about ten folk who are getting kitted out now to go hunting for Coo.' Darnell flinched at the word hunted. It was a little too close to comfort. 'Now, you've met Roger, who is a useless tracker, so I'll be leaving him here to keep you company, but I'm Ma Fran. I run the bakery for this zone of settlements. Coo loves my bread. Says he can never manage to make his own. It's the good quality flour I get. My brother is in the City proper and gets it delivered for me. Now who are you sonny?'

'Darnell, Ma'am, uh, Ma Fran.'

'You must be from south of the mountains. No northern boys ever have manners that good.'

'Yes Ma'am – sorry, Ma Fran.'

'Nothing to apologise for. Now, there's blankets and pillows on the sofa. Feel free to rug up if needed. Leave the lights on though so I can find my way back.' She laughed at this, a great honking cackle that echoed in the high-ceilinged room. 'You hungry?'

'No, thank you, Ma Fran. But the hot drink is much appreciated.'

'Well, there's bread and jam on the counter. Help yourself. Don't touch the whiskey though. You're too young to drink. But there's tea and more cocoa near the kettle. I see the posse arriving.' She got up and shrugged on a raincoat and pulled a plastic hat over her frizzy greying hair. 'Roger!' she yelled as she pulled on her gumboots. 'Roger come here, you stupid old dog.'

Roger came bounding in, tail wagging, threatening to knock things flying.

'Sit Roger. That's a good boy,' she said as he plonked his furry self down on the rug beside her. 'You look after him okay?' Darnell went to answer before he realised she was talking to the dog. 'Friend. Protect. Good boy.'

She bent down and grabbed her torch and a bundle of rope. 'Get some rest kid. Roger will keep you safe and sound. He may be stupid but he won't let anyone hurt you. He has a good sense of people. If he'd not liked you, I would have greeted you with a rifle. Now you crawled out near the jetty you said?'

'Yes, just before it near the big tree. I looked around but couldn't see him.'

'It's okay, two of the folk coming used to be City river patrol. If they can't spot him, he's further downstream than breath would give him. Here they are. I'm off. Rest.'

Darnell nodded and pulled a pillow off the couch. He lay down beside the fire, he could finally feel his hands defrosting and he'd finally stopped shivering. He heard Roger moving behind him, and with a *humpf*, Roger lay down behind Darnell, his thick coat instantly feeling warm against his back. It was just what he needed

***

Roger was growling. It was a terrifying noise, deep and thunderous. When he barked it was even deeper. A knock on the door followed by a shout made Roger more agitated.

'Hello! Is anyone home?' Darnell didn't recognise the voice

and Roger certainly was not impressed with whoever was behind it. Darnell wiggled his way across the carpet and grabbed a fire poker. It was heavy and sharp. He needed the protection.

The door knob jiggled, then another knock at the door. Then it went quiet. Roger moved his attention now as though following the man through the wall with x-ray vision. Darnell scooted behind the couch. He certainly didn't want the man to see him through the window. He heard a knock on the window pane. 'Hello! Anyone there? Hello doggy,' he heard the voice say through the window. Darnell stayed as still as he could. The man walked back to the door and jiggled at it again. This time Darnell heard a thump. He was trying to get through the door. Roger was now snarling. It was ferocious, and drool dripped from his exposed teeth. Darnell crouched as low as he could as the door slammed open with a splintering crash.

'Come out Darnell. I know you're in here. I followed your footprints through the... Argh!' He was cut off as Roger lunged at him and clamped onto his arm. The man had been holding a gun. It clattered to the floor. He tried to shake Roger off but the dog was not letting go. Even after a few punches Roger held fast. 'Get off me you stupid Mutt! I will snap your neck in two.'

Darnell couldn't let that happen. The fight was two against one so they had a chance. He jumped from behind the couch and ran towards the man, poker raised above his shoulder. He swung at the man's head; the man ducked just in time to miss most of the blow. The sharp point sliced across his head, gouging out a chunk of scalp.

'You little shit!' the man exploded, trying to swing at Darnell. Because of Roger's vicelike grip and at least forty kilogram bulk, the man was slow. Darnell swung again, this time cutting the man's face and glancing the poker off his other wrist. The man screamed a string of expletives as Darnell backed away from him. He felt something bump against his foot as he stepped back. It was the man's gun. As he bent to pick it up, Roger lost his grip. Despite tearing a good chunk from the man's arm, the man was free to swing his right hand and punched Roger in the face. The dog yelped as it fell over, blood splattered across its grey wiry coat. It took a moment for Darnell to realise it was the man's blood, not Rogers. Roger was getting back on his feet, a new growl rumbling through the air.

'Give me the gun kid. You're not going to shoot me.'

Darnell raised the gun to the man's chest, keeping just out of his reach.

'Give me the gun or I will break that dog's neck before I beat you to within an inch of your pathetic freak life. Now, you blank scum. Give me the gun!'

Roger lunged again but this time the man was ready. He kicked at Roger, sending the dog flying.

'Next time I snap his neck. Don't push me. Now give me the fucking gun!'

Darnell felt himself go cold. Could he actually shoot this man? Next thing he knew he heard the click of a rifle being loaded.

'No one hurts my fucking dog. Get on your knees now!' It was Ma Fran. She was dripping a puddle of rain but he saw she held a rifle up to the man's back. She prodded him with it. 'Knees or I will shoot. Unlike the boy, I will.'

The man dropped to his knees.

'Hands on your head. I don't care how much you're bleeding.'

The man complied. Darnell saw behind Ma Fran that a group of people stood on her porch, all in rain gear, and several more held rifles.

'Ma, I'll do a perimeter search in case this turkey has friends,' a man said before dashing off.

'Sheriff, you wanna come cuff this bastard?' Ma Fran said, prodding the man in the back again.

'Sure thing, Ma. Sir, you have forcibly entered the house of a resident of my jurisdiction. Now I'm no City Authority, but as Sheriff of this township, I have the ability to hold you in a cell until I can get the Authority to come get you. Now it's a Friday night so you're looking til at least Monday til I can get one of my runners to take a message to the City proper. You have the rights of remaining silent until the City has taken you into custody. And Sir, if I were you I would exercise those rights at least until you are safe in a cell where Ma Fran can't get to you because no one hurts Roger.' The Sheriff snapped some handcuffs on him and dragged him to his feet. Even cuffed, the rifles stayed aimed at the captive. 'Dave, Cecil. Will you escort this here gentlemen to the cells until I can get there? Keep a gun on him, he ain't a nice one.'

'He got blood everywhere too,' Ma Fran said as she placed the rifle down on the blood-splattered carpet and went over to Roger. He was whimpering now the man had gone, and was trying to stand. His back leg looked broken from what Darnell could see. Ma Fran was using the sleeve of her shirt to wipe the blood from his face. 'My poor baby. You did a good job. Good boy. Now lay down and let me look at that leg.'

Ma pulled off her rain gear and began to attend to Roger.

'Ma'am, I'm so sorry. I tried to fight back,' Darnell said, his hands beginning to shake. He dropped the gun and the fire poker that he was holding in his other hand. 'Roger saved my life.'

'Nothing to worry yourself over, child. It looks like it's probably just a sprain but I'll get it looked at. Sheriff, is Dr Grant out there?'

Before he could answer a young man in waders and a plastic poncho came in supporting a large man. It was Coo.

'I can look at Roger as soon as I can get this man down on a chair.' Darnell rushed over to help. They got him into a chair and Dr Grant went over to Roger. By now, the other people from the search party had taken their rain gear off and had sat themselves in front of the fire. A woman with long grey braids was passing around the bottle of whiskey.

'Coo. Are you okay? Coo, can you hear me?' Darnell said.

Coo tried to lift his head.

'You're okay, boy. Oh goodness, you're okay.'

'Where were you? I looked for you,' Darnell asked.

'Hey young man, let him get his breath. He was holding on to a log five minutes down river. He's lucky it was still half rooted to the ground. Sir, you need to get some dry clothes on.' He turned to the rest of the room. 'Where's his pack?'

'By the door,' the woman with the whiskey called.

The man got the pack and helped Coo up. 'Let's go get you changed then in front of that fire.'

Darnell went over and sat by Ma Fran, Roger and Dr Grant. 'How is he?'

'Good news is I don't think it's broken, just bruised. I'll get some of the others to help me bring him to the medical centre so I can have a proper look but Roger should be back on his feet after a few days,' Dr Grant said. Darnell began to stroke Roger's fur. There were flecks of blood mingled with the tackiness of his dirty fur, but Darnell didn't care. Roger really was a lifesaver.

'He may not be much of a smart dog, Ma Fran, but he's loyal and has a heart as big as the sun. If it weren't for him I'd have been shot.'

'What did he want?' Ma Fran asked, looking up from Roger.

'I don't know. Roger got to him before he really said much.' The lies again, so easy.

'I'm glad he did. People like that don't usually want more than to cause havoc. We haven't had any thieves out this way in years. See what I mean about Roger though? He knows good from bad.'

Coo came back out supported by two men this time. He did not look in a good way at all. A bruise was beginning to bloom on his face and he held his arm still against his chest. They lay him down on the couch and covered him with a blanket.

'Hey, kid. Leave him to sleep. He's not doing too well.

Should be fine in the morning with some sleep,' one of the men said. Darnell just nodded. 'Hey Ma Fran, these two okay to stay with you tonight?'

'As long as one of you boys will help Dr Grant get Roger over to the medical centre.'

'Sure thing Ma.' Roger was now standing but held the sore leg up off the ground. 'I'll stay with him til morning and bring him home again.'

'Okay folks, it's late. Go home. I have a mess to clean and two unexpected house guests.'

The crowd filed out, three of them now carrying Roger who looked back at Ma Fran with a pitiful stare. His ratty grey fur, still flecked with the man's blood, looked like an old man's. 'You'll be fine Roger. I'll see you in the morning.'

Coo had already begun to snore on the couch from beneath his blankets. Darnell was warm enough physically but a cold shiver ran through his body as his mind fully comprehended what had happened here tonight. Coo had nearly drowned, and he had nearly been shot. He looked over at Ma Fran looking at her door.

'Now what in the hell am I supposed to do about that tonight,' she said, looking around. 'Boy, you in a state to help me push that cupboard over in front of the door?'

'I... I guess so. I'm pretty strong I guess. So yes Ma'am, I mean Ma Fran.'

She chuckled at him and pushed the door into position. The cupboard was full of books so it was going to be heavy. They got behind it and pushed it until it blocked the doorway entirely.

'There. That'll do until I can get Davy to come look at it. Okay let's make you up a bed, and we'll leave this gun and fire poker nearby just in case.'

She lay down some pillows on the rug by the fire where he had dozed before and covered them with one of the blankets to create a makeshift mattress. 'It's not much I'm afraid but it's soft and warm and that's more than you'd get out there.

I'll see you in the morning. Holler if you need me.'

Darnell lay down on the pillows and starred at the ceiling wondering when this would all be over with.

CHAPTER NINETEEN
Zale

'What the hell is Sphere?' Zale asked.

'I can't tell you that,' Frank said.

'I'm pretty sure we have the right to know, Frank. Is that even your name?'

'Son, don't get that tone with me. I am a farmer. I have been for thirty years. I've been here for ten of those years. My Name is Franklin Ulysses Hermitage. I was Agent 9MFM4. If I tell you more, then you will most certainly die and I can't have more blood on my hands.'

'What does that even mean?' Zale demanded. The crowd was starting to close in to listen to the argument, especially hearing only Zale's side.

'Get these people back to the hall. I will make the area safe and we will take those bodies down. I will try to explain. Just for goodness sake, be quiet.'

Zale turned to Allen, 'Take them back to the hall. Wait with them. I'll be there soon. Try and get them to settle and make sure we get everyone's names.'

Allen nodded and called to the crowd at the top of his voice. 'If everyone can head back to the hall and we will stay there until Frank checks the area. There may be more landmines at the perimeter and I don't want more casualties.'

A mumble raced through the crowd.

'NOW!' ordered Frank. His booming voice scared most people there and they began to walk towards the City hall again.

'Let me guess,' Zale said once everyone was out of ear shot. 'Drill Sargent?'

'I led a crew, so I guess you could call me a drill sergeant.'

'Led a crew doing what exactly?'

'Training new recruits to go after high-risk criminals. The Sphere has an antigravity chamber below ground. It's where the lifers go. They just sit there, unable to move until their organs finally give up.

'There aren't any high-risk criminals though, not in years?'

'That you know of. Most are blanks that either test out of the Cube or get moved to Sphere due to being unresponsive to training.'

'So the Cube is real?'

'Indeed. I was offered a job there as head facilitator once after I retired from the force. Blanks don't get many options; they either go off-grid, are killed or are put in the Cube. In addition, once they're in there, very few will see adulthood or the sky again.'

'While we talk I need some things to throw at the land mines. I doubt they've rigged more than the gate so if we can get them gone, we can get the bodies down.' They spent a few moments tossing chunks of brick and random items towards the gate. After a few explosions, they finally felt the area was clear and went to cut the bodies down. It was not pleasant. By the time Zale had helped Frank lay the last one down on the ground, they were covered in blood and dirt.

'You're going after them, aren't you?' Frank asked.

'I don't know…'

'Don't lie to me. I saw Allen running up the tunnel with those packs. Let me come with you. I at least know my way around.'

'Why did you leave?' Frank said nothing. 'Frank, why did you leave?'

'My second-born son was deformed. No, not a blank. He was genetically broken. Had no legs, couldn't talk. Doctors said we shouldn't have let him go to full term. That it was breaking the genetic purity of Oasis.'

'But he wasn't blank?'

'No, that was the thing. He was marked. Same spot I was. My wife wanted to keep him. I guess I did, too. Sphere told me to allow the City to euthanise him or they would euthanise my family. I refused. I saw cracks in the system. If my son was marked, it meant he was mutagen free. They couldn't allow the public to see that it could fault. So I quit. My son never made it home from hospital. Medical complications they said, but I was a sharp shooter. Had eyes like a hawk. I saw the injection point. The missus and me moved our firstborn and ourselves out to the exclusion zone and began to farm out there. They say the soil is tainted but that's bullshit to keep the civilians away from the fences. When my boy died in a tractor accident, the missus and I realised we needed people. I'd heard about Condor Point from a Sphere buddy who kept me up to date on the goings-on of the City. He arranged safe passage for us up here and we've been here since. Mary died three years ago. Doc said it was a bad heart but I say it was a broken one. Losing two babies is not easy on anyone. I didn't believe in the system. It had failed me. It was a lie. The marks mean nothing.'

'Then what are they for?'

'They link you to a genetic match, for sure. But it's not a naturally occurring thing. It has to be man-made. There are too many flaws in it, you see. So let me come with you, please. I have no family and I can't seem to fit in here even after all this time, so I want to help.'

'Frank, they need you here. Without the council or the Colonel, the people of Condor Point need a leader. They need you.'

'Then can I give you a tip? If your hunt leads back to the Black Sphere, don't go in. Once you go in you will never come back out. Not alive, not dead. You will either get anti-gravved or reconstituted into genetic slurry. And make sure to take them by surprise. Do either of you even have military training?'

'Allen was a junior grunt before we came here'

'So that's a no then. You need to be quiet. If you go after that woman, she is special. She's got to have some genetic enhancement.'

'They're illegal. No one can have genetic enhancements.'

'Unless they work for Sphere. That's how I'm so strong. It's worn off a bit after all these years but that was just one of the enhancements back then. That woman looked mid-twenties at the most so who knows what she had pumping through her, but it certainly isn't run-of-the-mill blood.'

'We have guns.'

'Congratulations. She will probably use them to shoot you before you know she's even there. For the last time, let me go. Put Schonell in charge. Or Mrs Wade. Everyone loves Mrs Wade. Or Allen. He's good with people. Leave him here to look after everyone. Save his life by making him stay.'

'He won't let me go.'

'Don't tell him. Let's just go. By the time he realises we're not coming to town hall, we'll be three clicks into the forest.'

Zale didn't know how to answer. The idea of knowing that Allen was safe and sound at home with the rest of the towns people made him much more comfortable, but would Allen understand if he just disappeared?

'How will he know I'm okay? He'll know where I've gone.'

'No, he'll know what your plan was but not know where you're going. Did you have a plan?'

'Sort of?'

'Okay, so you had no plan. Look, there are two packs and even though you have a pocket full of ammo and want to take that woman down as much as I do, running in all gung ho and waving around a pencil in a sword fight is not going to keep you or Allen alive. With me, I know a few back ways in. I don't have clearance but if we run into anyone, I can say I was in deep cover to infiltrate a group of blanks. They'd believe me. Infiltrations have been on going and some agents were gone for years.'

'Okay. But I get to leave him a note.'

'No, no note, no clues, nothing. Let's go before they send a rescue team out. Your partner seems rather efficient. He'll make a good town leader.'

'Do you know where the Colonel is? Normally he would have made a situation broadcast but nothing has come in.'

'I know, that worries me too. I doubt he met the same fate as these four. He's tougher than that but he might have been captured. Have faith in him though. He's never let us down before.'

'Have you met him? I mean, met him in person?'

'I knew him in days gone by but since he became Colonel? No.'

'He was one of them, wasn't he? From the Sphere?'

'Sort of. Look, enough talking. Let's go get the packs and head off. How were you planning on following her?' Frank said as they began the walk up the hill. He veered to the right so as to go behind the town hall and Zale followed.

'Blood trail. I shot her in the leg, I think.'

'That will only get us so far, she won't be stupid enough to let it bleed. As soon as she was safe enough she'll have patched it and called for evac. Luckily, they won't have risked the flyers so it'll be a ground vehicle, which means tracks.'

'Flyers?'

'Oh, there is so much you don't know. But not now. Keep moving.'

They marched in silence until they got to where Allen had stashed the packs. Frank looked inside them and nodded.

'You boys certainly know how to pack at least. I recommend putting the holster on. There will be scouts in the area still I'll wager. And they'll have heard the explosions. Hopefully they will head towards them expecting a mob.'

Zale struggled into the holster and put the pack on after pulling a torch from its depths. He swept the beam across the ground until he found a splash of blood. Frank walked over and had a look.

'Must have got her pretty good. It's not an arterial bleed but it's no bullet graze. You also got her more than once, judging by how the blood has fallen, but she'll be limping until she can get something in her for the pain.'

They followed the splashes of blood, now black against the dirt and blades of grass, until they got to a low brick wall. There was a blood stain on the wall and an empty tube of superglue sitting on it. This was where she had stopped to fix herself.

'Superglue?' Zale asked, picking up the tube.

'That's not just superglue, its stem glue. Combo of a glue compound and stem cells. They were experimenting with it when I was there. It seals the wound and the stem cells recreate the damaged cells. She'll be at full use of her leg, except for a dull pain, in hours. And she's got several of those up her sleeve on us.'

Frank bounded over the low wall. The bricks were old and, in places, moss had begun to cover them with green fur. You could see the repairs on the wall from years of mending by mortaring the old bricks back together.

'This is the perimeter wall.'

'Yes son, it is. It's not dangerous. They just want you to think that. Come on. Over you come.'

'Are you sure it's safe? I don't want to come all this way to get radiation sickness and grow an extra eye or something.'

'I lived there and still look the same. Not sick, never have been. Our animals were happy and healthy.'

Zale climbed over the wall, a piece of brick crumbling off in his hand. He looked at it; it was more mortar than brick, he saw. Broken and crumbling just like his town. He tucked it into the pocket of his pants. A way to take a bit of Condor Point with him.

'She would have come here for evac. No civilians – well, not many anyway. We need to look for flattened grass or tracks closer to the fence.'

'I can't go to the fence.'

'Why?'

'The beasts will come over and pull me through.'

'That's a story made up by our great-great-grandparents to keep kids from going near it. It seems it was stuck in your head as you grew up too. Interesting.'

'Frank, I liked you better as a bumbling farmer.'

'You won't when they're trying to kill you.'

'Why didn't you try and stop them?'

'I didn't think they'd kill the little girl. We had morals… well, we had a code we stuck to. It wasn't up to us who lived or died. We just brought people in. Shoot to wound not to kill was how we tried to live.'

'Yeah well, her shooting that little girl in the head wasn't to wound her. It was to kill, and scare the living fuck out of everyone in that shelter. Where were you when it all happened? Surely you recognised the uniforms,' Zale hissed.

'Of course I did. I was at the back of the room. I didn't have a weapon and I would be no use to anyone if I was shot. I'm not a coward, Zale, I was trying to think ahead. And I really didn't think they'd kill the girl, honestly. Now please let's just find these tracks.'

They skimmed the area in both directions before finally spotting not a track but a small house. It was more of a shack. It couldn't have been more than two rooms with a tin roof but it sat against the fence. The sparse brown grass around it was long and wild. The dirt around it was dusty and hard like that in the Badlands. It was dead soil.

'It's a safehouse,' Frank whispered. 'She might still be waiting for evac.'

'Should we have a look?' Zale asked. He still felt wrong being this close to the fence but Frank had lived out here so surely he'd have aftereffects from it if it wasn't safe and he doubted Sphere would put a safehouse out here and endanger its people.

'It's the old banishment house for this area. I had heard of it being used as a safehouse but never got out this way when I was an agent.'

'The banishment house?'

'The family of blank kids stayed there when they used to banish blanks out to the Badlands. There'll be a gate around here too, although it'll be welded shut.'

'They did what?'

'Shh,' he hissed as the light went on. 'There's someone still in the place.'

A large shadow passed in front of the window. It certainly was not the woman. They heard shouting but couldn't make out what was being said from there they stood.

'We need to get closer,' Frank said, shimmying his way along the fence. Zale followed, trying to be as quiet as possible. They were halfway there when a gunshot rang out, piercing the night. A flock of roosting birds took off into the blackness. The shadow collapsed out of view.

'Frank, she'll kill us,' Zale whispered, trying not to make too much noise. As they came up on the house they could hear more talking.

'Just get him over the fence. Let the Badlands have him. He had no family, did he?' came the voice of a softly-spoken man.

'Not anymore. He had a sister at Condor Point. Didn't like that we removed her.' This voice was most certainly the woman.

'So that's why he was here. I was wondering. I don't get many visits out here. Try to remain as far away as possible from any action these days.'

'I apologise for the mess, Sir.'

'Evac will handle it. How's your leg?'

'Mending, Sir. Stem Gel is great for through-and-throughs if you have enough of it. You told us there were a few armed folks who could shoot, but some were sharp shooters. Lost at least twelve agents.'

'How many humans?'

'Nine, Sir. The rest were BGMs.'

'Black status recruits from red status are always great for

these operations. How many sleepers we have left in there?'

'At least two that I know of. One may have died in the bunker blast though. Not sure where he was when it blew.'

'Fair enough. If he's smart he would have stayed back. Now go rest your leg, Agent. I need you ready to go in the morning. Evac will be driving up and then we have a special mission for you.'

'Retrieval?'

'Yes. But no casualties there. Too many people we have onside in the area. I need it to be quick and clean. You'll need some civilian clothes. I'm sure base will find something that fits. Your cover will be provided.'

'Why me for a retrieval?'

'We've lost six agents trying to get this one and I want him for black status. It won't be easy though. He won't want to come easily and even a BGM couldn't get him. We haven't heard from that agent and he was due to report in three hours ago. Presumed dead like the others.'

'Sounds like my sort of recovery. I'm up for it, Sir. Goodnight.'

'Goodnight, Agent.'

They heard footsteps moving to the back of the shack, now only the raspy breath of the man remained.

'Frank?' Zale whispered as quietly as possible. 'What's a BGM?'

'Blank Genetic Modification. It's too much to explain now. We need to move. I recognise that voice and I need to see if I'm right. Stay here. Don't move. If you hear gunshots, run.'

'But Frank…'

'No, just do as I say, okay?'

Zale sat down against the side of the house. He couldn't bear to put his back to the fence, regardless of what Frank had said. He slipped the gun from its holster and made sure he was ready. He heard Frank walk around to the front of the house and open the door. Why was the old man not getting up?

'I knew it was you,' he heard Frank say. 'I'd know the

Colonel's voice in my sleep. How are you?'

Zale couldn't believe what he was hearing. The Colonel? Condor Point's reigning Colonel who looked after them like some omnipotent god?

'Long time no see? Come here and let me see what a civilian life has done to you? You're still big, just a tad bronzer from the sun.'

'That's what happens without being stuck in the Sphere.'

'What brings you out here?'

'I just had to know if you were okay. I see you are.'

'I'll be fine and if I wasn't you know you're next in line for Colonel, Frankie.'

'No one's called me that in a long time.'

'You won't come back?'

'You know I can't. Some warning would have been nice, by the way. Could have been blown to pieces.'

'Eh, I know you're a smart boy, Frankie. Just like your old man,' the Colonel said.

'You'd know, wouldn't you, Dad?' Frank said. Zale thought he was going to be sick.

CHAPTER TWENTY
Almara

I felt like throwing up. The motion of the train wasn't something I was at all used to. My nerves were on edge too. Every time the voiceover announced a station I'd jerk awake fully, scared to miss my stop. The passengers slowly thinned until there was only a few standing people, scattered throughout the carriage. I stretched out my legs, glad for the extra room. My knees gave a satisfying pop as I stretched them.

It had to have been at least an hour or two since we left. I could now see the lights flashing by the shuttle windows as we moved out of the mountains and into the northern reaches of Oasis. I got to my feet, slowly unfolding my cramped-up body, shaking out the stiffness. I needed to be ready to get off and I knew that next time I dozed off could be the time I fell asleep fully. Although I knew vaguely where I was going, I would rather do the trip with Ahn.

'Northern Groves Station approaching. Please exit on the left of the carriage. Northern Groves approaching,' the voiceover said. That was our stop. I moved to the left side of the carriage and rested my hand on the silver door release button. The shuttle slowed to a halt and I saw the station pull into view. It wasn't as big a station as I'd expected but there were already at least six people behind me waiting to get off and several at the other door.

There was a ding and the door release button lit up in green lights. I pushed it in and waited… it didn't work. *What if it could tell I was blank?* I thought to myself. I pressed it again, prodding at the button, hoping it would register. The doors finally slid open and I was forced onto the platform by the people behind me.

'It's okay love, does it to the best of us,' said an old man as he walked past. I breathed a sigh of relief and began to search for Ahn. I didn't want to call out but as the crowd thinned, I still couldn't spot him.

It was then I heard the scream. A troupe of City Authority guys had swarmed the platform with guns drawn. A woman dashed towards me, yelling for help. I turned my head away, scared that the Authority might recognise me. I had no idea if our faces had been plastered across the network yet or not. She went sprawling across the tiled floor and one of the uniformed Authority dove onto her, restraining her. He pulled her to her feet.

'Ma'am, you are coming with us. You are under arrest for stealing from the City. You have no rights.' With that, he dragged her, screaming, away. They weren't here for us after all. But as they took the woman I noticed the rest of the Authority had not left the platform. I started moving towards the exit, my hair down and covering my face. I glanced up to see them showing a photo to passengers if they were leaving. Next I knew, a hand grabbed my arm. I snapped my head around, ready to fight, but it was Ahn.

'Stay quiet, walk fast but don't run. They're asking around about us. We need to split up. Go out of the station and head about a hundred paces up the road and wait for me there. See if you can hide.'

I nodded and he let go of me, veering to the left and giving us distance. I put my head back down and kept walking. Outside of the station was cold. After being in the controlled temperatures of the shuttle and the station, the wind sent a chill up my spine. People spread out, moving towards the local bus stops and car parks. I felt suddenly very isolated but kept walking. I started to count my steps. One, two, three…

At a hundred I stopped and looked either side of me. There was a carpark on one side, the cars few and far between, and the other side was a park. I decided to head to the park. There were no lights on there so if I stayed low I should be able to blend into the shadows. I sat under a table and tried to keep an eye out for Ahn.

The City Authority had spilled out into the night as well. They headed to the carpark and began sweeping flashlights under cars.

'Please stay over there. Please,' I whispered to myself. The silence was as heavy as a winter coat on my shoulders but nowhere near as warm. I saw movement out of the corner of my eye and heard a whispered voice.

'Almara, are you over here?' Once again, Ahn had found me.

'Ahn, under here,' I whispered back. I saw him emerge from behind a slide in the nearby playground.

'Come on, while they're busy.'

I scrambled to my feet and rushed to where he stood. He motioned for me to follow him and we dashed across the grass and deeper into the shadows. I saw a soft glow from behind a fence in front of us. Whatever it was, that was where we seemed to be heading. Ahn went up to the fence and began running his hand up the length of it. I could barely see him except for a gentle glow on his hair from above. When he stopped suddenly, I nearly ran into him.

'Sorry, I found the gate,' he said, and he stuck his hand through to undo the latch.

'The gate to where, Ahn?' I asked as it swung open, bathing us in warm light.

'Northern Groves. Oasis' main producer of fruit. This is the orange grove. You can smell it.'

He was right. The sweet citrus burst assaulted my nose. It was fresh and made my mouth water. It'd been so long since I'd had fresh fruit. The Cube only served things that came out of cans. I looked around at the orange globes hanging from the trees under the lamps.

'I didn't know oranges fruited when it was this cold.'

'Genetically modified trees fruit all year. That's why they're under the heat lamps. Keeps them warm enough to produce.'

'Won't we get caught in here?'

'We'll be fine. The last shuttle just left so the only staff will be a few overnighters and we should be able to get past them. Just keep your voice down and be careful.'

Ahn began to walk down the row between the trees. The ground below us was mainly soil with sprouts of grass poking through. I saw an orange on the ground, its bright skin such a contrast to the dark earth below it. I bent and picked it up. I would wait until we were sitting before eating it. I wanted to savour it. I tucked it into one of the large cargo pockets on the side of my pants and continued following Ahn. As we moved through the fruit groves, the trees changed. First to grapefruits then limes then lemons. That was when we reached a road.

The road was narrow and paved with large cement slabs. It was darker in the centre as no lights hung above it but it was easy to see the tyre tracks printed in mud on them. But they were narrow. Not car or truck tracks but the buggy carts and wagons they used to shift the fruit.

'Do we run across?' I asked, looking at Ahn.

'Yeah, the coast seems clear, go now.'

We bolted across the road and into an apple orchard. It smelled even sweeter on this side of the road. I could feel my mouth watering as I wondered how much fruit I could shove in my pockets for later. I picked up an apple, bright red with splashes of green. That went into the opposite cargo pocket. We were walking briskly but I still had time to marvel over the sheer number of trees. Peaches, apricots, and even cherries went by, with me seizing fallen fruit from the ground and pocketing it. Some would get a few soft spots but it'd still taste better than tinned.

I saw darkness at the end of the orchard and Ahn dashed

ahead of me. I saw him at another gate as I approached. I didn't want to leave the sweet-smelling orchards of Northern Grove behind but we needed to find somewhere safe to bed down for the night. Behind the grove was a patch of bushland that was spindly and dry-looking. These were trees with no care given to them. As we walked through, I felt twigs snapping underfoot. The ground here was dry; the rain must have gone around it.

'Why don't they extend the groves out into this area?' I asked, looking back towards the fence with its distant glow of grow lights.

'It's a nature break. Gives the wild animals a chance of keeping their habitats. Things like deer and wild pigs. There's a few of these around, especially in these mountain areas. Mind you there's a few houses dotted through them from people who have gone off-grid.'

'Off-grid?'

'The simple life. No plumbing or electricity. No real connection to the City. I mean, don't get me wrong, the City knows where they are. But apart from making sure they aren't growing or selling contraband, they leave them well alone. There should be a small township not far from here. But I'd rather find an off-gridder. Most of them are fairly welcoming if you're running from the City. My wife used to keep a register of the off-grid folk as part of her job. The list grew longer every year. It always amazed me how many there were.'

'And there are some around here?'

'Plenty behind the groves. Most of them pick up a little work sorting fruit for the things they can't grow or barter for. A few credits and the reject fruit make for great pay checks, plus free seeds. There should be one coming up soon.'

I hoped he was right. My feet hurt and now I was sure I had several cuts from the twigs that kept jabbing at me from the malnourished trees. In the distance I heard the hoot of an owl and the running of water.

'Is there a river near here?"

'Still a ways off but yes. How did you know?'

'Listen. You can hear it. It sounds like bubbling water.'

Ahn stopped and strained his ears. 'You're right, Almara. Well, that's what we need to head towards. Water sources are vital for those off-grid.'

'Surely the City could run plumbing out here from the orchard.'

'Then they would have a hold over the off-grid family. It's better to live without for them.'

I couldn't imagine that. Even in the conditions in the Cube I had always had access to plumbing and electricity. But it was something I realised I may have to get used to. Was the place we were going off-grid?

We walked on in silence, only the sounds of our feet snapping twigs and crushing dry, fallen leaves could be heard above the owls and the river. The water was getting louder too. I sped up my pace as I saw the first glimmers of water in my flashlight beam. Despite the cold, my face was warm from the walking. I dropped to the ground and splashed the cold water on my face. Ahn laughed behind me.

'Don't fall in, for goodness sake. That's all we need, for you to get sick. Let's follow the river upstream. We should find a house soon. Looks like the sun will be up soon. too,' he said, looking towards the sky. It was no longer the inky black of night, but was now flushed with a purple tint. In the growing light I saw a small building ahead. It was a log cabin by the uneven wall surface I could see. By the time we were near, we heard the door open with a gentle squeak and the muttering of an old man. Being isolated does that to a person. I should know.

Not wanting to startle him, Ahn cleared his throat. The old man cocked his head and turned around. By now the sky was the colour of peaches turning into plums, enough light that we were all visible to each other.

'Oh, ya scared the bejeebus outta me. Don't get folk through here. You Authority checkin in or from over at the

Grove?' the man said, his voice cracking with age and misuse. You don't need much volume muttering to yourself. The old man started to cough.

'No Sir, we're just passing through, heading north,' Ahn said.

'What's north? Plenty of work in the grove. And why not take the shuttle?'

'Heading to Condor point.'

'Ah, I get cha now. She's a bit young for you though ain't she? Sure they still have coupling laws in the Point even with their anti-Authority ways.'

'Oh no. We're just friends. Travelling together,' I blurted out.

'Ah well, I suppose you need supplies. I haven't got much though but happy to give you some preserves. Too old to do much hunting these days so I don't have no meat.'

'No Sir, we have provisions. We were actually wondering if we could rest here a while. We've been on the road all night,' Ahn said.

'Oh, if that's all, I'd be happy to oblige. I don't have much room but I have an old couch and a small bed you are welcome to use while I work, if that'll suffice?'

'Thank you, Sir, we would be very grateful. Happy to share some of our supplies to make a meal if you're wanting.'

'That would be nice. Got any meats in there? Been so long.'

'I think I have a few packs of beef stew with your name on them.'

'Oh, my name, I forgot, I'm Jaylon,' the man said, holding out his hand.

'I'm Ahn and this is my friend Almara.' We shook hands and he ushered us back inside.

'Either of you two know how to make rabbit traps?'

I shook my head. Ahn did the same.

'Ah, thought I'd ask. It's been a while since I made one and this old brain of mine just plum forgot how to do it. Luckily, I can still grow plenty and when the grove gives me some work

I go buy some dried meat in the next town. Miss the real stuff though. Used to be a dab hand with a bow, but not strong enough now and guns are too expensive for me. Probably blow my hands clean off...' Jaylon continued to mumble to himself as he found a pot and lit his stove.

Ahn pulled out three dehydrated meal packs of the beef stew and emptied them into the pot. 'Six cups of water we need Mr Jaylon, Sir. I can go get it from the stream.'

'Oh no, I made my own plumbing. Look at this,' he said, turning the tap. I heard a pumping sound before water began to gently pour into a bowl beneath the tap. He scooped out six cups and splashed them into the pot.

He smiled an almost toothless grin at us. 'Still got something tickin' up here in the noggin.'

I laughed. Jaylon was a character, but you could tell the isolation certainly had got to him over the years. While Ahn watched the pot, Jaylon decided to show me to his room.

'You can sleep in my bed. More comfy than the couch, darlin. Drop your bag and come help me light the fireplace.'

I put my bag against the wall and took off my jacket. It was warm in the cabin from the woodstove, but if there was a fireplace too, I couldn't complain about that. Mother had never liked them, even the gas ones most had in the City, because she thought they were dangerous. We ended up with a digital one that emitted heat through its digital faceplate.

While we busied ourselves, I could hear Ahn in the kitchen. How delicious that stew smelled. Even though it was just freeze-dried it would still taste better than the cardboard-like meat and mash I'd eaten for the last seven years. So far, every bite of food I'd tasted had been better. My tastebuds were waking up. My mouth was watering. Jaylon and I got a good fire going as we began to hear cupboards being opened and closed in the kitchen.

'Top right above the stove,' Jaylon called out to Ahn, who, by the time we had been seated around the scratched wood table, was already ladling the stew into bowls. The stew was good. We ate in silence. I was too hungry to stop until I had scraped the bowl clean and I saw Jaylon and Ahn doing the same. This City grade stuff from CropServ was top notch. However, I was still peckish. I pulled the fruit out of my pockets.

'Gatherin' in the Grove I see. I won't tell if I can have the seeds. Actually, let's make it a proper fruit salad,' he said, jumping up to get a fruit basket. He then got three knives and a plate.

'Jaylon,' I asked as I peeled my orange, 'how long have you been out here?' I popped a segment of orange into my mouth. It was delightfully sweet.

'Well I'm eighty-seven, Molly died six years ago. Paul got snake bit and died forty years ago, and he was fifteen, so ...' he counted on his fingers,'...sixty years, give or take.'

'Wow,' I replied. 'That's an awfully long time out here. Molly, she was your wife?'

'Indeed she was. Betrothed at birth pretty much. She was a day older than me, well, twenty-two hours, but I'm the only one that counted that. Both of us were born in the same birthing centre. Our marks were clear as day. Mine on my chest, hers on her forearm. We pretty much grew up in each other's pockets. But we liked it that way.'

'Meant to be,' I said with a smile. 'Do you not get lonely out here?'

'Do now without Molly. But it's too long since I've been to the City. I'll most likely die out here. I get enough talk when I go to the Grove to help sort fruit. Can't do much more than that and tend to my gardens these days. A nice chap from the Grove runs to the nearest township for me if I need something but mostly I just talk to myself.'

'You're doing quite a good job on that fruit,' Ahn said, looking at the perfectly peeled and chopped fruit Jaylon had put on the plate, unlike our hacked-at pile that was half mush. He laughed and mixed it all together on the plate and we started eating. I savoured every bite. I could so easily get used to this but something told me not to. That the Cube was where I'd end up again, except blue status, being poked and prodded until I died.

I froze midbite, the fruit's sweetness becoming sickly as I felt the bile rising in my throat. I swallowed the mouthful and thought I was going to gag. Jaylon looked over to me.

'You okay lass? Not choking are ya? You gone whiter than Molly's sheets after a good wash.'

'Uh… I'm just a bit tired,' I said, trying to swallow the bile down. I took a deep breath and blew it out slowly to calm my nerves. 'Sorry. It's been a long day and I'm not used to as much walking as we've done the past two days. If you gentlemen don't mind I will go to bed.'

'Of course, love. Only just made the bed fresh this morning when I got up so nice and clean for ya. You got some good timing.'

I gave a smile to the men and shuffled down the hallway. I was filthy. I quickly slipped into something clean from my bag and tucked myself in. This was no plush mattress but it was still comfortable enough and with the men talking out at the table, I fell asleep.

***

A furious yelling woke me. It was late afternoon, the sky out the window starting to dull. It was out the front but I couldn't tell how close. I pulled on my jacket and boots and made myself ready to run if needed.

'I ain't been stealing!' I heard, finally making out the crackled voice of Jaylon. 'They're my damn trees. You can't touch em. I grew them with seeds I was paid with at the Grove. Go ask Paula, or Evie or Ben. They gave em to me with twenty credits for three days of sortin' fruit up there. I was on limes, if you need to know. I always do limes and apples.' Then a mumble from whoever else was out there. 'Yes, I do mind if you go inside. It's my house and it's not City run. The trees are mine and if you touch them I will…'

I heard a thunk sound and silence. Had they really knocked out an old man? If they came inside, they would find me. He had no cupboards in the room but the bed was high enough off the ground for me to fit under and the heavy valance would keep me hidden. I pushed my bag below and then wiggled under myself. It reminded me way too much of the day I was captured in the Archive library. I heard footsteps. They were getting closer. Next thing I knew I saw someone drop to the floor and lift the valance. I was going to be caught... I was going to be taken back to the Cube.

CHAPTER TWENTY-ONE
Zale

The Colonel was working with those people. Frank was working with those people. Frank was the Colonel's son! Zale's head was spinning. He needed to run. He got to his feet and looked around. He didn't even really know where he was. That woman was still in there.

'Zale. You may as well come in. I know you heard everything,' Frank called.

Should he run or should he stay?

'If you run I'll send her out after you. You won't get far. We know this area well. Just come inside.'

Zale's heart was racing, thumping in his chest. Frank was right. He didn't know where he was and if he ran it was more than likely they would find him before he could get back to Condor Point. He went towards the stairs up to the porch. The door was open. Frank was in the doorway, waiting for him.

'We're friends here, Zale. I wouldn't have brought you here if I didn't think we could be friends.'

Zale stopped at the door. 'You killed children. You killed a little girl.'

'No, Zale, they did. I didn't. I'm one of you just like my father here.' He stepped to the side revealing the Colonel. He was old and sitting in a wheelchair, his legs covered with a blanket. A large pink scar ran down his face in much the same place as Zale's but this was not from a mark removal. This scar was a burn, the skin around it was puckered and uneven, his eye was milky white and his lip was curled up with scar tissue.

'You're the Colonel. You're supposed to protect us. Not send dogs in to destroy us.'

'It's a matter of numbers my dear boy. Condor Point is only allowed to exist because of me. If it were up to the City alone, you would all be in jail and the blanks would be where they are meant to be. In facilities, being used to enhance our lives.'

'But we've done nothing wrong.'

'Incorrect. You are going against City Sanctioned regulations. While the numbers at Condor Point are small, there has been a twenty percent growth rate this year alone. There needed to be a cull.'

'So you shot a small child. Your own son is going against City regulations, or is that a lie too.'

'Zale, everything I told you is true. I just believe that there should be some control. My father is that control. He allows us to exist without too much interference. THEY allow us to exist. However, we have to do what we're told.'

'You call killing innocent people allowing us to exist?'

'I think you need to see why we do what we do.'

'And how am I supposed to do that.'

'042!' the Colonel called. The woman appeared in the doorway.

'Sir?'

'Call in an evac to the Sphere. You need to get these two dropped at intake before you head to Ellintown.'

'I'm not going anywhere with her. She's a psychopath!'

'No, she's loyal. She does what she's told. She is a good soldier despite her shortcomings.'

'She's a murderer! Frank, I need to leave. I need to get back to Condor Point.'

Frank moved to block the door. The woman walked into the back room. Zale could hear her talking. 'I don't want...'

'I thought you'd be more open-minded, Zale,' Frank said. 'We don't like the killing and personally I think it could have been done a lot less stressfully, but I don't make the rules.'

'Who the hell does?'

'The City. The City looks after us.'

'The City makes us couple with people we don't love. The City murders innocent people.'

'The City keeps us safe from blanks and the beasts outside. If it wasn't for the City you wouldn't have been born.'

The woman came back out. 'Sir, an air evac will be here in five. I advised cooperating prisoner and chaperone.'

'So now I'm a prisoner?'

'You don't have clearance. The only way to enter the Sphere is with clearance or as a prisoner. Cooperate and you will not need to be restrained. If you do, I cannot guarantee your safety.'

'Zale, sit down,' Frank said quietly.

'No.'

'Just sit the fuck down, Zale. We'll be leaving quite soon anyway. Air evac is imminent.'

'Air evac?

'Drone air shuttle. It's cloaked so it can't be seen from below. You've probably heard them a hundred times and never thought anything of it.'

'But air travel is forbidden? I didn't even think we had the technology for it anymore.'

'Of course we do. But City has sanctioned its use for Sphere missions only.'

'Then couldn't we connect with other regions? We can't be the only region left?'

'The blanks destroyed everything we stood for. We are the last region left as far as our intel goes and therefore we stay inside our borders.'

'The blanks won then.'

'No,'

'But they did. We have Oasis and they have the rest of the world?'

'They live like the savages. They are with their beasts patrolling the wastelands they created.'

'Can we not go and see if there are other regions? See if the blanks will take those that no longer want to be marked?'

'They will kill you. You may have carved a mark out of your skin but you are still not one of them. They will set the beasts on you at once. We have a treaty. They stay away from us and we stay away from them. Their technology won't have advanced without our superior knowledge, so they know they cannot win. Even though our numbers may be smaller, we have intelligence and technology on our side.'

'But how can you know?'

'It is not your job or mine to know. If the City needs that information they will get it. For now, as far as you or I know, the City is safe and we do not leave the borders.'

'Drone incoming,' the woman said, as she looked towards the window. A bag was slung on her back and her belt was restocked with ammo and her weapons. Zale could see two handguns, two medium length blades, two short knives and a taser. As she turned her head he noticed a scar on her throat, still shiny and pink.

'Zale, get your pack,' said Frank as he pulled his onto his shoulders.

'Do we...'

'No more questions,' the woman snapped. 'If you say one more word I will slice you through the middle. Speak only when spoken to. Do you understand?'

Zale nodded, too scared to even answer. She pulled his weapons from reach. He nearly opened his mouth to protest but she shot him a glare. He knew not to say a thing.

'These will be returned to you after you leave the Sphere. If they detain you, you will most likely never see them again. If they detain you, you will most likely never see the sky again.'

'042, he's not a prisoner. He may not understand, but with information from Sphere he will come around. Won't you, Zale?' said Frank.

Zale still stood in silence. He wasn't even sure if he was breathing anymore, he'd frozen up so much. He heard a humming sound in his ears getting louder.

'Drone landing in five. Please make your way to the stairs until it has landed,' 042 said. Zale looked at her. She was almost like a robot in her demeanour but she was human. He could see it in her eyes. They were steely grey and tinged with sadness. There was a lot going on behind them. More than the murderous rage he felt from her. She was a blank, so this was her only option at some type of freedom. He couldn't imagine a life of kill-or-be-killed. Her eyes met his for a second and he saw her lips part as if to say something to him but she turned her head away.

The noise was strange. It sounded like the thrumming of a thick guitar string but thousands of times louder. It was almost like hearing movement rather than sound. It reverberated through his chest and he began to feel a little nauseous. Frank must have noticed.

'Breathe through your nose. It'll stop you throwing up. It's quiet on the inside.'

The black drone landed in the long grass, flattening a vast circle of it into the dirt. A door opened and Frank pushed Zale towards it. The sooner they were inside the better.

It was like a small black room, the walls fitted with seats. Frank pushed him into one and pulled the seatbelt tight around him before strapping himself in. 042 got in and the door closed, bringing a heavy silence over them. Zale felt like he'd gone momentarily deaf.

'Better?' Frank asked with a smile.

'How do we not hear them?'

'We do, it's just a lot further away.'

'Locked and loaded,' 042 said into her comms as she strapped herself in. Zale felt the drone begin to move. With no windows it was a little off-putting but he was sort of glad to not see the ground rushing away from them.

'042, this is Sphere Control. You are on course with

prisoner and chaperone. We will have Eighty-three waiting to collect them. Your drone is programmed to take you to Ellintown for your next mission. Briefing notes on arrival.'

'Thank you, Sphere Control. If this mission involves the chance of me being shot again can I please get more med gel with those briefs. I'm all out.'

'Roger that, 042. Enjoy your trip.'

The trip was quiet. By the time they reached Black Sphere, Zale was finally beginning to feel like he wasn't going to be sick everywhere. Frank still helped him out of the drone. A man in the same black outfit as 042 approached them as 042 gathered the brief and a med kit and went back in the drone. He was beginning to feel sick again when Frank pushed him into a waiting elevator. The doors closed and again the blessed silence of soundproofing washed over him.

'Welcome back, Agent. To confirm identity before entering the facility please state your name and passcode and the name of the prisoner.'

'Franklin Ulysses Hermitage. Agent 9MFM4. Passcode 451F. Prisoner is Zale from Condor Point. He is here willingly and knows he has no rights within this facility.'

'Agent 9MFM4, your prisoner will be assigned a lock-in number once he is processed. Is the scar a removal or is he blank?'

'Removal. He should still be citizen chipped.'

'I should be what?' Zale blurted.

'You should be quiet, prisoner,' the receiving agent snapped.

'Hey, I'm here of my own volition…'

'But you are still a prisoner and if you do not stop talking you will no longer be seen as cooperating with Sphere. Do you understand?' Zale nodded. 'Do I need to secure you?'

'No…' he mumbled. He took a deep breath. This was getting to be too much. He could feel the bile rising in his throat as his anxiety began to well up. He felt tight in the chest and began to sweat. 'No no no no no,' he chanted under his breath. A panic attack would not be helpful. He hadn't had one since before he got to Condor Point. He felt clammy and his hands began to shake as he tried to pull enough oxygen into his lungs. He could feel them looking at him, their eyes boring into him, and all that did was make it worse. He closed his eyes and tried to conjure up an image of Allen but all he could see when he closed his eyes were the dead, the splatters of blood. His fellow Condor Point people dying, and he couldn't do anything to help it.

'Zale? Zale, are you okay?' he heard Frank ask through the fogginess of his brain. The sound was muffled but a high-pitched squeal had begun. He tried to open his mouth to talk but nothing came out except a choked cry. He felt the floor fall out from underneath him and his head hit the concrete, then he blacked out.

Zale came to with a groggy feeling in his head. He tried to sit up but a wave of nausea crashed over him.

'Stay still, Zale,' Frank said. 'They shot a tranq dart at you. I didn't even realise what they'd done at first, but you looked like you might go a little nuts on us there. You've been out for a while. Your body needed to rest. You've had a few big days.'

He opened his eyes slowly, expecting bright lights and stark white, but they seemed to be in an old-fashioned office. Slowly turning his head, he looked around. Frank sat in a dark leather chair next to him, the leather's studs punctuating the edges. He was on a lounge of the same leather. The light was warm and the walls were lined with bookshelves. The ceiling above was a rich burgundy with inset lights, the mouldings gilded in gold filigree.

He had only seen rooms like this in the movies. There were so many books. He remembered the library back home having a book section, but these were old, leather-bound books with foiled titles on the spine. Even the leather of the couch felt real; it had that worn buffing of a well-loved leather. No one had used real leather for furniture in years. It was just too expensive to manufacture now that synthetic leather was longer lasting and looked just as good.

Zale finally managed to prop himself up without throwing up in the process. He looked over at Frank, who looked out of place in this fine room, now dressed in black coveralls of the Sphere staffers. Zale tried to talk but nothing more than a crackled gasp passed his lips.

'You need some fluids, boy,' Frank said as he brought a straw to Zale's parched lips. The water was cold and refreshing and it made his head feel less foggy. He licked his lips and coughed away the dryness.

'Where… where am I?' he croaked.

'My father's office. I thought it would be a little less overwhelming than the medical wing. That and you don't need to see the things going on down there.'

Zale swung his legs over and sat with his head in his hands.

'If you're going to throw up tell me. If you vomit on the rug the Colonel will kill me. It's pre-war. Just like the books.'

'So all this time…'

'Yes, freedom has been given and freedom has been taken away. The blanks must be controlled. All the fairy stories that have been passed down through the years are true.'

'The beasts?'

'We haven't recreated them yet. We're still trying but the technology was lost in the war when we got cut off by the wastelands.'

'The jets? Couldn't we go over to find other colonies.'

'It's not safe, Zale. We are safer in our region of security. We don't know if any other colonies of marked people even survived. The wasteland is all around us. So we stay here.'

'But how do we know the blanks and beasts still roam around past the wasteland?'

'Are you willing to risk your life to find out?'

'I… But… How can you just pretend there's nothing out there when you have the means…'

'The means, sure, but with the breeding program in its infancy and the lack of trust we have with the blanks we've trained it's not something we can risk. If a blank turned and gave away our location and details of our community, it could spell doom for us all.'

Zale looked up at Frank. His skin was sallow and his eyes red-rimmed. His scar stood out in stark contrast to the rest of his skin.

'What if I volunteered?'

'Don't be stupid, boy. You'll die out there. The savages will tear you limb from limb. That's if you make it through the wasteland. The radiation levels near the fence may be lessened now but for all we know, a few miles on and you could be in cancer country.'

'I want to see Allen.'

'He's back at Condor Point.'

'Get me Allen. Bring him here now. I know you can do that. The Colonel has the means.'

'If he comes here, you may never get back to the community you love so much.'

'Tell me truthfully. Will I, as of this moment, ever have the chance to go back with what I now know?'

Frank sighed and leaned back in his chair. He picked up the glass of scotch that sat on the side table and took a sip.

'Tell me, Frank!'

'No. As of now, you will never get back to Condor Point. Either you will be relocated to a facility to work for Sphere or you will be imprisoned if you do not wish to cooperate.'

'Then bring me Allen. Or get the Colonel on comms so I can ask him.'

'You'd be damning him to the same fate.'

'He loves me. I know he would rather be damned with me than never know where I went. I assume he would be told I was a casualty otherwise.'

'You're even smarter than I thought you were, Zale. I was impressed with how you dealt with Mrs Peters. Actually, I was impressed with how you handled all of the bunker incident. Okay, stay here. I will go talk to my father. His damnation is on your shoulders.'

'And mine is on yours.' Zale said as Frank got up and left the room. Locking it behind him.

CHAPTER TWENTY-TWO
Darnell

Darnell woke, shivering. The fire had died down in the fireplace and he had thrown his blanket off at some point. It was still early morning, he thought. Something nagged at him though, as if some unspoken warning had pulled his blankets off him to wake him.

He looked over at Coo, who was sleeping on the couch. His snores tore through the silence and were punctuated with little, gasping splutters. His blanket was cocooned around him. He was safe and tucked in tight. He couldn't do this anymore. He couldn't keep risking other people's lives for his own. Coo had nearly drowned and Roger could have been shot. And who knows what the man would have done to Ma Fran?

He decided he needed to go on alone. He padded through the cabin to the laundry to dig out his clothes. He left Coo's sitting in the hollow belly of the machine. He pulled on his jacket as he went back to jam the clothes into his pack. He pulled on his boots and backpack and headed for the door. He paused at the entry; he should leave Coo a note not to worry himself about where Darnell had gone. On the table was a note pad and pencil ready for messages and shopping lists.

He scribbled a note apologising for running off on Coo, and thanking Ma Fran for everything she had done for him. He added *send love to Roger*. He had saved Darnell's life after all.

His handwriting had never been the neatest but this would have to do. He wanted to get going before anyone woke up. He tiptoed out the door and closed it behind himself with a barely audible click. He turned to go down the stairs when a voice startled him.

'And where do you think you're going, young man?' It was Ma Fran, sitting in a weathered rattan chair behind the dog house.

'Ma, you nearly scared the life out of me. Uh, I'm just going for a walk.'

'Lies. Tell Ma where you're going,' she said as she took a long swig of her steaming cup of coffee.

'I can't risk anyone else over me. I'm going to head upstream.'

'Unless you're packing an inflatable raft, I'm not sure how you're going to achieve that,' she said, chuckling to herself. 'You were going to try and steal one, weren't you?'

'No, Ma'am, I…'

'Nonsense, I'd have done the same. I have a better idea. You're heading to Ellintown?'

'Yeah, Mum's friend lives there.'

'Joe is heading into Ellintown in an hour or two. I can get you onto his cart. What about Mayor Coo?'

'That would be great. Coo can look after himself. I've already caused too much trouble for him. Send him home if you can.'

'I'll keep him here til he's strong enough to be moved, if I can get him to stay still once he's realised you're gone.'

'I just can't…'

'Yeah I know. Well, if you're ready, let's get to Joe's. He's three houses into the forest.' Darnell could see this town would be huge but fully quiet. She placed her coffee cup down and told Darnell to follow.

It wasn't far. They passed two more cabins before they hit a third by the roadside.

'Hey Ma, what can I do for my loveliest creature today?'

'Hey Joe, you still do your run to Ellintown?'

'In fifteen minutes. You got some requests or stuff to sell?'

'Not exactly. This young man, Darnell, needs to get to Ellintown to see an old family friend. His boat got taken in the storm last night. Poor little blighter nearly drowned. I'll owe you a roast duck next time I get one.'

'Roast duck with stuffing and potatoes?'

'Deal. I'll even pop in a whiskey or two for ya,' Ma said with a chuckle. She turned to Darnell with a smile. 'There you go, Darnell. Be nice to Joe and he'll be nice back and get you where you're going.'

'Thanks, Ma Fran. For everything.'

Darnell sat down on the edge of the porch as he watched Joe secure the tarp over his wares. There wasn't much in there. He wondered why such a trip with so little.

'Okay kiddo. I have to pick up a few things along the way but we'll be in Ellintown in about four hours if that serves ya kind. You know your uncle's address?'

'Uh, no, Sir. Just his name. It's been a long time since I've seen him.'

'Well, I can get you to the City records office. Actually no, we will drop into the Jig. It's a bar that also backs onto the general store in Ellintown. Lou-Lou who runs both knows everyone and she owes me a bottle or two so I'm heading there anyway. Need to get Ned's truck too. I'm bringing back some big items and my horses are getting old.'

Darnell nodded as he climbed up on the seat next to him. Four hours seemed an awful long time. The horses began their brisk trot and after about an hour they had reached Ned's homestead. An old truck sat in front of the house. It was already stacked with pieces of scrap metal, buckets and a pig.

The horses were unbridled and taken to a barn by a young man. Darnell stood near the wagon, not wanting more people to get hurt from being near him. The two men pushed the crates into the truck and Joe tossed an apple over the top of the pen for the pig in the truck. It happily munched away on it with a squeal of delight.

The men chuckled about things and Darnell was sure Joe had forgotten about him when he heard his name.

'Darnell, come over and say hello. Ned doesn't bite or nothing.'

Darnell walked over and shook Ned's hand. He only glanced at the man's face, choosing to stare at his feet.

'You are a quiet one, aren't you?' said Ned, patting Darnell on the back of his shoulder. 'Let's get you on the way to your uncle.'

Darnell muttered a thank you as Joe looked at him.

'Hop in the truck, Darnell. I won't be long,' Joe said. The truck door slid open as he approached.

Darnell scrambled in and Joe was soon climbing in beside me.

'She don't look like much but this truck is strong as guts. Ex-City truck. They sell 'em after they hit ten years old. I could never afford one but Ned trades in scrap metal he salvages and does a few City contracts. Used to go into town himself but just can't do it anymore, so he lets me and a few other folks borrow it when we need it.'

'Don't you need a permit?'

'I have one, don't you worry about that. I used to work for the City myself. Had a permit at sixteen. I assume you don't have yours?'

'Wouldn't know what to do with it, to be honest.'

'You from the City?'

'Born there but don't remember it. Been off-grid most of my life with my mum.'

Joe turned the key in the truck and a gentle motor began to hum. 'Well, let's get you to the Jig so you can see your uncle.'

The truck lurched into life and they were off with a dust trail behind them. Darnell hadn't been in a car before as far as he remembered. It was certainly faster.

They stopped five more times on their way to Ellintown.

Darnell saw how much bigger the colonies were getting. He still couldn't fathom the size of Ellintown, much less what the big City would be like. Finally, the truck approached the entry to the town. It was a wide arch with vines entwined around its metal frame. It was big enough that three trucks on top of each other would fit height-wise, and easily four across. Next to the gate was a City Authority guard in a small gatehouse. Darnell tried to stay calm.

Joe pulled up and leaned his head out of the window.

'Hey Smithy, how are you?' he asked. The Authority looked up and cracked a smile.

'Joe! Good to see you. Long time, no see. What you bringing through today?'

'Mainly Ned's scrap. Got a pig for the farmers markets, some produce, cheese, and some quilts.'

'You heading to the Jig?'

'Where else?'

'Lou-Lou might be interested in the pig. She wants to expand her breeding stock.'

'Might head there first then.'

'You're good to go through. Might see you at the Jig tonight then?'

'Maybe so. See ya later, Smithy.'

Joe waved as he drove them through the gate. Darnell's eyes went wide at the town in front of him. It was a far sight from the colonies they had been stopping at. Even the bigger of them were still small. Ellintown was a semi-metropolis. Its buildings rose several storeys high. There were no plain houses surrounded by trees. The buildings were all glass and metal. The roads were slickly paved and the more they drove the thicker the crowds got. So many people going about their lives. How was he supposed to find one man in this City? How was this woman Lou-Lou to know a single man in a town of thousands?

They drove through the streets until they got to a street backing onto a field of land. It was the most green space he'd seen since they got here. The sign above the door proclaimed it was the Jig. Joe pulled the truck up on the side of the road between the Jig and its nearest neighbour, the Ellintower – a tower of shiny glass walls that rose into the sky.

'Here she is, kiddo,' Joe said, sliding out of his seat. 'Come on, I'll introduce you to Lou-Lou.'

They walked to the large open doors. The smell of alcohol and seared meat wafted through and hit Darnell in the face before he was even off the doorstep. The lights were dim, and tables were full of people eating and drinking. They pushed their way to the bar.

'Isn't it a bit early for people to be drinking?' Darnell asked.

'Most of em probably just got off nightshift. This is dinner for them.'

'Hey Joe, looking for Lou-Lou?' the woman behind the bar asked.

'Yeah Ginn, she here or still in bed?'

'You ask that like you think she sleeps?' Ginn said with a giggle. 'I'll go grab her from the office. You and your friend here want your usual before I go?'

'Usual for me, something softer for the kid.'

'Ah okay,' she said placing two glasses on the bar. In one she dropped three ice Cubes and a good swig of whiskey, the other got ice and some frothy liquid Darnell hadn't seen before.

'Double on the rocks for you Joe, and a lemonade for the kid. I'll be right back.'

Ginn disappeared through the wooden door behind the bar. Joe swallowed his whiskey in one gulp, reached over the bar and poured himself another.

'Drink up kid. It's sweet. You'll like it. No booze in it.'

'I'm not a kid, you know,' Darnell mumbled taking a sip. It was certainly different from anything he'd ever had. His mother and he never had anything like it at the cabin as far as he remembered.

'Yeah but you look like a deer caught in a set of headlights with all these people so I'm thinking you haven't been to big towns before either. Not something you want to do drunk.'

He finished his second drink as Ginn came through the door with a portly woman in a red dress with a mop of long black curls cascading down her back. She had an air of confidence about her but also exuded warmth. She pushed through the bar gate and wrapped her arms around Joe, kissing him on each cheek.

'Joe my dear. How are you? And how many extra whiskeys did you pour while Ginn was getting me?'

Joe laughed at this, throwing his hands up in mock surprise. She playfully whacked him in the arm.

'Smithy said you were looking for a pig.'

'You won't like it out in the pens, Joe.'

'Ha ha, not me. I've got a hog in the truck. Ned wants to sell her.'

'What's he want for her?'

'Two hundred credits.'

'I'll give him one-fifty and a bottle of single malt?'

'Sold. I also need a few other things from you.'

'Sure thing. Firstly though, who's your little friend there?' she said, nodding at Darnell.

'Oh, this is Darnell. You might be able to help him. He's looking for his uncle. No address but I thought if anyone would know him you would. What's his name again, kid?'

'Uh... Oscar Greatfoot.'

'You certainly don't look like you're related to him, at least not by blood. He is as dark as the night sky and you are sun kissed but pale. Yeah, I know him. He doesn't come in much now but one of my boys runs groceries out to him once a week. He's pretty old. Let me see if he has an order to go today.' She pulled a notebook from her pocket and flipped through it, eyes scanning the page. 'You're in luck. He has a delivery this afternoon. You can go with one of the boys. Save Joe here getting lost. He's on the outskirts of town now. You sure you want to get mixed up with him though? There's a lot of rumours flying about him. Even though he's getting on in years.'

'Like what?' Darnell asked.

'He's ex-Authority. That always comes with baggage, you know?'

Darnell nodded even though he didn't really know what she meant.

'Well, he's family,' Darnell said quietly.

***

That afternoon Darnell rode alongside the delivery boy in his van. It was an odd experience as it was much faster and smoother than the trip in with Joe. The boy didn't say much so Darnell stayed quiet. He was more used to silence, and watching the bustle of the streets around him was far more interesting than small talk. As they drove further out, the high rises made way for smaller apartments and houses, then they reached a group of lowset houses in a gated community.

'This is us,' the delivery boy said as he pulled up in front of the last house in the row. It was too much like a cardboard box for Darnell's liking and he still felt too crowded-in, even out here. He grabbed his pack, and then grabbed some of the grocery bags, while the delivery boy lifted a box out of the back of the van.

At the door, the boy elbowed the doorbell and they heard a muffled voice from inside. The door slid open to reveal a thin man with wisps of white hair tufting from his dark skin. His eyes were tinged with yellow and his skin was as wrinkled as a dropped sheet.

'Come in, come in,' he mumbled. 'Nice to see Lou-Lou finally got you a helper. Just drop the stuff on the counter. I can put it away.'

The delivery boy did just that and pulled a delivery slip out of his pocket.

'Sign please,' he said before pocketing the slip and turning to leave. Darnell had better say something.

'Uh Sir, I don't know if you remember me. My name is Darnell. My mother Sharon sent me to see you.' It seemed to take a moment but he saw the man's eyes go wide in recognition eventually.

'Darnell! I didn't recognise you. It's been so long. Come sit with me,' he said as the door slid closed. Darnell watched as the old man became rather active compared to the frail old man that he had appeared to be. He motioned for Darnell to follow him. Darnell followed him down the hall and into a small room at the back. The old man slid the door shut behind them and sat down.

'This is a safe room. No signals can get in. They monitor me now. I just know it. If you're here that means something bad has happened to your mother. I honestly thought I'd never see you before I died.'

'How did you know my mother?'

'We worked together. I helped her leave the City. Promised her I'd be there for you if you ever needed me. Help you to integrate. I'm a bit long in the tooth but my mind is still all there. She left me a box for you.' He got up and opened the cupboard, pulling a wooden box from the shelf. It was plain save a wood-burned design on the top.

'Your dad made this for her. She wanted to make sure you got it.' He passed the box over and Darnell held its weight with a heavy heart. A box would never fill the hole his mother had left. He flipped the latch and opened the lid. In it was a box of photos, an envelope and a box of money. There was plenty there. He could go anywhere he wanted.

'You can stay here tonight. We'll work out what to do with you. We can get you artificially marked, and get you a fake citizen ID. Any ideas where you want to settle?'

'I want to go home.'

'Back to the big city? I guess. I can try and get onto your dad...'

'No. I want to go back to the cabin. That's my home. When you think it'll be safe, that's where I need to go.'

'It'll never be safe there.'

'But...'

'But nothing, it'll never be safe. I think we should settle you in a township. Not too big, not too small. Enough people to not be noticed in but too many to get personal. I need to make some calls. Stay here.' With that, he got up and left Darnell alone in the room. The door locked with a click. Darnell tried the handle but it wasn't budging.

He was getting sick of being locked in places against his will. He sat on the floor and started looking through the pictures in this wooden box of his mother's. After a few minutes the door unlocked and the old man pushed his pack through the opening.

'It's safer for you in here. They can't scan you.'

Then the door was closed again. After rifling through all the things in the box, Darnell started moving things out of his bag to make room. He had money now, so he pulled out some food to eat. Next to the cans, he had placed the notebook about Ava. He really should have left this behind. He wasn't sure how to get it back to Coo. Maybe Lou-Lou would be able to help with it. He ate and flicked through the pages, reading snippets here and there. He was bored but looking around the room turned up nothing more than empty cupboards and empty drawers.

He finished his meal and sat on the floor to get comfortable. The chair had become hard against his back. He strained his ears to listen for any noise outside, but apart from the random shuffling of the old man walking past and the odd mumbling it was mostly quiet. Suddenly the door flew open. It smacked against the wall with a crash. He pushed himself into the corner. A woman stood in the doorway. The old man cowering behind her.

'I'm sorry, Darnell. I'm so sorry.'

Darnell flicked his eyes between the two. The woman was dressed head to toe in black, her features sharp, her dark hair tied back tight against her scalp, a pink scar shining across her throat.

'Darnell Anderson. You are under arrest for fighting against the Authority. You will be remanded to the Sphere. You have no rights. Please stand and turn away with your hands behind your back. Failure to comply may result in injury and or death.' She spoke with no emotion, her voice a monotone, robotic and trained. He stood but couldn't take his eyes off her. He knew that face.

'Turn around, Darnell, before I need to draw my weapon.'

He was stunned but finally found his voice.

'Ava?'

CHAPTER TWENTY-THREE
Almara

'Almara, are you under there?'

It was Ahn. In the dim light I could see his eyes searching for me in the gloom.

'Yes,' I whispered. 'Come under with me.'

Ahn squeezed himself under the bed next to me. There wasn't much room but it was going to be the safest option for us both. If they found Ahn, I was as good as dead.

'I think they killed him,' Ahn said.

'What? Killed who?'

'Jaylon. It went silent so quickly. I didn't mean for him to get hurt.'

I could hear Ahn suppress a sob. The Authority started to kick at the locked door of the cabin. I could hear the wood start to splinter and the weight of their bodies slamming through. They stumbled in as the door gave way. I took a deep breath and tried to hold it. The silence was deafening.

They started to trash the living area. I heard smashing pottery and snapping wood. Broken furniture was thrown, and I smelled smoke from the fire wafting through the air. They were going to burn the cabin down. We had to get out. Their heavy boots stomped towards the bedroom door. I felt my heart thudding in my head. I slowly let out the breath that I was holding and tried to breathe as quietly as possible. Ahn was still sobbing but he was down to the silent shake of his body.

The Authority shoved into the room and smashed and kicked at anything that wasn't tied down or too heavy move. They pulled the blankets off the bed and rifled through the belongings on the low shelves against the wall.

From above the noise of smashing items, I heard a wail of pain and then the sound of Jaylon beginning his ranting.

'You bastards! What are you doing to my place? I'll set you bastards on fire.'

He smashed his way towards the Authority and I heard the thud as someone hit the floor.

'I'll teach you to touch my stuff!'

A second thud hit the ground. I peered out through the gap between the valance and the floor. The Authority people lay sprawled across the floor.

'Where are you poppets hidin? You still alive in here? Help me put out this damn fire. Bastards.'

I wiggled out from my hiding spot and saw Ahn doing the same on his side of the bed. But after that I froze. The bitter smell of the smoke burnt my nostrils. I had never really dealt with fire and had no idea what to do next.

'Jaylon! You're okay. I was sure they'd killed you,' Ahn said. Jaylon was standing there with blood dripping down his face, a large branch in his hand, the end tipped with gore.

'They got me a good 'un but I'm tougher than they realised. The smoke brought me around. They broke my garden, so my garden broke them. Now come on, before the whole place burns down.'

Ahn grabbed my hand and we rushed out to the well and began passing buckets of water into the house until the flames were out. So much was ruined in the house. The furniture in the lounge was black with soot and the window glass had shattered. I started picking up the sodden items on the floor that were salvageable and laid them out on the porch to dry. Ahn and Jaylon went into the bedroom and stripped the Authority folks to their underwear. I saw Ahn hand Jaylon the money from their pockets.

I helped them put the Authority guys into Jaylon's cart before they took them away down towards the farms. A few empty whiskey bottles and they would be found in such a position that they would never be believed. The bloody stick Jaylon had whacked them with went too.

When they got back I had finished moving the wet items onto the porch and the ruined objects into a pile by the side of the house.

'Saved as much as I could,' I said, nodding to the spread of items. 'The window is gone so you might want to board that up and I'm not sure if the couch will survive.'

'All good, lassie. I'll get back on my feet soon enough. I can salvage most the garden and I have a larder with enough supplies in it until it's back. Ahn said you might get some use out of those uniforms so they're all yours.'

'I'm just glad you're safe. Do you think they'll come back?' I asked as I picked up my bag.

'If they do it'll be on their own terms so I can shoot them for trespassing. Out of uniform they can't do a thing. In it they won't come back or I'll report them for setting the fire.'

Ahn came back outside with his bag, shoving the uniforms in as he approached.

'We better hit the road.'

'Take their truck. I don't want it nearby and it might get you where you're going a little faster. It should be out on the road at the end of the trail through the trees. If it's a new-fangled one with the back windows you'll be set for a peaceful drive.'

We said our goodbyes and went up the trail. I only looked back once, to see Jaylon on his hands and knees, already replanting uprooted fruit trees.

'Do you think he'll be all right, Ahn?'

'Folks like him go on forever. I'm sure he'll be fine.'

The path began to open up as we neared the road. I could see the back end of a black car. It was shiny and new with a City crest on each door. The windows were heavily tinted and it looked like it would be good in all terrains. I tried the door handle; it was unlocked so I hopped in the passenger side and threw my pack in the back seat as Ahn got behind the wheel.

He pulled the keys from his pocket and closed the door. I hadn't been in a car for so long but the small space and new plastic smell brought back memories from when I was a child. My mother took me to the City doctor every year the day before my birthday for them to see if I had got my mark yet. They would run test after test. Trying to work out what part of my genetics had eaten away at the mark. I remember the look in my mother's eyes while they jabbed me and spoke about me as though I wasn't there. Tears welled in them and behind the smile she plastered on her face, I could always see and sense her fear and apprehension. Now I knew why.

She knew one day they might take me away. That whatever agreement she had struck with the Authority to let me stay in the community would be wiped clean and she would lose me. Or that one of those needles they gave me would be poison instead of gene therapy. I don't know what they were putting into me but I'd be sick for days after. Sometimes my skin would itch and flake; one time my hair started falling out. And she saw all this happen knowing that it was keeping me with her.

I felt my heart begin to race as Ahn started the car. It gently rumbled into life. The pane behind the wheel lit up and a voice began to talk.

'Welcome back, officers,' it said, a little too sweetly. 'Your battery is at seventy-four percent. Without sunlight or recharging you have twenty-one hours of battery remaining. Drive mode: auto drive off. Please fasten your seatbelts before the vehicle is in motion. Thank you.'

We both looked at each other and shrugged, following the request for seatbelts. Better safe than sorry I guessed. After we had both clicked in, the voice continued. 'Seatbelts engaged. Drive mode: auto drive off. Thank you.'

Ahn smiled and we began to drive. I stared out the

window, looking at a world I hadn't seen in so many year pass by me. I was lost in thought when I felt the car pull to a stop. I jolted awake, expecting the worst. All I could think was we were surrounded by Black Sphere operatives. Ahn turned off the ignition and got out of the car.

'Ahn?' I called quietly after him. 'Ahn, where are we?'

'Just need to stretch my legs. You should too. We're about five minutes from a small town. We should see if these uniforms fit us in case we have to get out of the car.'

I hopped out and went around to Ahn, who was sizing up the uniforms. He kept the bigger of the two and tossed me the other.

'Mine might be a tad snug, yours a tad long but we should get away with it.'

We both stripped down and changed. I had to roll the sleeves and pants legs up a little but we both looked convincing. We got back in and drove into town. It wasn't all that big but the tech it held meant we were nearing the City central zone. Shuttle buses zoomed through and City monitors were on every corner. The tinted windows should keep us unnoticed but getting out would be the unsafe option. Ahn negotiated traffic and we decided to drive through if we could.

'After this town, if we head north I should be able to drive straight through to the main highway up to the outer parts of Oasis.'

I could see the signpost for the northern areas; we were nearly free of the City monitors. All of a sudden, a woman jumped in front of the car waving her arms. Ahn went to slam on the brakes but the auto braking kicked in.

'Vehicle auto brake engaged. Collision averted,' the car sang back at us.

'Help me!' the woman begged, running to Ahn's window and slamming her fists onto the glass. I jumped in my seat, startled by her unexpected panic. 'Help me please.'

Ahn looked at me and I shrugged. If we kept driving, it

would be suspicious for an Authority officer to ignore a plea for help. But if we got out, we might get picked up on the City monitors. Ahn lowered his window to halfway, enough to see the woman face to face.

'How can I be of assistance, Ma'am?' he said, trying to keep his voice calm. I turned my head so she couldn't see me. I'm sure out of the two of us, if they had put out a wanted notice, it would be my face that would be widest spread. The woman looked panicked and I almost expected her to try to crawl in through the window.

'I'm being followed. There's a man following me and I think he has a gun. Please, can you get him?'

'Uh, Ma'am, we don't have any restraints on hand as we're a… archival team, not combat trained. But we can take you to the Authority station. They will send out a collection team for the man.'

Then please, take me to the Authority station. I'm worried he's going to get me.'

He glanced over at me again.

'Uh, hop in, Ma'am. We're from another town so you'll have to give us directions.'

She got into the back and pulled the door closed. She was shaking and her eyes were wide. Her breathing was so ragged, she had to have been running.

'You're safe with us, Ma'am. Now, which way are we going?'

She directed us to a large white building with the City crest emblazoned on the double storey doors. I remembered these doors from my own City. City buildings looked the same in every town, it seemed. Ahn pulled up at the front and the woman got out.

'Are you not coming in?' she asked.

'No Ma'am, we were just driving through. Head on in. We'll wait here til you're inside.'

'Thank you, officers,' she said as she slammed the door and took off up the stairs. Ahn wound up the window and sighed with relief. We started driving through the City again and soon were back at the town line. As we went past the sign for the northern towns, a red light began to flash on the dashboard.

'That doesn't look good,' I said to Ahn.

'Do you think we should just ignore it?'

'How would I know? I've been living in a Cube most of my life.'

The car began to slow.

'Authority car forty-three, you are now leaving your designated area. Please turn back or submit outer area authorisation.'

'Oh shit,' Ahn mumbled. The car came to a halt.

'Authority car forty-three, you are now leaving your designated area. Please turn back or submit outer area authorisation. Failure to comply will result in auto drive being activated.'

'Shit, shit, shit. Get out of the car, Almara.'

I pulled at the door handle but the locks had engaged. We were trapped.

'Just drive back into town,' I yelled. Ahn tried to commandeer the steering but it was too late. The red flashing light was now a steady red glow.

'Auto drive activated. Please remain seated.'

The steering wheel folded and disappeared into the dash and the pedals sank into the floor.

'I'm sorry, Almara. I'm so sorry,' Ahn said softly.

'Ahn where are we going?' He said nothing, just lowered his head into his hands. 'Ahn. Look at me. Where are we going?'

'The City. It'll take us back into the City if we're lucky.'

'How is that lucky?'

'The other option is the Black Sphere. Hope for the City, Almara. Hope that's as far as we go.'

As the car began to move, the windows turned solid black so we couldn't see out. I felt the seatbelt tighten slightly over my chest. I thought I was going to throw up. I tried the door once more. It wouldn't budge and the windows wouldn't go down either. I looked over at Ahn. He hadn't moved, his face still in his hands.

'Don't you give up on me, Ahn. Don't you dare.'

'I'm so sorry. We're going to be arrested. Treason charges. We... we... oh, we are so going into suspended animation. Almara, I should have let you stay in the Cube. At least you could have lived a longer life. They will put you down or worse. I'm so sorry.'

I reached out and slapped him across the back of his head.

'Snap out of it, Ahn. We can do this. Pull your shit together, man. Don't just give up on me!'

He looked up at me with wide, red-rimmed eyes and I saw a look in them that I hadn't seen in my life. It was hollow and dark.

'I'm so sorry, Almara. I want you to know that it wasn't my choice.'

'What wasn't your choice?'

'It was all the truth, everything I told you was the truth. Please don't doubt me.'

'Ahn what are you talking about? Of course I believe you.'

'You won't. You'll think it was all lies but I promise there's a reason. I never wanted you to get hurt.'

'Ahn, this isn't your fault.'

'Yes. Yes, it is.'

'How? Tell me how this is your fault.'

'They have my daughter.'

'Who has your daughter?'

'Sphere has my daughter. They threatened to kill her like they did to my wife.'

'Why do they have your daughter?'

'They needed leverage. I knew too much. Then they gave me a mission. To test my loyalty, to test you.'

'Loyalty?'

'They think I'm loyal to them but my loyalty lies squarely

with my daughter. I haven't seen her in years and they only allow me a letter once a month. If I didn't they would take the last part of my reason for living away.'

'Ahn, what are you trying to say?'

'This was all part of the plan. I give you to Sphere after testing you in the field, they give me my daughter and let us live out our lives in a City apartment with a meaningless office job for me and an education for her. A nice City pension at the end. I had to do it. Forgive me.'

'Ahn... Ahn, are you saying this was all some test for me?'

'For us both I guess.'

I sat in silence. I could hear Ahn sobbing softly. He was obviously remorseful. I on the other hand was just angry. Not at him. He was doing what he had to. The black windows allowed no light through. The ceiling lights merely reflected my own face back at me. Where my eyes were in my reflection were merely dark smudges in the pale vista of my face. Maybe I really was a monster.

'How long?' I asked looking back over at Ahn.

'What?' he replied, looking like I'd pulled him from a deep sleep plagued with nightmares.

'How long do I have until we get to Sphere? How long do I have as a free person?'

'About an hour but you won't notice it.'

'Why? What does that mean?'

'Sedation should kick in soon.'

'You drugged me?'

'No, they drugged us both. The air filtering into the car since the windows blacked out has been laced with a sedative. We should start to feel sleepy soon.' He yawned as though trying to prove himself. 'There's no way to escape it.'

'But why would they...' My head started spinning a little and my mouth felt dry.

'Your kind are considered dangerous and you've been selected for black level. That, and they don't really trust me fully. They know I was doing this against my will. Now we are this far they see it as insurance.'

'I… I don't feel too well,' I mumbled.

'It's okay. When you wake up we'll be there.'

Spots started dancing in my vision. I heard Ahn mutter the word sorry before I went under.

CHAPTER TWENTY-FOUR
Darnell

'What did you call me?' she said, her hand coming off her weapon. Her eyes, once sharp and emotionless, seemed to soften and go wide.

'Ava. You're Ava. Your uncle helped me.'

'My... uncle?'

'Coo. Your uncle Coo. He's been looking for you... for so, so long. I have his book. Look.'

Darnell picked the book up from where it dropped from his lap. He flipped it open to the picture sketched in ink. It was a few years old, and she'd become leaner and sharper in the face but there was no mistaking that it was her.

She snatched it from him, hands shaking slightly. Flipping the pages, she saw images of herself as she grew up flicking past.

'I haven't heard my name in such a long time. Ava. I remember being called that.' She shook her head as though trying to free a memory.

'Ava, what have they done to you?'

'I've... I've been enhanced. I'm useful like this. Not just a genetic anomaly.'

'You're still a person, Ava.'

'I'm a BGM. I'm strong now. I am number 042. If you play your cards right, you could be a BGM too.'

'You're not a number. You're Ava. Daughter of Cora. Niece of Coo. You are not just your genetic status.'

'I… I…'

'Ava.'

'I'm… Ava. It feels wrong. That is no longer my name.'

'Let me go, Ava. Let me go back home to my cabin. Let me live out my life in peace. Let me bury my mother.'

'Your mother. In the cabin?'

'You know?'

'I shot her.'

'Is she dead?'

'No, she's not. She's sedated while they heal her.'

'Take me to her.'

'That means going to the Sphere. From there you will never leave.'

'I have to see her. I just want to see her one last time.'

'If you don't become Black Sphere you will end up in suspended animation until your mind is liquefied.'

'Just take me, Ava. But promise me something?'

'What?'

'Contact Coo. He misses you. And get out if you can. Hell, go to my cabin. Live out your years there. Just learn who you are again. Find the person you truly are. Find Ava.'

She tucked the book into one of the pockets of her pants, and stepped forward towards Darnell.

'I have to restrain you.'

'I understand.'

She pulled a pair of restraints off her belt and fastened them around his wrists. She picked up his bag, zipping it closed, and motioned for him to follow her.

'You've killed several of my colleagues.'

'You tried to kill my mother.'

She looked over at him and nodded. 'Fair enough.'

She pulled him into the black van parked outside the house. She slid the door closed and plunged him into darkness.

The ride was bumpy and Darnell was jolted awake several

times but when the van finally stopped and he heard the engine turn off, he became more alert than ever. He expected the doors to open but they remained shut, keeping him in the dark. He could hear muffled voices outside but couldn't make out any words. Finally, after what felt like forever, the van door slid open, the bright light blinding him momentarily.

'Be quiet. I've told them you're drugged and require medical attention. I'm going to take you to see your mother.'

Ava pulled him out and shouldered his pack. Darnell's eyes still felt blurry from lack of sleep and the bright lights, so pretending to be out of it was no more an effort than dragging his feet a little. He wanted to look around. He could see the white of the walls, a metal strip dividing it in two. The floor was black and glossy, a blurred reflection starring back at him. His shoes squeaked as he walked, the only other noise was the clicking of Ava's boots.

They reached a set of double doors that she pushed them through. Beyond was a bustling emergency room full of beds and rushing doctors. They took a door to their left and entered into a long hallway. It was quieter here. Halfway down the hall she stopped him, scanning her hand on the security panel. He heard a click as the door unlocked. The room was small. It held only one bed, but it looked almost cosy.

He'd expected a prison cell, but the light was a warm yellow, the room was a pale green and the woman in the bed was dressed in a pale yellow gown. A tube snaked into her arm from a drip of clear fluid and her vitals beeped steadily along on the monitor next to her. She was asleep. A thick bandage wound itself around her throat and Darnell noticed other dressings under the gown.

She was alive. Against all odds, he'd found her.

'Is she…'

'She's lightly sedated but you should be able to wake her.'

'The bandages?'

'She was shot several times. Med gel has been used but they won't use the stem gel on prisoners, so she had to undergo some surgery. I'm afraid she can't talk anymore. The damage to her voice box was too severe.'

Darnell walked over to the bed and stared at his mother's almost lifeless form. He saw her gently breathing, but the rise and fall of her chest was shallow. He placed his hand on her arm. With the restraints holding his wrists together, it was awkward but he'd get around it. She felt so much thinner after only a few days.

'Mum? Mum it's me, Darnell.' He shook her arm a little. He didn't want to shock her awake. He saw her eyes flutter but they remained closed. 'Mum?'

Finally they began to open and stay open. She was looking at him blankly but then she finally connected with what she was seeing. Her eyes went wide. She tried to move to hug him but winced at the pain. A croaked whisper escaped her lips.

'Don't move, Mum. You've been hurt. You can't talk. But yes, it's me.'

She smiled up at him. He hugged her, overwhelmed, and knelt down to be on her eye level. She looked around the room until her eyes settled on Ava. The look of terror that crossed her face was one he wouldn't soon forget. She tried to talk again, but hoarse whispered breath and flailing arms were her only available reactions. She winced in pain at the movement.

'It's okay, Mum. I know. This is Ava. I know she hurt you but she's helping me. She let me come and see you. She didn't have to.'

Darnell's mother's heartrate was beeping a quick staccato beat on the monitor and he patted her arm to try to calm her down. She nearly pulled the drip from her arm with her flailing. She was trying in vain to talk with her hands, realising her voice would do her no good.

'Mum,' he said gripping her arm. 'It's okay.'

'Mrs Anderson,' Ava said, still standing on the far side of the room, 'I'm not going to hurt you. Darnell asked to see you and I wanted to make it up to you both. I'm sorry. I... I was made to follow orders. I was only doing my job. Darnell is showing me an alternative.'

She finally started to calm down but Darnell could feel that her limbs remained tense.

'Darnell, we have to go,' Ava said.

'But we only just got here.'

'And if the doctors do rounds and see us in here, all three of us will end up spending our lives in suspension. Say goodbye to your mother.'

'Will she ever get out of here?'

'If we leave now, and don't get caught, then yes.'

Darnell looked between Ava and his mother. He didn't want to leave her side, but if it meant the chance that his mother may eventually be released he would do whatever he could.

'I love you, Mum. If I can, I'll come back to see you again, okay?'

A tear rolled down her cheek and she opened her mouth to speak before remembering that nothing would come out. She clutched his hand, kissing it tenderly as Ava ushered him out the door, her fingers sliding free when he got too far away from her. He looked back at her and he felt like someone had punched him in the stomach. He finally had her back, and then she was gone again. He held back the sob that was tearing up his throat, and turned away from her as she gave a weak wave at him.

'Where am I going?' he said, emotion stripped from his voice to hold it in check.

'The black room.'

'Do I dare ask?'

'You'll be processed and sent into sensory deprivation. I assume you will end up in black level training, working with the other BGMs. You managed to take several people out without any training so with a few modifications you'll be a top notch BGM agent.'

'But I didn't mean to take ANYONE out!'

'Even better. It means you have the instinct somewhere inside you.'

'I don't get any say in this, do I?'

'You will. You choose BGM training or the testing floor. I doubt they would bother with suspension for a blank to be honest. You either become a living, human pin cushion, or a cadaver human pin cushion.'

They exited the med ward and she directed him to the elevator at the end of the hall. She scanned her hand again and the doors opened.

'Unauthorised passenger detected. No citizen chip detected. Proceed to processing and black room.' The elevator chimed. Darnell had never been in an elevator before. It felt at first like the floor was going to fall out from underneath him. It lurched as it came to a stop and the doors slid open, revealing a grey room with a metal desk in the middle. An overweight, older woman sat behind the desk, coughing into a large floral handkerchief. She looked up, pushing her glasses back up the bulbous nose.

'Can I help you, Agent?' she asked, her voice rough and gravelly. She seemed to be bored even at the prospect of helping them.

'New recruit for BGM testing,' Ava said, pushing him towards the desk.

'Do you have the paperwork completed?'

'Sorry, no. This was a last-minute capture from the Colonel.'

'You need to complete these,' the handkerchief woman said, passing a clipboard over to Ava.

They went over to the metal bench against the wall. The room was cold.

'So do I need to...' Darnell began.

'No, I'll fill these out. It'll be faster. I know your file. I have a photographic memory thanks to my modifications.'

'Ava?'

'Don't call me that here. You will refer to me only as Agent.'

'Agent then. What happens to my stuff?' he said, nodding towards his pack.

'It will be sorted. Food and weapons will be removed. Civilian clothing and personal items will be stored until you are assigned a room. If you are selected to be an agent, you will have access to these items unless they are deemed dangerous. By the time they finish your training though you may not want reminders of your past. I was young when I came here so I had nothing but the clothes on my back, as do most BGMs. Having someone of your age come in is rarer, but after the modifications are completed and your objectives are planted in your mind, most prefer to leave it behind because you can't ever go back.'

'Has anyone ever tried to go back?'

'A few. Most are killed. A few are banished. The rest get their minds wiped and are sent to the medical labs as test subjects.'

'They use us as lab rats?'

'Pretty much. The rats don't seem to last as long.' She smiled a crooked smile at him. She had meant it as a joke but Darnell felt cold.

'There's no way out of here now, is there?'

'No, not really. I will see if I can convince the Colonel to release your mother. He has a soft spot for me. Apparently, I look like his long dead daughter. She will be able to go back to the cabin and live out her life in peace there. Or return to the City to live with your father.'

'But I'm either to become like you or a lab rat.'

'Or a corpse. The former is obviously the better option. It's not too bad. You'll be faster and stronger than anyone else and they look after you, feed you, educate you and in between missions, the Sphere isn't too bad a place to be.'

'But I become a monster. I have to kill people.'

'Kill or be killed, Darnell.' She finished off the last form and pressed her thumb to the registration square at the bottom. It glowed before showing a shadow of her thumbprint.

They went back to the desk. The woman didn't look up. Ava stood staring at her. When the woman still didn't look up after a few moments, Ava dropped the clipboard onto the desk. The woman looked up slowly.

'Please place personal belongings in the crate provided and attach this label.' She handed Ava a large sticker with 643 printed on it. 'Then proceed to testing room twelve for assessment. Stay with the subject until the adjudicator arrives.'

She motioned towards the double doors behind her. Ava placed Darnell's bag into the crate. 'Empty your pockets, Darnell. You won't want anything but your clothes on you.'

He did as he was told until his pockets were empty. Ava stuck the label onto the side of the crate and led Darnell through the double doors. Beyond the doors was a black hallway. The walls and ceiling now matched the dark floor. Thin strip lighting ran down the centre of the ceiling and small glowing numbers were illuminated on each of the doors.

At door twelve, Ava knocked. When there was no answer, she opened the door on a dark room. There was no light until they stepped across the threshold. Bright white light flooded the room as the door clicked closed behind them. A metal bench sat against one wall. The wall opposite the door sported another door of blackened frosted glass.

'I will be back for you after they finish your deprivation session. Just do as you're told.'

The frosted glass door slid open and a small woman stepped through. She was dressed in a suit of soft grey fabric, her white shirt buttoned tight around her throat. Her blonde hair hung to her shoulders, dead straight and streaked with grey. Without another word Ava left.

The woman approached Darnell and undid his restraints. The frosted door slid open again and she pulled him through it into darkness.

CHAPTER TWENTY-FIVE
Zale

Zale sat in the book-lined room for hours. He watched the clock hands tick past until he couldn't stand it anymore. He had paced the room, he had pulled books from the shelves and pushed them back, unread. He was going stir-crazy. The urge to pull the books from the shelves and throw them at the ticking clock was growing as the incessant noise grated at his nerves. He needed to use the bathroom and his stomach had begun to growl.

His eyes scanned the room for a way to communicate with the outside world but there was nothing he could see, not even a computer hidden in the desk. This room was purely archaic. He had more tech back in his cabin at Condor Point.

He went to the doors, large and doublewide and made from the same dark timber as the rest of the room. He banged his fists against them.

'Hey? Let me out!'

The doors barely rattled. The wood must be a veneer on top of metal. He was screwed. He bashed again. Even if it was futile, it would at least help his rising rage level.

'Goddammit, Frank! Open this fucking door!'

He heard a click and reached for the handle but before he had a chance, he saw it turn and it swung out away from his hand.

'Is that language necessary, Zale?' It was Frank. He held a tray in his other hand, which had food and two bottles of drink on it.

'I've been in here for hours. I need the bathroom.'

Frank placed the tray down on the desk. 'This way, son.' He led him down the hall to a communal bathroom. When he'd finished, Frank was waiting for him at the door.

'Let's go get you fed and watered and have a chat,' Frank said, returning to the study. Zale followed after him. He was getting rather hungry. They sat and ate, although Frank did more talking than anything.

'I've spoken to the Colonel. One of our operatives in Condor Point will get Allen for you. But I will ask you again, are you sure you want to bring him here?'

'Can I go back to him?'

'No. Your life is here now, at least until we know where your loyalties lie.'

'Then he comes here. You can tell him whatever you want but I'd prefer if he knew the truth before he left.'

'I can arrange that. We need to get you settled and debriefed. And organise for you to be trained in something useful. You won't have any security clearance just yet, but we have civilian-level jobs and living areas. You may end up cleaning or dishwashing but the pay is fair and everything you need is on site.'

'What about our families?'

'The ones you haven't spoken to in years? They'll know as much as they do now. I've looked you up, Zale. I haven't spent the past hours chatting to my dad about the clouds. I have your citizen file on my desk, along with Allen's. Neither of you has made contact with your families since you moved to Condor Point. In all the excitement, the Condor Point residents will assume you've been taken.'

'Who's the operative in the Point?'

'We have a few. Most legitimately want to be there. The newest, that doctor fellow Greyson, agreed in order to keep his sister from being pulled into the program – she's a blank. They escaped us, for years. Had her living in a hidden room in the basement of their house. He hadn't met his mate, so it was just the two of them. She was a smart girl. We could have made her a fine BGM. He said he'd do anything, so we held him to that. Trained him up, her too and sent him up to the Point.'

'That explains his sharp shooting.'

'He was a fast study. So was she. If they ever change their mind on where they want to be, they will fit into our programs quite well. I think he liked the idea of her being able to live freely, seeing she never had before. Now,' he said, wiping his hands briskly, 'we need to take you down to residential and get you signed in. There will be some paperwork, but that can wait until we get Allen here. Save the double up.'

'We can live together?'

'We have a few couple's rooms. Normally for matched pairs but Colonel has signed off on it for the two of you. But expect a few looks. The City rules are fairly indoctrinated here – nowhere near as accepting as the Point.'

'We lived with that for years before moving to the Point, we can get used to it again.'

'Well, follow me,' Frank said gathering the tray and bottles up and heading out the door.

The residential area was a rabbit warren of hallways on the second floor above ground level of the Sphere. Row upon row of white doors with numbers stencilled on them stretched out in front of him.

'451 is vacant. It's nothing fancy but very few rooms here are. You get a room, kitchenette and bathroom. You'll be given uniforms, and civilian clothes can be purchased from the vendors here.'

Frank passed a swipe card key to him. 'This is yours, don't lose it. Please don't leave the room until I get back. Go have a shower. There's a uniform in there that should fit, and then have a rest if you can. The City Ordinance and Sphere rules are on the table. I recommend you read them so you understand what is expected.'

Zale swiped the key card and the door slid open. The room was so basic and simple. It was almost clinical. But Frank was right, he needed a shower. Walking past the table with the two manuals on it, he found the bathroom, a towel, soap and uniform waiting for him on the countertop.

He'd flicked through the manuals on the table but wasn't really retaining anything. He wasn't ready to be indoctrinated completely. There was a television screen but when he turned it on, there was nothing more than static. He flicked it off and flopped on the sofa. He didn't plan on sleeping , he was too nervous. He startled at the sound of the door sliding open. Frank stood there with Allen. He was a sight for sore eyes.

Zale jumped up and threw himself at his true mate.

'You came,' he whispered into his chest, his voice cracking with raw emotion.

'Of course I did. I would have gone into the Badlands to be with you.'

'That was nearly an option,' Frank said with a laugh. Zale and Allen turned to face him.

'Frank, that's not funny,' Zale said.

'Wait, that happens?' Allen demanded.

'I'll leave Zale to fill you in on the goings-on. You're a permanent resident as long as you pass probation.'

'And if we don't?' Zale asked.

'Please refer to section seven of your citizen manual. I'll leave you folks to it. There's a computer terminal in the coffee table. Your log-on details are in there too. Your work orders are emailed every Friday. Training starts tomorrow at nine. I'll come get you at eight forty-five.'

Zale nodded. Allen still looked stunned at everything happening around him. The door closed behind Frank. Zale went over to the couch and Allen followed.

'He was joking, right?'

'Let's see,' Zale said.

He flicked to section seven: Law and Order in Black Sphere. He ran his finger down the index for the section until he found the section marked Probation. He skimmed the first part which ran over training, and penalties for being late or obstinate. Then at the end was a section marked *Failure to meet probation.*

'Should a Sphere resident fail to meet probation requirements, be it through behaviours or inability to be trained, the resident shall be imprisoned if the behaviours are believed to be rectifiable. If behaviours are not rectifiable or violate one of the laws listed in section seven point three, resident will be moved to a secure facility if of use, or will be banished out of Oasis.'

'Holy shit, they can do that?' Allen exclaimed.

'Honestly I wouldn't put it past them. I'm surprised they don't just euthanise people who aren't of use.'

'Well it certainly explains why everyone is so... obedient here.'

'We should probably read this stuff then call it a night. Early morning for us both. Go grab a shower and I'll get food ready.'

The next morning, Zale and Allen were up early. They were used to rising with the sun in Condor Point. Even without the sun to alert them, their internal body clocks seemed to still be in sync. They had read the manuals through and most of it was fairly straightforward. Destructive behaviours were not tolerated, nor was tardiness or substance use. Neither of them smoked and they had never been big alcohol drinkers at the Point, so it was of no great consequence to them. The thing they worried about though was not being able to speak up about what they were required to do in the Sphere. For their level of clearance most the jobs would be reasonably mundane, but if they saw anything they were not to question it.

Zale had always been a little outspoken. He struggled to ignore injustice and some of the practices here were most likely to raise his eyebrows at least. Allen would remain silent but things would gnaw at him. It worried Zale what this could do to them. And if they got enhanced security clearance, what would they have to do?

The door buzzed as Frank arrived. They had nothing to take with them. Zale felt odd being emptyhanded and in the plain uniform. Like he'd been stripped of all personality. He reached for Allen's hand and he gripped it hard.

'You might want to restrain from public affection. At least until folks get used to you,' Frank said, nodding at their hands. 'I know you're a bit nervous, first day an' all, but it's okay. I've got you something nice an' easy to do, training will be just the one day, then you'll be working. I've even managed to get you on the same shift roster. It's not in a public area so you won't need to interact too much, except at meal times if you eat in the mess hall. Be good to start doing that too. Get people used to you being together and all. No one will start anything but you will get odd looks and some may not socialise much with you. Most keep to themselves.' He handed them the booklets he carried in his big hands.

'Take these. They're your idiot's guide to your new job. I also have these,' he said, handing them two small glass tablets. 'They're comm devices but until you get out of probation they can only be used as a map and to check your work order emails. Press your finger on the screen for five seconds then you can either scroll through the location directory or search for specific rooms. If it's blue you can go there. Red is restricted.'

They had been wandering through the halls and Zale was certain they would never be able to find their way back without these new toys. Frank stopped in front of a large frosted glass door. The plaque above the door was just a number. *Was everything in this place just numbers?* Zale thought to himself.

The doors slid open silently and more of the same clinical white walls and white plastic furniture awaited them.

'How do you get around here without getting lost?

Everything looks the same.

Frank laughed. 'You get used to it after a while. The numbers start making more sense and then you start to notice the little things.'

'Like what? The angle of the seats?'

'Look towards the edge of the floor. There are thin coloured lines. Each section has a colour. You follow the line to get to the section. Or just use the fancy toys I just gave you. Here we are, boys. Training room thirty-four. Your trainer is Susan. Welcome to the world of Deprivation tank monitoring.'

'Wait, what? Deprivation what?'

'Deprivation tank monitoring. It's okay. You're not going in one. You just sit and monitor them.'

'But there are people in them?'

'Yes, it's our way of deprogramming blanks before we train them. They're only in there for a few months at most.'

'A few months?'

'They settle after a few days. Then you just make sure they don't have a seizure or pull out their tubing.'

'And if that happens?'

'We euthanise them.'

CHAPTER TWENTY-SIX
Almara

I could hear mumbling. There had to be people outside the car. I tried to open my eyes but they remained closed against my will. I tried to move but I couldn't even manage a toe wiggle, let alone anything useful. I realised I wasn't sitting up anymore. The muffled voices were getting clearer. Where was I?

Red swirls danced in front of my eyes as lights were turned on. Finally I felt my eyelids flicker. Pins and needles began to prickle at my face but I still didn't have a full range of movement. I strained to open my eyes. It felt like lifting a barrel over my head. Eventually, I managed it but the light above me was blinding so I shut them tight again. The voices were now clear and I certainly wasn't in the car anymore. I opened my eyes just a little, trying to minimise the light abuse.

I saw the people in the room as black smudges in the corner. Two of them. Memories began flooding back into my head. Ahn. Ahn had done this. But they had his daughter. I hoped Black Sphere would keep their word but I doubted it. He knew too much and he was merely fodder to them.

'How long until we can talk to her?' I heard one of the voices ask. I shut my eyes completely and pretended to be asleep.

'The other guy is still out cold and he's bigger so she might be a while yet.'

'Yeah but he's normal. She's one of them.'

'Very true, can't be too careful with them. She's strapped in though, so we should be okay. The arms and legs are usually the last to get feeling back after that much gas. So, if we can catch her before she gets all feeling back it would be ideal. Her vitals are good, so shouldn't be more than a few hours.'

I vowed to stay as still as possible until my legs were back to feeling. If I had to run, I'd rather not faceplant in my first few steps. If I cooperated, I might get to see the sky again.

Concentrating on keeping my breathing even and my body calm was easier said than done. I could feel my adrenaline levels rising as more of my body began to tingle with feeling. I stole a quick glance at the people in the room. Their backs were turned still, poring over some papers. I stretched the muscles in my face. It ached, my jaw stiff. I felt like I needed to crack it but couldn't risk it. I took a deep breath and tried to relax.

'Did she just move?' one of the figures said from their corner. They came over to me and I felt them pry my eyes open and shine a light. I tried not to flinch but I knew my eyes would react.

'Pupils are responding to light. She'll be able to move soon.' The man bent over and looked into my held-open eye. 'I know you can hear me. I'm going to let go of your eyelids. Blink in answer if you can.'

I let my eye close. I wanted to remain still but there was no point in dragging this out now they knew I was conscious. Blinking a few times to stop my eyes hurting I opened them fully.

'Ah, a little more awake than we thought. Okay, princess, we need to go through some things and then there will be some questions. Do you understand? Blink once for yes, twice for no.'

I blinked.

'Great. You are now at Black Sphere research facility for training and redeployment of blank individuals. It is also the housing for the City Life Holding Facility for those deemed too dangerous to be put into our prison system.

'You are here to be trained as a Sphere Operative if you are deemed able to be educated. If you fail any stage of the education process you will be delegated to the Research Department as a test case or you will be euthanised. This is not a choice you make. Do you understand?'

I blinked again.

'Your first step is to be purged of outside influences. We do this via sensory deprivation. You will be immersed into a tank of stasis gel. You will have feeding, breathing and expulsion tubes inserted. You will be able to open your eyes and breathe normally but if you struggle or try to remove any of the tubes, you will be considered a failure. You will wake up in the tank so we understand there is a transition period of shock but after that just relax. Once we register a calm brain pattern you will be taken out of the tank to begin training. Do you understand?'

I blinked. My vision was clear now and I could feel the warmth of feeling returning to my hands. My legs were just prickly feeling, with no ability yet to move them. The second person in the room stepped up beside me and shone the light into my eyes again.

'Should we anesthetise her before she gets more active and start the tubing?'

'Nah, we have to wait til she has all feeling back, otherwise it could paralyse her. She's a top-rated candidate, we can't waste her.'

I tried to clear my throat but my mouth was so dry all I managed was a raspy hacking noise.

'Do you need a drink? Can she drink?' the second person said, turning to the other man.

'She can have a little water. Not much though.'

He brought a glass over and lifted my head to take a sip. While he was distracted, I began to wriggle against my hand restraints. They would knock me out again soon so if I was going to get free I had to do it soon. There was some give on the straps. My arms still felt like jelly and trying to coordinate myself without jerking at the restraints was not easy.

'That's all you get, love. Sorry.'

'Don't talk to her like that.'

'Like what?'

'She's a blank, not a human. Don't apologise.'

I cleared my throat and they both looked at me. 'I may be a blank but I can still hear you,' I croaked.

'And the beast can speak,' the older of the two said. 'Do you have any questions?'

A thousand things ran through my head but only one thing kept coming to the top. 'Ahn. The man who brought me in, is he okay?'

'He followed orders in the end. Thought he'd gone rogue for a moment the way he busted you out, but he did the right thing in the end. When the security officers got you outside the farms he was given the ultimatum, which he chose to follow in his favour. He'll end up sweeping the halls for a few months but he'll come good in the end. He's trainable.'

'Thank you,' I mumbled. 'Tell him I don't blame him.'

'Will do, Miss,' said the younger of the two.

'What did I say about addressing her like that?' the older one snapped. 'Do you want me to report you?'

'Sorry, Sir. Won't happen again.'

'Go gather the anaesthetics and tubal kit for when she's ready.'

The younger man left the room.

'Now, the next part won't be pleasant. If you want to get through it, just do what is expected. They will have you tubed for euthanising so if you make too much of a fuss they won't hesitate. It'd be a shame to lose a specimen like yourself but they don't have time to fix you. You'll end up as a scientific test corpse and nothing else.'

'Will it hurt?'

'The sensory dep? It's more uncomfortable than anything, I've been told. You won't so much feel anything as experience things. It'll be totally dark. You will hallucinate. You will either calm and de-program or go mad.'

'It works like the suspended animation then, but awake?'

'Pretty much. How do you know about suspended animation?'

'I read a lot before I was put in the Cube. After that, reading materials became rather scarce.'

The man laughed. 'Most of you can barely read when you get here. Only the ones that really want to learn ever get taught. So reading materials aren't really part of the Cube budget. It's not City Lockup. Now relax while the sedative goes out of your system. I'll be back soon.'

He left me in the silent and glaringly white room. I started my attempt to wriggle my hands free as I felt sensation coming back into my thighs. My arms felt less like articulated slugs now, but my hands were still mostly useless. I twisted my wrists back and forth until I felt the restraint finally refuse to give any further at the widest part of my hand. I barely hesitated. This was going to hurt but I was still jellylike enough to not feel it as much as I normally would have. I yanked and forced the matter when it didn't work the first time. I felt my hand dislocate and bit my lip to stifle the scream that rose in my throat.

I looked down at my red skin. God, it seemed to pulse with heat and pain. I could still move all my fingers so I hadn't done any permanent damage, I hoped. Uncertainly, I popped the joint back in, swallowing the automatic sob of agony. The pain began to decrease immediately once everything was back in place. I could partially prop myself up now so I looked at the restraint of the other hand. Despite the rigidity of the metal clasp I saw that it was held shut with a push bolt on the side of the bed.

It took a few tries with my throbbing hand but I managed to pull the bolt free and free my hands. I sat up. I wasn't really sure what I could do next. My legs were still numb and if I ran they would surely kill me. I had no idea where I was or how to get out. They would easily catch me. Even wearing coveralls like security, the grey would be a stark contrast to the clinical white that I assumed would be spread throughout the whole facility. Or at least the levels I had access too. I checked the walls but saw no ventilation panels. The only exit was the door the man had walked through and a small cupboard in the corner. I would fit in there but it wouldn't be much of a hiding spot. I leaned forward, undid the restraints on my ankles, and drew my legs under me. I had to pull them in with my arms to get in a comfortable position but it felt good to be sitting up finally. I heard the door click open as the man returned.

'Wait, how did you…'

'I was cramping so I slipped one hand out and the rest was easy. It's okay, I'm not going to hurt you. Where would I go?'

'You need to lay back down.'

'Please, just let me sit comfortably as my last request before I'm shoved in a tank of goo and hallucinations.'

'If you try and run I will shoot you,' he said, pulling back the corner of his coat to reveal a stunner. 'It won't kill you but it'll hurt and you won't be all that comfortable.' He stared at me, like breaking eye contact would give me a chance to run.

'It's okay. I'm not gonna pull anything. I'm not stupid.'

'Your kind are unstable. I don't trust you.'

'You're the one with the gun, not me. Anyway, I can't feel my legs yet so if I try to run I won't get far.'

He stood staring at me. I had gone through so much and here I was being stared down by a City doctor, if that's what he was, with numb legs and the beginnings of a headache throbbing behind my eyes.

'So what's your name?' I asked. If we were going to be stuck staring at each other, I didn't want to sit in silence.

'Why do you need to know?' he asked, taking a step back.

'Don't look so scared. I was just making conversation. It's not like I'm a witch who wants to use your name to control you. Blanks can't do that. Hate to tell you but we really aren't all that different to you.'

'You are not the same as us. You are a genetic abnormality that poses a risk to the genetic purity of the City.'

'Indoctrination, I see. How many times did they make you repeat that over and over before it stuck?' He didn't react. 'Have I gained the skill to strike you dumb? Fine, I'll give you a name then. You look like a Bob. Hi Bob. I'm Almara.'

'No, you're not. You don't have a name.'

'Well, Bob, my mother gave me this name. You can refer to me with nothing but numbers all you want but I will always be Almara.'

'My name's not Bob.'

'Then what is your name?'

'Doctor Ross. I'm Doctor Ross.'

'Doctor Ross. Now was that so hard?' I felt my feet begin to prickle as feeling flooded back into them. If I could grab his gun... No. It was too much of a risk. Before I got the chance for another snide comment, the younger man rushed in, pushing a cart full of tubing and rattling trays full of needles. He stopped so suddenly as he entered the room that several syringes clattered to the floor and rolled away.

'It's okay,' I said, realising he had noticed my apparent freedom. 'I don't bite. So, what's your name?'

'Uh...' His gaze flicked between me and Doctor Ross. After a nod of okay he turned back to me. 'Silas. I'm Silas. And you are?'

'Almara, although according to the doctor here I don't have a name anymore. Just a number.'

He laughed nervously. Doctor Ross cleared his throat and cast his eyes towards the scattered syringes.

'Oh, sorry, Doctor,' he mumbled before dropping to the floor to gather them up.

'Can you stand, 482?' Doctor Ross asked me.

'Really? You can't even use my name after I've told you.'

'Can you stand, 482?'

I shook my head and swung my legs off the side of the table. I wiggled my toes. They were still a little numb but I had enough movement that I should be able to stand up. I slid off the table, holding onto the edge just in case they failed me. I wobbled a little and my knees tried to buckle out from under me but I managed to stay up. I gingerly released the table.

'Ta-da!' I announced. Doctor Ross did not look impressed, but Silas gave me a smile. I liked that guy.

'Okay 482, please remove your clothing and lay back on the table.'

Silas blushed as I unzipped the coveralls. My body was nothing to write home about but I guessed he hadn't seen many half-naked girls. Most people only saw their partners. I had never seen a naked man myself. And if the City got its way the only way I would see one would be on a dissecting table or in a changing room, or maybe in a book. I knew the basics but there were no pictures in the biology books I'd read as a child. The Cube's library was highly lacking. It was a bit cold as I kicked the grey coveralls over towards Doctor Ross. I looked at the metal table I'd been strapped to.

'Can you put a sheet on the table or something? I would rather not literally freeze my ass off and it's already nippy in here.'

Silas pulled a cellular blanket from the storage cupboard and had laid it onto the table before Doctor Ross could say anything. He pulled a second one out and held it out to me.

'To keep you warm,' he said, still averting his eyes. I took it from him with a smile and finished stripping down. The table was still cold on my bare skin, but covering my naked self with the blanket certainly stopped the worst of it.

'Thank you, Silas.'

'No problem, Almara. At least the tank will be body temperature so you won't be cold in there.'

'482. You will refer to her as 482. She needs to get used to the proper way of things again. A few days of so-called freedom has spoiled her.'

Silas ducked his head and went back to reorganising the cart's contents onto a surgical table. Six syringes sat in a row, the liquid colours darkening from clear to a dark amber colour.

'Although we do not require your consent 482, I am legally obligated to read you the following statement. 482, as per City Ordinance you are to be anesthetised and prepped for sensory deprivation treatment. This treatment will be for a minimum period of two weeks. If you do not complete this treatment, you understand that there are consequences that may involve suspended animation or euthanasia. After the treatment is complete, you will be admitted to our training facility for aptitude testing. Do you understand?'

'As I don't have a single choice in this matter, sure. Why not.'

'I will now insert a cannula and Silas will begin the anaesthetic process.'

I turned my arm to expose my inner elbow and watched as Silas' hands stopped shaking as he picked up the cannula needle. He had been nervously trembling seconds ago. He put a tight tourniquet around my upper arm and prodded at my inner elbow for a vein. I'd had enough blood drawn in the Cube to know how this all worked. But something no one in the Cube had ever done was say sorry.

'This may hurt a little,' he said as he pressed on my vein. 'I'm sorry. After a few minutes you won't feel anything at all until you wake up in the tank.'

I nodded and closed my eyes. I hated this part. I felt the needle push into my skin and through to my vein. The first batch of anaesthetic was pushed into me. I heard him say 'just relax' before I felt the warmth of unconsciousness.

CHAPTER TWENTY-SEVEN
Darnell

'Just relax, 643,' the woman said, leading him to a chair.

'My name is…'

'Your name is now 643. You will refer to me as the Adjudicator.'

'But…'

'No buts. If you continue to argue I can cancel your adjudication at any time. Please remember that.' Her voice was soft but he knew she meant every word of it. 'Please sit back and place your hands on the armrests as indicated.'

She pressed a button and restraints clamped around his wrists. His first urge was to pull against them.

'Don't worry, this won't hurt. It's just so our readings don't get skewed by movement.' She fastened a belt around his chest then pulled a type of helmet from the ceiling, wires streaming out of it like crazy hair. She fastened it under his chin and stepped back behind her desk.

'Now try to remain as still as you can. This will scan your brain and biometrics for aptitude and latent skills. You will also feel a prick at your wrists as we take a blood sample. I recommend you close your eyes.'

Before he could question why, he felt a zap of static that felt like it permeated all the way into his brain. His eyes started to throb with pressure so he did as advised and closed them. It was the strangest sensation. He felt like someone was pulling his memories out of his head and prodding at his eyeballs. He felt the prick at his wrist for the blood-taking but his limbs felt so far away and separated from his body.

He had no idea how long he sat there but finally the buzzing stopped and he felt his head relax. His neck felt stiff. He had been clenching his jaw so tight that when she removed the helmet it took a few moments for him to open his mouth again. She unbuckled his chest restraint and the wrist straps disappeared into the arms of the chair. The woman placed a glass of water on the desk in front of him.

'Drink. It will help.'

He nodded, his shaky hands barely able to grip the cup. As his eyes focused, again he saw the computer screen scrolling through diagrams and graphs. He placed the empty cup back on the table and she put it in the bin as a new page came up on the data tablet on the desk surface. The top corner flashed green.

'Interesting,' she mumbled, reading over the data. Darnell tried to read it from where he was sitting but the angle was all wrong.

'Interesting good or interesting bad?'

'Just interesting. Also you don't have a citizen chip or a bio marker chip that most blanks get. You must have been hidden quite early in life. Do you know how old you were when you were removed from civilization?'

'Mum said I was just a baby when we left.'

'And you lived off the land? A farm?'

'Mostly. Mum got some supplies in the early days but we grew and fished enough to look after ourselves.'

'Your vitamin D levels are great. Must be from all the sun. Most blanks are deficient because they spend so much time locked away... if they live to maturity, of course.'

'What does that mean?"

'Left to live without City interference you would probably have died of natural causes by 25. Genetic abnormality does that. We enhance you so you can become more resilient. Blank DNA is easier to alter because it is not normal. That's why you aren't allowed to breed.'

'So I don't really have a choice here, do I?'

'Honestly, no. I'm not one to pussyfoot around things. You go through training and become a BMG or you end up as a lab experiment. They're trying to recreate the beasts at the moment. So far it has not been very successful.'

'But what about basic human rights?'

'As per City Ordinance, you are not human. You are a genetic abnormality. If they wanted to dump you in the wastelands they could. This is kinder by half. At least the beasts can't get you in here.'

'But I could become one…'

'Well, you passed this phase of BMG testing. Physically you are a perfect candidate. You will do well with agility, tactical training and combat. So no beastification for you if you do what you're supposed to. You're genetically disposed to impulsive behaviour but with analytical thinking that can be enhanced as well. Biologically, your body will take the genetic manipulation well, although that's common with blanks. Now all we have to test is your resilience. Have you heard of sensory deprivation before, 643?'

'In theory.'

'Then this will be easier for you. Please remove your clothes and put on this gown,' she said, handing him a flimsy hospital gown.

Darnell looked around for somewhere to change.

'643, please disrobe. Here is fine. It's nothing I haven't seen before. It's either the robe or I leave you naked and strap you to a gurney like we do for some intakes.'

He turned his back on her and changed into the gown. It was barely long enough to cover him and was open at the back. He turned back to the woman who was holding out a small basket. 'Clothes in the basket. They will be laundered and returned after testing. Please follow me.'

She went through the doors into a black room with an operating table on it. Darnell did not like the look or smell of this room. Even though it smelled like the med wing, there was another layer of scent he couldn't place, but it felt like fear.

A young woman met them by the table.

'I am Dr Garin. Please untie your gown at the back and lay on the table.' He did as told, the cold metal biting at his bare back and buttocks. He looked over for the Ajudicator but she had left in silence.

'Now, we do not require your consent, 643, but I am legally obligated to read you the following statement. 643, as per City Ordinance you are to be anesthetised and prepped for sensory deprivation treatment. This treatment will be for a minimum period of two weeks. If you do not complete this treatment, you understand that there are consequences that may involve suspended animation or euthanasia. After the treatment is complete, you will be admitted to our training facility for aptitude testing. Do you understand?'

Darnell nodded.

'Do you have any questions?'

'How do I… uhhh… go to the bathroom in the tank?' Darnell mumbled. He felt silly asking but thought it was a valid question.

'We will have a waste removal system attached to you so if you need to go it will be moved away. You will also have a feeding tube inserted. This will deliver all needed nutrients to your system.'

'Can I open my eyes in there?'

'You can but you won't see anything. It's pitch black. You will feel suspended but will be able to move, albeit slowly. Also, on a personal recommendation, when you wake up in the tank, don't freak out or try to remove the tubes. If you struggle you fail.'

She began the anaesthetic process and soon Darnell was asleep.

When he came to, Darnell felt strangely cocooned. He opened

his eyes against the thick goo he was suspended in. It pushed against him as he tried to move. As much as he could push his arms around, he felt like he was swimming in jelly. It was like he was suspended in the womb ready to be birthed. Even with his eyes open, the gel caressing his eyes, it was dark.

His throat hurt, the tube making him feel like he was choking. He tried to grab at it but the goo slowed him down long enough to remember the warning not to struggle. He closed his eyes and tried to breathe. Closing his eyes made no difference in the lightless room but it was comforting. It wasn't dark, he was just asleep, he tried to tell himself. In the silence, he felt his thoughts begin to click through his head.

How long was I unconscious for?

How is my mother?

Will I ever see her again?

Could I drown in here?

Is anyone actually watching?

Can they see me?

If so, why can't I see them?

Am I going to die in here?

They started to get muddled together. No wonder this was deemed as training. He had no idea how he was going to last two weeks. At least he knew he could rest in here. No more running or being scared of what was around the corner. This would be his prison but it would also keep his mother safe.

He started to zone out, colours flashing by on the back of his eyelids. He started nodding off and soon fell asleep.

He drifted in and out of sleep, colours and memories flashing through his head. He had no idea how much time had passed, or even if the things he was thinking were real. He heard a tapping sound. Then again. Tap tap tap. Tap tap tap. Was there someone there, just beyond his senses? He felt the gentle reverberations through the glass and the goo.

He felt himself wake up more now. He was definitely hearing the tapping. He remembered he was inside a tank of sorts, but he had no idea how big, or far ahead the glass was.

Was there someone on the other side? He held his breath to pinpoint where the tapping was coming from. It was to his left. He swam his way through the thick goo towards the sound.

He pushed his arms out in front of him until he felt the hard, smooth surface of glass. Tap tap tap. He felt it through the glass now. He tapped back in return. He wasn't alone. There was someone on the other side of the glass. Were there multiple tanks, side by side? The taps stopped. He tapped again. Had it all been in his imagination? There was no reply. One last try. Tap tap tap. Silence. He'd imagined it after all.

He rested, pushing his head against the glass, when a single tap echoed through this head. His eyes flew open. He tapped again. It was real. The tap repeated now like before but faster, more insistent. But now what? He didn't know any codes. He pressed his face to the glass trying to see through, but it was impossible. There was no trace of light. The glass was the same temperature as the goo they floated in, but it was not just him. He wasn't sure which was stronger, the joy at company or the horror that someone else was going through this with him.

Another set of taps came but this time it was from another side. Could there be even more? How many blanks were there trapped in this soundless, lightless hell? He made his way sluggishly over to the noise and tapped back. This time the response was immediate. He heard his neighbour tapping on their glass too.

CHAPTER TWENTY-EIGHT
Zale

Training was slow. Susan, although a lovely woman with a kind voice, was not cut out for teaching. She droned on and vaguely pointed at buttons and levers on the test control panel. Allen was good at remembering this sort of thing, Zale was not. He felt his mind wandering several times, only to be reefed back into the reality of his latest job skill.

By the end of the day his head was swimming. Allen assured him that he remembered enough and Susan had loaded their device with a map of all the buttons. If the subjects behaved, it was more a monitoring job: keeping track of vitals and making sure the tubes stayed clear. If anything happened there was a big red button to alert the tank heads. They then made the call on the future of the subject.

He collapsed into a chair when he got to the apartment. Allen looked at him as he started making food.

'Does it feel wrong to you?' Allen asked quietly.

Zale sat up a bit straighter, looking over at his partner. He looked tired and grey. 'A bit, I guess.'

'You guess? We are monitoring people stuck in sensory deprivation against their will because they aren't normal. Do you realise we aren't normal? They could do this to us.'

'They won't do this to us. We aren't blank. No weird genetic markers with us. We have no value to them.'

'That's even worse. We're disposable. They can exile us, or worse, at the drop of a hat.'

'We just need to follow instructions until we become one of the team.'

'Did you not see how they looked at us? How they stared at you, and our scars from mark removal? We are breaking their rules, and only because you made a deal with the Colonel are we alive.'

'Allen, I had no choice. It was this or I was going to be separated from you. You didn't have to come.'

'Of course I did! After all we've been through to be together, you think I would just leave you? If we're going to be exiled I intend to be with you through to the end. If that means starving to death in the wasteland, so be it.'

'We just have to keep our heads down and follow the rules. We have food, shelter and a job and they're letting us be here.'

'I know,' he said, leaning over to kiss Zale on the head. 'I know.'

***

Zale and Allen followed their data pads to the tank monitoring room. After a day of training, they were being thrown into work. They each had a tank to monitor, sitting next to each other. Susan met them at the door.

'Please swipe your security passes at your terminal. This logs your work hours. Due to the nature of your job, I will bring your lunch in for you so there is no need to leave except to use the bathroom. One at a time though so someone is in the room at all times.'

Zale nodded as Allen brought up the data pad map of the control panel, resting it on the glass of the tanks in between the two. He took his seat in silence. Susan looked between the two of them and asked if there were any questions. Allen sat staring at the tank. Allen shook his head and took his seat as Susan left the room.

They both looked up at their respective subjects. In Allen's tank a young man floated suspended in goo, tubes snaking their way from his body. In front of Zale was a young woman, her dark hair floating like snakes around her pale face. They were both still asleep. They were new into the tanks so the monitoring of their vitals was important because the anaesthetic wearing off could lead to shock. Them freaking out because they were trapped in a tank of goo that they weren't in before could also happen.

'I'm sorry, Allen,' Zale whispered.

'Sorry for what?'

'Sorry for bringing you here. To deal with this,' he said, waving him arms around him.

'It's fine. We just need to follow our monitors and try not to doze off in boredom.' He turned back to look at his monitors. The heartrate of his subject beat a steady pattern on the monitor, the oxygenation levels were steady. Everything looked fine. He glanced over at Zale's monitor. 'Hon, it looks like your girl is waking up. Heartrate is speeding up.'

Zale looked up at the girl. Her eyes were wide but she remained still except her head which she was trying to turn in the goo to look around. Her head turned back and stared straight at Zale.

'They can't see us, can they?'

'Why?'

'She's looking at me. Like, looking right at me.'

'It's one-way glass. They can't see out, we can see in. They just see darkness.'

'Seriously, look. She's looking right at me.'

Allen leaned over to take a look.

'That is a little creepy. Her vitals are settling at least. No need to stress.'

The girl blinked but kept her gaze fixed on Zale's face. He moved over to the right towards Allen. The girl's eyes followed him. How could she know where he was? He rolled his chair the other way to the edge of the tank. This time her head moved slowly until she made eye contact. Zale stood up, his chair clattering to the floor behind him.

'Zale, what the hell?' Allen choked out in shock.

'She can see me, Allen. Watch!' Zale dashed over to where Allen now stood, but the girls head remained turned slightly to one side, her eyes blank.

'Hon, I think the quiet has got to you. She can't see through the glass. Neither of them can.'

'She watched as I moved. Her head turned and followed me. You have to believe me.'

'It must have just looked like she was watching you. It's just a coincidence. Just relax. We're stuck here for the rest of the day until next shift.' Allen went and picked up Zale's chair, then led him over to it, sitting him down. 'Just watch her vitals. Don't even look at her unless something looks off on the monitors.'

They sat without a word as the monitors beeped steadily along. Zale tried not to look up at the girl's pale figure but after a while his eyes drifted up to her face. She was looking right at him again. He pushed back from the desk again, the chair this time rolling across the room only to bounce off the wall and spin wildly to the side. He leaned over the console and placed his hands flat against the glass. It was warmer than he'd expected.

'Zale, what the hell are you doing? Do you want to get banished or ground up into dog food?'

'She can see me, Allen. She can see me, I know it.'

'No, she can't. It wouldn't be sensory deprivation if they could see out, would it?'

'How do you know we're not the test subjects here, Allen?' Zale spat, his chest heaving with every breath. His eyes were wild. 'She can see me.'

'Zale, just breathe. Go sit against the wall and take a break. I can monitor them both for a while.' Allen tried to steer Zale towards a corner of the room away from the tank but he stood his ground. 'Come on.'

Zale bowed his head in defeat and went to step away when he raised his hand and knocked on the glass. Allen forcibly pulled him away this time.

'Why did you do that? If she heard that and reacts badly it could kill her.' Allen pushed Zale into the corner of the room and shoved him into a sitting position on the floor. 'Now stay there and try not to get us killed.'

Zale looked up and saw the girl was moving. 'She's still watching me.'

'You just knocked on the tank. She's looking at the noise, most likely.'

They looked over at the monitors. The boy was awake again, staring ahead of him as though looking at a faraway sunset beyond an endless sea.

The girl had swum lower and was looking in Allen's direction. He had to admit it was a little off-putting. He settled back in his chair and closed his eyes. The steady beep of the monitors lulled him into a shallow sleep.

A burst of quickened beeps jolted him awake. His chair rolled back as he went forward. It nearly landed him on the floor. He caught the chair before it went too far and looked at the monitors. Whatever anomaly had caused the beeps had righted itself. The boy was once again asleep and the girl floated at the bottom of the tank looking out at Zale. Zale was fast asleep against the wall, muttering to himself.

It was nearing midday; lunch would be coming soon. Allen got up and went over to Zale, shaking him gently awake. He woke suddenly, a yelp escaping his sleep-numbed mouth.

'Hey hon,' Allen whispered. 'A minder should be here soon. You need to get up.' Allen helped Zale to his feet and onto the chair.

'I see she's still being creepy,' Zale said, nodding towards the girl. She had swum a little higher in the tank but remained fixated on them.

'Yeah, I admit it is a bit off-putting.' He pushed Zale in his chair back up to the desk. The girl reached her hand out and touched the glass, the palm of her hand a white shape pushed into blackness.

They watched as it slid down and away from the glass;

finally, she lowered her head. Only a moment passed before the doors hissed open to the clatter of a meals trolley.

The woman pushing the trolley was not who they had been expecting. This was no civilian worker.

Zale jumped to his feet, knocking his chair flying. 'Get out!' he screamed. He grabbed Allen by the arm and pulled him back.

'It's just lunch delivery,' the woman said. Her voice was soft but firm. Her black jumpsuit was topped off with heavy boots and tightly tied-back hair.

'You killed her! She was four years old!'

'Zale, what are you talking about?'

'He's referring to my mission to your camp. I was following orders.'

'You were ordered to kill a child? Does that not ring any alarm bells?'

'I'm a BMG. If I don't follow orders I die. I get recycled. You are not in any danger from me.'

'Are you sure about that? How do we know you aren't going to poison us? How do we know there's even food under those covers?'

'I'm not hiding grenades under the cloches. If I wanted to kill you, you'd be dead already. You should know I don't fuck around. My name is Ava. A lot has changed since the incident at Condor Point. I don't expect you to trust me but there is some reading material under your plates. I implore you to read it. The Colonel is pandering to your life together for now but it won't last.'

'See? She's threatening us, Allen,' Zale spat as he pulled Allen further away from Ava.

'Zale, just listen to her. You must admit that the Colonel allowing us in here is not normal. If he intends to use us as an example, I'd like to be forewarned, especially from the person most likely to kill us.'

'Thank you, Allen. Please eat. Someone will come to talk with you further when they collect your food trolley. The documents underneath the plates need to remain hidden though. If anyone else comes in do not expect them to be on your side. Trust me on that.'

'So, trust you to trust no one. Got it,' Zale said. Allen nudged him with his elbow.

'Ava, thank you. We understand,' Allen said. Ava turned on her heels and exited the room. A moment of silence passed between the two men.

'I'm not eating it,' Zale muttered.

'Don't be a child. She's right. If she was sent to kill us she'd have shot us point blank. It seems she follows orders and Sphere doesn't seem to fuck around. They wouldn't bother with poison, would they? It's not like they need a cover-up in their own walls. And who would come looking for us? Condor Point probably thinks we're dead and no one here cares about two men who go against City Ordinance and have no marks by choice. We're only one step up the food chain from the two kids in the tanks.'

Allen pulled both cloches off the food trolley to reveal pale slices of meat and a selection of cubed vegetables.

'See? Bland, mass-produced food. Mixed veg and mystery meat. It's probably all synthetic too.'

Zale grunted and set down his chair. Allen pulled his chair over and began to eat. After a few mouthfuls, he looked up at Zale who had pushed his chair up to the other side of the trolley. 'See hon, I'm fine. It's not the best food but it's better than nothing.'

Zale's stomach let out an audible growl. He sighed and began to eat. He saw the corner of a manila folder sticking out from under his plate, another poked out from the under the other plate. Allen finished his food and pulled his free. He opened it gingerly, pulling out a collection of pages, paperclipped on one corner. Zale saw the red ink of a confidential stamp on the top page.

Allen flipped through the pages, his brow furrowed in concentration. Zale finished his meal and pulled out the folder under his plate. Before he opened it, he looked over at Allen.

'Well, what's yours?'

'It's the Emergency Disengagement Protocol for Sensory Deprivation Tank Subjects. Shouldn't this have been a part of our training?'

'Why would she give us that? If there was an evacuation, surely there would be a tech to take them out of the tanks.'

'Listen to this: Standard Procedure is to leave subjects in tanks during any evacuation procedure. Life support systems should sustain life through any natural disaster. If not, they are deemed as collateral loss. Emergency Disengagement is only to be used to remove sanctioned subjects early if a technician is not available. This procedure should be used only on active agents undergoing treatment who are urgently needed for missions.'

'So, they just let them die?'

'They use these on their own agents! They could put us in there. Do you think that's...'

'The plan for us? No, I'm pretty sure we just become pet food if we screw up.'

Allen folded the papers and shoved them into his pocket. 'Just in case,' he muttered before nodding to his folder. 'What's in yours?'

Zale opened the folder in his lap and pulled out another collection of papers just a little thicker than Allen's had been. Rather than a furrowed brow, Zale's eyes lit up wide. He flicked to the next page and then the next, his mouth falling open in what Allen thought was shock or amazement.

'What is it?'

'We aren't alone...'

'Of course we aren't, Oasis is...'

'No, outside our region. We're region twelve. There are other regions. There could be more people like us.' He kept flicking through them and a photo fell from the papers. It was a copy, faded along creased lines like it had been looked at over and over again. It showed a boy standing next to a patrol vehicle, except it was unmarked and bright red in between smears of dirt.

In the vehicle was a man smiling at the camera. It wasn't the man, or even the oddly-coloured vehicle that drew his attention, it was the background. Behind them was a fence... THE fence. Zale knew this was taken from outside the fence because the Colonel's house was visible through the wires.

The next page was headed with *Blank Community External Communication*. It listed thirty frequencies. 'I... I... I think this means there's something else out there.'

He showed the papers to Allen. 'This means banishment is freedom.'

'But the beasts... the radioactivity of the wastelands... it's all a lie?'

'To keep us in. This photo; you recognised something.'

'It's from outside the fence looking in. That's the Colonel's house. I've been there.'

'Do you know this man?'

'No, neither of them is familiar but they are both outside and I see no marks.'

'Marks can be hidden but how would they get a car outside? I guess that means it came from outside too.'

Allen flicked to the page after the frequencies and began to read.

'Regions are still contained. No breaches of fences. Blank community zones are ready for new citizens. Please cease killing citizens in Regions. Marked Regions will remain under its own rules. *END COMMUNICATION*'

They don't need to kill them. They're choosing to kill them rather than let them be free. Why?'

'Who knows.'

They sat in silence until Allen gathered all the papers and added them to the papers in his pocket.

A tapping sound broke through the quiet. They looked up to see the girl looking at them her hands now pressed to the glass. She knocked again.

'Not this shit again,' Allen said. Zale got to his feet and tapped back. She smiled and tapped again. Zale responded before watching her swim her way to the side of the tank to the glass between her and the boy. She tapped again, waiting a few moments before tapping again. The boy stirred. Tap tap tap. The boy pushed through the goo, hands out in front of him as though he was guiding himself with the vibrations of the tapping.

He reached the glass, pressing the palms of his hands on the glass. The girl tapped again and this time the boy responded in turn. Zale was grinning, watching this interaction. He tapped the glass again. Zale watched, waiting for the girl to tap back but she looked at the glass, a quizzical look on her face. The boy rested his head on the glass. Finally, she tapped back and he responded, both tapping in incessant bursts. Zale stepped forward but Allen pulled him back. The boy looked like he was trying to push his face through the glass now.

Zale broke free of Allen's grasp and ran to the boy's tank, knocking on the glass. The boy's head darted away from the glass wall he rested against. He pushed off and swam towards the corner of the glass box and replied. Zale all but giggled. All three of them began tapping in unison.

'Zale, stop,' Allen said. ' Someone is coming.' Zale stepped back but the boy continued his tapping. The girl had stopped though, floating calmly in the corner of the rank. The boy pressed his palms flat against the glass and rested his forehead against it too. A look of despair grimaced across his face. It was a look of absolute abandonment.

Allen and Zale went back to their seats, Allen sliding the now-empty folders under the food trays. They tried to gather their composure as the door to the room slid open.

A woman, maybe late forties, entered the room. Unlike most of the staff she wore black pants and a plain white blouse. Her hair was tied back but a few loose curls had begun to escape, framing her face. She also wasn't wearing the customary boots, but simple flats, that clicked on the hard floor as she entered.

'Hello gentlemen,' she said, glancing at each of them in turn, her eyes wandering over the tanks for a second.

'Afternoon, Ma'am,' Allen managed to say. He saw Zale start to open his mouth and kicked his foot to stop him.

'Uh, hi,' Zale muttered, his eyes flicking over to the tanks and their occupants.

'Let me introduce myself. My name is Harley. I work here in communications. I was the one who sent the blank woman with the files. Have you read them?'

After a pause Allen and Zale both nodded. Allen wondered if this was a test that would send them to the mincers.

'Do you understand what those files were?'

'Is it...' Zale began.

'Just a yes no response please. Just in case,' the woman said, motioning her head towards one of the cameras mounted on the wall.

'Yes Ma'am. I think we do,' Allen replied. 'We have questions though.'

'If you didn't I'd have been sorely disappointed. But now is not the time. Ava will be back soon. Help her by using the instructions.'

'But...' Allen interjected.

'Now, now Allen. I know you must feel betrayed and confused by everything you've been through but I need you to trust me. Your civilian status on base may have been sanctioned by the Colonel but there are those here who see you as criminals and those people are in the majority, especially in this facility. Mark removal and unsanctioned relationships can be taken badly here, and I fear that persecution lies in your futures, just as it does for these two,' she said, gesturing to the tanks.

'And what do you get out of this?' Zale asked.

'For myself? Nothing but satisfaction, probably death. But for you and Ava and the others, I want to give you back your lives.'

'We had lives before Sphere sent in a kill squad.'

'Not a life in a closed commune. I want you to have true freedom in a place without fences.'

'So why do you care so much?' Allen asked. 'You're obviously marked, and you don't even know us'

'Because of her,' she said, indicating the girl in the tank. 'That girl is my daughter.'

CHAPTER TWENTY-NINE
Almara

I could sense something was happening. I seemed to sense a lot in this tub of goo they'd trapped me in. I could feel the presence of others on two sides of the tank, and now I had confirmed there were people there. It had been silent for a while now. I had arranged myself into a pseudo sitting position, floating suspended in the jelly.

I had no way of telling the passing of time in the sightless and sound-muffling existence except for the beat of my heart, which I could feel and hear thudding in my chest. So when I felt myself moving, at first I thought nothing of it, an illusion of my isolation, until I realised I really was moving, the goo draining away from me.

At first I froze, unsure what it meant or if I should be fighting the pull down. Then a thought crossed my mind. What if the drain hole was how they sucked you into stasis, or some kind of meat grinder? I started to swim against the pull. I had to be swimming my way up. My head broke the surface and cold air enveloped face. I blinked the vestiges of goo from my eyes. Everything was blurry and my eyes burned from the change in temperature and lack of moisture. I swam to the nearest edge of the tank, the top now sliding open to reveal dim lights my eyes that nonetheless still seared at my retinas like a thousand suns after my inky blackness. I reached for the lip of the tank and tried not to let my slimy hands slip too much on the metal. My blurred vision was not helpful in the slightest. Flailing, trying desperately to claw my way out, I felt more of my skin being exposed to the air. My hands slipped and I fell back into the goo, realising that the edge of the tank was just getting further and further away from my grasp. I threw my hand up with one last attempt to pull myself out when I felt a hand take a hold of my wrist and begin to pull.

I was yanked from the goo. A sucking sound echoed as my naked body came free, pulled onto the cold metal grating surrounding the tank. I could finally rub my eyes to clear out the last of the gunk. I blinked as they began to acclimatise, then came face to face with a harsh-looking woman. A black coverall and black boots at first made me want to recoil, but surely if she was helping me out I had to trust her. I saw the gun at her hip. That meant I had no choice but to at least go along with her. She helped me remove my breathing tubes, and despite thinking I would throw up, the first breath of real air I took was delightful and fresh.

'I...' I croaked. My voice was beyond rough, my throat scratched from the intubation.

'Don't try and talk. Your throat will be delicate. I am B...' She paused. 'My name is Ava. I'm here to help you escape. Now what comes next may hurt,' she warned me as she started removing all my tubes and monitors. I stayed silent as she worked. I was too exhausted and frankly, overwhelmed, to argue.

When she'd finished, she draped a towel around me.

'Get dry, get dressed and tie your hair back tight like mine. I need to help the others.'

I looked over to where the other tank was to see two men in coveralls with a naked boy around my age being pulled from his tank. He grabbed at the breathing tubes. Ava slapped his hands away but it was too late. He pulled it free then threw up a stream of water. The boy gagged as he collapsed onto the metal grating. I turned away to finish drying myself, peeling off the remnants of the medical tape stuck to my body.

I pulled my damp hair into a tight ponytail at the base of

my neck like Ava's and picked up the coveralls. They were black with a spherical logo embroidered on the chest. I pulled them on and zipped it up to my neck. It was nice to be clothed again. The fabric was surprisingly soft but thick. It was nothing like the thin uniforms in the Cube.

I sat again to pull on the socks and boots, tucking the slightly long legs of the coveralls into the top of the socks. The only thing left was the belt of pouches. As I clipped it around my waist I heard the boy cry out. Removing the catheter had hurt enough for me; I couldn't imagine how it would have felt for him.

I heard boots on the floor behind me and turned to see Ava with a man who had a pink scar across his face. I tried not to stare.

'Almara, this is Zale. Over there is his partner Allen, and our fellow blank Darnell.'

Zale held his hand out to shake. I'd never met a gay couple before. It was unheard of, or at least unspoken of, but then again, so were blanks like me.

'Are you...' I began.

'Gay?' he answered. 'Yes.'

'I was going to say blank,' I mumbled.

Zale laughed. 'Oh, no. Allen and I had our marks removed. Hence this lovely scar.'

'Sorry. I didn't mean...'

'It's okay. Pleased to meet you, Almara. May I ask you a question?'

I nodded as I saw Allen and Darnell appear behind him. 'Could you see through the glass of the tank?'

'No.' It struck me as odd he would ask that. 'Why?'

'I told you!' Allen cried.

'It looked like you were watching us. Then the tapping...'

'I could sense someone outside, like when someone is staring at the back of your head and you just know.'

'Is it a blank thing?'

'Don't look at me,' Darnell said. 'I'm no psychic. My skills end at running and catching fish.'

'Well, running may come in handy,' Ava said. 'We need to move soon. New shift will be in in a little under two hours. We need to be at least near the launch room. Preferably as soon as possible. But first we need to get to the comms room to meet Harley.'

My heart leapt unexpectedly.

'Did you say Harley?' I asked, curious.

'Yes, Almara. It's your mother, Harley. She's been working in Sphere for the past six years. When she saw your image on the intake listing, she pulled me aside.'

'Why you?' Zale asked. 'You don't seem the type to disobey City Ordinance.'

'Zale, things have changed since we first met. Darnell helped me see through some of the lies. I approached Harley for help to verify some information. She's head of communications. She has all the files. She found me. I had a name. A name I didn't remember. I have a family and they've been looking for me. I wasn't abandoned like I was told. I was stolen.'

'Just like me,' I muttered.

'She's been looking for you too, Almara. Since the day they took you. I was there when the bulletin came in about you but I was assigned to recover Darnell. Now I know he can fight and shoot too but I wasn't sure if you could fire a gun. I put a taser on your belt. Looks like a gun but won't kill. Don't tase yourself though. I'm strong but not enough to carry you at a decent speed. If you get shot, or fall, we will leave you. That goes for any of you. They will shoot to kill.

'Now follow me. Walk straight. Talk to no-one. Leave all the talking to me. I'm hoping to get to Harley 's office without being questioned, but we need to be prepared. ' We all nodded.

'When we go out the door, the light is going to be bright. Just a warning, as compared to in here it's quite a contrast and I don't want you looking like blind mice.'

I prepared to squint as Ava pushed the door release. The

metal slid back into the wall, flooding the area we stood in with yellow-white. She stepped through, looking both ways before motioning us forward. I followed closely behind her, Darnell behind me, and Zale and Allen bringing up the rear.

Ava had been right. It was beyond bright in the stark, white hallway. Our new boots squeaked as we walked and I tried to blink the glare away. My heart was racing. I rested my hand on the taser. Feeling the cold metal under my fingers was at least somewhat comforting, but I looked over at Ava to see her hands swinging gently by her sides. I lowered my hand again. I had to fit in. I felt someone walk up beside me. It was Darnell.

'Do you think this is just part of the training?' he whispered to me.

'No, they wouldn't bring up my mother by name,' I said quietly. 'Was she telling the truth about you helping her?'

'I guess. Her uncle helped me. When I was hiding in his safe room I found a book. He's been trying to find her. Keeping notes, little sketches when he had a chance to see her in passing... I guess she knows now.'

'If she feels the relief I'm feeling right now, realising my mum didn't abandon me to the City, then I understand.'

'Guys,' Ava hissed. 'Shut up. We're approaching a more populated area.'

Darnell slowed until he fell back into line behind me. I glanced over my shoulder but Darnell was already concentrating on his own feet. We turned the corner of the empty white corridor into a wider main thoroughfare. More populated was an understatement. Was she taking us through the barracks? People in black coveralls like the ones we were wearing were everywhere, guns at their hips, in and out of the frosted sliding doors that punctuated the white expanse of wall. Most looked under thirty, with the exception of a handful of older folk carrying their data pads and nothing else. The younger soldiers carried folders and crates, some pushing trolleys. There was little chatter, the bootfalls echoing in the air. In the distance, I could hear orders being barked. As it got louder I realised we were entering a hall of training rooms. A hall full of new faces. We'd fit right in.

We finally turned another corner but the hall ahead was short and ended at a set of metal doors – an elevator. A screen next to the door had a faint blue glow around its sphere logo. Ava rolled up her sleeve and held her wrist up to the panel. It lit up green and the doors slid open. Two women in grey civilian coveralls stood at the back, each holding a box. They looked at Ava and lowered their heads, avoiding eye contact. We followed Ava into the elevator before watching the doors close. At least this time we were going up. At level three the two women got out. Level four was our destination.

The doors slid open on a busy hallway. Although the floors and ceilings were still the stark white of the rest of the facility, the walls here were all glass. A ramble of people rushed around in the rooms beyond, full of computer screens glowing pale blue onto the skin of the operators. Even those walking between rooms had their heads buried in reams of paper or were all but glued to their data pads. I looked back at Darnell whose mouth was open and eyes wide. Had he never seen tech before? Maybe he hadn't, I thought. I didn't know his story but it seemed it was very different to mine.

'This way,' Ava said, pulling us from our staring. We followed, weaving between people. The glass walls stretched on for several hundred metres until it was interrupted by black frosted glass I couldn't see through. Etched in white on the door was the title *Director of Communications*.

Ava knocked once and a panel slid into a recess in the door, revealing another scanning plate. Ava put her wrist up to it like she had at the elevator and after a few barely audible sounds, the door slid open to a bank of computers and a wall of monitors.

The shape of a woman was silhouetted against the brightness of the screens, but as she turned I knew it was my mother. I stood still. I wanted to run to her as much as I felt like screaming at her. I still couldn't see her face but I could smell her rose perfume. I'd always hated the cloying sweetness of it that hung in the house as a child, but now the scent brought tears to my eyes. I thought I'd forgotten it but now everything came rushing back.

'Almara?' she whispered. All I could do was nod my head. 'I've finally got you back.'

She ran towards me and I started to sob as she threw her arms around me. I didn't want to let her go.

Eventually she stepped back. She looked the same as I remembered except for a few grey hairs and a few lines beginning to show on her face. She wiped the tears away from her eyes and gestured to the seats.

'Sit, please. Everyone sit,' she said, settling back on her chair. 'Ava, thank you for helping with this. I know you are fighting what you have always known but now you have proof otherwise.'

We all sat except for Ava; she relaxed against the wall. She didn't really seem the sitting-down type, and even in this position her hand rested on her gun.

'Now,' my mother started. 'Let's see if I have you three around the right way. Darnell, I know you because I saw you in the tank.' Darnell blushed. 'But Allen and Zale... Zale?' She said, pointing to the man with the scar across his face. He nodded with a smile. 'Excellent, that makes you Allen.'

'That's right, Ma'am. I don't mean to seem rude. The documents that Ava delivered; they are a little confronting.'

'I understand,' she said. 'I promised you I would answer your questions so I will explain as much as I can.'

'What documents, Mother?' It felt so good to speak to her again. 'What did you find?"

'I found you, and the others, a way to be free, but getting you there will not be easy.'

'But where? One of the camps?' I asked.

'No, outside.'

'Outside what?'

'Outside the region.

'But there's nothing out there but wasteland and the beasts.'

'That is what the City wants everyone to believe.'

'I've had that rammed down my throat as history in the Cube for seven years! My genetic abnormality, my defects, the risk I pose was always punctuated with stories of the beasts and the blanks that roamed, mutated from the radiation left from the war.' I doubted my defects but never that there was an option outside.

'That's why there is no civilian air travel. We have the tech, and Sphere has stealth aircraft, but they are all region-locked. They power down just after the fence but that's all we need.'

'No offence, Ma'am, but how do you know all of this?' Darnell asked.

'Several months ago, I intercepted a virus. Well, we thought it was a virus. I stopped it in time but when I was removing it from the system it activated a video file. It was from outside. I'll show you.'

She pushed a button on the desk and the wall of screens behind her all went black as they went to act as one large screen. 'It's a tad corrupted so the visuals aren't perfect but you will understand.'

A pixelated image appeared on the screen and after a few crackles and squeals, a voice began.

'The Marked War nearly tore our world apart. The marked began to lose ground and agreed to be moved into reserves; regions of marked people to live their way of life without us unmarked tainting their ideals. This message is not for them. This message is for the ones who want to break free of marked control. We know you birth unmarked children. You have banished some into the wasteland. I can only imagine what you do to the ones you keep, considering what you tried to do during the war.

'We also open our arms to marked folk not following City Ordinances: gay, re-partnered, transgender, intersex or even just those wanting to choose their own paths. We do not judge.

'Go to the wastelands beyond the fence. I promise you it is safe. We created it ourselves. Keep walking away from the fence. We will find you. You have been lied to.'

The video crackled and the screen went black, flickering once before returning to its multiple camera feeds.

'You need to release it,' Darnell said. 'You need people to know.'

'Even if I got it back on the network, I'm not the only person in comms security. Only Sphere knows about the other marked regions, even less know about the blanks beyond the wasteland.'

'So we get punished, segregated and tortured in the case of Darnell and your own fucking daughter, for the sake of oversensitive genetic purist bullshit from before the war?' Zale snapped. 'People are dying. Those that aren't killed are brainwashed into mercenaries who can't think for themselves. Who don't flinch at shooting a child in the face!' Ava flinched now, but Zale was far from finished. 'Don't you look at me like that Ava. You shot a four-year-old at point blank range and barely blinked,' he snapped before turning back to Harley. 'How would you have felt if they'd just broken down your door and shot Almara when she was little? They do this! And it's not just here! How many regions is this going on in? How many kids are getting killed for breeding purity? Is there anything actually wrong with the genetics of blanks? Do you even know? How is all of this… this… bullshit better than freedom?'

Zale was fuming. Allen tried to calm him with a hand on his arm but he flinched away. 'SAY SOMETHING!' he screamed at Harley.

'There are laws. There are agreed-to conditions to our sanctuary. We need to remain in the regions. Technically we can't even transfer blanks out. It's only through banishment that we release people and it's only the kind hearts of those who rescue that saves them. Trust me, I've looked.'

'And if the blanks all disappeared overnight...' Ava began.

'Exactly. It would be too obvious,' Harley replied. 'But I can save you. We need to get to a flight room.'

Zale's shoulders slumped in defeat. I saw a tear roll down his pink-scarred cheek.

'From the flight room,' Harley continued, her voice softer now, 'Ava will fly you to the fence. From there I can't promise anything but it seems the blanks must somehow monitor the perimeter. They should meet you. A full ration pack and med kit will be in the mini jump jet. It should last a week easily in case they're a little slow.'

'So how will we proceed, Ma'am?' Ava asked.

'I'll lead you through as far as I can. One of my colleagues will meet you at the transport dock and take you to the flight room.'

'Can we trust them?' Allen asked.

'As much as I can. They think you're fresh blanks going to the training facility up north. However, I want you to remember this: if Ava says run, you run. Follow her and keep up. She knows the way and is your best chance of escape.'

'You aren't coming with us?' I asked.

'Not yet sweetie. I have to try and fix things here.'

'Excuse me, Ma'am,' Darnell interjected softly. 'My mum. She's in the infirmary. Can she come with us? I'm all she really has and vice versa.'

'Not yet, Darnell.' Harley said.

'Then I'm not going.'

Ava looked over to him, her shoulders heavy.

'She's right, Darnell. For us to escape we can't have dead weight. Your mother is still sick. I'll bring her with me when I follow you.'

'Wait, you're not coming either?' I asked. I had been hoping to have someone capable at survival with us.

'I'll be hanging back at the fence for a while, helping Harley ferry through other blanks. Also, I'm the most likely to survive in the forest, being hunted.'

'I promise, Darnell, we will send your mother as soon as she is able to travel.'

'Can't we just hole up somewhere until we can all go together?' I asked.

'That would be unwise. Small groups are harder to catch and harder to spot. We need every advantage we can get. Now no more discussion. Harley, if you would like to lead the way.'

My mother got up and picked up her data pad. 'Follow me. I will take you to the storage lockers. There are packs with clothes and water for you. We may also need to arm you.'

'Already done, Ma'am,' Ava said. 'All have standard issue, except your daughter. I have given her a taser for safety.'

'She will need a gun. A real one. And you all need ammunition. I also need to remove your trackers.'

'Our what?' Darnell asked.

'Citizen trackers are for I.D. but when they put them in at school age you also get a tracking chip. They called them booster shots.'

Without another word, the door slid open at my mother's touch and we filed out in the same order we had been in before. Maybe we were getting used to this regimented life. We headed back down the glass-walled corridor and turned a corner to a white-doored room. So far no one had batted an eyelid at us.

We filed into the room. The lights overhead started flickering on at our presence.

'Ava, can you please go collect packs, ammo and a gun for Almara. We will be in the med aisle.'

Ava jogged off, boots squeaking the rhythm of her steps. We followed Mum two aisles over, where a little alcove was cut into the wall. Inside were walls of boxes marked with a cross. First aid supplies. The names on the boxes were mostly unpronounceable. I assumed them to be medicine. To one side was a table with several devices laid out. Most of them had pointy shiny parts. This was not going to be pleasant.

'Who wants to go first?' Harley asked.

'I will,' Darnell said. 'Mine will be easy because its fresh.'

'Fresh?' I asked.

'Never got chipped before I got here.'

He sat on the stool next to the metal table as Harley picked up two objects. One was a small bar-shaped item that beeped after it was turned on. The other was a gun of some type with several needles sticking out of its tip. Moving the bar over Darnell's skin, it started to beep faster, finally letting out a high-pitched whining noise. She pressed the button on the bottom and I saw it stamp an ink circle onto Darnell's skin. She put down the tracking bar and lined up the needle-filled gun with the ink.

She pulled the trigger. Darnell squealed as she pulled the gun away. There was a small hole in his skin weeping blood, but I could see a tiny capsule in the needles of the device. Harley squirted some gel over the hole to stop the bleeding and said, 'Next'.

Soon we were all sans trackers except Ava. She returned as Mum had reloaded the extraction needles. Ava handed each of us a backpack and some ammo, which we stored in our belts. She also handed me a gun. I felt its weight. I put my hand on my taser but I hoped I'd never have to use either.

'Put the taser in your pack,' Ava said as Harley searched for her tracker. She barely winced when the needles pulled her tracker from her neck. Harley started cleaning up but stopped to look at us all.

'Go now. I can't go to the next floor without looking suspicious. They're your responsibility now, Ava.'

The corridors seemed to have filled with even more people in the short time we'd been in the stock room. Our packs looked out of place and every glance made me tense up.

I looked over to our group. We all had our heads down, staring at our booted feet. All except Ava who walked in front of us with her head high, a stoic look plastered on her face. Her hand hovered near her gun though now, the holster unclipped for easy access. I hadn't seen her do that.

I'd put the real gun on my pack and left my taser on my belt. I felt safer that way, but I unclipped my holster too. I felt following her actions would be the best bet at surviving if someone caught on.

I glanced up to see we were heading towards another elevator, but as we got closer, Ava turned sharply and went for the stairwell. I sighed inwardly; more stairs. These past few days I had climbed more stairs than I had in the entirety of my previous life. We all went through the door and crammed ourselves onto the small stairwell landing. Darnell looked up at the flights stretching above us.

'Uh, how many floors…'

'It's okay, just the one flight of stairs, then we enter the lift on the barracks floor. It'll look more natural you entering the lift from there.'

'What about our lack of tracking chips? Would it not pick up that we were tracer-less? Can you even get in the lift without it?' I asked. We had our citizen chips but were they what determined our access, or had that been the tracking chips? That's what I'd been told in the Cube.

'Tracking is purely for locating and even then, they aren't as good as they used to be. My citizen chip will be enough. It will also override the need to check your chips like in the last elevator. It will either deem you prisoner transport or a training group.' I hoped she was right. 'And keep your heads up. You're soldiers, not livestock.'

Ava began her ascent and the rest of us followed. She was good to her word, and we exited on the floor above. The elevator was surrounded by people. I heard Zale muttering curses under his breath. He was acting twitchy and I saw his hand fall to the handgun at his side. He glanced up at my staring and I shook my head as he made eye contact. He acknowledged me with a nod and we remained silent.

The group were recruits, empty-eyed teens, obviously blanks already in brainwash mode. They filed into the elevator as the doors slid open. A man in a matching black coverall stepped in behind them.

'Enough room for you and your recruits, soldier,' he called to Ava.

'Gotta keep this lot away from the recruits. Special project. Not allowed to socialise,' Ava said. The lie flowed so easily from her lips. The other soldier nodded and pressed the button for his floor.

The door closed on the group and Ava scanned her chip to bring the elevator back. She stood perfectly still. I tried to mimic her but the panic in my eyes had to be an obvious giveaway.

'Soldier!' a voice boomed down the hallway. I could see the others flinch out of the corner of my eye but we regained our composure quicker than I expected.

Ava turned and saluted. 'Sir!' she called. The man looked at us. 'You need to teach these greenies to show some respect for superiors. How fresh are they?'

'Very green, Sir. I'm taking them for their first outsider training.'

'Greensticks, learn quick. When approached by an officer who outranks you, which is almost everyone in black, you salute. Clear?'

'Yes, Sir,' we all muttered.

'Soldier, you need to work them hard. They're softer than my grandmother's feather bed. They're so soft, they'd make better mystery meat than cannon fodder if you leave them like this.'

'Yes, Sir,' Ava said as the elevator dinged and doors opened.

The man turned and continued his march down the hallway. Darnell sighed in relief.

'File in,' Ava said, holding the door open for us.

CHAPTER THIRTY
Darnell

When the elevator door opened, the floor was nothing like the white expanses of hallways they'd been dealing with. Darnell had seen the flight floor when he arrived but the others looked around in wonder. It was still stark white and over-lit, but from this angle all they could see was metal reaching up to the roof, a large top door open to the sky. The sun was setting, the expanse above on fire with colours of orange and pink. The moon, a sliver of white, peeked out from the side of the opening, a light spattering of stars could be seen where the sky was turning the bruised purple of plums.

Darnell tried to work out where he had exited the floor and saw a row of platforms on the far side of the room. The small aircrafts lined up there like fat insects, shiny and round. There were a few empty platforms towards the end, but they could see the few straggling aircrafts coming through the ceiling, silhouetted against the colourful expanse.

'This way,' Ava said, and they followed behind her like a mother duck. Darnell noticed everyone held their heads up with mock confidence now. They almost looked like soldiers. 'We need to get to the flight platform.' Ava pointed to the aircraft area Darnell had been looking at. 'Stay close. There are hazards. Don't get run over.'

They skirted several vehicles, the last pulling in as they reached the first set of stairs. The huge door that allowed the ground vehicles access began to move. It was mostly dark but

Darnell thought he made out patches of green grass on either side of the road leading in. Almara looked out and stumbled, her attention on the draw of freedom.

'Careful,' Darnell said, grabbing at her arm.

She looked at him like she'd forgotten where she was for a moment.

'Did you smell it?' she asked. 'The breeze that came in? It smelled like grass.'

He stared at her for a moment. 'You don't get out much, do you?'

'No, I've been locked in the Cube for seven years.'

Darnell said nothing. He'd never thought about how much freedom he'd really had, away from City Ordinance. He saw Ava shoot them a glare and followed on.

A woman with a data pad approached them from near one of the vehicles. 'Soldier?' she said as she stopped in front of Ava.

'Yes, Sir?' she responded, saluting the woman. Darnell looked at the others and saluted as they did.

'I don't have any tours or outgoings listed for tonight. Any reason you're bringing grunts onto my floor? You are in violation of safety procedures.'

'Sir, there should have been orders from Head of Communications come through. This is a recon training exercise. Last minute, but necessary for a special project,' Ava said, without a shred of doubt in her voice.

'Well, you're not on my list. Who confirmed it?'

'Unsure, Sir. Just following orders.'

At this moment a short woman in a red coverall of the mechanics corps came dashing down the stairs. Her hair was curly and escaping the attempted braid that hung down her back. In her hand she held a scrunched piece of paper. She came to a stop in front of them and after pushing her glasses up, she held the paper out.

'Sir, is this about the last-minute recon flight?' the mechanic asked.

'Yes, Petia. Did you approve it?'

'It came pre-approved. Uh, it's from the Colonel.'

'Let me see that. You didn't think to come and tell me?' she asked, snatching the paper from her hand. Ava stayed still as a rock. Darnell had a slight tremble in his hands. This was taking too long.

The woman looked at Petia and shook her head before turning to Ava. 'You are cleared for flight deck access soldier. Make sure the grunts don't break anything.'

'Yes, Sir.' Ava turned and began to walk away, heading towards the stairs. The heard Petia run up behind them. 'Sorry for that, Soldier. It came through a little later than I expected. Follow me. I have your ship prepped.

Suddenly sirens filled the air. Ava stopped, Almara nearly running into her back.

'Oh, don't mind those. Just means one of the blanks have gone walkabout. They always find them. Take them down to the testing labs or the grinders. It should stop soon.' Petia yelled over the sirens.

They were two flights up when the door on the ground level burst open and a cloud of black-clad soldiers poured in. Ava stopped and grabbed Almara by the wrist.

'RUN! Get to the third ship and shut the door. I'm right behind you.' She all but shoved Almara up the next step and drew her gun. Petia was running next to Almara.

'Why are we running?' she yelled.

'We're the blanks gone walkabout. Get down,' Almara exclaimed. A bullet flew past her shoulder as she said this and struck Petia in the arm. The mechanic cried out in shock, slapping a hand over the instant wound, and Almara frantically pulled her down out of the line of fire. 'I'm sorry, oh god, I'm sorry. I think you'll be okay. Just stay there.'

They were shooting from below and their aim was obscured by the stairwells and Ava's wild shots. She'd fire, then move up a few steps. Darnell pushed Almara to move, feeling Zale and Allen on his heels. As they hit the walkway to the aircrafts, the flight deck door flew open, spewing more soldiers.

'Run!' Zale screamed. Almara didn't even look back. She saw the aircraft, door sitting open waiting for them and pushed herself to run as fast as she could. She was at the first craft now when she heard more gunfire. Turning, she saw the soldiers gaining. As they ran past the stairwell entry Ava took out two soldiers before rushing the next batch.

A scream ripped through the air over the bullets as Allen's thigh exploded with blood. He fell to the ground. Ava had reached them now.

'Run, you idiots!' she ordered as she backed past, still firing. She barely glanced over. 'Zale, leave him. It's too late.'

Zale was trying in vain to hold Allen up and drag him. Ava fired past them once more, taking out a few more approaching soldiers.

'I can't,' Zale said, tears beginning to stream down his face. 'He's all I have.'

'Oh, for fuck's sake. Shoot at them and I'll take him.' She grabbed Allen around the waist and hauled him over her shoulder, still trying to shoot. As she ran out of ammo, Zale began to fire. He wasn't a great shot but he worked as enough of a distraction to get them to the aircraft relatively unscathed.

She all but threw Allen in and climbed into the pilot's seat. As Zale closed the door, several shots pinged off the metal.

'Buckle up folks, this is gonna be a bumpy ride!' Ava called as the craft began to lift off.

CHAPTER THIRTY-ONE
Zale

The mini aircraft set down in the flattened grass outside the Colonel's house. A shiver of horror ran through Zale's body. There was already the stench of betrayal around them.

The gel seemed to have stopped the bleeding in Allen's thigh at least. He still limped but he could manage better than he would have without the wound gel. Ava pulled a syringe from the med kit and approached Allen.

'What's that?' Zale asked. He still wasn't sure he trusted Ava fully.

'It's just a local anaesthetic. Just a little to dull the pain in his leg. He can't run on it.'

'But no one knows exactly where we are, right?' Almara asked. 'I mean, except for Mum?'

'Naivety can only get you so far. Shots were fired. Your tanks are empty. We have maybe a five-to-ten-minute head start on them. My comm appears to have been silenced so I can't hear them. Now let me numb his leg and get out of this vehicle.'

'Where are we headed?' Almara asked, passing the packs out to Darnell.

'We need to stick together and stay quiet. The lights are off but that doesn't mean that the house is empty. He's there most of the time.'

Almara nodded, jumping down out of the aircraft. She shouldered one of the packs, then another. Darnell followed her lead. Zale would need to help Allen.

Ava injected the anaesthetic into Allen and helped Zale get him down to the ground. She grabbed the last pack and the first aid kit, before motioning for the group to follow her. They moved as quietly as they could towards the side of the dark house. The sun was mostly set now and the pink on the horizon line made the ruins in the distance light up like they were alive.

'The wasteland looks so much less scary knowing someone else is out there,' Zale whispered. 'It's almost beautiful.'

'Why have they never tried to break into the regions? We have tech and food and medicine…' Darnell began.

'Maybe they do too. Maybe they have more. We have no idea on their level of tech. The beasts are theirs, remember?' Zale said.

'Has anyone ever seen one?' Almara asked. Silence fell over them. Finally Ava spoke up.

'They're mech suits. Bio mech suits, actually. There's one in the lab. The driver was hardwired into it. Suit got shorted and it fried his insides. Cooked his brain. Even after all the years we've had the suit, when it's opened it smells like burnt meat.'

'So they aren't mutations?'

'Like the tape said, the radiation is a myth. A lie to keep us inside. There may have been bombs dropped but they certainly weren't outside every region.'

'So the Badlands are what, then?'

'Exclusion zones, I'm guessing. Stop the regions being visited like a zoo. Keep marked on the inside and blanks at a distance.'

'Then why not let us just go?' Zale asked.

'Because then blanks couldn't be used and the marked might leave. We are two species who, when mixed, cause wars. We don't need another war over genetic markers. Now be quiet.'

They were behind the house now. The grass was long here.

There was not a huge amount of space between the house and the fence but enough that Zale could still act as a crutch for Allen.

The gentle rustle of the grasses against the thuds of their boots made Zale cringe. They were so loud. He was pretty sure everyone could hear his heart thumping too.

Finally they were past the house and heading towards a large shed. Zale saw the gate he had passed on his way here last time. They made it to the gate to see a heavy padlock chaining the gate shut.

Allen flopped to the ground amongst the long grass, only his head visible. Zale let out a laugh before stifling it in his hand.

'You look like a potato, peeking through the dirt,' Darnell said as he too began to giggle.

'Be quiet,' Ava hissed, but soon they were all giggling under their breath. It felt good to laugh.

Finally getting themselves under control, Almara looked up at Ava from where she had fallen to the ground. Ava stood emotionless near the gate.

'So what are us grass potatoes supposed to do about the big-ass padlock on what I assume is our way out?'

'I have a lockpick. It will be no issue, but the drones that are closing in on our position will be a problem.'

'What drones?' Allen asked, looking around.

'I can hear them. Enhanced hearing was one of my bio upgrades. They're still a few minutes out and don't operate outside the fence. None of the tech does. Just like Harley said.'

'So what are you waiting for? Pick the fucking lock,' Allen said urgently. Ava nodded and pulled a ring of metal pins from a pouch on her belt. As she reached for the lock, Allen inhaled sharply and called, 'WAIT!'

Ava didn't jump but spun around glaring at them 'What part of quiet do you not understand?' she spat. 'What do you want, mark-traitor?'

'Isn't the fence electrified?'

'Would I be reaching for it if it was?' Ava said, turning back to the lock.

'Fair point,' Allen mumbled.

'Get up, potatoes,' Ava said as the lock fell into her hand. The gate swung open, beckoning them into their uncertain futures. 'Drones incoming. We need to be outgoing.'

There was no time for hesitation. Zale pulled Allen to his feet and pulled him through the gate behind Darnell and Almara. Ava stepped through as two drones came into sight. They flew up to the fence line, shining their mini spotlights on Ava's face.

'You have no jurisdiction here. You have no power outside the fence,' Ava screamed into the lights. She turned and pointed into the inky blackness that filled the land stretching ahead of them. 'A car is coming. You need to move forward and turn on your head lamps. I'm right behind you.'

Zale saw her toss the padlock at one of the drones before he took off, following Almara's flashlight. From the expanse of the wasteland, a jeep was coming to a stop ahead of them in a cloud of dust.

'Get in!' a man yelled from the driver's side. Almara fumbled with the door handle until she managed to open the car door. She pushed Darnell in and dashed over to help Zale with Allen. As Allen was lifted into the backseat, gunshots rang out behind them. The man in the driver's seat started to yell. 'Get moving folks. We have incoming company and I don't think we have much time.'

Almara turned towards the gunfire. Ava was shooting at the drones but new bobbing beams of light meant they would have more than drones to deal with soon.

'Ava, come on!' Almara yelled as another transport landed near the gate. She rummaged in her bag as she ran for her handgun. The taser would be useless. She wouldn't be a good shot but could provide a distraction at least. 'I'll cover you!'

The door of the plane opened and instead of black-clad soldiers spilling out, Almara saw it was her mother. Out of the corner of her eyes Harley saw Almara drop to the ground holding her head. Her eyes didn't know where to look. Looking at her mother she muttered, 'Mum?' Then, louder, 'Mum! Hurry!' Her mother began to trot towards the car, grabbing Ava's arm as she went past.

'We really need to hustle folks. We aren't supposed to fire on the marked and I don't have much ammo anyway!' the man called.

Almara saw Zale reaching out for her. Ava and her mother were halfway when Ava stopped. Harley stumbled but kept her footing. She turned to pull on Ava's arm.

'Ava, come on.'

'No.' Zale barely heard her speak but she did see an odd look cross her face. Behind them the soldiers were at the gate.

'What are you doing, Ava?' Zale called.

'I'm following orders,' was all she said before raising her gun and shooting Harley in the head. Harley's body crumpled to the dirt. Almara screamed and started to run towards her.

Zale jumped out of the car and dragged Almara against all her efforts and all but threw her in the car. The soldiers started to spill towards Ava, who still stood silently in the dust.

The man driving the car began to reverse, while Almara continued to scream, trying to get out of the car. Ava stared blankly after them. As the headlights receded, they saw Ava lift the gun to her temple and fire. The gunshot echoed through the night as the headlights fell away, the car turning and driving off into the dark.

EPILOGUE
Almara

The man who rescued us is quiet most of the time. His name is Raph. It's only when we stop to eat and rest that he talks. We mainly just listen. In total, we've been driving for two days but I can see the City looming ahead. They aren't ruins like we'd been told, but shining high-rises made of metal and glass. It almost looks like home.

This book is dedicated to Michael Willis.

In 2015, I wished on a shooting star. I asked for someone who would love me for who I am, that could look past my broken parts and make me feel whole again. I asked for someone to invigorate my mind, to be my muse and most of all someone that was meant to be in my life. Now I probably should have been more specific, but I got something so much more than what I intended and I still have no idea how I deserve a friend in my life quite like you. You are certainly made from the same star stuff as me and even though you weren't what I meant with that wish, you are what I needed. My muse, my nakama, my ka-tet, my fellowship. I'm so glad you are part of my life.

To the rest of you, thank you for putting up with me while I get frustrated over words I can't remember and scenes I can't work out how to write while juggling all the things in my life.

For more information on Sabrina visit
www.ouroborusbooks.com